U0165575

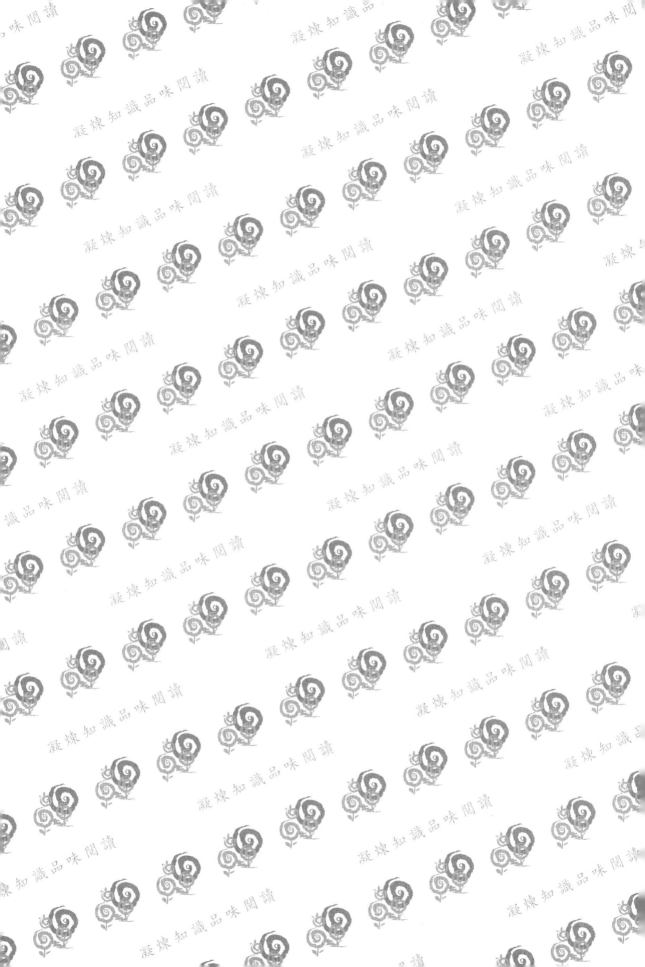

專為初學華語的外籍人士所設計

實用
生活華語
不打烊

Practical Chinese

初級篇

隨書附贈
華語聽力練習
光碟

你好

楊琇惠——編著

　　本書乃是《實用生活華語不打烊》系列教材的初級教本，亦即專為零起點人士所設計的會話教材。本書出版後，《實用生活華語不打烊》系列教材可謂趨於完備；學習者透過教材的引導，可從最基本的打招呼、購物、問路、交際等生活用語，一直學到深層的文化認知，漸次培養聽、說、讀、寫的能力。

　　在設計此初級教本之初，本編輯團隊一再思量：該如何以活潑有趣的方式來克服初學者對華語的恐懼，進而激發其持續學習的興趣？反覆思量的結果，決定改變傳統內容的設計，而特地加入了生動的日記寫作，以及唐詩、諺語的介紹。

　　首先，為什麼要加入日記呢？所以會加入日記，除了想要訓練學生的閱讀能力之外，主要是希望藉此來培養學生對中文寫作的信心。怎麼說呢？這得從零起點學習者的心態說起。一般外籍人士開始學華語時，多視漢字為洪水猛獸，紛紛敬而遠之，以為自己永遠也不可能學會漢字的符號系統，所以有些人一開始就表明了只想學聽、說兩項能力。然而任何一種語言的學習，若有所偏廢的話，必然很難提升語文的程度。尤其是處處充斥著同音字的中文，若只是會聽、會說，而不學識字、寫字的話，日後在聽聞一些較深入的會話，或是文本的書寫內容時，肯定會產生理解上的困難。是以我們希望透過文中女主角白愷俐的日記書寫，來讓同學知道，或許一開始學中文時只會兩三句話，但是經過一段時間的學習後，只要有心，便可以將幾乎通篇都是英文的日記，變成全篇都是中文的書寫。期望這種循序漸進的做法，能增強學生學習漢字的信心，並舒緩其對漢字書寫的恐懼。此外，由於日記的內容乃是重覆課文會話的陳述，所以學生在閱讀日記時，不但可以練習簡單的閱讀，還可以再次復習課文的重點。

　　再者，為何會在一本初級會話的書中加入唐詩和諺語等素材呢？這麼做的主要目的同樣有兩點，一來是為了讓教材更加豐富、多元，以引發學習者對華語的興趣；二來是希望能由此來介紹一點中華文化及用語習慣給同學。

　　《實用生活華語不打烊》系列，在初、中、高級完全出版之後，學習者固然可以循此來學習。可是由於每個人的學習狀況不同，所以中間難免會有級數上的落差，甚至出現無法跟上級數的情形。對此，本編輯團隊日後擬再編幾本輔助性的教材，如趣味成語、詩詞欣賞及常用華語300句等等，以供級數出現落差時使用。

　　本系列套書能順利出版，要感謝的人非常多。首先要感謝國立台北科技大學教學卓越計畫的援助，讓筆者得以獲得充分的資源來完成華語教材的編撰。還要感謝Brian Greene在英文教案上的撰寫與校稿，及郭謦維、鄒蕙安兩位同仁在文案上所提供的創意點子及細心的校對。以及美編黃甄媚小姐的用心，讓整本書能呈現活潑亮麗的樣貌。除此之外，五南出版社黃副總編惠娟及胡天如小姐，在校稿及錄音上的協助更是讓筆者銘感五內。

　　最後想說的是，華語教學之路既遙且遠，要達到完美的境界，還需長時間不斷的學習與修正。因此，若各位先進發現本書不足之處，還請不吝指教。

楊琇惠

2009年12月
北科大通識中心

Chinese Characters

Principles

Chinese characters are one of the features of the Chinese language that sets it apart from other world languages. As there is no alphabet in Chinese, individual Chinese characters represent both sound and meaning. Although there are different estimates of the total number of Chinese characters ranging from 20,000 to over 40,000, there is consensus that a knowledge of between 3,000 to 6,000 frequently occurring characters is sufficient for literacy.

Although it is true that Chinese characters came originally from pictographs, in contemporary Chinese, only a handful of characters are, strictly speaking, pictographs. The majority of characters appearing in contemporary usage (approximately 90%) are of a form that combines a phonetic (sound) component along with a semantic (meaning) component. These pictophonetic compounds provide clues to the character's pronunciation and meaning. However, generally speaking, the exact pronunciation-initial, final, and tone-and meaning of a given Chinese character must be memorized, especially for many fundamental characters that provide no explicit clues to their pronunciation and/or meaning-for example 我 (wǒ *I/me*), 要 (yào *to want/neeed; will*), and 去 (qù *to go*). This is the main factor that makes learning to read and write Chinese so time intensive for native and non-native speakers alike. But do not despair. Once a student has attained a character base on the order of 1,000 characters, guessing the gist and pronunciation of unfamiliar characters becomes much easier, because new characters often include components that have already been memorized.

Chinese characters are composed of three building blocks: strokes, components, and radicals. These building blocks are assembled to create characters based on established conventions of order and spatial arrangement. Whether learning to recognize characters or to write them, knowing the principles of character composition lies at the heart of understanding written Chinese-and that includes both traditional and simplified characters.

Traditional characters, otherwise known as full-form or complex characters, are in current use in Hong Kong, Macau, Taiwan, and various overseas Chinese communities throughout the world. They were also used in China prior to 1956 and therefore appear in countless historical documents, printed materials, and various forms of art originating from China. In addition, many traditional characters are in use in both written Japanese and Korean. Traditional characters are featured in this book.

Simplified characters are currently used in China. Their use was promulgated in the mid-1950s to increase literacy, render characters easier to write, and, in the name of modernization, to make a decisive break from the past. The simplification of entire characters and/or character components is based on cursive script, which dates to the Han dynasty. It is because of the long history of cursive script that many simplified characters made it into Japanese during the Tang dynasty through a process of linguistic borrowing and are still in use today. For example, modern Japanese uses the simplified character for "country/nation" 国 (guó), rather than the complex form 國 (guó), not because of mid-1950s language reform in China, but because when the character was borrowed into Japanese during the 8th century, the simplified form already existed with the prevalence of cursive script used at that historical moment.

Since Chinese characters have a long history of development, their use is regulated and standardized by various governmental and educational bodies, and because they are the topic of scholarly research and debate, there is contention when it comes to writing and rendering certain characters and their component parts. While studying Chinese, a student should always be aware that individual teachers and particular textbooks may present characters in slightly different ways. Like any living language, Chinese is in constant flux and represents the various linguistic habits and needs of its numerous users. Therefore, which stroke order, for example, might be "right" according to one native speaker might be "wrong" according to another.

Strokes

Stokes are the fundamental units of Chinese characters. They are combined, following certain principles of construction, to form components, radicals, and complete characters. Similar to alphabetical order in English, stroke order determines how components, radicals, and characters are organized in dictionaries. For example, the mouth radical 口 (kǒu), with three strokes, comes before 木 (mù), the tree/wood radical, which is composed of four strokes. Characters that share a common radical are arranged by the number of strokes in the part of the character that appears after the radical. Therefore, in a dictionary, 你 (nǐ *you*) with its five strokes in addition to the radical 亻 (rén *person*), appears after 他 (tā *he/him*), which has only three strokes in the component next to the 亻 radical.

Radicals like 丨 (gǔn) and 丶 (zhǔ) are composed of a single stoke, as is the character 一 (yī). With more strokes comes increasing complexity. The character 家 (jiā *home; family*) has ten stokes, the character 黨 (dǎng *faction; political party*) has twenty strokes, 驫 (biāo *horses*) has thirty strokes, and 齉 (nàng *stuffy nose*) has thirty-six strokes. At fifty-two strokes, 𪚥 (bèng) is so rare that many people do not even know how to pronounce it! But as you learn more about Chinese characters, you will discover that even a complicated character like 䨻, which signifies the howl of a storm, is not really that complicated. Essentially, it is made up of four 雷 (léi *thunder*), each of which is composed of a 雨 (yǔ *rain*) over a 田 (tián *field*). These are, in turn, built from eight and five fundamental strokes, respectively, which are all listed below.

Table 1   Fundamental Stokes

Stroke	Chinese Name	English Meaning	Description
、	點 diǎn	dot	small dash
一	橫 héng	horizontal	rightward stroke
丨	豎 shù	vertical	downward stroke
㇀	提 tí	rise	flick up to the right
㇏	捺 nà	press down	falling to the right and fattens
ノ	撇 piě	throw away	falling to the left
㇚	鉤 gōu	hook	added to other strokes; always down and to the left
㇂	彎 wān	bend	concave to the left

Using the strokes above, we can write the character 永 (yǒng), which means perpetual, eternal, or always. Note 1) the order in which the strokes are written and 2) the direction in which is stroke is written. The beauty of this example is that it neatly summarizes many of the key concepts of both stroke order and stroke direction using a single, ubiquitous, and useful character.

Figure 1   Direction of Strokes and Stroke Order for 永

Stroke Order

In addition to paying close attention to the direction in which a stroke is written, one must be aware of the order in which the strokes themselves are written. There are some slight variations, but in general, the following principles guide native Chinese speakers when they write in Chinese.

1. Left to right, top to bottom（三、川）

This is a key principle of character writing that applies to simple characters, like 三 and 人, as well as complex characters like 語, which can be divided into two parts. The left part, 言, is written first, followed by the right part, 吾, and both of these parts are written from top to bottom.

2. Horizontal before vertical（十）

In characters and components that have two strokes that cross each other, as with 十, the horizontal stroke is generally written first.

3. Cutting strokes last（必）

Vertical strokes that cut through a character are written after the horizontal strokes they cut through. For example, 中, 事, and 津 follow this rule.

Horizontal strokes that cut through characters are written last, as in 母.

4. Diagonals right-to-left before diagonals left-to-right（文）

Right-to-left diagonals（ノ）are written before left-to-right diagonals（乀）.

5. Center verticals before outside components（水、小）

Vertical center strokes are written before any strokes on the sides. Notice how this principle differs from cutting vertical strokes: Center verticals do not pass through or cross the outside strokes.

6. Outside before inside（回、日、月）

In characters that have an outside border enclosing other components, the outside strokes are written first and the inside strokes are written last. Characters with an incomplete outside border, like 同 and 月 follow this principle. When there is a bottom stoke that closes the outside border, like in 日, it is the last to be added.

7. Left vertical before enclosing（口）

This rule is closely related to the previous "outside before inside" principle, and is most clearly demonstrated with the stroke order of 口. The left vertical stroke | is written first, followed by the top and right-hand stroke ㄱ , which are written together as a single stroke. Finally, the stroke across the bottom is added to close the box.

8. Bottom enclosing strokes last（這、道）

Any strokes that appear at the bottom of a character are written last. Since the lower-most stroke in 這 is part of the common radical 辶 (chuò), the entire radical is written last. Notice that this principle is similar to "outside before inside" and "left vertical before enclosing." However, the difference is that this bottom stroke is not part of a border surrounding the entire character.

9. Dots and minor strokes last（戈）

Dots and small strokes like at the upper right of 戈, the left of 寸, and the bottom right of 玉 are written last. Notice how the overall stroke order of 戈 follows several principles: horizontal before vertical, then the cutting stroke that falls to the left, and finally the dot at the upper right.

Components

A 1997 report by the National China Linguistics and Character Committee identified 560 individual components among a sample of 20,902 Chinese characters studied. From further statistical analyses, among these more than twenty thousand characters, there are 4,000 that are most frequently used in modern Chinese and known to university-educated Chinese native speakers. In this 4,000-character subset, there are 440 components. Components are a set of discrete units of meaning used in building characters, and this set includes radicals. All components can be used to create Chinese characters, but only some

(214) can also stand alone as their own characters and/or function as radicals. It is for this reason that this subset of components known as radicals is used to organize dictionaries- there are simply too many components to do this efficiently. However, an awareness of components is still necessary to improve one's literacy of Chinese characters. While all radicals are components, not all components can serve as radicals.

The following table presents some character components that are frequently encountered while studying to read and write Chinese characters that do not appear in typical dictionary radical indexes. The table can be used in conjunction with a Chinese dictionary for a deeper understanding of the relationship between components and a particular character's overall meaning.

Table 2 Frequently-Occurring Components

Component	Pinyin	Strokes	Meaning	Example
丶	yí	1		分
丂	kǎo	2	obstruction of breath	考
丩	jiū	2	to join the vine	糾、收
乄	wǔ	2	five	腦、爽
厶	sī	2	private	台、公、能、參
兀	wù	3	cut off the feet	元、光、先、完
巛	chuān	3	river	經、巡
彑	jì	3	snout	互、綠
罒	wǎng	4	net	深、探
乍	zhà	5	first time	怎
癶	bō	5	legs	發
卯	mǎo	5	stop	留、聊
占	zhān	5	to divine	站、店
臼	jiù	6	mortar; head	兒、舀、寫、閣
咼	guǎ	6	joint cleaned of flesh	剮、過
冏	jiǒng	7	bright	商

Radicals

As mentioned earlier, radicals are a special subset of components and there are 214 of them. With radicals, characters can be grouped into semantic categories. Radicals allow for characters to be arranged in dictionaries for quick reference and provide clues to a character's meaning and, to a lesser extent, a character's pronunciation. They are generally arranged by their number of strokes, from one（一 yī *one*）to seventeen（龠 yuè *Chinese flute*）, depending on the dictionary.

Based on where in the character they are located, and because of the simplification of characters in China, some radicals have two forms.

The ability to identify an unfamiliar character's radical is necessary to look it up in a dictionary, and even if you do not have a dictionary at hand, the radical can often offer clues about a character's meaning and pronunciation. Of course, dictionaries can be used to look up characters from their pronunciation as well. But since the pronunciation of any character cannot be known with certainty until it has been memorized, using radicals to find characters in a dictionary is a fundamental skill that must be mastered early in the study of Chinese.

The following table does not list the complete set of 214 radicals, but does present many that appear frequently and provides examples of where they appear in selected characters. Used in conjunction with a good Chinese dictionary, these radicals will be very useful while learning the characters that appear throughout the lessons in this book.

Table 3　Frequently-Occurring Radicals

Radical	Pinyin	Strokes	Meaning	Common Name	Alternate Form	Example
一	yī	1	one	yī bù		七、丁、上、下 三、丈、並、丘
	gǔn	1	vertical line	gǔn bù		中、串
亅	jué	1	hook	jué bù		了、事
冫	bīng	2	ice	bīng bù		冷、冬、冰
亻	rén	2	person	rén zì páng	人	你、代、今、企
勹	bāo	2	encompass	bāo bù		包、勿
刂	dāo	2	knife	dāo bù	刀	利、刑、分、剪
廴	yǐn	2	stride	yǐn bù		廷、延、建
阝 [left]	fù	2/3	mound	fù bù	阜	阿、院、陸、除
阝 [right]	yì	2/3	state	yì bù	邑	那、都、郭、郵
氵	shuǐ	3	water	sān diǎn shuǐ	水	河、江、永、泉
忄	xīn	3	heart	shù xīn páng	心	忙、快、您
宀	mián	3	house	mián bù		字、家、安
广	yǎn	3	shelter	yǎn bù		店、庫、廁

彳	chì	3	step w/ left foot	chì bù		得、律、從、待
土	tǔ	3	soil; earth	tǔ bù		在、地、堂、壁
艹	cǎo	3	grass	cǎo zì tóu	艸	草、花、茶、華
口	kǒu	3	mouth; opening	kǒu zì páng		吃、問
囗	wéi	3	surround	wéi bù		四、回、固、圈
尸	shī	3	lying body	shī bù		屋、局、屎、尿
女	nǚ	3	female	nǚ bù		媽、婆
扌	shǒu	3/4	hand	tí shǒu páng	手	把、打、拿、摩
犭	quǎn	3/4	dog	quǎn bù	犬	狗、狂、獎、狀
木	mù	4	wood	mù bù		本、林、李、朵
戈	gē	4	weapon	gē bù		我、成、或
日	rì	4	sun	rì bù		明、早
曰	yuē	4	speech	yuē bù		書、會、曲
牛	niú	4	cow; ox	niú bù	牛	物、特、牟、犁
火	huǒ	4	fire	huǒ bù	灬	炒、災、熱、煮
戶	hù	4	door plank	hù bù		房、所
辶	chuò	4	walk(ing)	chuò bù	辵、辶	進、這、過、退
攵	pū	4	hit	pū bù	攴	收、改、放
斤	jīn	4	ax	jīn bù		斯、新
月	yuè	4	moon	yuè bù		有、朋
月	ròu	4	flesh	ròu bù	肉	胖、肥、腐
王	yù	4/5	jade	yù bù	玉	玩、現、璧、瑩
穴	xuè	5	cave	xuè bù		空、穿
疒	chuáng	5	disease	chuáng bù		疼、痛、疫、病
目	mù	5	eye	mù bù		看、盲、相、眼
石	shí	5	stone	shí bù		研、磨
禾	hé	5	crop	hé bù	禾	秋、租、穎、秀
礻	shì	5	sign	shì zì páng	示	社、神
衤	chǎ	5/6	cloth	yī zì páng	衣	被、裳
羊	yáng	6	goat; sheep	yáng bù	羋、羊	羚、美、善、群
虫	huǐ	6	small animal	huǐ bù		蟲、蚊、蛋
竹	zhú	6	bamboo	zhú zì tóu	竹	笑、等、笨
臼	jiù	6	mortar; head	jiù bù		舊、舅
糸	mì	6	thread	mì bù	糸	絲、線、紅

言	yán	7	words	yán bù		說、話
豕	shǐ	7	pig	shǐ bù	豕	豬、象
貝	bèi	7	shell	bèi bù		貴、質
見	jiàn	7	to see	jiàn bù		視、觀、規、覺
足	zú	7	foot	zú bù	足	距、跑、蹩
豸	zhì	7	reptile	zhì bù		貌、豹
雨	yǔ	8	rain	yǔ bù		電、零
食	shí	8	food	shí bù	食	飯、餓、養、餐
金	jīn	8	metal	jīn bù	金	釘、銀、鑒
門	mén	8	door(way); gate	mén bù		間、閱
隹	zhuī	8	short-tailed bird	zhuī bù		雖、雀、隼、集
頁	yè	9	head	yè bù		頂、頭、題、顧
馬	mǎ	10	horse	mǎ bù		馮、駕、騎、驚

NOTE: Entries with two stroke counts, e.g. fù (2/3) or yù (4/5), indicate, as in the former, that there are either two ways to write the same radical, or as in the latter, that the two forms of the radicals differ by the addition or deletion of one stroke.

Notice in the preceding table that radicals can be rendered in slightly different ways depending on where they are and how they interact with other components in a given character to maintain the character's overall harmony. This will be addressed in the following part of this chapter and in some of the character writing and radical exercises in later chapters.

How Characters Components and Radicals Are Arranged

Chinese characters can be best understood as occupying a two-dimensional square. Indeed the paper on which all learners practice character writing-native speakers and students of Chinese as a second language alike-consists of a grid of boxes in which to write the characters. Within the box-like confines of any Chinese character, the components and radicals of that character can be arranged spatially in a number of ways. The underlying principle of arrangement is driven by the need to maintain a character's overall balance.

Below is a catalogue of several fundamental ways that components and radicals are assembled to build Chinese characters. Being familiar with them will improve both your recognition of Chinese characters as well your ability to write them from memory. In addition, with an awareness of the modular nature of Chinese characters, you can more readily a) make connections between characters that share a common component or radical, b) invent mental strategies to remember characters, and c) recognize the ubiquitous nature of pictophonetic compounds-characters assembled from a sound component and a meaning component.

1. single component

   Some characters consist of only a single radical or component, and the character is made to fit within a box of uniform size.
   EXAMPLES: 日、月、人、子、本、天

2. top/bottom

   The components and radicals of many characters are arranged from top to bottom.
   EXAMPLES: 台、英、笑、要、書、早

3. left/right

   Many characters have their parts arranged from left to right.
   EXAMPLES: 漢、語、她、好、找、吃、誰、胡、那

4. bounded left/right

   Another class of characters have their parts arranged left to right, but one of the components surrounds the other on two sides.
   EXAMPLES: 有、房、可、句、這、還

5. surrounded on three sides

   In this group of characters, one component surrounds another component or components on three sides.
   EXAMPLES: 開、問、凶、函、區、匯

6. inside/outside

   There is a group of characters that consists of parts within other parts.

EXAMPLES: 回、因、國、圓、園、四

7. top/middle/bottom

These characters consist of three parts stacked on top of one another.
EXAMPLES: 賣、累、草、舊、密、舅

8. left/middle/right

In this set of characters, three components are arranged from left to right. Often a radical can be added to another character with two parts to form a new one. This is frequently done by adding the radical to one side-usually the left-of another character.
EXAMPLES: 湖、瑚、哪、娜、謝、做

9. one above two / two above one

These characters feature three components that are arranged in a triangular fashion to maintain symmetry. One component resides either above or below two others. This is common when one radical or component is longer than it is tall.
EXAMPLES: 品、花、節、想、努、熱

There is a special class of one above two characters that feature the same radical in triplicate.
EXAMPLES: 姦、森、晶、犇、鑫、蟲

10. one beside two / two beside one

Characters like these feature three parts arranged to allow a taller radical or component to stand beside two smaller components.
EXAMPLES: 錢、鞋、認、夠、影、封

Kinds of Characters

Chinese characters can be classified into six types based on their relation to what they are signifying and their composition.

While it is true that some Chinese characters are pictograms, it is important to realize that most frequently used characters in modern Chinese are pictophonetic compounds（形聲字 xíngshēngzì: shape-sound character）.

The table below summarizes the six types of characters and supplies examples of each.

Table 4　Character Types

Type	Chinese	Pinyin	Definition	Example	Amount*
Pictophonetic Compound	形聲字	xíngshēngzì	Character contains two components: One suggests the meaning, and the other is derived from another character with the same or similar pronunciation.	嗎 (mouth + mǎ = ma *question marker*) 媽 (woman + mǎ = mā *mother*) 罵 (two mouths + mǎ = mà *scold*) 湖 (water + hú = hú *lake*) 語 (words + wú = yǔ *language*)	90%
Pictogram	象形字	xiàngxíngzì	Character resembles the object signified.	日 (*sun* rì) 月 (*moon* yuè) 木 (*tree* mù)	4%
Logical Aggregrate	會意字	huìyìzì	Character combines pictograms to symbolize an abstract concept.	明 (*sun* + *moon* = *bright* míng) 好 (*woman* + *sun* = *good* hǎo) 林 (*two trees* = *woods* lín)	4%
Ideograph	指事字	zhǐshìzì	Character illustrates abstract concepts directly.	上 (*up* shàng) 下 (*down* xià) 凹 (*concave* āo) 凸 (*convex* tū)	1%
Associate Transformation	轉注字	zhuǎnzhùzì	Different characters that have similar meaning and have bifurcated from a common character.	追、逐 The characters 追 (zhuī) and 逐 (zhú) both mean "chase" or "pursue," and have bifurcated to form new words related to their common meaning.	0.5%
Borrowed	假借字	jiǎjièzì	An existing character is used to represent an unrelated word with similar pronunciation.	自、萬 The character 自 (zì) originally was a pictograph of the nose. Since pointing to the nose refers to self, this character was borrowed to mean self. 萬 (wàn) is a pictograph of a scorpion. It was borrowed to represent its modern meaning, 10,000.	0.5%

*NOTE: An estimate of the amount of each character type as a percentage of the total number of characters in contemporary use.

Characters and Words

Are Chinese characters "words"? In general, yes. Single characters do represent the sound and meaning of nouns, verbs, adjectives, adverbs, and other parts of speech. However, it is important to remember that, in modern Chinese, characters are frequently combined to create two-, three-, and four-character compounds that are themselves discrete words and polysyllabic compounds.

For example, and this is but one of many, although the character 排 (pái) means to arrange or put together, it almost never appears by itself as a word in modern Chinese. In contemporary usage, 排 frequently appears in combination with other characters to form words like 排隊 (páiduì *to line up*), 安排 (ānpái *to arrange*), 排球 (páiqiú *volleyball*), 排水管 (páishuǐguǎn *drain*) and 排山倒海 (páishān-dǎohǎi *overwhelming*).

The precise relationship between Chinese characters and words, including the concepts of prefix and suffix, is a complex one about which linguists have not yet reached consensus. A student of Chinese need only be aware that there is a relationship between characters and words. An awareness of this will be enough to aid in the acquisition of new vocabulary.

Learning Chinese Characters

For native speakers of Chinese, learning to recognize and produce characters begins with the onset of formal education and, of course, after learning how to speak. As such, learning Chinese characters for native speakers is an exercise in matching visual symbols with oral/aural concepts and habits that are already firmly established. For non-native speakers, in contrast, learning oral/aural and reading skills in Chinese generally occurs simultaneously. This means that students need to quickly come to grips with managing two new and rather arbitrary sets of information (spoken words and their written analogs) in the target language. This is no easy task.

Fortunately, the number of methods available for learning, practicing, and referencing Chinese characters is just as large as the number of intelligences, learning styles, and personalities that students, motivated enough to tackle Chinese, bring to the language-learning table. There is no single "right" way to learn to read and write Chinese. Experiment with as many methods as you can and stick with the ones that work best for you.

While native speakers spend years from pre-school to junior high school in constant exposure to characters, continually practicing writing and reading, second language learners of Chinese often are suddenly plunged into the Chinese language, bombarded with new information, and obligated to quickly get up to speed in the four modalities: listening, speaking, reading, and writing. In this situation, low-tech approaches like using flash cards to memorize the form and pronunciation of Chinese characters and grid paper to practice writing them are both indispensable. Memorization speeds up the process and writing develops muscle memory. And there is simply no substitute to using a proper paper dictionary to look up words using either pronunciation or radical.

Higher-tech approaches like electronic dictionaries, computer software, and online resources certainly compliment traditional methods of character acquisition and will definitely become part of your learning arsenal. You will find that although typing and writing characters are completely different animals, they are mutually reinforcing. Whatever you do, the key is constant practice with a healthy mix of methods until you reach a mastery of that critical mass of fundamental characters. When that moment arrives, learning to read and write Chinese becomes markedly easier.

Conclusion: The Beauty of Chinese Characters

For native speakers and second-language learners alike, learning to read and write Chinese is a time-consuming and challenging process. Despite the difficulty, many students of Chinese report that learning Chinese characters is the more interesting part of studying Chinese language.

By approaching the task using the set of techniques and principles outlined in this chapter and in the various exercises throughout the book, students should be able to make connections between characters, which makes the process of memorization, recognition, and production a little easier. While it is true that mastering the phonetic and semantic components of the roughly 3,000 characters required for literacy is no simple task, an awareness of how they are constructed and related to one another provides you with powerful mnemonic devices to guide the exercise and management of character acquisition.

Chinese Phonetics

Principles

To facilitate communication among speakers of the hundreds of mutually unintelligible Chinese dialects, Standard Mandarin Chinese (SMC) has long been promoted to serve as the common language of communication throughout the Chinese-speaking world. With this, SMC pronunciation is precisely what the name implies: standardized. Chinese language authorities and native speakers alike place great importance on proper pronunciation, not only to enable communication over great expanses of time and space, but also to demonstrate one's command of language and culture. To pronounce SMC properly is to emulate the model, and only by emulating the model can one's pronunciation be judged as standard（標準 biāozhǔn）. It is "biāozhǔn" rather than "excellent" or "beautiful" that is most commonly used to complement a speaker's pronunciation. Be prepared to hear this word many times-and with varying degrees of sincerity-in your SMC studies. On the other hand, if your pronunciation varies too far from the standard, you risk creating misunderstanding. In this case, your stereotypical "foreigner" pronunciation is liable to be playfully mimicked, and your ideas taken less seriously. Therefore, like native speakers, you need to strive to get the sounds right.

Any student of SMC, which is the pronunciation presented in this book, needs to quickly come to terms with the three major phonetic elements of SMC: initials, finals, and tones.

The pronunciation of SMC is based on the Beijing dialect. SMC can be transliterated, or romanized, using the Latin alphabet in a number of ways. This book uses Hanyu Pinyin, which presents SMC using 21 initials, 38 finals, and 5 tones. There are approximately 400 possible combinations of these initials and finals that form the commonly occurring syllables in SMC. (See page XX for a table listing all the possible pinyin combinations.) Most of these syllables can then be pronounced with different tones, each corresponding to different Chinese characters.

All syllables in SMC, and for that matter, most morphemes (the smallest sound unit in a language that represents meaning) correspond to a Chinese character, which in turn, represents a word. Each syllable is formed from a combination of three elements: initial, final, and tone. Most syllables combine all three, but some (stand-alone finals) omit the initial.

The following table presents the classic example of assembling initials, finals, and the five tones to demonstrate the fundamentals of pronunciation in SMC.

Table 1 Monosyllabic Chinese Words and Their SMC Pronunciation using Hanyu Pinyin

媽		麻		馬		罵		嗎	
mā		má		mǎ		mà		ma / ma	
m	ā	m	á	m	ǎ	m	à	m	a
initial	final & 1st (high, level) tone	initial	final & 2nd (rising) tone	initial	final & 3rd (falling-rising) tone	initial	final & 4th (falling) tone	initial	final & 5th (neutral) tone
mother		sesame; hemp		horse		to scold		question marker	

The next table rearranges the five words just presented to form a sentence. You will notice three things. First, word order plays a crucial role in rendering the overall meaning. In this interrogative sentence, the syntax is: (subject) (verb) (object) (question marker). Second, the tone is an integral part of the final and determines the meaning of each word. Third, notice how single characters can be combined to form two-character, disyllabic compounds-in this case, it is 媽媽 (māma / mā·ma *mother*).

Table 2 Mono- and Disyllabic Chinese Words and Their SMC Pronunciation using Hanyu Pinyin (I)

麻媽媽罵馬嗎？											
麻		媽		媽		罵		馬		嗎	
má		mā		ma / ma		mà		mǎ		ma / ma	
m	á	m	ā	m	a	m	à	m	ǎ	m	a
initial	final & 2nd tone	initial	final & 1st tone	initial	final & neutral tone	initial	final & 4th tone	initial	final & 3rd tone	initial	final & neutral tone
sesame; hemp		mother		(suffix)		to scold		horse		question marker	
麻		媽媽				罵		馬		嗎	
Sesame		mother				to scold		horse		?	
Does Mother Sesame scold horses?											

The third table follows the same logic of the first two and presents a realistic sentence that a student of SMC can immediately use to describe precisely what he or she is doing by looking at this book.

Table 3 Mono- and Disyllabic Chinese Words and Their SMC Pronunciation using Hanyu Pinyin (II)

我學習中文。									
我		學		習		中		文	
wǒ		xué		xí		zhōng		wén	
	uǒ	x	üé	x	í	zh	ōng		uén
initial	final & 3rd tone	initial	final & 2nd tone	initial	final & 2nd tone	initial	final & 1st tone	initial	final & 2nd tone
I; me		to learn; to study		to practice; to be used to		center; middle		language; literature; culture	
我		學習				中文			
I		to study				Chinese			
I study Chinese. / I am studying Chinese.									

Note that some finals can stand alone as syllables-finals, for example, beginning with "u" that function as stand-alone syllables are written in pinyin with a "w." Also notice how characters/syllables can be combined to form both compound verbs and nouns. In this case, the verb "study" is formed from two characters with related meaning. The word "Chinese" is a compound noun formed from two discrete characters: an adjective and a noun. Other parts of speech including adverbs and prepositions can be created in the same way. With respect to pronunciation, the two syllables of both of these words receive virtually equal stress. The result is that despite having three words, when this sentence is uttered, the listener will hear five sounds spaced equidistant in time. This is part of the reason why SMC has been labeled, mistakenly, as being a monosyllabic language.

In actuality, SMC is a syllable-timed language. This means that, for the most part, each syllable receives equal stress. That, combined with a writing system in which there is a one-to-one correspondence between syllable and character, contributes to the inaccurate notion that SMC is a purely monosyllabic language. Although it is true that each syllable can be a discrete word, most words are multisyllabic compounds formed from monosyllabic words. These multisyllabic words have meanings more subtle, specific, or specialized than their component parts possess alone.

Because meaning can be conveyed at the level of the syllable in SMC, tones are very important. In principle, any combination of initial and final can be pronounced four, and sometimes, five different ways, with respect to tone. Take for example the initial-final combination "ma" shown in Table 1. Although the initial "m" and final "a" remain constant throughout the table, the pronunciation of the compound, and consequently, the meaning, is altered solely with the change in tone. This is precisely why tones are of ultimate importance in SMC phonetics. Also, since most languages do not apply tones to individual syllables, SMC tones are often one of the hardest skills for most students of Chinese as a second language to master.

The key to learning SMC tones is through listening to SMC and trying to emulate what you hear. You must absolutely place your full attention on learning to distinguish the differences between the five tones when listening to SMC as well as articulating the proper tone of any initial-final combination you say. If you do not do this, you not only risk being incomprehensible, but it is also likely that you will say something you do not mean to say.

Always attend to the initial, final, *and* tone of any item you happen to be studying or speaking. Every SMC syllable has a tone, and with that tone comes the proper meaning of the word associated with that syllable. In terms of initial-final combinations, SMC has hundreds of homonyms and near-homonyms. The key to differentiating between many of these identical or semi-identical initial-final combinations is by assigning them different tones. Do not think of words as initials, finals, *plus* a tone. The tone is an *integral* part of the word. In particular, it is an integral part of the final. You need to learn to hear tones and produce them properly in context to facilitate communicative competence.

What is Hanyu Pinyin and Why Study It?

Numerous romanization systems have been created to render Chinese using the Latin alphabet. There are more than ten of these for SMC and Hanyu Pinyin is one of them.

Hanyu Pinyin was created in China during the 1950s for native and non-native SMC speakers alike. Because of the close relationship China shared with the Soviet Union at that time, the system borrowed some phonetic components from Eastern European languages. This fact explains the frequent use of "x" and "z" in Hanyu Pinyin to represent some sounds in Chinese, which often confuses people who wrongly think Hanyu Pinyin is a form of English.

Like all romanization systems used to represent SMC, Hanyu Pinyin is an abstraction of sorts. Since Chinese uses characters instead of an alphabet, and because some of the phonetic features of SMC do not exist in other languages, any method of romanization is at best merely a way to *remind* the speaker or learner how to properly pronounce words in Chinese. Regardless of the romanization system, the standard pronunciation of a given character in SMC is the same. Therefore, no matter if rendered as tz'u^2, tsz2, cíh, cí, tsyr, or even ㄘˊ, the pronunciation of 詞 (speech; statement) remains the *same*.

Each romanization system has some unique advantages and disadvantages, but these differences are largely trivial. From a functional point of view, the choice to use one or another is essentially arbitrary. After all, the only real point of romanization is to learn the relationship between the sounds that exist in SMC as spoken by native speakers and their representation in pinyin. Hanyu Pinyin *is not* English, nor is it any other language. Do not confuse the letters you see with those of another language. Just relate them to the sounds in SMC you are hearing as you learn it.

Although Hanyu Pinyin is no better than many other romanization systems, it is also no worse; in the end, Hanyu Pinyin is the system most worth learning because it is the most widely used. The United Nations uses it as do libraries throughout the world. More and more electronic devices feature Hanyu Pinyin as a character input option. News of China, including place names and proper nouns, is regularly reported using Hanyu Pinyin in western-language media. Since the fundamental idea of promoting SMC is to satisfy the Chinese-speaking world's need for a lingua franca, a standard romanization system is necessary for teaching the language as well as for putting it into print in the western world. Hanyu Pinyin has become that standard transliteration system.

As you study Chinese, Hanyu Pinyin will be one of the best friends you have. Mastery of Hanyu Pinyin will allow you to quickly pronounce new vocabulary and look up words in Chinese dictionaries. It will also allow you to efficiently write Chinese characters on almost any computer. Moreover, since writing Chinese characters quickly-if at all-can be quite difficult, Hanyu Pinyin will allow you to easily write down SMC words that you hear. Once you have the pinyin written down, then you can remember how to say the word you heard as well as look it up in a dictionary. Although Hanyu Pinyin is a supplement to learning SMC, it is a very useful one. Eventually, like a native speaker, you will transition to writing Chinese characters instead of pinyin. But if your memory abandons you for a particular character, which is likely, you will always have Hanyu Pinyin to fall back on.

How Do I Pronounce Hanyu Pinyin?

Hanyu Pinyin uses certain Latin letters and diacritic symbols to represent the initials, finals, and tones of SMC. The discussion below first introduces tones. Following that, the letters used by Hanyu Pinyin to represent the sounds of SMC are presented. The pronunciation of each Hanyu Pinyin initial, final, and final combination is explained with reference to how the vocal organs are used to produce those sounds. Corresponding pronunciations in English are also provided. However, since these are, at best, only approximations, listening to the sound files included with this book is *mandatory*. Remember, Hanyu Pinyin is only a crutch to rely on until you are able to relate from memory the SMC pronunciation of a word with its corresponding Chinese character or characters.

Overview of the Five Tones

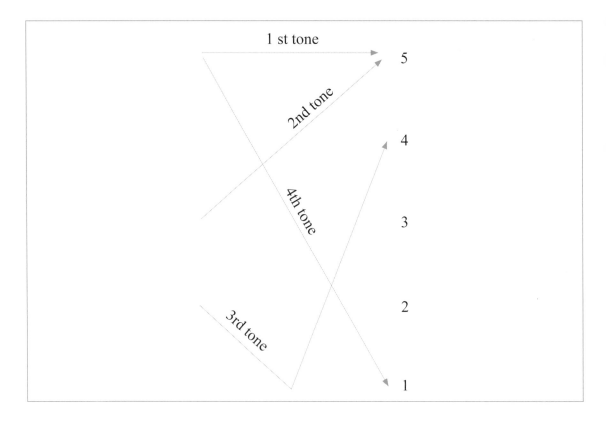

SMC has five tones.

1. The 1st tone (high, level tone) is spoken high and the voice neither falls nor rises. It is indicated with a level [-] diacritic: mā

2. The 2nd tone (rising tone) starts with the voice lower than the 1st tone but ends with the voice just as high. It is indicated with a rising [/] diacritic: má

3. The 3rd tone (falling-rising tone) starts with the voice lower than the second tone, dips low, and then rises to a tone lower than the 1st or 2nd tone. It is indicated with a falling-rising [v] diacritic: mǎ

    3.1 The 3rd tone is a changeable tone. When two 3rd tones come together, the first 3rd tone should be changed into a 2nd tone. For example, nǐhǎo（你好 *hello*）should be pronounced níhǎo.

3.2 When a 3rd tone is followed by a 1st, 2nd, 4th, or neutral tone, the 3rd tone should be pronounced as a half 3rd tone. In other words, it is a low tone, as in jǐnzhāng（緊張 *nervous*）and jiějué（解決 *to solve*）. Both jǐn and jiě start low, drop even lower, and then *do not* rise in tone.

3.3 Only under the following conditions should the 3rd tone be pronounced as a proper 3rd tone:

a. When a 3rd-tone word is spoken is on its own. For example, the monosyllabic expression hǎo（好 *good, okay*）is pronounced with a proper, complete 3rd tone.

b. When a 3rd tone is at the end of a sentence or a phrase. For example, fànghǎo（放好 *to place* [something] *properly.*）in the sentence 請你放好 (qíng nǐ fànghǎo *please put it down*). Take note that in this sentence, because 請你 (qǐng nǐ) contains two 3rd tones, the first 3rd tone changes to a 2nd tone.

3.4 When a sentence has three 3rd tones next to each other, it can be changed into one of the following two patterns:

a. 2nd, 2nd, proper 3rd. For example, wǒ hěnhǎo（我很好 *I am fine*）can be pronounced wó hénhǎo.

b. half 3rd, 2nd, proper 3rd. For example, wǒ hěnhǎo（我很好 *I am fine*）can also be pronounced wǒ hénhǎo.

4. The 4th tone (falling tone) falls rapidly from high to low. It is indicated with a falling [\] diacritic: mà

5. The 5th tone (neutral tone) is a short, light tone. It can be indicated with a dot [·] diacritic (·ma), or left unmarked (ma). The best way to remember how to pronounce the neutral tone is to remember its length and pitch as follows:

5.1 The syllable before the neutral tone should be pronounced longer.

5.2 The pitch of the neutral tone varies depending on the tone that precedes it. If a neutral tone is preceded by a 1st or 2nd tone, both of which end at a high pitch, the neutral tone should be voiced at a lower pitch than the preceding tone. When preceded by the 3rd tone, the neutral tone is voiced at a higher pitch than the preceding tone and, in fact, at a pitch higher than the neutral tone following the 1st and 2nd tone. Finally, when preceded by the 4th tone, the neutral tone is pronounced at an even lower pitch than the preceding tone.

Table 4   Absolute Pitch of Neutral Tone Based on Pitch of Preceding Tone

word	pinyin	meaning	absolute pitch of neutral tone
喇叭	lǎba / lǎba	horn	highest
伯伯	bóbo / bóbo	uncle	
玻璃	bōli / bōli	glass	
兔子	tùzi / tùzi	rabbit	lowest

The following table summarizes the characteristics of the five tones.

Table 5   Hanyu Pinyin Final "a" Combined with the Five Tones and the Initial "b"

1st tone (high, level tone) ā	2nd tone (rising tone) á	3rd tone (falling-rising tone) ǎ	4th tone (falling tone) à	5th tone (neutral tone) a / a
The 1st tone is indicated by placing the level diacritic [-] above the main vowel. It has a long sustained sound.	The 2nd tone is marked with the rising diacritic [/] above the main vowel. Start from the middle of the tone range and end at the high pitch of the first tone.	The 3rd tone is indicated by placing the falling-rising diacritic [v] above the main vowel. This tone starts at a low pitch, drops to the lowest pitch, and then, depending on the surrounding tones, either stops or rises to a pitch slightly higher than the starting-point.	The 4th tone is marked with the falling diacritic [\] above the main vowel. It initiates high and ends low. The tone falls quickly. The 4th tone is shorter in duration than the 1st and 2nd tone.	The neutral, or 5th tone, is commonly unmarked, or can be indicated by a dot diacritic [·] placed to the left of the word. It is a short, light tone.
bā 八 eight	bá 拔 to pull out	bǎ 把 a handle; to hold	bà 爸 father	ba / ba 吧 particle indicating imperative tense, agreement, or uncertainty

Tone Changes with 一 (yī) and 不 (bù)

As mentioned earlier, tones in SMC are sometimes changeable. This is called tone sandhi. For example, the 3rd tone changes to a 2nd tone when appearing before another 3rd tone. Another common tone sandhi occurs with the words 一 (yī *one*) and 不 (bù *no; not*) when they precede words pronounced in the 4th tone. Specifically, yī becomes yí when it is followed by 4th tone, and bù becomes bú when it precedes a 4th tone. Take note of the examples below.

yī （一 *one*）+ yàng （樣 *kind*） → yí yàng （一樣 *the same*）

yī （一 *one*）+ wàn （萬 *ten thousand*） → yí wàn （一萬 *ten thousand*）

bù （不 *not*）+ shì （是 *to be; is*） → bú shì （不是 *is not*）

bù （不 *not*）+ yào （要 *want; must*） → bú yào （不要 *do not want; don't*）

Where should I mark the tones?

Tones should be marked on a vowel in a final. If a word has a compound final with more than one vowel, the tone should be marked on the main vowel of the final. Main vowels are listed in the following order: a, o, e, i, u, and ü. As the vowel "a" appears first in this list, the tone in the word liao should be marked on the vowel "a" like this: liāo liáo liǎo liào. Likewise, since "e" comes before "u," the tones for the combination "xue" are marked like this: xuē xué xuě xuè. However, there are exceptions. For example: tuī tuí tuǐ tuì and liū liú liǔ liù. Therefore, when learning new vocabulary words, pay close attention to which vowel is emphasized and where the tone is marked.

Initials

There are 21 initials in SMC. The table below arranges the initials by their place of articulation, the position of the tongue, and whether the sound is aspirated. Aspiration is an audible breath that accompanies or comprises a speech sound.

Table 6   Hanyu Pinyin Initials with Respect to Articulation and Aspiration

labial	dental	velar (back of tongue)	palatal	retroflex	alveolar	aspiration
b	d	g	j	zh	z	non-aspirated
p	t	k	q	ch	c	aspirated
m	n					non-aspirated
		h	x	sh	s	aspirated
	l			r		non-aspirated
f						aspirated

The following figure shows the parts of the mouth used in making the SMC initials.

Figure 1   Places of Articulation

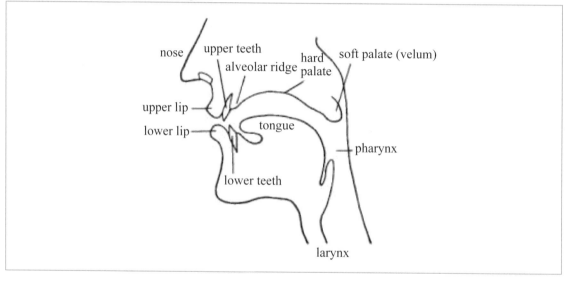

Labials

The labial initials are formed with the lips. The tongue remains relaxed. With the labials, as with the other initials that follow, pay close attention to which sounds are aspirated and which are not.

b is pronounced like the **b** in "**b**ay," but is pronounced more lightly than in English. It is unaspirated, like the **p**, in "s**p**it."

p is pronounced like the **p** in "**p**en," but is accompanied by a stronger puff of air than in English. It is aspirated, like the **p** in "**p**it."

m is pronounced like the **m** in "**m**an." Start the sound with the lips together. The sound is slightly nasal, so you should feel a vibration in the nasal cavity.

f is pronounced like the **f** in "**f**ive." It is aspirated. The upper teeth contact the lower lip and air is forced out between them.

Dentals

The dental initials are formed by placing the tip of the tongue behind the upper front teeth, and then bringing the tongue down as the sound is produced.

d is pronounced like the **d** is "**d**ay," but is pronounced more lightly than in English. It is unaspirated, like the **t** in "s**t**op."

t is pronounced like the **t** as "**t**en," but is accompanied by a stronger puff of air than in English. It is aspirated like the **t** in "**t**op."

n is pronounced like the **n** in "**n**ame." It is unaspirated.

l is pronounced like the **l** in "**l**ike." It is unaspirated.

Velars

The velar initials are produced with the throat interacting with the back of the tongue.

g is pronounced like the **g** in "**g**o," or the **k** in "s**k**i," but is pronounced more lightly than in English. This is the only velar that not aspirated.

k is pronounced like the **k** in "**k**ite," or "**k**ey," but is accompanied by a stronger puff of air than in English. It is aspirated.

h is pronounced like the **h** as in "**h**ow," but is pronounced further back in the throat, and is accompanied by a stronger puff of air than in English. It is aspirated.

Palatals

The palatal initials are formed with the lips slightly parted and stretched tightly. The tongue is flat and pressed against the lower front teeth, touching the flat ridge behind the upper front teeth. Since the tongue is kept flat, it is the shape of a blade. Keeping the tongue stationary, the jaw is lowered slightly allowing for the formation of sound.

j is pronounced like the **j** in "jeep," with the flattened edge of the tongue forward behind the lower teeth. The sound is squeezed out between the top of the tongue and the hard palate as the jaw opens slightly. It is not aspirated.

q is pronounced like the **ch** in "cheap," with the flattened edge of the tongue forward behind the lower teeth. The sound is squeezed out between the top of the tongue and the hard palate as the jaw opens slightly, accompanied by a flow of air. It is aspirated.

x is pronounced like the **sh** in "sheep," with the flattened edge of the tongue forward behind the lower teeth. The sound is squeezed out between the top of the tongue and the hard palate as the jaw opens slightly, accompanied by a flow of air. It is aspirated.

Retroflexes

The retroflex initials are formed by curling the tip of the tongue back and touching it against the roof of the mouth. The tip of the tongue should touch the hard palate at a point somewhere behind the alveolar ridge (the hard ridge behind the upper front teeth) and the soft palate.

zh is pronounced like the **j** in "jet," but with the tongue curled up and back, the tip touching the roof of the mouth. Like the Hanyu Pinyin **j**, it is unaspirated.

ch is pronounced like the **ch** in "chance," but with the tongue curled up and back, the tip touching the roof of the mouth. Like the Hanyu Pinyin **q**, it is aspirated.

sh is pronounced like the **sh** in "shine," but with the tongue curled up, the tip touching the roof of the mouth. Like the Hanyu Pinyin **x**, it is aspirated.

r is pronounced with the tongue beginning curled back like the **l** in "laugh," but with the tip not quite touching the roof of the mouth. Then say the **wr** part of "wrong." The tongue does not move and sound comes out from the throat, but it is unaspirated.

Alveolars

The alveolar initials are made with the tip of the tongue and the alveolar ridge. For each, begin with the top of the tongue pressed against the alveolar ridge and the tip touching the back of the upper front teeth. Keep the tongue flat and lower it slightly to make the sound.

z is pronounced like the **ds** in "rea**ds**." Like Hanyu Pinyin **j** and **zh**, it is unaspirated.

c is pronounced like the **ts** in "ca**ts**." Like Hanyu Pinyin **q** and **ch**, it is aspirated.

s is pronounced like the **s** in "**s**nake," but is pronounced more strongly than in English. Like Hanyu Pinyin **x** and **sh**, is it aspirated.

Finals

The table below lists the 38 finals and final combinations found in SMC.

Table 7   Hanyu Pinyin Finals and Final Combinations

	i	u	ü
a	ia	ua → wa	
o		uo	
e	ie		üe
ê			
-i*			
er			
ai		uai	
ei		uei → ui	
ao	iao		
ou	iou → iu		
an	ian	uan	üan
en	in	uen → un	ün
ang	iang	uang	
eng	ing	ueng → weng	
ong	iong		

*Follows these initials: zh, ch, sh, r, z, c, s

The following diagram shows the part of the mouth where each of the vowel sounds in SMC finals is produced. Refer to the chart as you read descriptions of the individual finals that follow.

Diagram 1   SMC Vowel (Finals) Chart

	front	central	back
high	i ü		u
mid	ei	e	u o
	en		
low	ai		a

Mid-Front and Low-Central

a is pronounced like the **a** in "father." Open your mouth wide and say, "Aah." It is articulated at the low, central position in the mouth.

ai is pronounced like the **i** in "dine." It is articulated at the mid, front position in the mouth.

an is pronounced with the **a** in "car." With the addition of **n**, the Pinyin **an** is somewhere between English "an" and "on," articulated at the low, central position in the mouth. Start with the **a** in "car," and then touch the front of your hard palate with the tip of the tongue.

ang is pronounced like the **ong** in "wrong." Articulate an **a** at the low, central position and then touch the soft palate with the back of your tongue.

ao is pronounced like the **ow** in "now." It is a diphthong (double vowel). To articulate it, begin at the low, central position, and finish in the mid, back position.

Table 8　Initial-Final Examples

	a	ai	an	ang	ao
m	mā 媽 mother	mǎi 買 to buy	màn 慢 slow	máng 忙 busy	māo 貓 cat

Mid-Front and Mid-Central

e is usually pronounced like the **u** in "**u**p," and articulated at the mid, central part of the mouth. However, after **i** or **y**, it is pronounced like the **e** in "**yet**," and articulated in the mid, front area of the mouth.

ê is pronounced like the **ay** in "d**ay**." It is used by itself and pronounced in the 1st, 2nd, 3rd, and 4th tone as an interjection to express affirmation, agreement, disapproval, surprise, or to attract attention.

ei is pronounced like the **a** in "l**a**te." It is a dipthong that begins low front and ends mid front.

en is pronounced similar to the **en** in "t**en**." Maintain the mid-central **e** sound and then touch front of your hard palate with the tip of your tongue.

eng is pronounced like the **ung** in "r**ung**." Begin with the mid-central **e** and then touch your soft palate with the back of your tongue.

er is pronounced somewhat like the word "are." The **r** is voiced with the tongue curled. **B**egin with the mid-central **e** and then curl the tongue back.

Table 9　Initial-Final and Stand-Alone Final Examples

	e	ei	en	eng	er
g	gè 個 measure word	gěi 給 to give	gēn 跟 with	gèng 更 even more	
no initial	yě 也 also				èr 二 two
NOTE: When "e" is a stand-alone final, a "y" is added					

Glides with "i"

i, after **b**, **d**, **j**, **l**, **m**, **n**, **p**, **q**, **t** and **x**, is pronounced like the **ee** in "s**ee**." Pull your lips back and push your tongue up towards the hard palate without touching it completely-air needs to pass over the tongue. It is articulated in the front, high part of the mouth.

Table 10   Initial-Final Examples

bǐ 筆	dì 地	jī 機	lì 立	mǐ 米	nǐ 你	pí 皮	qī 七	tǐ 體	xī 西
brush-pen	land; soil	machine	to stand	rice	you	skin	seven	body	west

-i, after the retroflexes (**zh**, **ch**, **sh**, and **r**), is voiced similar to the **e** in "h**er**." After the alveolars (**z**, **c**, and **s**), the voiced sound is similar to the "bu**zz**" of a bee.

Table 11   Initial-Final Examples

zhǐ 只	zǐ 子	chī 吃	cí 詞	shí 十	sì 四	rì 日
only; just	son	to eat	word(s)	ten	four	sun; day

ia is pronounced like the **yaw** as in "**yaw**n." It is a dipthong that begins high front, and ends low central. As a stand-alone final, it is written **ya**.

ian is pronounced similarly to the Japanese unit of currency, the "**yen**." This dipthong begins high front, moves mid central, and ends with the tip of the tongue touching the alveolar ridge. As a stand-alone final, it is written **yan**.

iang is pronounced with the **y** of "**y**es" followed by the **ong** of "s**ong**." Begin high front, move low central, and then finish by pressing the back of the tongue against the soft palate. As a stand-alone final, it is written **yang**.

iao is pronounced like the **yow** in "**yow**l" or the **eow** in "m**eow**." It is a tripthong (triple vowel). Start high front, move low central, and then finish mid back with the lips rounded. As a stand-alone final, it is written **yao**.

ie is pronounced like the **ye** in "**ye**t." This dipthong begins high front and ends mid front. As a stand-alone final, it is written **ye**.

in is pronounced like the **ene** in "Ir**ene**." It is articulated high front. Sustain the **i** sound, then touch front of your hard palate with the tip of your tongue. As a stand-alone final, it is written **yin**.

ing is pronounced like the **ing** in "s**ing**," but with a more nasal sound. Articulate in the high, front position. Sustain the **i** and then touch your soft palate with the back of your tongue. As a stand-alone final, it is written **ying**.

iong is pronounced with the **ee** in "s**ee**," followed by the **o** of "n**o**te," and finally the by the **ng** of "si**ng**." The articulation begins high front and moves mid back with the back of the tongue touching the soft palate. As a stand-alone final, it is written **yong**.

iu is pronounced like **yo** in "**yo**del." This articulation of this dipthong moves from high front to mid back. As a stand-alone final, it is written **you**.

Table 12   Initial-Final and Stand-Alone Final Examples

	ia	ian	iang	iao	ie	in	ing	iong	iu
x	xiā 蝦 shrimp	xiàn 線 thread; line	xiāng 香 fragrant	xiào 笑 to laugh	xiè 謝 to thank	xīn 新 new	xìng 姓 surname	xióng 熊 bear	xiū 修 to repair
no initial	yá 牙 a tooth	yān 煙 smoke	yǎng 養 to raise	yǎo 咬 to bite	yé 爺 grand-father	yín 銀 silver	yìng 硬 hard	yǒng 永 always	yòu 右 right

NOTE: When finals beginning with "i" stand alone, a "y" is added.

Mid-Back and High-Back

o is pronounced somewhat like **o** in "m**o**rning," but with the mouth not open as wide. Begin with your lips forward in a tight circle and your tongue at the bottom of your mouth. As you make the sound, slowly lower your jaw and open your lips, keeping your tongue at the bottom of your mouth, leaving a hollow space above it. Articulated at the mid, back position in the mouth.

ong is pronounced with the **o** in "n**o**te" followed by the **ng** in "si**ng**." It is articulated in the mid back position. Say **o** and touch your soft palate with the back of your tongue.

ou is pronounced like the **o** in "v**o**te." Begin low back and end mid back.

Table 13   Initial-Final and Stand-Alone Final Examples

	o	ou	ong
m	mó 摩 to rub, touch	mǒu 某 some	
d		dòu 豆 bean	dòng 洞 hole
no initial	ó 哦 oh; ah	ōu 鷗 a gull	

High-Front and High-Back

u is pronounced like **oo** as in "too," except after **j**, **q**, **x** and **y**, where it is pronounced differently-see **ü** below. Push your lips forward and make a narrow gap through which your breath can pass. Your lips should be shaped like they are when you say "boot." The articulation is high back. As a stand-alone final, it is written **wu**.

ua is pronounced like the **wa** in "watch." As the articulation moves from high back to low back, the mouth opens from a rounded-lip shape to a semi-smile. As a stand-alone final, it is written **wa**.

uai is pronounced like "why." This is a tripthong. The articulation begins high back, moves low front, then finishes mid front. As a stand-alone final, it is written **wai**.

uan is pronounced with most initials like the **wan** in "wander." Begin high back, glide to low back, and then bring the tongue tip up to touch the alveolar ridge. As a stand-alone final, it is written **wan**. Do not confuse with **üan** (see below).

uang is pronounced with the **w** of "way" followed by the **ong** of "long." Say **ua** and then touch your soft palate with the back of your tongue. As a stand-alone final, it is written **wang**.

ue is pronounced like **üe** (see below). As a stand-alone final, it appears as **yue**. It is also used with the initials **j**, **q**, and **x** to form the syllables **jue**, **que**, and **xue**.

uei is written in pinyin as **ui** and is pronounced like "way" Begin high back and glide to a position high front. As a stand-alone final, it is written **wei**.

uen is written in pinyin as **un** and is pronounced like the **oo** in "moon," followed by the **un** of "under." The pronunciation of **un** is **u** + **en**. Say **u** first, then **en**. The articulation moves from high back to mid front, and then the tongue tip moves up to touch the alveolar ridge. As a stand-alone final, it is written **wen**. Do not confuse with **ün** (see below).

ueng is written in pinyin as **weng** and is pronounced like the **oo** in "book" followed by the **ng** in "lung." Since the final **ueng** does not combine with any initials, it is an exclusive stand-alone final. As such, it always appears written as **weng**. The articulation glides from high back to mid central, and then the back of the tongue moves up to touch the soft palate.

uo is pronounced with the **w** of "wet" followed by a sound like the **o** in "hot" with the mouth not open as wide. The articulation begins high back and ends mid back. As a stand-alone final, it is written **wo**.

ü appears with the initials **n**, **l**, **j**, **q**, and **x** to form the syllables **nü**, **lü**, **ju**, **qu**, and **xu**. As a stand-alone syllable, it appears as **yu**. The diacritic dots above the "u" are omitted with **ju**, **qu**, **xu**, and **yu** because these initials cannot be combined with **u**. One the other hand, notice that the dots are used above the "u" following "n" and "l" because these initials can be combined with "u." The pronunciation of "nü" and "nu" is different, as is the pronunciation of "lü" and "lu." To produce the **ü** sound, start by saying "yī." As you say it, keep the position of your jaw stationary but round your lips as if you were going to whistle. It is similar to the umlaut "ü" in German or the French "u." Say the **ee** in "s**ee**" through tightly pursed lips-the shape they make when you say the "**sh**" of the English word "fi**sh**."

üe is pronounced like **u** as in French "**u**ne," followed by **we** as in "**we**nt." The articulation begins high front and moves mid front. As a stand-alone final, it is written **yue**.

üan is pronounced with the **u** in French "**u**ne," followed by the **an** in "isl**an**d." The articulation begins high front, moves mid front, and concludes with the tongue tip moving up to touch the alveolar ridge. It combines exclusively with the initials **j**, **q**, and **x**. As a stand-alone final, it is written **yuan**.

ün is produced by saying the **ü** sound, and then touching the front of your hard palate with the tip of your tongue. As a stand-alone final, it appears as **yun**. When combined with the initials **j**, **q**, and **x**, it appears as **jun**, **qun**, **xun**. Notice the diacritic dots are omitted. Because these initials are never combined with **u**, there is no ambiguity.

Table 14   Initial-Final and Stand-Alone Final Examples

	u	ua	uai	uan	uang	ueng	ui	un	uo	ü	üe	ün	üan
h	戶 hù a n account	花 huā flower(s)	壞 huài bad	換 huàn to exchange	皇 huáng an emperor		回 huí to go back	混 hùn to mix	貨 huò goods				
j										句 jù a sentence	爵 jué feudal title	菌 jùn bacteria	卷 juǎn to roll up
l	鹿 lù a deer			亂 luàn disorder				輪 lún a wheel	羅 luó a surname	驢 l a donkey	略 lüè a plan		
n	奴 nú a slave			暖 nuǎn warm					諾 nuò to consent	女 nǚ woman	虐 nüè cruel		
	無 wú without	挖 wā to dig	歪 wāi crooked	晚 wǎn night; late	網 wǎng a net	翁 wēng an old man	未 wèi not	問 wèn to ask	握 wò to hold	雨 yǔ rain	約 yuē to arrange	暈 yūn dizzy	院 yuàn a courtyard

NOTE: When finals beginning with "u" stand alone, a "w" is added. For the stand-alone finals beginning with "ü," a "y" is added.

Before we conclude our discussion of Hanyu Pinyin finals, practice reading the vowels below.

$$\bar{a} \quad \bar{o} \quad \bar{e} \quad \bar{\imath} \quad \bar{u} \quad \bar{\ddot{u}}$$

Use the vowel chart on page XX as well as the recording accompanying this book to guide you. If you read them from left to right, you should notice that the shape of your mouth will start off quite open, and then gradually become narrower.

Table of Possible Initial and Final Combinations

This table shows all of the syllables that can be formed in SMC by combining the various initials and finals. It also shows which finals can stand alone as syllables. Notice that many combinations are not possible. For each possible stand-alone syllable or syllable combination, an example character is given with its corresponding Hanyu Pinyin.

請參閱本書下一頁所附之「Potential Combinations of Nanyu Pinyin Initials, Finals, and Jones in Standard Mandarin Chinese」表。

Conclusion

The two characteristics of modern Chinese that make it particularly challenging for students are Chinese characters and tones.

With its relatively limited number of vowels and consonants, the articulation of sounds in SMC is not particularly difficult. Depending on your native language, there are a few sounds that will take some time to master, but overall you will find the consistency of vowels and consonants and their combinations predictable and far from impossible to master. However, SMC has tones, and coming to terms with them is a common source of frustration for students.

Many textbooks and language courses fail to emphasize an important aspect of tones, and for that reason, this book is going to reveal it now in hope that you keep it in mind *every time* you speak SMC: The key to mastering tones is to pay close attention to starting and ending points of each tone-this is the secret behind making them sound distinctly different, and making your Chinese sound remarkably standard.

ie	iu	ian	in	iang	ing	iong	u	ua	uo	uai	ui	uan	un	uang	ueng	ü	üe	üan	ün
ye 也 yě	you 有 yǒu	yan 言 yán	yin 陰 yīn	yang 陽 yáng	ying 影 yǐng	yong 用 yòng	wu 五 wǔ	wa 挖 wā	wo 我 wǒ	wai 外 wài	wei 為 wéi	wan 萬 wàn	wen 文 wén	wang 王 wáng	weng 翁 wēng	yu 魚 yú	yue 月 yuè	yuan 元 yuán	yun 雲 yún
bie 別 bié		bian 變 biàn	bin 賓 bīn		bing 冰 bīng		bu 不 bù												
pie 撇 piě		pian 片 piàn	pin 品 pǐn		ping 平 píng		pu 普 pǔ												
mie 滅 miè	miu 謬 miù	mian 面 miàn	min 民 mín		ming 明 míng		mu 目 mù												
							fu 福 fú												
die 爹 diē	diu 丟 diū	dian 點 diǎn			ding 丁 dīng		du 度 dù		duo 多 duō		dui 對 duì	duan 段 duàn	dun 盾 dùn						
tie 鐵 tiě		tian 天 tiān			ting 聽 tīng		tu 土 tǔ		tuo 脫 tuō		tui 推 tuī	tuan 團 tuán	tun 吞 tūn						
nie 嚙 niè	niu 牛 niú	nian 年 nián	nin 您 nín	niang 娘 niáng	ning 寧 níng		nu 努 nǔ		nuo 諾 nuò			nuan 暖 nuǎn				nü 女 nǚ	nüe 虐 nüè		
lie 列 liè	liu 六 liù	lian 臉 liǎn	lin 林 lín	liang 兩 liǎng	ling 令 lìng		lu 路 lù		luo 落 luò			luan 亂 luàn	lun 論 lùn			lü 綠 lǜ	lüe 略 lüè		
							gu 古 gǔ	gua 瓜 guā	guo 國 guó	guai 乖 guāi	gui 貴 guì	guan 關 guān	gun 滾 gǔn	guang 光 guāng					
							ku 哭 kū	kua 跨 kuà	kuo 擴 kuò	kuai 快 kuài	kui 葵 kuí	kuan 寬 kuān	kun 昆 kūn	kuang 狂 kuáng					
							hu 湖 hú	hua 化 huà	huo 火 huǒ	huai 懷 huái	hui 會 huì	huan 還 huán	hun 昏 hūn	huang 黃 huáng					
jie 節 jié	jiu 就 jiù	jian 見 jiàn	jin 金 jīn	jiang 江 jiāng	jing 京 jīng	jiong 炯 jiǒng										ju 局 jú	jue 覺 jué	juan 捐 juān	jun 君 jūn
qie 切 qiè	qiu 求 qiú	qian 千 qiān	qin 秦 qín	qiang 強 qiáng	qing 青 qīng	qiong 窮 qióng										qu 去 qù	que 缺 quē	quan 全 quán	qun 群 qún
xie 寫 xiě	xiu 休 xiū	xian 先 xiān	xin 信 xìn	xiang 想 xiǎng	xing 行 xíng	xiong 凶 xiōng										xu 許 xǔ	xue 學 xué	xuan 選 xuǎn	xun 訊 xùn
							zhu 住 zhù	zhua 抓 zhuā	zhuo 桌 zhuō	zhuai 跩 zhuǎi	zhui 追 zhuī	zhuan 尊 zhuān	zhun 准 zhǔn	zhuang 壯 zhuàng					
							chu 出 chū		chuo 戳 chuō	chuai 踹 chuài	chui 吹 chuī	chuan 川 chuān	chun 春 chūn	chuang 床 chuáng					
							shu 書 shū	shua 刷 shuā	shuo 說 shuō	shuai 帥 shuài	shui 水 shuǐ	shuan 栓 shuān	shun 順 shùn	shuang 爽 shuǎng					
							ru 如 rú		ruo 弱 ruò		rui 瑞 ruì	ruan 軟 ruǎn	run 閏 rùn						
							zu 租 zū		zuo 做 zuò		zui 最 uì	zuan 鑽 zuàn	zun 尊 zūn						
							cu 粗 cū		cuo 錯 cuò		cui 脆 cuì	cuan 余 cuān	cun 存 cún						
							su 素 sù		suo 所 suǒ		sui 隨 suí	suan 算 suàn	sun 孫 sūn						

Potential Combinations of Hanyu Pinyin Initials, F

initial \ final	a	o	e	ê	-i	er	ai	ei	ao	ou	an	en	ang	eng	ong	i	ia	iao
a	a 阿 ā	o 哦 ó	e 惡 ě	ê 欸		er 二 èr	ai 愛 ài	ei 欸 éi	ao 凹 āo	ou 歐 ōu	an 安 ān	en 恩 ēn	ang 昂 áng			yi 一 yī	ya 鴨 yā	yao 要 yào
b	ba 八 bā	bo 波 bō					bai 百 bǎi	bei 北 běi	bao 保 bǎo		ban 班 bān	ben 本 běn	bang 棒 bàng	beng 甭 béng		bi 比 bǐ		biao 表 biǎo
p	pa 怕 pà	po 破 pò					pai 排 pái	pei 配 pèi	pao 跑 pǎo	pou 剖 pōu	pan 盤 pán	pen 噴 pēn	pang 胖 pàng	peng 碰 pèng		pi 皮 pí		piao 票 piào
m	ma 馬 mǎ	mo 末 mò	me 麼 me				mai 買、賣 mǎi mài	mei 美 měi	mao 毛 máo	mou 某 mǒu	man 慢 màn	men 門 mén	mang 忙 máng	meng 孟 mèng		mi 米 mǐ		miao 秒 miǎo
f	fa 發 fā	fo 佛 fó						fei 非 fēi		fou 否 fǒu	fan 飯 fàn	fen 分 fēn	fang 方 fāng	feng 風 fēng				
d	da 大 dà		de 的 de				dai 代 dài	dei 得 děi	dao 到 dào	dou 都 dōu	dan 但 dàn		dang 當 dāng	deng 等 děng	dong 東 dōng	di 地 dì		diao 掉 diào
t	ta 他、她 tā		te 特 tè				tai 太 tài		tao 套 tào	tou 頭 tóu	tan 談 tán		tang 堂 táng	teng 疼 téng	tong 痛 tòng	ti 題 tí		tiao 條 tiáo
n	na 那 nà		ne 呢 ne				nai 奶 nǎi	nei 內 nèi	nao 腦 nǎo		nan 南 nán	nen 嫩 nèn	nang 囊 náng	neng 能 néng	nong 弄 nòng	ni 你 nǐ		niao 鳥 niǎo
l	la 拉 lā		le 了 le				lai 來 lái	lei 類 lèi	lao 老 lǎo	lou 樓 lóu	lan 藍 lán		lang 狼 láng	leng 冷 lěng	long 龍 lóng	li 里 lǐ	lia 倆 liǎ	liao 了 liǎo
g	ga 咖 gā		ge 哥 gē				gai 改 gǎi	gei 給 gěi	gao 高 gāo	gou 夠 gòu	gan 肝 gān	gen 跟 gēn	gang 剛 gāng	geng 更 gèng	gong 公 gōng			
k	ka 卡 kǎ						kai 開 kāi		kao 考 kǎo	kou 口 kǒu	kan 看 kàn	ken 肯 kěn	kang 康 kāng	keng 坑 kēng	kong 空 kōng			
h	ha 哈 hā						hai 還 hái	hei 黑 hēi	hao 好 hǎo	hou 後 hòu	han 漢 hàn	hen 很 hěn	hang 行 háng	heng 橫 héng	hong 紅 hóng			
j																ji 及 jí	jia 家 jiā	jiao 角 jiǎo
q																qi 其 qí	qia 掐 qiā	qiao 橋 qiáo
x																xi 西 xǐ	xia 下 xià	xiao 小 xiǎo
zh	zha 炸 zhà		zhe 這 zhè		zhi 直 zhí		zhai 窄 zhǎi	zhei 這 zhèi	zhao 找 zhǎo	zhou 周 zhōu	zhan 站 zhàn	zhen 真 zhēn	zhang 張 zhāng	zheng 正 zhèng	zhong 中 zhōng			
ch	cha 茶 chá		che 車 chē		chi 吃 chī		chai 柴 chái		chao 超 chāo	chou 臭 chòu	chan 禪 chán	chen 陳 chén	chang 長 cháng	cheng 成 chéng	chong 蟲 chóng			
sh	sha 殺 shā		she 蛇 shé		shi 是 shì		shai 曬 shài	shei 誰 shéi	shao 少 shǎo	shou 手 shǒu	shan 山 shān	shen 深 shēn	shang 上 shàng	sheng 生 shēng				
r			re 熱 rè		ri 日 rì				rao 繞 rào	rou 肉 ròu	ran 然 rán	ren 人 rén	rang 讓 ràng	reng 仍 réng	rong 容 róng			
z	za 雜 zá		ze 責 zé		zi 自 zì		zai 在 zài	zei 賊 zéi	zao 早 zǎo	zou 走 zǒu	zan 贊 zàn	zen 怎 zěn	zang 髒 zāng	zeng 曾 zēng	zong 總 zǒng			
c	ca 擦 cā		ce 策 cè		ci 詞 cí		cai 才 cái		cao 草 cǎo	cou 湊 còu	can 慘 cǎn	cen 參 cēn	cang 倉 cāng	ceng 層 céng	cong 從 cóng			
s	sa 卅 sà		se 色 sè		si 死 sǐ		sai 賽 sài		sao 掃 sǎo sào	sou 搜 sōu	san 三 sān	sen 森 sēn	sang 桑 sāng	seng 僧 sēng	song 送 sòng			

目　錄
Contents

序　(3)

Chinese Characters　(5)

Chinese Phonetics　(19)

Potential Combinations of Hanyu Pinyin Initials, Finals, and Tones in Standard Mandarin Chinese

1 Claire White　白愷俐 (Bai Kaili)

Claire White is an easygoing girl from Vancouver, Canada. As an Aries, she is very optimistic and always open to new things. Her father, a pastor, makes her a pious Christian, and her mother, an English teacher, endows her with a talent for language learning. She has just graduated from college, where she majored in music. She has come to Taiwan to learn Chinese simply to give herself another way to see things. She is 22 years old.

2 Joshua Chamberlain　張志學 (Zhang Zhixue)

Joshua Chamberlain is Claire's best friend in the Chinese classroom. He is a frank, adventurous, knowledgeable young man from Los Angeles, the United States. He has a pure mind and seldom thinks too much; he is always ready to do something and never hesitates before taking actions. He had studied biology for two years when he went to Sydney, Australia to study biochemistry, where he made some good friends from Taiwan. He decided to learn more about Taiwan more and comes to study Chinese. He has fallen completely in love with Claire, although he is one year younger than she is.

3 William Smith　陳偉立 (Chen Weili)

William Smith is a designer who works for a transpacific advertising company from San Francisco, the United States. He is 33 years old, married, and he comes to Taiwan in order to live with of his wife, Lin Anhui 林安惠, and her family. They met when Anhui studied design in California. William is diligent in his work, devoted to his marriage and family, and prefers a peaceful life to an exciting one. To Claire and Joshua, William is always the right one to talk to when they need good advice.

4 Fatoumate Jammeh　賈法杜 (Jia Fadu)

Fatoumate Jammeh is a clever 19-year-old muslim girl from Banjul, The Gambia. Having won a scholarship, she comes to Taiwan to study medicine at National Taiwan University. Members of her family went to different places around the world to work or to study. Her greatest hope is to build a hospital in a rural area of The Gambia to cure her fellow people of disease.

5 Kim Higyeong　金希京 (Jin Xijing)

Kim Higyeong comes from Seoul, South Korea to Taiwan in order to study politics in a Taiwanese graduate institute. She is now working temporarily in a Korean company. She is highly interested in diplomacy, politics and other social sciences, and of course, she also would like to find a good boyfriend in Taiwan.

6 Gao Lishan　高立山

Gao Lishan is a Taiwanese college student. He majors in computer science and works as a part-time programmer. He is renting a room in the building where Claire lives, and happens to be Joshua's language exchange partner.

7 Fan Huimei　范惠美

Fan Huimei is Lishan's good friend, who majors in history at the university where Lishan studies. She is also one of Claire's neighbors.

第一課 早安！您好！
dì   yī kè   zǎoān   nínhǎo

 ● 對話 一 *Dialogue One*
duìhuà yī

(On the street.)

1
鄰居 ： *2*小姐，*3*早安！
línjū   xiǎojiě   zǎoān

4
愷俐 ： *5*先生，早安！*6*你好嗎？
kǎilì   xiānshēng   zǎoān   nǐhǎo ma

7 *8*   *9* *10*
鄰居 ： 我很好，你呢？
línjū   wǒ hěn hǎo   nǐ ne

愷俐 ： 我*11*也很好，*12*謝謝！
kǎilì   wǒ yě hěn hǎo   xièxie

13
鄰居 ： 再見！
línjū   zàijiàn

愷俐 ： 再見！
kǎilì   zàijiàn

● 生詞 *Vocabulary*
shēngcí

1 鄰居 neighbor
2 小姐 lady, miss
3 早安 good morning
4 愷俐 Kaili (Chinese name of Claire
          White, a Canadian girl)
5 先生 sir, mister
6 你好嗎？ How are you?
7 很 quite
8 好 to be fine, good
9 你 you
10 呢 (interrogative marker)
11 也 also
12 謝謝 thank you
13 再見 goodbye

● 對話二 *Dialogue Two*
duìhuà èr

(In Hanlai Chinese Language Center.)

老師：小姐，您好！
lǎoshī　xiǎojiě　nínhǎo

愷俐：先生，您好！您是老師嗎？
kǎilì　xiānshēng　nínhǎo　nín shì lǎoshī ma

老師：我是老師。
lǎoshī　wǒ shì lǎoshī

愷俐：老師好！
kǎilì　lǎoshī hǎo

老師：你好，你是 學生 嗎？
lǎoshī　nǐhǎo　nǐ shì xuéshēng ma

愷俐：我是 學生。他也是 學生 嗎？
kǎilì　wǒ shì xuéshēng　tā yě shì xuéshēng ma

老師：他不是 學生，他也是老師。
lǎoshī　tā bú shì xuéshēng　tā yě shì lǎoshī

愷俐：謝謝老師！
kǎilì　xièxie lǎoshī

老師：不客氣！
lǎoshī　bú kèqì

愷俐：再見！
kǎilì　zàijiàn

老師：再見！
lǎoshī　zàijiàn

● 生詞 *Vocabulary*
shēngcí

14	老師	teacher
15	您好	Hello! (polite)
16	是	to be
17	學生	student
18	他	he
19	不	not
20	不客氣！	You're welcome!

日記 *Claire White's Diary*
riji

Dear Diary,

I have decided that I'll keep a diary to record everything happening to me in Taiwan since I enrolled in a Chinese language course today. The most important thing is that I hope one day I can write solely in Chinese. Oh, English, I will definitely say 再見 to you when I finish this diary!

After a long, long flight ..., I arrived in Taiwan a week ago. My father helped me find a place to stay, and now I've moved into a nice, neat flat in Taipei. 謝謝 God that I could live in such a quiet and clean place, and my neighbors are so kind and polite.

When I was moving in, a kind young man living next door to me came to help; not only that, he taught me some useful expressions in Chinese. 他是好鄰居. I hope one day, to him, 我也是好鄰居!

I enrolled at the Chinese Language Center this morning. I believe I WILL meet a 好老師, and I WILL become a 好學生! To prove it, I will transform this diary into a Chinese reader very soon. If you don't believe me, just wait and see!

Claire

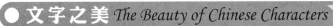

文字之美 *The Beauty of Chinese Characters*
wénzì zhī měi

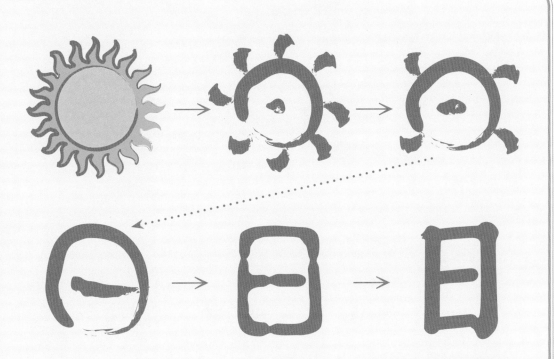

The character " 日 " (rì) has meanings such as "Sun," "day," and "daytime," and its form is derived from that of the Sun. The box framing the character was originally round. However, because square characters are more convenient in writing, 日 evolved to its present shape. The stroke at the center of the character symbolizes the Sun's source of energy, and conveys both the heat and light emitting properties of the Sun.

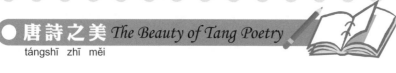

唐詩之美 *The Beauty of Tang Poetry*
tángshī zhī měi

登鸛雀樓 Ascending the Heron Lodge　　王之渙 Wang Zhihuan
dēng guànquè lóu

王 之 渙
Wáng Zhīhuàn

白 日 依 山 盡 ， 黃 河 入 海 流 。
bái　rì　yī　shān　jìn　　huáng　hé　rù　hǎi　liú

欲 窮 千 里 目 ， 更 上 一 層 樓 。
yù　qióng　qiān　lǐ　mù　　gèng　shàng　yì　céng　lóu

Sunset behind the mountains, Yellow River flowing seaward.

With the desire to see farther, the higher one can climb.

The three-story Heron Lodge is located in southwestern Shanxi Province. Tang Dynasty (618–907) poets would visit this place to enjoy the view and write poetry.

The first line of the poem depicts a scene of grand scale, which suggests the eternal processes of nature. The second line captures the impression of witnessing such a view, and simultaneously draws a parallel. Literally, one can climb higher to see farther, and figuratively, one can understand more by striving to advance.

Wang wrote the poem at the height of the Tang, and both the notion and possibility of advancing oneself, or "moving up," reflects the optimism of the period.

發音 *Pronunciation*
fāyīn

First tone (high level tone)

一	安	居	先	生	師	他
yī	ān	jū	xiān	shēng	shī	tā

yī yí yǐ yì

Second tone (mid rising tone)

您	鄰	學
nín	lín	xué

mā má mǎ mà ma

Third tone (low falling-rising tone)

早	好	小	姐	愷	你	我	很	也	老
zǎo	hǎo	xiǎo	jiě	kǎi	nǐ	wǒ	hěn	yě	lǎo

wēn wén wěn wèn

Fourth tone (high falling tone)

俐	謝	再	見	是	不	客	氣
lì	xiè	zài	jiàn	shì	bù	kè	qì

tāng táng tǎng tàng

Neutral tone (toneless, short)

嗎	呢
ma	ne

xiān xián xiǎn xiàn

qiāo qiáo qiǎo qiào

Attention! Tone Changes

1. 不 takes the second tone when it precedes the fourth tone.

Compare:

不安	不學	不好	不是
bù ān	bù xué	bù hǎo	bú shì

2. When two falling-rising tones (third tones) appear in a row, the first one is changed into a rising tone (the second tone). Pinyin will NOT show this change.

For example:

小姐	你好	很好	也好
xiǎo jiě	nǐ hǎo	hěn hǎo	yě hǎo

● 文法 *Grammar*
　　wénfǎ

1. In Chinese, verbs remain the same in form regardless of changes in person and number. 是 (shì), an equative verb (EV), is not an exception. Equative verbs equate two nouns (or nominal expressions) as in: I am a teacher 我是老師. The word order in most instances is the same in both English and Chinese. 不 (bù), an adverb, indicating negation, precedes verbs, adverbs or adjectives.

Number	Person	Pronoun	EV (not)	N
singular	1st 2nd 3rd	我 你 他／她	（不）是	老師 lǎo shī
plural	1st 2nd 3rd	我們 你們 他／她們		學生 xuéshēng

🍎 們 (men) is a plural marker when it follows personal pronouns.

2. Chinese adjectives (SV) in their positive form normally require an adverb. When no other adverb is used, 很 (hěn) will be prefixed to the SV. Although 很 (hěn) is translated as "very", when used before an SV it usually has no meaning.

S	A	SV
我		好 hǎo
你		高 gāo (tall)
他／她	很	忙 máng (busy)
我們		累 lèi (tired)

🍎 S: subject, A: adverb, SV: stative verb

3. 也 (yě), an adverb, is similar to "also" in English, but it appears before the predicate.

For example:

他也是學生。　He is also a student.
tā　yě shì xuéshēng

我也很好。　I am also good.
wǒ yě hěn hǎo

4. In a Chinese interrogative sentence, there is no inversion of verbs and subjects; instead, an interrogative marker 嗎 (ma) is attached to the end of the sentence.

For example:

你好嗎？　How are you? (Literally, it means "Are you fine?")
nǐhǎo　ma

你是 學生 嗎？　Are you a student?
nǐ　shì　xuéshēng　ma

5. When the content of the question is already clear from context, 呢 (ne) often follows the noun or pronoun to form a "how about S?" question, and the predicate in the question can be omitted.

For example:

A:你好嗎？
　nǐhǎo　ma

B:我很好，他呢？　How about him?
　wǒ hěn hǎo　　tā　ne

A:你是 學生 嗎？
　nǐ　shì　xuéshēng　ma

B:不，我是老師。你呢？　How about you?
　bù　　wǒ shì lǎoshī　　nǐ　ne

LESSON 1

第1課 第2課 第3課 第4課 第5課 第6課 第7課 第8課 第9課 第10課 第11課

● 換你試試看 *It's Your Turn!*
huàn nǐ   shìshikàn

Challenge 1

Please choose the correct pinyin.

1. (　　) 小　　A. jiǎo　　B. xiǎo　　C. qiǎo
2. (　　) 早　　A. sǎo　　B. zǎo　　C. zǎ
3. (　　) 安　　A. ān　　B. āng　　C. gān
4. (　　) 您　　A. nǐ　　B. níng　　C. nín
5. (　　) 好　　A. hǎo　　B. kǎo　　C. hǒu
6. (　　) 學　　A. xué　　B. jué　　C. xuè

Challenge 2

Draw a line to match the correct translation.

A. Good morning. How are you?

B. I'm fine, thanks. And you?

C. No, I'm not a teacher.

D. He is also a student.

E. Are you a student?

a. 我很好，謝謝。你呢？
　 wǒ hěn hǎo , xièxie.　 nǐ ne?

b. 他也是 學生。
　 tā yě shì xuéshēng.

c. 我不是老師。
　 wǒ bú shì lǎoshī.

d. 早安。你好嗎？
　 zǎo ān.　 nǐ hǎo ma?

e. 你是 學生 嗎？
　 nǐ shì xuéshēng ma?

Challenge 3

You meet a person in a Chinese language center. Greet him and then ask him if he is a student. (Write your answer in Chinese characters and pinyin.)

Challenge 4

For each character given below, form a sentence using the pattern "我很SV" and write down the pinyin as well.

For example: 高→我很高。 Wǒ hěn gāo.

1. 累→

- -

2. 忙→

- -

3. 好→

Challenge 5

I. Fill in the blanks in the following dialogue with 嗎 or 呢.

A: 你好＿＿＿？
nǐhǎo

B: 我 很 好。你＿＿＿？
wǒ hěn hǎo　nǐ

A: 我是老師，你也是老師＿＿＿？
wǒ shì lǎoshī　nǐ yě shì lǎoshī

B: 我也是老師。
wǒ yě shì lǎoshī

A: 他＿＿＿？
tā

B: 他不是老師，他是學生。
tā bú shì lǎoshī　tā shì xuéshēng

II. Insert the words in parentheses at the appropriate place(s) in each sentence.

1. 他學生。（是）tā xuéshēng (shì)

→

2. 我好，謝謝。（很）wǒ hǎo xièxie (hěn)

→

3. 我是 學生，你是 學生？（也，嗎）
wǒ shì xuéshēng   nǐ shì   xuéshēng   (yě   ma)

→

4. 我很好，他好。（很，也）wǒ hěn hǎo tā hǎo (hěn yě)

→

III. Rearrange the following sentences to form a dialogue. Use numbers to indicate the correct order.

☐ A: 你是學生嗎？nǐ shì xuéshēng ma?

☐ B: 早安！zǎoān!

☐ A: 早安！zǎoān!

☐ B: 他是老師。tā shì lǎoshī.

☐ A: 我是學生，他呢？wǒ shì xuéshēng, tā ne?

☐ B: 我不是學生，你呢？wǒ búshì xuéshēng, nǐ ne?

☐ A: 謝謝老師。xièxie lǎoshī.

☐ B: 不客氣，再見。búkèqì, zàijiàn.

● 聽力練習 *Let's Listen!*
tīnglì liànxí

I. Listen and circle the right tones.

1. jiē jié jiě jiè
2. yē yé yě yè
3. dā dá dǎ dà

4. shēng shéng shěng shèng
5. mō mó mǒ mò
6. kē ké kě kè

II. Choose the best description for each dialogue.

1.( ) A. They greet each other in the afternoon.

B. They say good-bye to each other in the morning.

C. They greet each other in the morning.

D. They say good-bye to each other in the afternoon.

2.( ) A. There are two teachers.

B. There are two students.

C. There are no teachers.

D. There are no students.

3.( ) A. The man is happy.

B. The man is busy.

C. The man is fine.

D. The man isn't tired.

字型練習 Let's Write!
zìxíng liànxí

丿	亻	亻丿	亻𠂊	㑓	你	你					
你	你	你									
nǐ		你	你								

𡿨	女	女	女乛	好	好						
好	好	好									
hǎo		好	好								

丨	冂	日	日	旦	早	早	是	是			
是	是	是									
shì		是	是								

丿	𠂉	𠂉	𠂉	𠂉	𠂉	𦥑	𦥑	𦥯	學	學	學
學	學	學									
xué		學	學								

ノ ニ ニ 牛 生

生 生 生
shēng 生 生

ㄧ ㄇ ㄇ ㄇ ㄇㄧ ㄇㄈ ㄇㄈ ㄇㄈ 嗎 嗎 嗎 嗎 嗎

嗎 嗎 嗎
ma 嗎 嗎

ノ 一 千 手 我 我 我

我 我 我
wǒ 我 我

ㄧ ㄇ ㄇ ㄇㄧ ㄇㄈ ㄇㄈ 呢 呢

呢 呢 呢
ne 呢 呢

㇆	㇆丨	也			
也	也	也	yě	也	也

㇒	亻	亻㇆	亻㇆丨	他	
他	他	他	tā	他	他

一	十	土	耂	耂	老
老	老	老	lǎo	老	老

㇒	丨	㇒丨	⺊	⺊	𠂤	𠂤一	𠂤冂	𠂤币	師
師	師	師	shī	師	師				

Note

LESSON 2

第二課 您貴姓？
dì èr kè nín guì xìng

 ● 對話一 *Dialogue One*
duìhuà yī

(In the classroom.)

老師：各位¹同學²，大家³早⁴！
lǎoshī　　gèwèi tóngxué　　dàjiā zǎo

同學：老師早！
tóngxué　　lǎoshī zǎo

老師：我是楊⁵老師，是大家的⁶華語⁷老師。
lǎoshī　　wǒ shì yáng lǎoshī　　shì dàjiā de huáyǔ lǎoshī

同學：楊老師好！
tóngxué　　yáng lǎoshī hǎo

老師：現在⁸，我們⁹來¹⁰認識¹¹同學。請問¹²，您¹³貴姓¹⁴？
lǎoshī　　xiànzài　　wǒmen lái rènshì tóngxué　　qǐngwèn　　nín guì xìng

恺俐：我**姓白**。
kǎilì　　wǒ xìng bái

老師：**名字**呢？
lǎoshī　　míngzi ne

恺俐：我**叫**恺俐。
kǎilì　　wǒ jiào kǎilì

老師：謝謝！**請**白同學問**下一位**同學。
lǎoshī　xièxie　qǐng bái tóngxué wèn xià yí wèi tóngxué

恺俐：同學，你好！請問你叫**什麼**名字？
kǎilì　　tóngxué　nǐhǎo　　qǐngwèn nǐ jiào shéme míngzi

志學：我叫**張**志學。
zhìxué　　wǒ jiào zhāng zhìxué

恺俐：志學，你好！
kǎilì　　zhìxué　　nǐhǎo

志學：恺俐，你好！
zhìxué　　kǎilì　　nǐhǎo

●**生詞** *Vocabulary*
shēngcí

1 各位　Everybody!;
　　　　Ladies and gentlemen!

2 同學　classmate, student

3 大家　everyone; everybody

4 早＝早安　good morning

5 楊　Yang (Chinese surname)

6 的　of, 's

7 華語　Chinese (the language)

8 現在　now

9 我們　we

10 來　to be about to;
　　　to let oneself

11 認識　to know

12 請問　may I ask...?

13 貴　your (polite)

14 姓1　surname, family name

15 姓2　to have the surname of

16 白　Bai (Chinese surname)

17 名字　name (full name or
　　　　given name)

18 叫　to be called as

19 請　to invite

20 下一位　the next one

21 什麼　what?

22 志學　Zhixue (name of one
　　　　of Claire's classmates)

23 張　Zhang (Chinese surname)

對話二 *Dialogue Two*
duìhuà   èr

(In the hallway outside the classroom.)

偉立：愷俐，早安！
wěilì   kǎilì   zǎoān

愷俐：早安！請問你是志學嗎？
kǎilì   zǎoān   qǐngwèn nǐ shì zhìxué ma

偉立：不是！我叫陳偉立，不叫志學。
wěilì   bú shì   wǒ jiào chén wěilì   bú jiào zhìxué

愷俐：偉立，對不起！
kǎilì   wěilì   duìbùqǐ

偉立：沒關係！
wěilì   méiguān xi

愷俐：請問，她是誰？
kǎilì   qǐngwèn   tā shì shéi

偉立：她是我的太太。她姓林。她叫林安惠。
wěilì   tā shì wǒ de tàitai   tā xìng lín   tā jiào lín ānhuì

愷俐：陳太太，你好！
kǎilì   chén tàitai   nǐhǎo

安惠：白小姐，你好！
ānhuì   bái xiǎojiě   nǐhǎo

生詞 *Vocabulary*
shēngcí

24 陳 Chen (Chinese surname)

25 偉立 Weili (name of one of Claire's classmates)

26 對不起 I'm sorry.

27 沒關係 Never mind.

28 她 she

29 誰 who?

30 太太 wife; Mrs.

31 林 Lin (Chinese surname)

32 安惠 Anhui (name of the wife of Chen Weili)

日記 Claire White's Diary
rìjì

Dear Diary,

Our Chinese teacher, Ms. 楊, gave each of us a Chinese 名字. Starting today, I will try to sign my Chinese 名字, 白愷俐, at the end of each day's diary entry. Yes, yes, I admit the characters are challenging, but so what? They look so nice!

My given name, 愷俐, sounds similar to my English name, Claire. Ms. 楊 told me that the two characters denote "joyful" and "clever." Great! That's what I want to be. And my surname, 白, the color white, is a literal translation of my English surname, White. Oh, right, Chinese surnames come before given names! So, my full name is 白愷俐! 我姓白, 我叫白愷俐!

I love my classmates. 偉立 is a nice guy who comes from America; I practiced Chinese pronunciation with him, and I found him to be such a fast learner! He remembered almost every detail that Ms. 楊 had said! And I should say sorry to him because I confused him with 志學, another guy in my class. 偉立姓陳, 志學姓張. 陳太太的名字叫林安惠. I promise I will never forget their 名字!

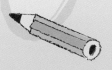  

白愷俐

● 文字之美 *The Beauty of Chinese Characters*
wénzì zhī měi

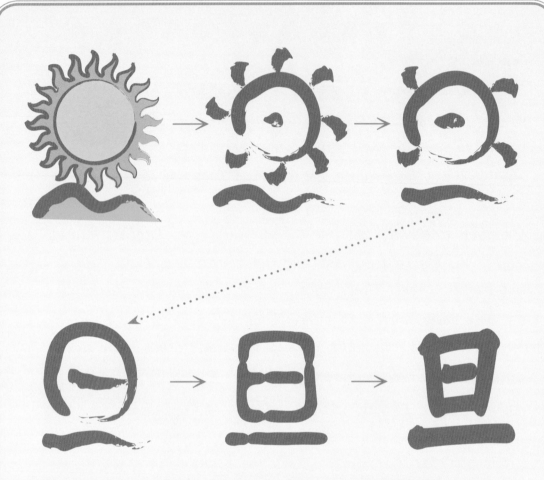

The character "旦" (dàn) refers to early morning or dawn and depicts the sun rising above the horizon. The components "日" and "一" are the sun and the horizon respectively. Since sunrise marks the beginning of each day, 旦 can also mean "start" or "begin."

● 諺語的智慧 *The Wisdom of Chinese Proverbs*
yànyǔ   de   zhìhuì

天 有 不 測 風 雲 ， 人 有 旦 夕 禍 福 。
tiān yǒu bú cè fēng yún   rén yǒu dàn xì huò fú

Heaven has unpredictable wind and clouds;
people have daily disasters and happiness.

↓

Something unexpected may happen at any time.

↓

Things like this happen sometimes.

Since 夕 (xì) means "dusk," the compound 旦夕 suggests a day—a short duration of time in the larger scope of things. As many unexpected things can happen on a daily basis, predicting one's lot in life is as impossible as forecasting the weather.

This proverb is normally used to comment on unfortunate circumstances after they occur, but it can also be used to express the unpredictability of an outcome before it happens.

For example, if your friend sustains an injury, you can comfort him or her by using this proverb. Likewise, if an earthquake leaves many homeless, it would be appropriate to use this expression—often just the first part of the proverb is used—to show your empathy.

Alternately, if your friend is making steady progress on a project, he or she might say, "At this rate, I'll be finished by Monday." However, since there are many factors—most beyond one's control—that could cause delays, you might be inclined to say, "A lot could happen, so don't plan on it," to remind your friend to remain realistic. You could also say "Don't count your chickens until they've hatched."
or you could try using this Chinese proverb!

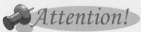

發音 Pronunciation
fāyīn

Let's practice the fourth tone.

ヽヽ	ヽヽ	ヽヽ	ヽヽ
貴姓	各位	現在	認識

ヽー	ーヽ
大家	安惠

ヽノ	∨ヽ	∨ヽ
志學	請問	偉立

ヽヽ∨	ヽノヽ
對不起	下一位

shuìjiào

zuòmèng

yìjiàn

jìnrù

yuànwàng

shìjiè

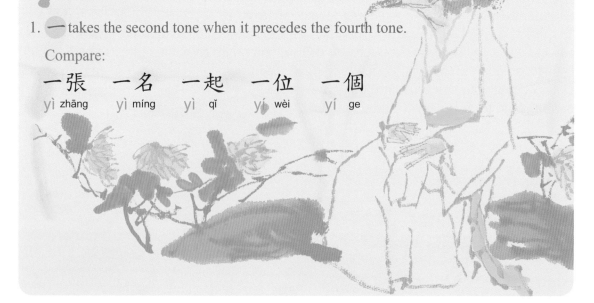

Attention!

1. 一 takes the second tone when it precedes the fourth tone.

Compare:

一張　　一名　　一起　　一位　　一個
yì zhāng　　yì míng　　yì qǐ　　yí wèi　　yí ge

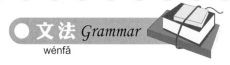

● 文法 *Grammar*
　wénfǎ

1. The equative verb "是 shì" equates two nouns (or nominal expressions) as in the following examples. "是 shì" is the most common equative verb (EV).

S	EV	N
我	（不）是	楊老師。
你	（不）是	張先生。
他	（不）是	陳偉立。
她	（不）是	我的太太。
白小姐	是	誰？
這 zhè (this)	是	什麼？

Two other equative verbs introduced in this lesson are "姓 xìng" (to be surnamed) and "叫 jiào" (to be called). Some sentence patterns are given below.

S	EV	N
你	姓	什麼？
我	姓	黃 Huáng。
		李 Lǐ。
		王 Wáng。
你	叫	什麼（名字）？
我	叫	愷俐。
		安惠。
		志學。

台灣常見的姓氏
the most common surnames in Taiwan

陳
林
黃
張
李
王
吳 Wú
劉 Liú
蔡 Cài
楊

2. Question words (QW) do not occur in sentences containing the interrogative particle "嗎". In this lesson, the QW "什麼" and "誰" are put in the object position.

S	EV	Object
白愷俐	是	誰？ shéi
志學	姓	什麼？ shéme
楊老師	叫	什麼（名字）？ shéme míngzi

3. In Chinese, the possessive marker "的 de" is added to the (pro)noun modifier preceding the noun which is modified.

(Pro)noun Modifier	Possessive Marker	Noun Modifier
我	的	朋友 (friend) péngyǒu
你	的	老師 lǎoshī
陳先生	的	太太 tàitai
白愷俐	的	學校 (school) xuéxiào

4. "來 lái" is used before a verb or verb phrase to indicate that one is about to do something. The usage is similar to "let" in English.

S	來 + V (VP)		O	Translation
大家	來	認識	同學。	Let's acquaint ourselves with our classmates.
我	來	問	下一位女生。	Let me ask the next girl.

● 換你試試看 *It's Your Turn!*
huàn nǐ shìshìkàn

Challenge 1

Please choose the correct pinyin.

1. ( ) 認　　A. shèn　　B. rèn　　C. chèn
2. ( ) 識　　A. xì　　B. qì　　C. shì
3. ( ) 關　　A. guān　　B. guāng　　C. gēng
4. ( ) 下　　A. xià　　B. xiá　　C. xiā
5. ( ) 貴　　A. kuì　　B. huì　　C. guì
6. ( ) 叫　　A. jiào　　B. jià　　C. jiù

Challenge 2

I. For each picture below, use the question words (QW) "誰" and "什麼" to form a sentence. Take turns asking and answering the questions.

For example:

陳老師

A：他是誰？　　他姓什麼？／他叫什麼？
　　tā shì shéi　　tā xìng shéme　　tā jiào shéme

B：他是老師。　他姓陳。
　　tā shì lǎoshī　　tā xìng chén

林安惠

A：

B：

張志學

A：

B：

王小姐

A：

B：

II. One student points to the picture and uses the pattern
"……是誰的……" to make a question, and the other uses
the pattern "是……的" to answer.

For example:

A: 王 小姐 是誰的同學？
　　wáng xiǎojiě shì shéi de tóngxué

B: 王 小姐 是白 先生 的 同學。
　　wáng xiǎojiě shì bái xiānshēng de tóngxué.

A: 楊老師 是 誰 的 華語 老師？
　　yáng lǎoshī shì shéi de huáyǔ lǎoshī

B:

林安惠

鄰居

吳小姐
wú

A: 林安惠 是 誰 的 鄰居？
　　lín ānhuì shì shéi de línjū

B:

A: 楊 日華 是 誰 的 太太？
　　yáng rìhuá shì shéi de tàitai

B:

太太

李先生
lǐ

楊日華

Challenge 3

I. Write your Chinese name in characters and pinyin.

II. Use the information on this Taiwan ID card to answer the questions below.

父	林大明	母	吳華俐
配偶	陳偉立		
出生地	臺北市		
住址	臺北市內湖區萬湖里1鄰 民權東路六段150巷165弄218號		

中華民國國民身分證

姓名 林 安 惠

出生年月日 民國 57 年 6 月 5 日

性別 女

發證日期 民國 94 年 7 月 1 日 (市) 換發

統一編號 A234567890

0000000105

1. 她叫 什麼 名字？
   tā jiào shéme míngzi

2. 她的 母親 姓 什麼？
   tā de mǔqīn xìng shéme

3. 她的 先生 叫 什麼名字？
   tā de xiānshēng jiào shéme míngzì

補充 生詞 Supplementary Vocabulary bǔchōng
父親（父）fùqīn (fù) father
母親（母）mǔqīn (mǔ) mother
配偶 pèiǒu spouse

Challenge 4

Match each with the correct translation.

(　) A. May I ask what your surname is?
(　) B. My surname is not Zhāng. My name is Chén Wěilì.
(　) C. She is my wife. Her name is Kǎilì.
(　) D. I am Mr. Chén, your new Chinese teacher.
(　) E. No, my name is Wěilì, not Zhìxué.

1. 我是陳老師，是你們新的華語老師。
wǒ shì chén lǎoshī　shì nǐmen xīn de huáyǔ lǎoshī

2. 她是我的太太。她叫愷俐。
tā shì wǒ de tàitai　tā jiào kǎilì

3. 不，我叫偉立，不叫志學。
bù　wǒ jiào wěilì　bú jiào zhìxué

4. 我不姓張。我叫 陳偉立。
wǒ bú xìng zhāng　wǒ jiào chén wěilì

5. 請問 您貴姓？
qǐng wèn nín guìxìng

Challenge 5

Read the narrative passage and answer the questions. (True/False)

陳偉立是學生，他正在學華語。他的華語老師姓楊，名日華，
chén wěilì shì xuéshēng　tā zhèng zài xué huáyǔ　tā de huáyǔ lǎoshī xìng yáng　míng rìhuá

偉立都叫他楊老師。楊老師不高，但嗓門很大。白愷俐是偉立
wěilì dōu jiào tā yáng lǎoshī　yáng lǎoshī bù gāo　dàn sǎngmén hěn dà　bái kǎilì shì wěilì

的好朋友。她也不高，但很漂亮，是個好學生。
de hǎo péngyǒu　tā yě bùgāo　dàn hěn piàoliàng　shì ge hǎo xuéshēng

(　) 1. 楊老師是陳偉立的學生。
yáng lǎoshī shì chén wěilì de xuéshēng

(　) 2. 陳偉立 正 在 上 華語課。
chén wěilì zhèng zài shàng huáyǔ kè

(　) 3. 白愷俐很漂亮，但不是個好學生。
bái kǎilì hěn piàoliàng dàn bú shì ge hǎo xuéshēng

(　) 4. 白愷俐的同學是 楊日華。
bái kǎilì de tóngxué shì yáng rìhuá

(　) 5. 白愷俐不高，楊老師也不高。
bái kǎilì bù gāo　yáng lǎoshī yě bù gāo

補充生詞 Supplementary Vocabulary	
嗓門 sǎngmén	sound of human voices
漂亮 piàoliàng	to be beautiful
問問題 wèn wèntí	to ask questions
認真 rènzhēn	to be earnest

LESSON
2

第1課 第2課 第3課 第4課 第5課 第6課 第7課 第8課 第9課 第10課 第11課

● 聽力練習 *Let's Listen!*
tīnglì liànxí

I. Listen and circle the right tones.

A.	xī	xí	xǐ	xì
B.	zhāi	zhái	zhǎi	zhài
C.	miāo	miáo	miǎo	miào
D.	qīng	qíng	qǐng	qìng
E.	yī	yí	yǐ	yì

II. Listen to the dialogue and mark the correct statements with "T" and the incorrect ones with "F".

補充生詞 Supplementary Vocabulary			
師丈 shīzhàng	the husband of someone's teacher	乖 guāi	to be well-behaved
女兒 nǚér	daughter	貴 guì	to be expensive
姐姐 jiějie	sister	便宜 piányí	to be cheap

句型 Supplementary Sentence Patterns
我遲到了。 I am late. wǒ chídào le
我來自……。 I come from… wǒ láizì…
（我）很 高興 認識 你/您。 Nice to meet you. (wǒ) hěn gāoxìng rènshì nǐ/nín
你叫……就好了。 Just call … nǐ jiào…jiù hǎo le

(   ) 1. This conversation happens in the teacher's house.

(   ) 2. Kǎilì praises her teacher's dress rather than her daughter.

(   ) 3. The surname of the teacher's husband is Zhāng.

(   ) 4. Kǎilì thinks that the house is very big and pretty.

(   ) 5. The teacher's husband thinks that the house is very expensive.

● 字型練習 *Let's Write!*
zìxíng liànxí

一 ナ 大

大 大 大
dà 大 大

丨 冂 口 叫 叫

叫 叫 叫
jiào 叫 叫

丿 ク タ 夕 名 名

名 名 名
míng 名 名

丶 ′ 宀 宀 字 宁 字

字 字 字
zì 字 字

ˊ ㄅ ㄉ 白 白 白 的 的

的 的 的
de 的 的

ㄥ ㄅ 女 女 女 女 姓 姓

姓 姓 姓
xìng 姓 姓

ˋ 宀 宀 宀 宀 宀 宀 家 家 家

家 家 家
jiā 家 家

ˊ ㄅ 什 什

什 什 什
shé 什 什

` 亠 广 庁 庄 床 庶 麻 麻 麼 麼 麼

麼
me
麼 麼

亠 言 言 言 訁 訃 計 訐 詐 詐 誰 誰

誰
shéi
誰 誰

言 言 言 言 訁 訮 詀 請 請 請 請

請
qǐng
請 請

丨 冂 冂 冃 冃 門 門 門 門 問 問

問
wèn
問 問

Note

第三課 我 喜 歡 爬 山
dì　sān　kè　　wǒ　　xǐhuān　　pá　　shān

 ● 對話一 Dialogue One
　　　　duìhuà　yī

(In the park near the Hanlai Chinese Language Center.)

志學：愷俐，早！
zhìxué　　kǎilì　　zǎo

愷俐：早！志學。
kǎilì　　zǎo　　zhìxué

志學：愷俐，你喜歡[1]不喜歡[2]爬山？
zhìxué　　kǎilì　　nǐ　xǐhuān　bù　xǐhuān　pá shān

愷俐：喜歡！我很喜歡爬山。
kǎilì　　xǐhuān　　wǒ　hěn　xǐhuān　pá shān

志學：太好了[3]！我也喜歡爬山！
zhìxué　　tài　hǎo　le　　wǒ　yě　xǐhuān　pá shān

愷俐：沒想到，我和你都喜歡爬山，喜歡運動！
kǎilì　　méi xiǎngdào　　wǒ hàn nǐ dōu xǐhuān pá shān　　xǐhuān yùndòng

志學：那下次我們一起去爬山，好嗎？
zhìxué　　nà　 xiàcì　wǒmen　 yìqǐ　qù pá shān　　 hǎo ma

愷俐：好啊！
kǎilì　　hǎo　a

志學：除了爬山之外，我還喜歡做飯，你呢？
zhìxué　　chú le pá shān zhīwài　　wǒ hái　xǐhuān zuò fàn　　 nǐ　ne

　　　你喜不喜歡進廚房？
　　　nǐ　xǐ　bù　xǐhuān　jìn chúfáng

愷俐：哦！我只喜歡吃美食，不喜歡做飯。
kǎilì　　ò　　wǒ zhǐ xǐhuān chī měishí　　bù　xǐhuān zuò fàn

志學：沒關係！下次我做飯給你吃，如何？
zhìxué　　méi guānxi　　xiàcì　wǒ zuò fàn gěi nǐ chī　　rúhé

愷俐：太好了！謝謝你！
kǎilì　　tài hǎo le　　xièxie　nǐ

●生詞 Vocabulary
shēngcí

1 喜歡 to like
2 爬山 to go hiking in the mountains; to go mountain climbing
3 太……了 too; really
4 沒想到 to one's surprise; didn't know
5 和 and
6 都 both, all
7 運動 to (do) exercise

8 那 then (concluder)
9 下次 next time
10 一起 together
11 去 to go
12 啊 ah
13 除了……之外 beside, other than
14 還 still; even; further
15 做飯 to cook; cooking

16 進 to enter
17 廚房 kitchen
18 哦 oh
19 只 only
20 吃 to eat
21 美食 fine food; delicacies
22 給 (dative marker)
23 如何 how

對話二 *Dialogue Two*
duìhuà èr

(On the mountain.)

志學：愷俐，你喜歡這裡²⁴嗎？
zhìxué   kǎilì   nǐ xǐhuān zhèlǐ ma

愷俐：喜歡，這裡好²⁵美²⁶啊！
kǎilì   xǐhuān   zhèlǐ hǎo měi a

志學：那我們就²⁷在²⁸這裡野餐²⁹好了³⁰！
zhìxué   nà wǒ men jiù zài zhèlǐ yěcān hǎo le

愷俐：耶³¹！你準備³²了³³些什麼？
kǎilì   ye   nǐ zhǔnbèi le xiē shéme

志學：我做了三明治³⁴和水果³⁵沙拉³⁶，希望³⁷你會³⁸喜歡！
zhìxué   wǒ zuò le sānmíngzhì hàn shuǐguǒ shālā   xīwàng nǐ huì xǐhuān

愷俐：哇³⁹！好⁴⁰好吃⁴¹喔！
kǎilì   wā   hǎo hǎochī o

志學：你喜歡就⁴²好！
zhìxué   nǐ xǐhuān jiù hǎo

生詞 *Vocabulary*
shēngcí

24 這裡 here, this place

25 好 so

26 美 to be beautiful

27 就 right

28 在 to be (somewhere)

29 野餐 to go on a picnic

30 好了 to be all right

31 耶 yeah

32 準備 to prepare

33 了 (perfective aspect marker)

34 三明治 sandwich

35 水果 fruit

36 沙拉 salad

37 希望 to hope

38 會 to be going to; will

39 哇 wow

40 好吃 delicious

41 喔 oh

42 就 (main clause marker, indicating that the condition in the subordinate clause suffices to verify the proposition shown in the main clause)

愷俐：志學，你當我的烹飪老師，好不好？
kǎilì　　zhìxué　　　nǐ dāng wǒ　de pēngrèn lǎoshī　　hǎo bù hǎo

志學：沒問題！可是我的收費很高喔！
zhìxué　　méi wèntí　　kěshì　wǒ　de shōufèi hěn gāo　o

愷俐：How much?
kǎilì

志學：A kiss.
zhìxué

愷俐：（臉紅了）那就算了……
kǎilì　　　liǎnhóng le　　nà　jiù　suànle

● 生詞 *Vocabulary*
shēngcí

43 當　to be, take the role as

44 烹飪　cooking (literary/formal)

45 沒問題　no problem

46 可是　but

47 收費　fee (literary/formal)

48 高　high

49 臉紅　to blush

50 算了　forget it

○ 日記 *Claire White's Diary*
riji

Dear Diary,

Last week 志學 asked me about what I like to do. I told him that 我喜歡爬山 , and he looked overjoyed because 他也喜歡爬山, and said he would like to invite me to go hiking. I said "yes" right away, since I was so eager to know what the mountains around Taipei would be like. Another plus was that he would 做飯給我吃. 我喜歡吃飯，可是 我不喜歡做飯!

The mountain scenery was fabulous! 好美喔! I loved the green, green grass, the colorful azaleas, the warm sunshine, and the melodious birdsong. I was so happy, and 志學 looked even more handsome against the pleasant background… But it's too soon for me to be falling in love ♥, because I know so little about him—I don't even know if he's religious or not!

But I have to admit that 志學 is a born cook. 他做了三 明治和水果沙拉， 三明治和水果沙拉 都很好吃!I thought about how wonderful it would be if I could cook as well as he can, so I asked him to teach me; I hoped that he could 當我的烹飪老師. Then he told me that 他的收費很高! When I asked how much he charged, unfortunately (or fortunately?) he said the tuition was a kiss! Come on! That was a bit over-the-top. 那就算了! I shouldn't decide anything until I know a lot more about him!

白愷俐

文字之美 *The Beauty of Chinese Characters*
wénzì zhī měi

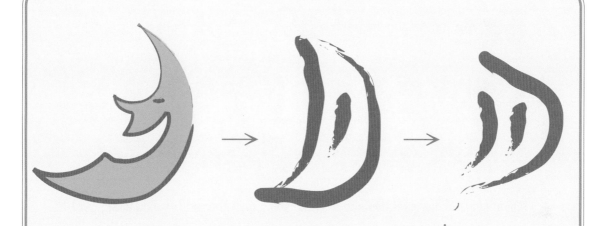

The character "月" (yuè) depicts the Moon. The half moon was used to create this character because people see partial lunar phases more often than the full moon.

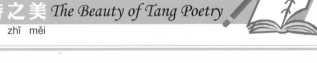

● 唐詩之美 *The Beauty of Tang Poetry*
tángshī zhī měi

竹 里 館 Inn Among the Bamboo　　　　王 維 Wang Wei
zhú　lǐ　guǎn　　　　　　　　　　　　　wáng wéi

獨 坐 幽 篁 裡 ， 彈 琴 復 長 嘯 。
dú　zuò yōu huáng lǐ　　tán qín fù cháng xiào

深 林 人 不 知 ， 明 月 來 相 照 。
shēn lín rén bù zhī　　míng yuè lái xiāng zhào

Sitting alone in the quiet bamboo grove, playing my zither and singing along.

Deep in the grove no one can hear me, the moonlight shining down from above.

Wang Wei (701–761) had a successful civil service career and rose to the rank of Chancellor in 758. Wang also studied Zen Buddhism, wrote poetry, and painted landscapes.

Many of his poems are known for the quiet, natural scenes they depict and their lack of human presence. His paintings share similar qualities. Wang's poetry, art, government service, and study of Zen can be best understood as being extensions of each other.

In this poem, the classic, solitary poet is described in relation to a much larger natural order. There is a sense that Wang is narrating a peaceful, visual scene that the reader is welcome to enter. Converting Wang's poetic details into a mental picture is a key to appreciating his poetry.

The overall composition includes human images—sitting alone, playing the zither, and singing along—juxtaposed with elements of the setting—the serenity and seclusion of the grove illuminated by the moon. It is a yin and yang of sorts that reflects Wang's ambivalence with Tang society. Alone among the bamboo, the narrator is insulated from the anxieties of official life.

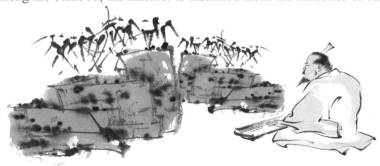

發音 *Pronunciation*
fāyīn

Let's practice the fourth tone.

＼ ＼	＼ ＼	＼ ＼
運動	下次	做飯

― ＼	― ＼	― ＼
希望	烹飪	收費

∨ ＼	∨ ＼	／ ∨ ＼
準備	可是	沒想到

Let's practice the first tone.

∨ ―	∨ ―	∨ ―
喜歡	野餐	好吃

／ ―	― ／ ＼
爬山	三明治

shìjì	wèidào
jīpiào	yōuxiù
diǎnxīn	hǎibiān

文法 Grammar
wénfǎ

1. Affirmative + Negative Questions ("A 不 A" pattern)

This is a type of question that requires a "yes" or "no" answer. Its function is equivalent to the question word "嗎" used in the interrogative sentence.

A	不	A		
好		好	=	好嗎？
美		美	=	美嗎？
貴		貴	=	貴嗎？
便宜	不	便宜	=	便宜嗎？
認識		認識	=	認識嗎？
喜歡		喜歡	=	喜歡嗎？
討厭		討厭	=	討厭嗎？
好吃		好吃	=	好吃嗎？

[便宜 piányí to be inexpensive, cheap]　[討厭 tǎoyàn to hate]

"便宜不便宜？" and "討厭不討厭？" are marked expressions, so they are used less frequently than 喜歡不喜歡？ and 貴不貴？

The adverbs 很 and 都 cannot be used with this pattern, and can only be used in the 嗎 type question.

Correct: 他們很喜歡嗎？

Incorrect: 他們很喜歡不喜歡？

Correct: 你和志學都認識她嗎？

Incorrect: 你和志學都認識不認識她？

Question	Affirmative Reply	Negative Reply
你喜歡不喜歡做飯？	喜歡。（我喜歡做飯）	不喜歡。（我不喜歡做飯）
你認識不認識林安惠？	認識。（我認識她）	不認識。（我不認識她）
偉立下次去不去爬山？	去。（他去）	不去。（他不去）

🍎 "Some native speakers say "你喜不喜歡他？" instead of "你喜歡不喜歡他？""

2. Tag Question (TQ)

This is a short statement that functions to ask for confirmation or a suggestion, and is added to an affirmative statement.

Affirmative Statement	TQ
你認識白愷俐，	對嗎？　（對不對？）
我們就在這裡野餐，	好嗎？　（好不好？）
我做飯給你吃，	如何？
坐公車去上課，	怎麼樣？

🍎 [坐公車 zuò gōngchē to take a bus]　[怎麼樣 zěnmeyàng what do you think]

3. 和 (hàn) and

This is a common conjunction used for nouns and pronouns. In contrast to its English counterparts, 和 (hàn) cannot join two verbs, adverbs, clauses, or sentences.

他和偉立一起去爬山。
愷俐和志學都是學生。
（我）希望你喜歡我的三明治和水果。

4. 都 (dōu) both, all

This adverb occurs before a predicate and refers to all the persons or things having the same quality described by the predicate. "都不" is the negative form and applies to all the persons or things mentioned in the sentence.

Affirmative	*Negative*
我和你都喜歡爬山。	我和你都不喜歡爬山。
愷俐和志學都喜歡野餐。	愷俐和志學都不喜歡野餐。

5. 還 (hái) in addition to

This adverb is placed before the verb and is used by the speaker to introduce an additional statement to complement the one s/he just said.

For example:

我喜歡做飯,(我)還喜歡爬山。
我學了華語,(我)還學了烹飪。 [學 xué to learn]

In the latter clause of a complex sentence, the subject, which is identical to the one in former clause, can be omitted.

相關句型 Related Patterns
除了⋯⋯之外,還⋯⋯
For example:
除了爬山之外,我還喜歡做飯。
除了吃飯之外,我還喜歡烹飪。

6. 了 (le)

This is a perfective aspect marker that follows the verb or verb phrase and indicates the completion of action.

媽媽	準備	了	水果給小孩。	Mom prepared fruit to give to the kids.
志學	吃	了	三明治。	Zhixue ate the sandwich.
我們	預習	了	第二課。	We previewed Lesson Two.

[媽媽 māma mother]　　[小孩 xiǎohái child(ren)]　　[預習 yùxí preview]

● 換你試試看 *It's Your Turn!*
huàn nǐ　shìshìkàn

Challenge 1

Please choose the correct pinyin.

1. (　　) 美　　**A.** něi　　**B.** měi　　**C.** lěi

2. (　　) 歡　　**A.** hūn　　**B.** huāng　　**C.** huān

3. (　　) 算　　**A.** suàn　　**B.** shùn　　**C.** shuàn

4. (　　) 爬山　**A.** pāisān　**B.** pàshāng　**C.** páshān

5. (　　) 運動　**A.** wèndòng　**B.** yùndòng　**C.** wèntòng

6. (　　) 可是　**A.** kěshì　　**B.** kěqí　　**C.** kěxí

Challenge 2

I. Use different interrogative forms to ask your classmates questions.

Example 1

你學華語。(嗎)

→　A：你學華語嗎？

→　B：是啊，我學華語。

Example 2

她很高。(A不A)

→　A：她高不高？

→　B：她不高。

1. 俊傑(jùnjié)吃了三明治。（嗎）

→ A：

→ B：

2. 烹飪課的收費很高。（A不A）

→ A：

→ B：

3. 陳美喜歡去爬山。（A不A）

→ A：

→ B：

4. 陳太太的先生做飯給她吃。（嗎）

→ A：

→ B：

5. 老師很累。（TQ是不是）

→ A：

→ B：

補充生詞 Supplementary Vocabulary	
烹飪課 pēngrènkè (cooking class)	書法課 shūfǎkè (calligraphy class)
華語課 huáyǔkè (Mandarin class)	繪畫課 huìhuàkè (painting class)
體育課 tǐyùkè (physical education class)	

II. Write a new sentence using the clues provided in parentheses.

1. 小偉(xiǎowěi)是我的朋友。小俐(xiǎolì)是我的朋友。
   (小偉和小俐，都)

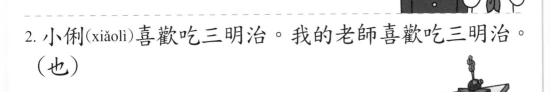

→

2. 小俐(xiǎolì)喜歡吃三明治。我的老師喜歡吃三明治。
   (也)

→

3. 師丈(shīzhàng)去爬山。我們去爬山。
   (和)

→

4. 老師準備了沙拉。老師準備了水果。
   (除了……之外，還……)

→

5. 志學當我的華語老師。他也當我的烹飪老師。
   (除了……之外，還……)

→

Challenge 3

Situation :

It's your first time to meet your language exchange partner. You need to introduce yourself, ask him/her some questions, and then discuss what he/she usually likes to do.

Hints:

1. Greetings.
2. Ask about what interests him/her.
3. Invite him/her to eat something with you.

Language to use:

1. 你好
2. 我叫……，你呢？
3. 喜歡不喜歡
4. 你 平常 喜歡 做 什麼？ (What do you usually like to do?) 　 nǐ píngcháng xǐhuān zuò shéme
5. 想不想 xiǎngbùxiǎng (Would you like to...?)
6. 怎麼樣 zěmeyàng (What do you think?)

Challenge 4

Look at the following message and choose the best answer.

| Send | Save draft | Attach ▾ | Spell check | Set priority to ▾ | X Cancel |

From: 志學 ▾　　　　　　　　　　　Show Cc & Bcc

To: 立山

Subject:

Show plain text

✂ 📋 📋 | Font Style ▾ Font Size ▾ | **B** *I* U̲ | ▤ ▤ ▤ | ▤ ▤ ▤ ▤ | 🌐 🔗 — 🖌 🔺 ☺

立山：
lìshān

你好！我想介紹一位華語課的同學給你認識。
nǐhǎo　wǒ xiǎng jièshào yíwèi huáyǔ kè de tóngxué gěi nǐ rènshì

她叫金希京，剛來台灣念研究所。
tā jiào jīn xījīng gāng lái táiwān niàn yánjiùsuǒ

她現在除了學華語之外，還學了書法。
tā xiànzài chú le xué huáyǔ zhīwài hái xué le shūfǎ

她很喜歡吃美食，可是不知道台北這裡有什麼好吃的。
tā hěn xǐhuān chī měishí kěshì bùzhīdào táiběi zhèlǐ yǒu shé me hǎochī de

我最近很忙，所以想請你帶她去夜市，
wǒ zuìjìn hěn máng suǒyǐ xiǎng qǐng nǐ dài tā qù yèshì

介紹台北的美食給她認識。
jièshào táiběi de měishí gěi tā rènshì

你明天6:00 p.m. 和她一起去夜市，如何？
nǐ míngtiān hàn tā yìqǐ qù yèshì rúhé

希望你明天有空！
xīwàng nǐ míngtiān yǒukòng

志學2008/1/12
zhìxué

補充生詞 Supplementary Vocabulary	
想　xiǎng　to want; would like to	什麼　shéme　something
位　wèi　a measure for person [polite]	最近　zuìjìn　recently
剛　gāng　just	忙　máng　busy
台灣　táiwān　Taiwan	所以　suǒyǐ　so
念研究所　niàn yánjiùsuǒ　to attend [a] graduate school/program	帶　dài　to take somebody
研究所　yánjiùsuǒ　[a] graduate school/program	夜市　yèshì　night market
台北　táiběi　Taipei	明天　míngtiān　tomorrow
有　yǒu　there is, there are	有空　yǒukòng　to be free

1. (　　) What is the purpose of this message?

   A. To wish someone happy birthday.

   B. To ask someone for help.

   C. To congratulate someone on graduation.

2. (　　) What time should Lìshān go to see Xījīng?

   A. Tomorrow evening.

   B. This afternoon.

   C. At 6:00 p.m. next Monday.

3. (　　) Who will take Xījīng to the night market?

   A. Kǎilì

   B. Lìshān

   C. Kǎilì's teacher

   D. Zhìxué

4. (　　) Which is NOT an adequate description of Xījīng?

   A. She is learning both Mandarin and calligraphy.

   B. She loves tasty food.

   C. She knows Taipei very well.

● 聽力練習 *Let's Listen!*
tīnglì liànxí

I. Listen and circle the correct tones.

A.	yē	yé	yě	yè
B.	cān	cán	cǎn	càn
C.	chū	chú	chǔ	chù
D.	hōng	hóng	hǒng	hòng
E.	fāng	fáng	fǎng	fàng

II. Listen to the dialogue and mark the correct statements with "T" and the incorrect ones with "F".

補充生詞 Supplementary Vocabulary

韓國 hánguó Korea	最（喜歡）…… zuì (xǐhuān)…… to like something the most
韓國人 hánguó rén Korean	
對了 duìle by the way	趕快 gǎnkuài in a hurry; to hurry
原來 yuánlái originally, actually	進去 jìnqù to enter; to go in
這裡／那裡 zhèlǐ/nàlǐ here/there	說得對 shuō de duì That's right.
有 yǒu there is, there are	等等我 děngděngwǒ Wait for me.

台灣小吃 táiwān xiǎochī Local Snacks in Taiwan

炒麵 chǎomiàn	fried noodles	水餃 shuǐjiǎo	dumpling(s)
炒飯 chǎofàn	fried rice	春捲 chūnjuǎn	spring roll
滷味 lǔwèi	soy marinated food	包子 bāozi	steamed stuffed buns

(   ) 1. It is the first time Lìshān sees Xījīng.

(   ) 2. Both Xījīng and Lìshān are Taiwanese.

(   ) 3. Xījīng first thought xiǎochī meant little rice.

(   ) 4. Both Xījīng and Lìshān don't like chǎofàn.

(   ) 5. Chǎofàn is one kind of well-known local snack in Taiwan.

● 字型練習 *Let's Write!*
zìxíng   liànxí

`丶 丷 ⺌ 兰 ⺷ 羊 羊 美 美`

美 美 美

měi   美 美

`丶 亠 宀 市 古 古 高 高 高 高`

高 高 高

gāo   高 高

`一 二 冫 冫 次 次`

次 次 次

cì   次 次

`丨 冂 口 叮 叻 吃`

吃 吃 吃

chī   吃 吃

㇏	㇐	㇐	㇑	㇑	㇑					

收 收 收
shōu 收收

㇐	㇐	㇐	㇑	㇑	㇑	㇑	㇑	㇑	㇑	㇑

費 費 費
fèi 費費

㇐	㇐	㇐	㇐	㇐	㇐	㇑	㇑	㇑	㇑	㇑

喜 喜 喜
xǐ 喜喜

㇏	㇑	㇑	㇑	㇑	㇑	㇑	㇑	㇑	㇑	㇑

歡 歡 歡
huān 歡歡

ノ メ 〆 关 关 希 希

希 希 希
xī 希 希

ヽ 亠 七 亡 セク セタ セダ セ夕 望 望 望

望 望 望
wàng 望 望

ノ 冖 冖 冎 冎 冒 冒 冒 軍 軍 運 運

運 運 運
yùn 運 運

ノ 二 千 台 台 旨 直 重 重 動 動

動 動 動
dòng 動 動

LESSON 4

第四課 我會説華語
dì sì kè wǒ huì shuō huáyǔ

 ● **對話一** *Dialogue One*
duìhuà yī

(Lishan and Huimei, two college students, live in the same building as Claire White. They are in the elevator.)

立山：惠美，你今天 不用 上課 嗎？
lìshān huìměi nǐ jīntiān bú yòng shàng kè ma

惠美：對啊，我今天放假。立山，你家住七樓吧？
huìměi duì a wǒ jīntiān fàngjià lìshān nǐ jiā zhù qī lóu ba

立山：對，我住七樓。惠美，你要到五樓吧？
lìshān duì wǒ zhù qī lóu huìměi nǐ yào dào wǔ lóu ba

惠美：我不是要回家，我要到八樓找明芬。
huìměi wǒ bú shì yào huí jiā wǒ yào dào bā lóu zhǎo míngfēn

(The door opens on the second floor and Claire steps into the elevator.)

立山：外……外國人耶！
lìshān wài wàiguó rén ye

惠美：怎……怎麼辦²¹，我的²²英文很²³爛耶。你來²⁴啦！
huìměi　zěn　　zěn mebàn　　wǒ de yīngwén hěn làn ye　　nǐ lái la

立山：Um... hello, which... which floor...
lìshān

愷俐：你好，我²⁵會²⁶說華語。
kǎilì　　nǐhǎo　　wǒ huì shuō huáyǔ

請²⁷跟我說華語，我²⁸想²⁹練習！
qǐng gēn wǒ shuō huáyǔ　　wǒ xiǎng liànxí

立山：哇，你好³⁰厲害喔！那小姐你要³¹上³²幾樓？
lìshān　　wā　　nǐ hǎo lìhài o　　nà xiǎojiě nǐ yào shàng jǐ lóu

愷俐：我要上³³四樓，謝謝。
kǎilì　　wǒ yào shàng sì lóu　　xièxie

立山：沒問題！(Presses the button for the fourth floor.)
lìshān　　méi wèntí

●生詞 *Vocabulary*
shēngcí

1 立山 lìshān (name of a boy)
2 惠美 huìměi (name of a girl)
3 今天 today
4 不用 not to have to
5 上課 to go to school
6 對 yes; you're right
7 放假 to take a day off
8 家 home
9 住 to live
10 七 seven
11 樓 floor, story
12 吧 (guess marker, " S 吧" shows that the speaker suspects S to be true)

13 要 will; to want to
14 到 to arrive at
15 五 five
16 回 to go/come back to
17 八 eight
18 找 to visit
19 明芬 Mingfen (name of a girl)
20 外國人 foreign national
21 怎麼辦 What shall we do?
22 英文 English
23 爛 rotten; poor
24 啦 (cause marker, " S啦" shows that the speaker needs the addressee to carry out S)

25 會 to be able
26 說 to speak
27 跟 with
28 想 to want to
29 練習 to practice
30 厲害 to be terrific, impressive
31 上 to go up to
32 幾 which (number)
33 四 four

惠美：我叫惠美，他叫立山，請問你叫什麼名字呢？
huìměi　　wǒ jiào huìměi　　tā jiào lìshān　　qǐngwèn nǐ jiào shéme míngzi ne

愷俐：我叫白愷俐，叫我愷俐就³⁴行了。
kǎilì　　wǒ jiào bái kǎilì　　jiào wǒ kǎilì jiù xíng le

惠美：愷俐，³⁵真沒想到你會說³⁶中文！
huìměi　　kǎilì　　zhēn méi xiǎngdào nǐ huì shuō zhōngwén

³⁷對了，立山住七樓，我住五樓，³⁸歡迎你³⁹有
duì le　　lìshān zhù qī lóu　　wǒ zhù wǔ lóu　　huānyíng nǐ yǒu

⁴⁰空來⁴¹坐坐；我們都會⁴²幫你的。
kòng lái zuòzuò　　wǒ men dōu huì bāng nǐ de

愷俐：謝謝你們！ (They arrive at the fourth floor.)
kǎilì　　xièxie nǐ men

啊，我要⁴³走了，再見！
a　　wǒ yào zǒu le　　zàijiàn

立山、惠美：再見！
lìshān　　huìměi　　zàijiàn

● 生詞 *Vocabulary*
　　shēngcí

34 行　to be fine　　　　39 有　to have
35 真　really　　　　　　40 空　free time
36 中文　Chinese　　　　41 坐　to sit
37 對了　by the way; ah yes　42 幫　to help
38 歡迎　welcome　　　　43 走　to leave

對話二 Dialogue Two
duìhuà èr

(Since Zhixue had a good time hiking with Claire, he wants to invite her to the National Palace Museum. They meet in the hallway at the Hanlai Chinese Language Center.)

志學：愷俐，我想邀你一起去故宮看展覽，好不好？
zhìxué　kǎilì　wǒ xiǎng yāo nǐ yìqǐ qù gùgōng kàn zhǎnlǎn　hǎo bù hǎo

愷俐：故宮是什麼呀？
kǎilì　gùgōng shì shé me ya

志學：故宮是一座很大的博物館，裡面有 很多中國
zhìxué　gùgōng shì yí zuò hěn dà de bówùguǎn　lǐmiàn yǒu hěn duō zhōngguó

文物，你一定會喜歡的！
wénwù　nǐ yídìng huì xǐhuān de

愷俐：好哇！我想去！會不會很遠哪？
kǎilì　hǎo wā　wǒ xiǎng qù　huì bú huì hěn yuǎn na

志學：有一點遠，所以我們要坐公車去。
zhìxué　yǒu yìdiǎn yuǎn　suǒyǐ wǒ men yào zuò gōngchē qù

愷俐：坐公車多沒意思，你可不可以開車載我去？
kǎilì　zuò gōngchē duó méi yì si　nǐ kě bù kěyǐ kāi chē zài wǒ qù

生詞 Vocabulary
shēngcí

44 邀 to invite
45 故宮 National Palace Museum
46 看 to see
47 展覽 exhibition
48 呀 (personal involvement marker, following the finals "a", "e", "i", "o", or "ü")
49 一 one
50 座 (measure word for large buildings e.g. museums)
51 大 to be big
52 博物館 museum

53 裡面 inside
54 多 many; much
55 中國 China
56 文物 cultural relic
57 一定 must
58 的 (assertion marker, "S的" shows that the speaker is sure that S will be true)
59 遠 to be far
60 哪 (personal involvement marker, following finals

ending with an "n" sound)
61 有一點 a little bit
62 所以 so; therefore
63 坐 to take (a vehicle)
64 公車 bus
65 沒意思 to be boring
66 可以 can
67 開 to drive
68 車 car
69 載 to give (somebody) a ride

志學：**真可惜**[70]，我不會開車。
zhìxué　　zhēn kěxí　　wǒ bú huì kāi chē

愷俐：什麼？**這樣**[71]不行喔，我**未來**[72]的**男朋友**[73]一定
kǎilì　　shéme　　zhè yàng bù xíng o　　wǒ wèilái de nánpéngyǒu yídìng

要會開車。
yào huì kāi chē

志學：**真的嗎**[74]？那我一定要**學會**[75]開車！
zhìxué　　zhēn de ma　　nà wǒ yídìng yào xuéhuì kāi chē

愷俐：**而且**[76]**最好**[77]是要會開**飛機**[78]。
kǎilì　　érqiě zuì hǎo shì yào huì kāi fēijī

志學：真的嗎？那我一定要 **賺**[79] 很多的錢[80]，
zhìxué　　zhēnde ma　　nà wǒ yídìng yào zhuàn hěn duō de qián

去學開飛機！
qù xué kāi fēijī

愷俐：（**心裡想**[81][82][83]）**不會吧**[84]？他**當真**[85]了！
kǎilì　　xīn lǐ xiǎng　　bú huì ba　　tā dāngzhēn le

●生詞 *Vocabulary*
shēngcí

70 真可惜 what a pity! / that's too bad!	76 而且 moreover	82 裡 inside
71 這樣 this way	77 最好 had better	83 想 to think
72 未來 future	78 飛機 airplane	84 不會吧 oh no; how could
73 男朋友 boyfriend	79 賺 to earn	that be possible?
74 真的嗎 really?	80 錢 money	85 當真 to be serious;
75 學會 to acquire the skill of	81 心 heart; mind	to mean business

日記 Claire White's Diary
rìjì

Dear Diary,

I have two new friends here: 立山和惠美. I met them in the elevator. They were so friendly. When they tried to talk to me in English, I told them 我會說華語, 請他們跟我說華語, because I really want to 練習. I am so lucky to have two more friends; 我可以跟他們練習中文!

Once again, 志學邀我 to a fabulous place: 故宮. I really like all of those old 中國文物. Since 我喜歡中文, of course 我也喜歡中國文物. But get this: 志學 told me that 故宮 is 有一點遠 from here, so 坐公車 去故宮 was his plan. 不會吧? Isn't he trying to date me? To show he really cares, he should at least 開車載我去, if not 開 a Porsche or Peugeot 載我去. 沒想到他不會 開車! Can you believe it? 志學 , as a man, was supposed to say " 沒問題, we'll take my car!" It's almost unforgivable that 他不會開車! After all, 我會開車! But abroad, 我不可以開車, because my license is only valid in Canada.

Anyway, I said "yes" to his invitation, so tomorrow 我們要去故宮看文物展覽. Why? Well, when he said 他不會開車, I told him that the basic requirements to be my 男朋友 include 要會開車 and 開飛機 . Then I saw the determination in his eyes when he said 他要學會開飛機! OK, I admit, maybe 我的心有一點melted, but at least I'm sure 志學 is reliable and good-hearted.

白愷俐

文字之美 *The Beauty of Chinese Characters*
wénzì zhī měi

The character "明" (míng) means bright. The "日" (rì) on the left and the "月" (yuè) on the right depict the Sun and Moon adding radiance to each other, and thus the combination suggests unlimited light.

● 諺語的智慧 *The Wisdom of Chinese Proverbs*
yànyǔ de zhìhuì

明 槍 好 躲 ， 暗 箭 難 防
míng qiāng hǎo duǒ   àn jiàn nán fáng

Bright spear easy to hide, dark arrow hard to guard against.

↓

Open attacks are easier to defend against than surprise attacks.

↓

Better an open enemy than a false friend.

The contrast between 明 and 暗 figures prominently in this proverb, and the two characters are both used in their figurative sense. Bright 明 suggests "obvious" and "in the open," and dim 暗 implies "concealed" and "secret."

This proverb is usually used to remind others to beware of treacherous, false, and otherwise just bad people. For example, if your friend tells you about how nice one of his or her coworkers is being, but you suspect that coworker is nothing but a big phony and probably saying bad things behind your friend's back for selfish ends, it would be appropriate to use this proverb.

You can also use this proverb to remind yourself to always be vigilant against the insincere and scheming types you may encounter on a daily basis.

It is usually the second part of this proverb that gets used, and quite frequently, it is shortened even further. For example, "You need to watch out for 暗箭," is a standard admonition.

● 發音 *Pronunciation*
fāyīn

Let's practice tones.

——	——	——	——
飛機	當真	今天	公車

╲╲	╲╲	╲╲
上課	放假	屬害

—╱	—╱	—╱
歡迎	英文	中國

╲╱	╲╱	╲╱
外國	練習	未來

╲╲	╲╲	╲╲╲╲	╱╲	╱╲
所以	可以	有一點遠	一定	一座

╱╲	╱╲	╲	╲	╱╲
不用	不會吧	去啦	怎麼	沒意思

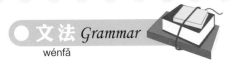

● 文法 *Grammar*
wénfǎ

1. The Auxiliary Verb 要 (yào): be going to

要 has many meanings. In this lesson, we introduce one of them. 要 refers to a future action, similar to the function of "be going to" in English.

你	要	到三樓嗎？ Are you going to the third floor?
惠美	要	到五樓。 Huimei is going to the fifth floor.
我	不要 búyào	走路去學校。 I am not going to walk to school.
他	不要 búyào	和我一起去爬山。 He's not going to go hiking with me.

🍎 If you want to emphasize your eagerness for doing something, you can add "一定" before "要". Think of it like "certainly" in English. The predicate is often under the control of the speaker and will most likely come true.

我		要學會開車。 I'm (certainly) going to learn to drive (a car).
我男朋友	一定	要賺很多錢。 My boyfriend is (certainly) going to make a lot of money.
我和我的太太		要去台灣旅行。 I'm (certainly) going on a trip to Taiwan with my wife.
我和家人		要到加拿大看楓葉。 I'm (certainly) going to Canada to see the maple leaves with my family.

🍎 [台灣 táiwān Taiwan]   [家人 jiārén family (members)]
　　[旅行 lǚxíng travel]   [楓葉 fēngyè maple leaves]

2. The Auxiliary Verb 會 (huì)

The three main meanings of 會 are shown in the following chart.

會₁ (is)	based on the speaker's knowledge of the world	故宮會不會很遠呢？ Is Gugong far?
會₂ (will)	based on the speaker's obligation or voluntary action	我們都會幫你的。 We'll help you. 希望你會喜歡。 (L.3) (I) hope you'll like it.
會₃ (can)	based on the speaker's capability	愷俐會說華語。 Kaili can speak Chinese.

🍎 會₃ usually infers a kind of learned ability, like speaking a language.

🍎 Some adverbs and adverbial phrases can be placed before "會" to show the degree of the possibility or ability. For example, "不太會" means "cannot ...very well",
(bú tài huì)
so "我不太會說中文" means "I can't speak Chinese very well". Conversely,
(wǒ bú tài huì shuō zhōngwén)
"很會" means "can... very well", so "我很會說中文" means "I can speak
(hěn huì)   (wǒ hěn huì shuō zhōngwén)
Chinese very well."

3. The Auxiliary Verb 想 (xiǎng)

想, used in this lesson, refers to a desire to do something. For example:

我想邀你去故宮。	I'd like to invite you to go to Gugong.
志學想到四樓找老師。	Zhixue wants to go to the fourth floor to see the teacher.
我現在想去吃東西。	I'd like to eat something.
你暑假想去花蓮玩嗎？	Would you like to go to Hualian this summer vacation?

🍎 [東西 dōngxi something]　　　　　　　[暑假 shǔjià summer vacation]
[花蓮 huālián refers to 花蓮縣 Huālián Xiàn Hualien County (on the east coast of Taiwan)]

An interrogative form of 想 is 想不想? (xiǎng bù xiǎng), which is equivalent to 想嗎?

你想不想學華語？ Do you want to learn Chinese?

老師，您想不想和我們去吃飯？ Would you like to go eat with us, professor?

志學，你明天想不想一起去看電影？
Want to go see a movie with me tomorrow, Zhixue?

[明天 míngtiān tomorrow]   [看電影 kàndiànyǐng see a movie]

4. The Auxiliary Verb 可以 (kěyǐ)

可以 has several meanings. In this lesson, we introduce one of them. Here, 可以 indicates possibility or is used to ask about someone's willingness, similar to "may" or "could" in English. "可以不可以" or "可不可以" follow the "A不A" pattern used in interrogative sentences, and are equal to the tag question "可以嗎".

你可不可以開車載我去？ Can you give me a ride?

我可以開車載你去台北。 I can give you a ride to Taipei.

老師，您可以再說一次嗎？ Professor, can you say that again?

偉立，請說慢一點，可以嗎？ Could you speak a little bit more slowly, Weili?

[台北 táiběi Taipei]   [再說一次 zàishuōyícì say (that) again]
[慢一點 mànyìdiǎn more slowly]

第1課 第2課 第3課 第4課 第5課 第6課 第7課 第8課 第9課 第10課 第11課

● 換你試試看 *It's Your Turn!*
huàn nǐ   shìshìkàn

Challenge 1

Please choose the correct pinyin.

1. (   ) 課   A. gè   B. hè   C. kè
2. (   ) 放假   A. fángjià   B. fàngjià   C. fǎngjiā
3. (   ) 不用   A. búyòng   B. bùyǒng   C. bùyòng
4. (   ) 而且   A. ěrqiě   B. èrqiě   C. érqiě
5. (   ) 館   A. guàn   B. guǎn   C. guān
6. (   ) 最   A. zuò   B. zòu   C. zuì

Challenge 2

I. According to the dialogue in this lesson, use the appropriate phrases
containing "會" from below to complete the following sentences.
Language to use:

會不會很遠	不太會說	會跟大家
huì bú huì hěn yuǎn	bú tài huì shuō	huì gēn dàjiā
不會做飯	不會幫你	會不會來
bú huì zuòfàn	bú huì bāng nǐ	huì bú huì lái

1. 王小姐：你的女 朋友 很會做飯，你呢？你會不會？
nǐ de nǚ péngyǒu hěn huì zuòfàn nǐ ne nǐ huì búhuì

白先生：我 _____ ，可是我很會吃飯。
kě shì wǒ hěn huì chīfàn

2. 陳先生：你會不會 說 華語？教我好不好？
nǐ huì bú huì shuō huáyǔ jiāo wǒ hǎo bù hǎo

白小姐：對不起，我也 _____ ，
duì bù qǐ

你可以去問 高偉立。
nǐ kěyǐ qù wèn gāo wěilì

3.陳小姐：林先生，請問林太太 _____？

　　林先生：她會來，她一定會來。
　　　　　　　tā　yídìng　huìlái

4.王先生：那家小吃店[diàn store] _____？
　　　　　　nà jiā xiǎochī diàn

　　王太太：有一點遠喔！我們開車去，好不好？
　　　　　　yǒu yìdiǎn yuǎn　ō　　wǒ men kāichē qù

5.老師：你明天 _____ 一起去嗎？
　　　　　míngtiān

　　學生：會啊！我很 想 去看故宮的展覽。
　　　　　　　　wǒ hěn xiǎng qù kàn gùgōng de zhǎnlǎn

- -

II. Practice using the question word "誰" to make sentences.

1. 我想要上五樓。
→誰想要上五樓？

2. 偉立暑假想去加拿大。
→

3. 希京真的很想學會開車。
→

4. 愷俐喜歡故宮裡面的文物。
→

5. 楊老師沒想到今天會下雨[xiàyǔ to rain]。
→

Challenge 3

Ask three classmates about their interests, what they are able to do, and what they would like to do in the future.

同學姓名	Interests	Abilities	Wishes

Language to use:

興趣　Interests xìngqù	特長　Abilities tècháng	願望　Wishes yuànwàng
喜歡做飯	會開車	想去故宮
喜歡吃三明治	會開飛機	想學書法
喜歡中國文物	會說英文	想學畫畫
喜歡爬山	會唱歌　(sing) chànggē	想當老師
喜歡看書 (reading) kànshū	會跳舞　(dance) tiàowǔ	想賺很多錢

Challenge 4

Read the following conversation and match the pictures of 故宮文物 with the appropriate names.

楊老師：愷俐早！
yáng lǎoshī　 kǎilì zǎo

愷俐：老師早！
kǎilì　 lǎoshī zǎo

楊老師：你們昨天去了故宮，對不對？
yáng lǎoshī　 nǐmen zuótiān qù le gùgōng　 duìbúduì

愷俐：對啊！故宮裡的文物都很美，我最喜歡的文物就是
kǎilì　 duì a　 gùgōnglǐ de wénwù dōu hěnměi　 wǒ zuìxǐhuān de wénwù jiù shì

　　書法和陶瓷。
　　shūfǎ hàn táocí

楊老師：除了書法之外，故宮裡面的畫也很有名。
yáng lǎoshī　 chú le shūfǎ zhī wài　 gùgōng lǐmiàn de huà yě hěn yǒumíng

　　　　清明上河圖，你們看了嗎？
　　　　qīngmíngshànghétú　 nǐmen kàn le ma

志學：我們當然看了，可是我最喜歡的是玉器。
zhìxué　 wǒmen dāngrán kàn le　 kěshì wǒ zuì xǐhuān de shì yùqì

　　翠玉白菜 真的 很 漂亮 呢！
　　cuìyùbáicài zhēnde hěn piàoliàng ne

愷俐：好可惜喔！故宮離學校有點遠，不然我真希望每天都
kǎilì　 hǎo kě xí o　 gùgōng lí xuéxiào yǒu diǎn yuǎn　 bù rán wǒ zhēn xīwàng měitiān dōu

　　去呢！
　　qù ne

楊老師：老師下次可以跟你們一起去故宮。
yáng lǎoshī　 lǎoshī xiàcì kěyǐ gēn nǐmen yìqǐ qù gùgōng

志學：太好了，一定會很有意思。
zhìxué　 tàihǎo le　 yídìng huì hěn yǒu yìsī

補充生詞 Supplementary Vocabulary
陶瓷 táocí (china)
玉器 yùqì (jade)
翠玉白菜 cuìyùbáicài (Jadeite Cabbage with Insects)
清明上河圖 qīngmíngshànghétú (Along the River During the Ching-Ming Festival)
離 lí (distant from)

1. (　　　　)　　　　2. (　　　　　)

3. (　　　　)　　　　4. (　　　　　)

A. 陶瓷　táocí

B. 書法　shūfǎ

C. 國畫　guóhuà　(Chinese painting)

D. 玉器　yùqì

聽力練習 *Let's Listen!*
tīnglì liànxí

I. Listen and circle the correct tones.

A. yāo   yáo   yǎo   yào

B. huī   huí   huǐ   huì

C. yuān   yuán   yuǎn   yuàn

D. yīng   yíng   yǐng   yìng

E. kē   ké   kě   kè

II. Listen to the dialogue and choose the best answer.

補充生詞 Supplementary Vocabulary

姊姊   elder sister
jiějie

電話   telephone; phone number   / 打電話   make a phone call
diànhuà   dǎ diànhuà

請問 您 找 哪位？   Who would you like to speak with?
qǐngwèn nín zhǎo nǎ wèi

她不在。   She is not in.
tā búzài

請問 你 有 什麼 事嗎？   Would you like to leave a message?
qǐngwèn nǐ yǒu shéme shì ma

(   ) 1. Where would this conversation most likely take place?

         A. In a doorway.   B. Over the phone   C. In a shop.

(   ) 2. Is Huìměi home?

         A. Yes, she is.   B. No, she isn't.   C. Not clear from the dialogue.

(   ) 3. Who is talking with Kǎilì?

         A. Huìměi's sister   B. Huìměi   C. Huìměi's neighbor

(   ) 4. What message does Kǎilì want to pass on to Huìměi?

         A. She wants to turn down Huìměi's invitation to see a movie.

         B. She wants to invite Huìměi to come over to her house.

         C. She asks Huìměi to give her a phone call.

(   ) 5. What does the person whom Kǎilì talks to think of Kǎilì's Chinese?

         A. It's terrific.   B. It's not very good.   C. It's quite poor.

● 字型練習 *Let's Write!*
zìxíng liànxí

丿 人

人
rén 人 人

丿 八

八
bā 八 八

丶 心 心 心

心
xīn 心 心

丨 山 山

山
shān 山 山

一 厂 厅 厈 亘 亘 車

車 車 車
chē 車 車

一 乙 云 云 至 至 到 到

到 到 到
dào 到 到

一 十 才 木 机 机 机 相 相 想 想 想

想 想 想
xiǎng 想 想

一 十 才 扌 找 找 找

找 找 找
zhǎo 找 找

丶 宀 广 广 庀 庐 庒 座 座

座 座 座
zuò 座 座

一 ナ 才 冇 有 有

有 有 有
yǒu 有 有

一 一 一 一 西 西 要 要 要

要 要 要
yào 要 要

丿 人 今 仐 亼 佘 侖 侖 侖 侖 會 會

會 會 會
huì 會 會

LESSON 5

第五課 你是哪一國人？
dì wǔ kè nǐ shì nǎ yì guó rén

● 對話一 *Dialogue One*
duìhuà yī

(In a classroom at the Hanlai Chinese Language Center.)

老師：大家好！
lǎoshī dàjiā hǎo

學生¹們：老師好！
xuéshēngmen lǎoshī hǎo

老師：上課²之前³，我想⁴先跟大家⁵介紹⁶一位⁷新同學，
lǎoshī shàngkè zhīqián wǒ xiǎng xiān gēn dàjiā jièshào yí wèi xīn tóngxué

　　　大家 掌聲⁸ 歡迎 她！(Everyone claps.)
　　　dàjiā zhǎngshēng huānyíng tā

法杜⁹：大家好，我叫法杜。
fǎdù dàjiā hǎo wǒ jiào fǎdù

志學：法杜，你好漂亮¹⁰！你是哪¹¹一國¹²人¹³呢？
zhìxué fǎdù nǐ hǎo piàoliàng nǐ shì nǎ yì guó rén ne

愷俐：我猜¹⁴法杜¹⁵應該是¹⁶美國人吧？
kǎilì wǒ cāi fǎdù yīnggāi shì měiguó rén ba

法杜： 我不是美國人，我是**甘比亞**人。
fǎdù　　　wǒ bú shì měiguó rén　　wǒ shì　gānbǐyà　rén

我會說**英語**，也會說**一點**華語。
wǒ huì shuō yīngyǔ　　yě huì shuō　yìdiǎn　huáyǔ

愷俐： 沒想到你是甘比亞人！
kǎilì　　méi xiǎngdào nǐ shì　gānbǐyà　rén

甘比亞在**非洲**，對不對？
gānbǐyà　zài fēizhōu　　duì bú duì

法杜： **沒錯**！
fǎdù　　méi cuò

老師： 我想請大家向法杜**自我介紹一下**，好嗎？
lǎoshī　　wǒ xiǎng qǐng dàjiā xiàng fǎdù　zìwǒ　jièshào　yíxià　　hǎo ma

希京： 好，我先！我叫**金**希京，我是**韓國**人！
xījīng　　hǎo　wǒ xiān　wǒ jiào jīn　xījīng　　wǒ shì hánguó rén

愷俐： 你好，我叫白愷俐，我是**加拿大**人！
kǎilì　　nǐhǎo　wǒ jiào bái　kǎilì　　wǒ shì　jiānádà　rén

● **生詞** *Vocabulary*
shēngcí

1 們 (plural marker, denoting a group of people)

2 之前 before

3 我 I, me

4 先 first

5 介紹 to introduce

6 位 measure for person (polite)

7 新 to be new

8 掌聲 clap; to clap

9 法杜 Fadu (name of a Gambian girl)

10 漂亮 to be pretty

11 哪 which

12 國 country, nation, state

13 人 person, people

14 猜 to guess, suppose

15 應該 should, to be supposed to

16 美國 the United States

17 甘比亞 Gambia, The Gambia, Republic of The Gambia

18 英語 English, the (spoken) English language

19 一點 a little bit

20 非洲 Africa

21 沒錯 that's right

22 自我介紹 to introduce oneself

23 一下 a little bit—softens a request or command

24 希京 Xijing (name of a Korean girl)

25 金 Jin (Korean surname)

26 韓國 Korea

27 加拿大 Canada

志學：法杜，你好，叫我志學就好。我**來自**美國。²⁸
zhìxué　　fǎdù　　nǐhǎo　　jiào wǒ zhìxué jiù hǎo　　wǒ láizì měiguó

偉立：我叫偉立，我和志學**一樣**是美國人。²⁹
wěilì　　wǒ jiào wěilì　　wǒ hàn zhìxué yíyàng shì měiguó rén

請多多指教！^{30 31}
qǐng duōduō zhǐjiào

法杜：也**請您**多多指教！大家都好**親切**呢！^{32 33}
fǎdù　　yě qǐng nín duōduō zhǐjiào　　dàjiā dōu hǎo qīnqiè ne

老師：**既然**大家都認識了，我們就**開始**上課吧！^{34 35}
lǎoshī　　jìrán dàjiā dōu rènshì le　　wǒmen jiù kāishǐ shàngkè ba

請同學翻到第十六頁！　(The bell rings ending class.)^{36 37 38 39}
qǐng tóngxué fān dào dì shíliù yè

老師：真**快**，**下課 鐘 響**了！我們 **明天 再見**。^{40 41 42 43 44 45 46}
lǎoshī　　zhēn kuài　　xiàkè zhōng xiǎng le　　wǒmen míngtiān zài jiàn

對了，同學回家**記得**要**複習**哦。^{47 48}
duì le　　tóngxué huí jiā jìdé yào fùxí ó

愷俐：老師，我們今天有**回家作業**嗎？⁴⁹
kǎilì　　lǎoshī　　wǒmen jīntiān yǒu huíjiā zuòyè ma

老師：**沒有**，**但要練習單字**，明天**考造句**！^{50 51 52 53 54}
lǎoshī　　méiyǒu　　dàn yào liànxí dānzì　　míngtiān kǎo zàojù

●生詞 Vocabulary
shēngcí

28 來自　to come from

29 一樣　the same as

30 請　please

31 多多指教　nice to meet you;
let's get along; (lit.) give me much advice

32 您　you (honorific)

33 親切　to be kind;
to be agreeable

34 既然　since, now that

35 開始　to start, begin

36 翻到　to turn to (page...)

37 第　(ordinal prefix), -th

38 十六　sixteen

39 頁　page

40 快　to be fast, quick

41 下課　to finish class; to dismiss the class

42 鐘　bell

43 響　to ring

44 明天　tomorrow

45 再　again

46 見　to meet

47 記得　to remember

48 複習　to review

49 回家作業　homework

50 沒有　no; not to have

51 但　but

52 單字　vocabulary (word)

53 考　to test

54 造句　making sentences

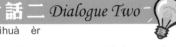

● 對話二 *Dialogue Two*
duìhuà èr

(To get to know Fatou, Claire invites her to lunch. They are eating in a Japanese restaurant.)

愷俐：法杜，你為什麼會想來台灣學中文呢？
kǎilì　fǎdù　nǐ　wèishéme huì xiǎng lái táiwān xué zhōngwén ne

法杜：因為我想在台灣念醫學，所以才來學中文。
fǎdù　yīnwèi wǒ xiǎng zài táiwān niàn yīxué　suǒyǐ cái lái xué zhōngwén

愷俐：你自己一個人來台灣嗎？
kǎilì　nǐ zìjǐ yí ge rén lái táiwān ma

法杜：對呀，我家人都不在身邊。
fǎdù　duì ya　wǒ jiārén dōu bú zài shēnbiān

我爸爸和我媽媽在阿根廷工作。
wǒ bàba hàn wǒ māma zài āgēntíng gōngzuò

愷俐：這麼遠！
kǎilì　zhème yuǎn

● 生詞 *Vocabulary*
shēngcí

55 為什麼　why

56 來　to come

57 台灣　Taiwan

58 學　to learn

59 因為　because

60 念　to study

61 醫學　medical science, medicine

62 才　(main clause marker—indicates that the proposition in the subordinate clause is necessary in order to verify the proposition in the main clause)

63 自己　oneself

64 一個人　alone

65 家人　family members

66 在身邊　to be around

67 爸爸　dad, father

68 媽媽　mom, mother

69 阿根廷　Argentina, Argentine Republic

70 工作　to work

71 這麼　so

法杜：是啊。我⁷²哥哥在⁷³挪威⁷⁴留學，⁷⁵姊姊在⁷⁶印度工作
fǎdù　　shì a　　wǒ　gēge zài nuówēi liúxué　　jiějie zài yìndù gōngzuò

我⁷⁷妹妹還住在甘比亞，⁷⁸但是⁷⁹明年她就要去
wǒ mèime hái zhù zài gānbǐyà　　dànshì míngnián tā jiù yào qù

⁸⁰俄羅斯⁸¹念書了。
èluósī　　niàn shū le

愷俐：哇，你們一家人都好⁸²有趣！
kǎilì　　wā　　nǐmen yì jiā rén dōu hǎo yǒuqù

爸爸媽媽在⁸³南美洲、姊姊在⁸⁴亞洲、哥哥在
bàba māma zài nán měizhōu　　jiějie zài yàzhōu　　gēge zài

⁸⁵歐洲！
ōuzhōu

法杜：對啊！⁸⁶分散⁸⁷於⁸⁸各⁸⁹洲呢！
fǎdù　　duì a　　fēnsàn yú gè zhōu ne

愷俐：有⁹⁰機會⁹¹的話，我也要去⁹²更多⁹³地方⁹⁴玩！
kǎilì　　yǒu jīhuì dehuà　　wǒ yě yào qù gèng duō dìfāng wán

法杜：那很好啊！愷俐，你想去⁹⁵哪裡？
fǎdù　　nà hěn hǎo a　　kǎilì　　nǐ xiǎng qù nǎlǐ

●生詞 Vocabulary
shēngcí

72 哥哥 elder brother	80 俄羅斯 Russia, Russian Federation	88 各 each, every
73 挪威 Norway, Kingdom of Norway	81 念書 to read books; to study	89 洲 continent
74 留學 to study abroad	82 有趣 to be interesting	90 機會 chance, opportunity
75 姊姊 elder sister	83 南美洲 South America	91 的話 if
76 印度 India, Republic of India	84 亞洲 Asia	92 更 even more
77 妹妹 younger sister	85 歐洲 Europe	93 地方 place
78 但是 but	86 分散 to disperse	94 玩 to play, to enjoy oneself
79 明年 next year	87 於 at, in, on (literary)	95 哪裡 where

恺俐： 嗯嗯······ (Looking around.)
kǎilì　　　en en

以後我想去日本留學！怎麼樣？
yǐhòu wǒ xiǎng qù rìběn liúxué zěnmeyàng

法杜： 太好了！以後我可以去日本找你，
fǎdù　　tài hǎo le　　yǐhòu wǒ kěyǐ qù rìběn zhǎo nǐ

順便去吃道地的日本料理！
shùnbiàn qù chī dàodì de rìběn liàolǐ

●生詞 *Vocabulary*
shēngcí

96 嗯　um

97 以後　later, later on, afterwards

98 日本　Japan

99 怎麼樣　How is it?
　　　　What do you think?

100 順便　conveniently

101 道地　to be authentic

102 的　(adjectival marker)

103 料理　cuisine (especially Japanese or Korean)

日記 Claire White's Diary
rìjì

Dear Diary,

We got a new classmate today! 她叫法杜 , and guess what :

她是甘比亞人! There's no doubt people worldwide want to learn

中文. Her Chinese is really good! That means she's smart. It also means

I'm going to have to make an effort to keep up!

她的家人住在 many different places all over the world—她爸媽

在阿根廷工作, 她哥哥在挪威讀書, 她姊姊在印度上班,

and 她妹妹也要去俄羅斯. It's amazing! I hope I can be as global as

she is one day—in fact, I've made up my mind! After studying Chinese,

我要去日本留學! 順便去吃道地的日本料理!

In order to prepare for the quiz on 造句, 法杜 came to my flat this

evening and we studied together. She is such a fast learner that she

absorbed everything we've learned up to now in less than three hours! She

could be the smartest person I've ever met.

白愷俐

文字之美 The Beauty of Chinese Characters
wénzì zhī měi

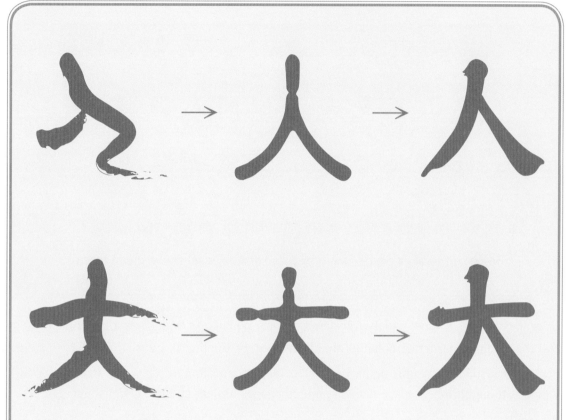

The character "人" (rén) resembles the spread legs of someone standing, and means person or people. The character "大" (dà), which means large, depicts someone standings with arms and legs wide, was originally used to mean person. However, since the posture it depicts shows a person at his or her largest, the character eventually came to represent the notion of big.

● 唐詩之美 *The Beauty of Tang Poetry*
tángshī zhī měi

鹿柴 Deer Park
lù zhài

王維 Wang Wei
wáng wéi

空山不見人，但聞人語響。
kōng shān bú jiàn rén   dàn wén rén yǔ xiǎng

返影入深林，復照青苔上。
fǎn yǐng rù shēn lín   fù zhào qīng tái shàng

No one can be seen on the empty mountain, yet perhaps I hear a voice.

Reflected sunlight pierces the grove, and shines again above green moss.

Deer Park is one of most widely translated of Tang poems. As Wang was a Buddhist mystic, and this poem in particular contains Buddhist imagery, the title in translation refers to a deer park where Buddha gave his first sermon. The literal translation of 鹿柴 is "deer firewood," which is thought to be a place name, conjures images of deer and trees, and suggests a place of refuge.

Like much of Wang's art, sanctuary is indeed a major theme in this poem and is articulated by contrasting the lack of human presence—no one can be seen and perhaps only a single voice can be heard—with an abundance of natural elements—sunlight, the deep grove of trees, and moss.

These details of color and light also demonstrate Wang's knowledge of painting. Although sparse, he uses them to depict a lush space that stands in stark contrast to the human-dominated bustle of Tang society in Chang'an. As a successful official, Wang was certainly able to function among people, and this makes their insignificance in his art all the more striking.

發音 *Pronunciation*
fāyīn

Let's practice tones.

＼＼	＼＼	＼＼	＼＼
介紹	漂亮	作業	但是

一＼	一＼	一＼	一＼
親切	因為	工作	機會

一一	一一	一一	一一
應該	非洲	歐洲	身邊

一／	一／	一／	一／
之前	中文	醫學	家人

／＼	／＼	／＼	／＼
來自	一下	一樣	十六

＼ˇ	＼ˇ	＼ˇ	＼ˇ
自己	一點	日本	料理

／一	／一	／一	ˇ／	ˇ／	ˇ／
明天	台灣	挪威	美國	以為	可能

／／	／／	／／	＼／	＼／	＼／
韓國	留學	明年	既然	記得	複習

● 文法 *Grammar*
wénfǎ

1. 哪 (nǎ/něi) **: which**

When asking for a specific piece of information among several possibilities, Chinese-speakers often use the pattern "哪(一) + classifier / measure word" (equal to "which (one)" in English) in order to ask the addressee to narrow down the information s/he has offered.

Therefore, "你是哪一國人" means "Which country do you come from?" "國" in this sentence is a classifier that indicates nationality; "哪一", a typical question word added before 國 , functions to determine someone's nationality.

你是	哪一國	人？ What's your nationality? / Where are you from?
我是	美國	I'm American. / I'm from the United States.
	加拿大	人。 I'm Canadian. / I'm from Canada.
	甘比亞	I'm Gambian. / I'm from The Gambia.

🍎 Some native speakers say "你是哪國人？" instead of "你是哪一國人？"

🍎 Nationality → 國名(name of nation) ＋ 人

To indicate the nationality of an individual, the character " 人 " (rén) is placed after the name of his/her country of origin.

For example:

America	美國	(Měiguó)
American(s)	美國人	(Měiguó rén)
China	中國	(Zhōngguó)
Chinese	中國人	(Zhōngguó rén)

2. 哪裡(nǎlǐ) : **where**

哪裡 is a question word used to ask for directions or locations.

For example:

偉立，你住在哪裡？	Where do you live, Weili?
妳週末想去哪裡？	Where do you want to go this weekend?
不好意思，請問這裡是哪裡？	Excuse me. Where am I? / Where is this?

🍎 Some Taiwanese speakers of Mandarin say "你是哪裡人？" if the speaker knows the nationality of the addressee is the same as his/hers. "哪裡" is used to ask for the specific city or county the addressee comes from.

3. 為什麼(wèishéme) : **why**

為什麼 is a high-frequency question word placed before verbs or adjectives that functions to ask the reason for something. The correlative conjunction pattern 因為……所以 is used to explain the reason for something. In contrast to English usage, 所以 (therefore; so) is often used at the head of the second clause following the 因為 clause.

Q：你為什麼想學英文？　Why do you want to study English?
A：因為我想要有更多的機會去國外工作。 Because I want a better chance to find work abroad.
Q：你妹妹為什麼喜歡日本？　Why does your (younger) sister like Japan?
A：因為她真的很喜歡吃日本料理，所以才喜歡日本。 She only likes Japan because she likes Japanese food.

🍎 [國外　guówài　overseas, abroad]

4. 在 (zài) . 於 (yú) : at, in, on

在 and 於 are location markers, corresponding to English prepositions like "in", "at", "on", and others, but can also function as verbs when followed by a place word as complement, such as in "在家" or "在台灣".

"於" is literary and it is preserved to this day in formal discourse such as newspaper articles.

在 Prep.	法杜的家人都分散於世界各洲呢！ Fatou's family members are spread out on every continent in the world!
	我的爸爸和媽媽都在美國工作。 My mom and dad work in the United States.
在 V	她的家人都在日本。 Her relatives are all in Japan.
	請問白愷俐在家嗎？＝ 在不在家？ Is Claire White at home? / Is Claire there?

🍎 The A 不 A term "在不在", equal to "在嗎", is used to ask if somebody is in. The affirmative reply "在" means, "Yes, (person) is in."

5. 一下 (yíxià) : a little bit; a short while

一下 used after a verb indicates that an action is of short duration and can express the notion "to give something a try". "我來介紹一下" and "我們來認識一下新同學" are expressions commonly used when people meet each other for the first time because 一下 softens requests and commands, rendering statements more polite. Other action verbs can be followed by the term "一下" as in the following examples.

請大家向法杜自我介紹一下。 Everyone, please introduce yourself to Fatou.
志學，你可以念一下二十五頁的課文嗎？ Zhixue, could you read the text on page 25?
我們想一下明天要去哪裡玩吧！ Let's think about where we should go tomorrow (for fun)!
請問一下，高鐵站在哪裡？ Excuse me. Where is the high-speed rail station?

🍎 [高鐵站 gāotiě zhàn high-speed rail station]

6. 就(jiù) **: right; main clause marker**

就 has two meanings. 就1 is roughly equivalent to the English adverbs "just" and "right." 就2 is more common, and as an adverb of relation, it is placed before the verb to indicate that the condition mentioned earlier has been satisfied to validate the main predicate.

就1 just, right	我們**就**在這裡野餐好了。 Let's just have the picnic here.
	這裡**就**是我們的學校。 Our school is right here.
就2 adverb of relation	我叫張志學，叫我志學**就**好。 My name is Zhang Zhixue, but you can (just) call me Zhixue / but Zhixue is fine.
	既然大家都認識了，我們**就**來上課吧！ Now that everyone knows each other, let's start class!

7. 了 (le) **: a modal particle to mark a change of state**

Differing from the usage of the perfective marker 了 following a verb, 了 in this lesson marks a change of state or a new situation and appears as a particle at the end of a sentence.

| 鐘響了，趕快進教室吧！The bell's ringing. Quickly, to the classroom! |
| 啊，我要走了，大家再見。Hey. I've got to go. (I'll) see you all later. |

8. 有 (yǒu) **: to have**

有 is a verb denoting possession or existence. The negative form is "沒有" (méiyǒu), never "不有"; the interrogative forms are "有……嗎" and "有沒有……".

| 明天有考試嗎？　Is there a test tomorrow? [lit.: Does tomorrow have a test?] |
| 愷俐，今天有沒有回家作業？Kaili, is there any homework today? |
| 啊，我沒有零錢搭公車了。Oh, I don't have any change for the bus. |

🍎 [零錢 língqián change]

9. 但(dàn) = **但是**(dànshì) **: but**

但(是) is a conjunction often used to introduce a phrase or clause that stands in contrast with or qualifies what has been previously stated.

沒有，但要練習單字，明天考造句。

No, but we need to review the vocabulary for a quiz on making sentences tomorrow.

陳老師的中文課很有趣，但中文真的有一點難。

Chen Laoshi's class is really interesting, but Chinese is a little bit difficult.

我妹妹還住在甘比亞，但是明年她就要去俄羅斯念書了。

My younger sister still lives in The Gambia, but she's going to Russia next year to study.

In contrast to 但是, 但 is more commonly used in conversation than in written Chinese.

For example:

今天沒有回家作業，但是，要記得練習單字。

今天沒有回家作業，但要記得練習單字。

There's no homework today, but don't forget to review the vocabulary.

---

10. 怎麼樣(zěnmeyàng) **: what do you think? how is it/that?**

怎麼樣 is a term used to ask for one's point of view or opinion like "如何" in Lesson 3. It can function independently or as a tag question attached to the main clause.

媽媽，我想和姊姊一起去美國留學，怎麼樣？

Mom, I want to go with my elder sister to study abroad in the U.S. What do you think?

明天我帶妳去吃漢堡，你覺得怎麼樣？

Tomorrow I'll take you to eat a hamburger. How's that? / How do you feel about that?

[漢堡　hànbǎo　hamburger]　　　　[覺得　juéde　to feel]

● 換你試試看 *It's Your Turn!*
huàn nǐ   shìshìkàn

Challenge 1

Please choose the correct pinyin for each word you hear.

1. (　　) 翻　　　　A. pān　　　B. fān　　　C. huān

2. (　　) 一點　　　A. yìdiǎn　　B. yídiǎn　　C. yìdiàn

3. (　　) 一樣　　　A. yìyàng　　B. yíyàng　　C. yìyáng

4. (　　) 親切　　　A. xīnqiè　　B. jīnqiè　　C. qīnqiè

5. (　　) 指教　　　A. zhǐjiè　　B. zhǐjià　　C. zhǐjiào

6. (　　) 沒有　　　A. méiyǒu　　B. méiyóu　　C. méiyòu

Challenge 2

Using the pictures as hints, substitute the green words and make a
conversation with one of your classmates.

1. A：他是誰？
   B：他是新來的同學。
   A：他姓什麼？
   B：他姓張。

鄭老師

→ A：
- -

　　B：
- -

　　A：
- -

　　B：

2. A：誰是賈小姐？

　B：我是賈小姐。

　A：請問你叫什麼名字？

　B：我叫賈法杜。

→ A：

　B：

　A：

　B：

高立山

[賈 jiǎ a Chinese surname]

3. A：你是不是美國人？

　B：不是，我是加拿大人。

　A：她也是加拿大人嗎

　B：是的，我和她都是加拿大人。

日本人

→ A：

　B：

　A：

　B：

4. A：你認識不認識金希京？

　B：我認識金希京。

　A：他／她是哪一國人？

　B：他／她是韓國人。

中國人

楊教授

→ A：

　B：

　A：

　B：

[楊教授 yáng jiàoshòu Professor Yang]

5. A：他不是醫學系的學生，她呢？

　　B：她也不是醫學系的學生。

　　A：誰是醫學系的學生？

　　B：王小姐是醫學系的學生。

歷史系

李小姐

→　A：

　　B：

　　A：

　　B：

Supplementary Vocabulary About Majors
系　xì　faculty; department
主修　zhǔxiū　major; specialty
醫學　yīxué　medical science
化學　huàxué　chemistry
資訊科學　zīxùn kēxué　information science, computer science
生物　shēngwù　biology
歷史　lìshǐ　history
政治　zhèngzhì　politics; political science
文學　wénxué　literature
音樂　yīnyuè　music
美術　měishù　fine art

Challenge 3

Match each of the conversations below with one of the five following contexts.

1. [Meeting someone for the first time]
2. [Talking about each other's nationality]
3. [Asking about someone's interests]
4. [Talking about each other's major]
5. [Asking about someone's family]

(   ) A：你喜歡不喜歡 中國 文物？
nǐ　xǐhuān bù　xǐhuān zhōngguó　wénwù

B：我很喜歡呢！我最喜歡的文物就是書法和國畫。
wǒ hěn　xǐhuān ne　　wǒ zuì　xǐhuān de wénwù　jiùshì　shūfǎ　hàn guóhuà

A：我也是。如果有機會的話，我可以帶你去故宮。
wǒ yě　shì　　rúguǒ　yǒu jǐhuì　　　　　wǒ　kěyǐ　dài nǐ　qù gùgōng

B：太好了，一定會很有意思。
tài hǎo le　　yídìng　huì　hěn yǒu　yì si

(   ) A：請問一下，你們是不是醫學系的學生？
qǐng wèn yí　xià　　nǐ men shì　bú　shì　yīxué　xì　de xuéshēng

B：不是喔！我們是生物系的學生。
bú　shì　ō　　wǒ men shì　shēngwù　xì　de xuéshēng

A：那妳呢？

C：我主修歷史。
wǒ zhǔ xiū　lìshǐ

A：是喔！我是醫學系的學生，很高興認識你們。
shì　ō　　wǒ shì　yīxué　xì　de xuéshēng　　hěn gāoxìng rèn shì　nǐmen

(   ) A：我們認識一下。我叫高立山。你叫什麼名字？
wǒ men rènshì yí　xià　　wǒ jiào gāo lìshān　　　nǐ jiào shé me míngzi

B：我叫 Joshua Chamberlain，

我的 中 文名字叫 張 志學，請多多指教。
wǒ　de　zhōng wén míngzi jiào　zhāng　zhìxué　　qǐng duōduō zhǐjiào

(   ) A：你一個人來台灣嗎？
nǐ　yí ge rén lái　táiwān ma

B：對啊！我的爸爸媽媽都住在美國。
wǒ　de　bàba　māma dōu zhù zài měiguó

A：那你有兄弟姐妹嗎？
nà nǐ yǒu xiōng dì jiě mèi ma

B：我有一個哥哥和一個姊姊。哥哥在挪威留學，
wǒ yǒu yí ge gē ge hàn yí ge jiě jie gē ge zài nuówēi liúxué

姊姊也來台灣工作了。
jiě jie yě lái táiwān gōngzuò le

[兄弟姐妹 xiōngdì jiěmèi brothers and sisters] [個 ge a measure word for general use]

(　) A：請問，您是哪一國人？
qǐng wèn nín shì nǎ yì guó rén

B：我是台灣人。你呢？
wǒ shì táiwān rén

A：我是甘比亞人，很高興認識你。
wǒ shì gānbǐyà rén hěn gāoxing rènshì nǐ

B：哇！沒 想 到甘比亞人的 中 文這麼厲害。
wā méi xiǎng dào gānbǐyà rén de zhōng wén zhème lìhài

Challenge 4

Introduce the three students below to one or more of your classmates by using the information in the registration form. Write down what you say using Hanyu Pinyin.

學生登記表　Student Registration Form

姓名 name	性別 sex/gender	國籍 nationality	主修 major	家人 family
張志學	男	美國	生物系	美國
白愷俐	女	加拿大	音樂系	美國
賈法杜	女	甘比亞	醫學系	哥哥—挪威 姊姊—印度

wǒ gēn nǐ jièshào yíxià.→

Challenge 5

Match each question with the best possible reason.

1. (　　) 為什麼你想去日本玩？
wèishéme　nǐ　xiǎng qù　rìběn　wán

2. (　　) 為什麼你喜歡我？
wèishéme　nǐ　xǐhuān　wǒ

3. (　　) 為什麼法杜要念醫學系？
wèishéme　fǎdù　yào　niàn　yīxué　xì

4. (　　) 為什麼你哥哥希望賺很多錢？
wèishéme　nǐ　gēge　xīwàng zhuàn hěn　duō qián

5. (　　) 為什麼你想來台灣？
wèishéme　nǐ xiǎng lái　táiwān

- -

A. 因為她想　當　醫生。
yīnwèi　tā xiǎng　dāng　yīshēng

B. 因為妳很漂亮，說話也很有趣。
yīnwèi　nǐ　hěn piàoliàng　shuōhuà yě hěn　yǒuqù

C. 因為日本料理太好吃了。
yīnwèi　rìběn　liàolǐ　tài hǎo chī le

D. 因為台灣人很親切，東西也很便宜。
yīnwèi　táiwān rén hěn　qīnqiè　dōngxī yě hěn　piányí

E. 因為他想給他女朋友買一座博物館。
yīnwèi　tā xiǎng gěi　tā　nǔ péngyǒu mǎi　yí zuò　bówùguǎn

[說話 shuōhuà saying, talking, or speaking]

● 聽力練習 *Let's Listen!*
tīnglì liànxí

Listen to the dialogue and mark correct statements with "T" and incorrect ones with "F".

Supplementary Vocabulary	
覺得 juéde to feel	電玩遊戲 diànwán yóuxì videogame
最近 zuìjìn recent, recently	討論 tǎolùn to discuss, talk about
難 nán to be difficult	客氣 kèqì polite; modest
語言交換 yǔyán jiāohuàn language exchange; language exchange partner	帥 shuài to be handsome
害怕 hàipà to be afraid (of sth.)	必須 bìxū must

(   ) 1. Since Zhìxué's language exchange partner helped him practice Chinese, Zhìxué doesn't think the test was difficult.

(   ) 2. Zhìxué's language exchange partner comes from The Gambia.

(   ) 3. Fatou thinks having a language exchange sounds interesting.

(   ) 4. Fatou hopes that her language exchange partner will be a handsome guy.

(   ) 5. Zhìxué's language exchange partner likes to talk about hiking.

字型練習 Let's Write!
zìxíng liànxí

| ノ | 人 | 仝 | 今 | 仐 | 金 | 金 | 金 | | | |

| 金 | 金 | 金 | | | | | | | | |
| jīn | | 金 | 金 | | | | | | | |

| 丨 | 冂 | 月 | 月 | 目 | 貝 | 見 | | | | |

| 見 | 見 | 見 | | | | | | | | |
| jiàn | | 見 | 見 | | | | | | | |

| 丨 | 冂 | 月 | 日 | 日 | 明 | 明 | 明 | | | |

| 明 | 明 | 明 | | | | | | | | |
| míng | | 明 | 明 | | | | | | | |

| 一 | 厂 | 厂 | 刃 | 來 | 來 | 來 | 來 | | | |

| 來 | 來 | 來 | | | | | | | | |
| lái | | 來 | 來 | | | | | | | |

丶	口	口	叮	叮	吲	明	哪	哪	哪

哪 哪 哪
nǎ 哪 哪

ノ	亻	亻	亇	位	位	位

位 位 位
wèi 位 位

丶	亠	六	立	立	辛	亲	新	新	新	新

新 新 新
xīn 新 新

丶	亠	六	立	立	辛	辛	亲	亲	新	親

親 親 親
qīn 親 親

| 丨 | 冂 | 冂 | 厈 | 同 | 同 | 同 | 國 | 國 | 國 | 國 |

國	國	國		
	guó	國	國	

| 丶 | 丶 | 氵 | 汀 | 汋 | 汌 | 洲 | 洲 | 洲 |

洲	洲	洲		
	zhōu	洲	洲	

| 丶 | 丶 | 氵 | 汇 | 汇 | 沪 | 湮 | 漂 | 漂 | 漂 | 漂 |

漂	漂	漂		
	piào	漂	漂	

| 丿 | 亻 | 仈 | 们 | 们 | 們 | 們 | 們 | 們 | 們 |

們	們	們		
	men	們	們	

Note

LESSON 6

第六課 她是我的室友
dì liù kè　tā　shì　wǒ　de　shìyǒu

● 對話一 — *Dialogue One*
duìhuà　yī

(Fatou plans to live with a classmate, and asks her classmates for information.)

希京：法杜，早安！
xījīng　　fǎdù　　zǎoān

法杜：早！(Sighs.) 怎麼辦呢？
fǎdù　　zǎo　　　　　zěn me bàn ne

希京：發生了什麼事呢？
xījīng　　fāshēng le shéme shì ne

法杜：請問我可以跟你一起住嗎？
fǎdù　　qǐngwèn wǒ　kěyǐ　gēn　nǐ　yìqǐ　zhù ma

這樣比較方便。我想 當你的室友！
zhèyàng　bǐjiào fāngbiàn　　wǒ xiǎng dāng nǐ de shìyǒu

希京：好可惜！我已經有室友了。對了，你可以去
xījīng　　hǎo kěxí　　wǒ yǐjīng yǒu shìyǒu le　　duì le　　nǐ kěyǐ qù

問愷俐！說不定你可以當她的室友。
wèn kǎilì　　shuōbúdìng nǐ　kěyǐ dāng tā de shìyǒu

法杜：謝謝你！那我去問她！
fǎdù　xièxie nǐ　nà wǒ qù wèn tā

(Fatou talks with Claire.)

法杜：愷俐，早安！聽說你一個人住，是嗎？
fǎdù　kǎilì　zǎoān　tīngshuō nǐ yí ge rén zhù　shì ma

愷俐：是啊！
kǎilì　shì a

法杜：我想 跟同學一起住，因為我覺得跟同學
fǎdù　wǒ xiǎng gēn tóngxué yìqǐ zhù　yīnwèi wǒ jué de gēn tóngxué

一起住比較方便。
yìqǐ zhù bǐjiào fāngbiàn

愷俐：我也這麼想！
kǎilì　wǒ yě zhè me xiǎng

法杜：愷俐，我當你的室友好不好？
fǎdù　kǎilì　wǒ dāng nǐ de shìyǒu hǎo bù hǎo

愷俐：好哇！
kǎilì　hǎo wā

法杜：真的很謝謝你！
fǎdù　zhēn de hěn xièxie nǐ

愷俐：不客氣！
kǎilì　bú kèqì

●生詞 Vocabulary
shēngcí

1 發生 to happen, occur
2 事 event, incident, thing
3 嗎 (interrogative marker)
4 比較 (contrastive) more
5 方便 to be convenient
6 室友 roommate
7 可惜 a pity
8 已經 already
9 問 to ask
10 說不定 chances are; maybe
11 聽說 I heard that; somebody told me that
12 覺得 to feel, think, consider that
13 真的 really

● 對話二 *Dialogue Two*
duìhuà   èr

(On Saturday, when Claire is helping Fatou move in her flat, Huimei comes Huimei comes over.)

法杜： 愷俐，你的**房**間好漂亮！我好喜歡**這個**房間！
fǎdù   kǎilì   nǐ de fángjiān hǎo piàoliàng   wǒ hǎo xǐhuān zhège fángjiān

愷俐： 真的嗎？你喜歡就好！
kǎilì   zhēn de ma   nǐ xǐhuān jiù hǎo

法杜： **當然**是真的！我覺得這個房間**比花園**還漂亮！
fǎdù   dāngrán shì zhēnde   wǒ jué de zhè ge fángjiān bǐ huāyuán hái piàoliàng

(The two laugh. The doorbell rings.)

愷俐： 請問是哪位？
kǎilì   qǐngwèn shì nǎ wèi

惠美： 是我，惠美！
huìměi   shì wǒ   huìměi

愷俐： **等**一下！我**馬上開門**！(Opens the door.)
kǎilì   děng yíxià   wǒ mǎshàng kāi mén

歡迎 歡迎，**不好意思**，我現在比較**忙**！
huānyíng huānyíng bùhǎo yì si   wǒ xiànzài bǐjiào máng

惠美： **別這麼說**！**咦**？請問這位是……？
huìměi   bié zhè me shuō   yí   qǐngwèn zhè wèi shì

愷俐： 她是我的室友，她叫**賈**法杜！她是**從**甘比亞來的！
kǎilì   tā shì wǒ de shìyǒu   tā jiào jiǎ fǎdù   tā shì cóng gānbǐyà lái de

法杜： 你好！叫我法杜就可以了。
fǎdù   nǐhǎo   jiào wǒ fǎdù jiù kěyǐ le

我**今年十九歲**。請問你叫什麼名字？
wǒ jīnnián shíjiǔ suì   qǐngwèn nǐ jiào shéme míngzi

惠美：法杜你好！我姓范，叫做惠美，我今年二十
huìměi fǎdù nǐhǎo wǒ xìng fàn jiàozuò huìměi wǒ jīnnián èrshí

歲。很高興認識你！
suì hěn gāoxìng rènshì nǐ

愷俐：惠美很年輕，不過法杜更年輕呢！
kǎilì huìměi hěn niánqīng búguò fǎdù gèng niánqīng ne

惠美：差不多啦！來，法杜，我送你一個禮物！
huìměi chābùduō la lái fǎdù wǒ sòng nǐ yí ge lǐwù

(She gives Fatou a candy.)

法杜：謝謝！我越來越喜歡這裡了！ (She tries the candy.)
fǎdù xièxie wǒ yuè lái yuè xǐhuān zhè lǐ le

這比什麼都好吃！
zhè bǐ shé me dōu hǎochī

惠美：那就太好了！需不需要我幫忙？
huìměi nà jiù tài hǎo le xū bù xūyào wǒ bāngmáng

愷俐、法杜：好啊，謝謝！
kǎilì fǎdù hǎo a xièxie

●生詞 Vocabulary
shēngcí

14 房間 room
15 這個 this
16 當然 of course, surely
17 比 than
18 花園 garden
19 等 to wait, await
20 馬上 right away, at once
21 開 to open
22 門 door
23 不好意思 excuse me
24 忙 to be busy

25 別這麼說 never mind, there's no need to apologize
26 咦 (exclamation uttered when surprised)
27 賈 Jia (a Chinese surname)
28 從 from
29 今年 this year
30 十九 nineteen
31 歲 years
32 范 Fan (a Chinese surname)
33 叫做 to be called as
34 二十 twenty

35 高興 to be happy
36 年輕 young
37 不過 but
38 差不多 not much difference
39 送 to give as a present
40 個 (measure word for countable things)
41 禮物 gift, present
42 越……越…… the more..., the more...
43 什麼 anything
44 需要 to need
45 幫忙 to help with something

日記 Claire White's Diary
rìjì

Dear Diary,

法杜  told me that 她要跟我一起住, and I said "sure!" because 同學一起住比較方便. 我們可以練習說中文, and we can help each other do the 回家作業, nice! I am a forgetful person, and I love to have somebody as clever as 法杜 to remind me of everything. And when I face difficulties doing my 回家作業 or preparing for tests, I am sure I will bother her very, very often! And the rent will reduce tremendously, too!

On Saturday 法杜 came here with a lot of luggage. She was so satisfied with her new home; she even said that 我們的房間比花園還漂亮! But I agree, 這個房間比我在加拿大的房間還漂亮. At that time 我們的鄰居惠美 came to bring some tasty candies to us (or me), and I used the chance to 介紹法杜給惠美認識, 也介紹惠美給法杜認識. Then we ate the candies that 惠美 brought along. Surprisingly they were so delicious that 法杜 said 她越來越喜歡台灣了 ♥, because the people are so kind and the things are wonderful. That's true to me, too!

白愷俐

尋找部首 *Let's Find Radicals*
xúnzhǎo bùshǒu

Most Chinese characters can be divided into parts, some of which denote the "group" to which the character belongs. For example, some characters share the same part and and their meanings are all related to "mouth." Therefore these characters belong to the "mouth" group and the part they share is called the mouth **radical**/**部首**(bùshǒu). A radical can change positions in different characters.

Radical 部首	口 kǒu	山 shān	田 tián	目 mù	言 yán	馬 mǎ	鳥 niǎo
Meaning 意思	mouth	mountain	field	eye	word	horse	bird
Examples 例字	和 可 同 問 唱 吃	岸 岩 岡 岳 峰 島	町 畝 界 畔 男 畢	眼 睛 睡 眠 看 相	說 話 詩 詞 警 語	馴 駐 駕 駛 駱 駝	鳳 鷹 鴿 鴉 鸚 鵡

● 文字之美 *The Beauty of Chinese Characters*
wénzì zhī měi

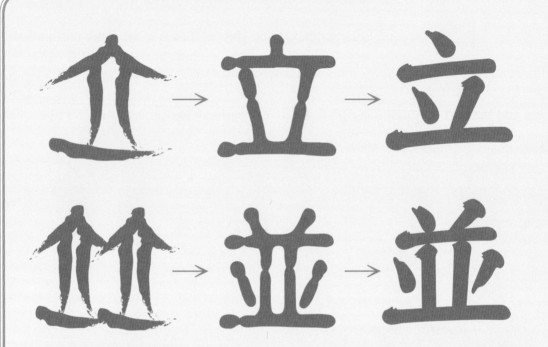

The character "立" (lì) has the meaning of stand or standing. The shape of the character looks slightly like a person, with hands and feet spread, standing on the ground. The horizontal stroke at the bottom of 立 represents the surface of the earth.

The character "並" (bìng), which means together, is composed of two 立 side by side. It depicts two people standing together with their hands and feet spread, and thus indicates people or things being together. In this way, it is often used as a conjunction (e.g. and, also, both) in written Chinese.

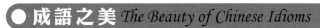

● 成語之美 *The Beauty of Chinese Idioms*

chéngyǔ zhī měi

頂 天 立 地
dǐng tiān lì dì

Top heaven standing ground

↓

Towering from earth to sky

↓

Upright and high-minded

This idiom describes someone, usually a man, who handles affairs in an open and above board way, and does so with vigor and boldness. Only someone who really stands out, like a respected civil leader or an honest politician, would be worthy of such a description. You can also use this idiom to simply describe someone who is tall.

For example, since Gandi stood by his principles, you could say, "He was a 頂天立地 person." You could also use this idiom to describe Yao Ming's height by saying, "He's 頂天立地."

標 新 立 異
biāo xīn lì yì

Mark new standing different

↓

Standing out as new and different

↓

New and original

This four-character compound also contains the character 立 and describes creating items, views, or opinions that stand out as being different from others. It is often used to comment on the importance of originality related to design, performance, and style. Since creativity and innovation are necessary to produce outstanding forms, this idiom is frequently used when discussing art-related topics.

For example, you could say, "Artists must 標新立異. Otherwise, how could their work be original?" You can also use the idiom in this way: "Teenagers often like 標新立異 and being different than others."

發音 *Pronunciation*
fāyīn

Let's practice tones and finals with the "a" sound.

ー ／	ー ／	∨ ＼	∨ ＼
花園	開門	比較	禮物

a　　大　八　他　爸爸　媽媽　沙拉
dà　bā　tā　bàba　māma　shālā

ia/ya　　家　亞　加拿大
jiā　yà　jiānádà

an　　但　山　男　展覽
dàn　shān　nán　zhǎnlǎn

ian/yan　　臉　錢　先
liǎn　qián　xiān

ang　　幫忙　當然
bāngmáng　dāngrán

iang/yang　　想　楊
xiǎng　yáng

楊 爸爸 想 養 馬，馬 媽媽 想 養 羊，
yáng bàba xiǎng yǎng mǎ， mǎ māma xiǎng yǎng yáng

大家 想 幫忙 他們 嗎？ 當然 想 幫忙！
dàjiā xiǎng bāngmáng tāmen ma？ dāngrán xiǎng bāngmáng

Father Yang wants to raise horses, and Mother Ma wants to raise sheep.

Are we willing to help them? Of course we are!

● 文法 *Grammar*
wénfǎ

1. 比 (bǐ) : to compare; compared to; than

When you want to have a positive or negative comparison between the difference of two or more persons or affairs, then the sentence pattern "**N1 (不)比 N2 SV**" can be used. If the compared sentence is a positive one, an adverb 還(hái) can add before the SV in order to strengthen the degree of the difference.

N1	(不)比	N2	(還)	SV	
這個房間	比	花園	(還)	漂亮。	This room is (much) prettier than a garden.
這個炒麵		那個炒飯	(還)	好吃。	This chow mein is (much) better than that fried rice.
華語	不比	英語		難。	Chinese is not as difficult as English.
立山		志學		矮。	Lishan is not as short as Zhixue.

🍎 [矮 ǎi to be short]

The negative comparative pattern, "不比" can be replaced with "NP1 / VP1 沒有 NP2 / VP2 那麼 + SV" as in the following examples:

N1	沒有	N2	那麼	SV	
台北的**天氣**	沒有	花蓮的天氣	那麼	好。	The weather in Taipei is not as good as it is in Hualien.
百貨公司的東西		夜市的東西		划算。	Things in a department store are not as affordable as they are in a night market.

🍎 [天氣 tiānqì weather]　[花蓮 Huālián refers to 花蓮縣 Huālián Xiàn Hualien County (on the east coast of Taiwan)]　[百貨公司 bǎihuògōngsī department store]　[夜市 yèshì nightmarket]　[划算 huásuàn profitable]

2. 比較(bǐjiào) : (contrastive) more

In contrast to "比", "比較" is not a transitive verb, so it cannot be followed by a noun. The other person or thing compared is usually mentioned compared, is usually mentioned earlier.

N1	比較（不）	SV	
這個房間	比較	漂亮。	This room is prettier.
林醫生		年輕。	Dr. Lin is younger.
寫書法	比較不	難。	Writing (Chinese) calligraphy is not as difficult.
跳舞		容易。	Dancing is not as easy.

🍎 In front of this pattern, you can also add "跟……比起來" to illustrate the thing being compared to. Example: "跟寫書法比起來，跳舞比較不容易"。

[跳舞 tiàowǔ to dance]

3. **越**……**越**……(yuè……yuè……) = **愈**……**愈**……(yù……yù……)

越 refers to a degree of process. There are two sentence patterns using 越. One is "越來越……". In this pattern, the degree of thesubject's process increases with time. The other one, "越 A 越 B", shows that the process of B changes resulting from the change of process A.

越來越…… = 愈來愈……
我越來越喜歡這裡了。　I like it here more and more.
物價越來越高，但**薪水**越來越低。 Prices are higher and higher, but wages are lower and lower.
天氣愈來愈**熱了**，你覺得呢？ The weather is getting hotter and hotter, don't you think?
我愈來愈覺得台北是個有趣的**城市**。 I think, more and more, that Taipei is an interesting city.

🍎 [物價 wùjià price of commodities]　[薪水 xīnshuǐ salary]
　[熱 rè to be hot]　[城市 chéngshì city]

越 A 越 B = 愈 A 愈 B
我們的房間當然是越大越好！Certainly, the bigger our room is the better!
我越看越喜歡這個禮物。The more I look at this gift the more I like it.
她們愈談愈高興了。The more they talk the happier they are.
妹妹愈吃愈胖了。The more (my younger) sister eats, the heavier she gets.

🍎 The parts of speech of A and B are either V or SV.
　[談 tán to talk; chat]　[胖 pàng to be fat]

4. 想(xiǎng) **vs. 要**(yào) **: would like to; want**

Among the many meanings of 要, one represents volition, and can sometimes be replaced by 想 as in the following examples.

他要學中文。→他想學中文。 He wants to study Chinese → He would like to study Chinese.
我要送禮物給法杜。→我想送禮物給法杜。 I want to give a gift to Fatou. → I would like to give a gift to Fatou.
偉立要跟我們一起去爬山。→偉立想跟我們一起去爬山。 Weili wants to go hiking with me. → Weili would like to go hiking with me.
志學要介紹語言交換給法杜認識。→志學想介紹語言交換給法杜認識。 Zhixue wants to introduce a language partner to Fatou. → Zhixue would like to introduce a language partner to Fatou.

🍎 In a positive sentence, 要 is similar to 想, but 要 is more affirmative and stronger intention. In a negative sentence, 不想 is a polite way to refuse and is used more frequently than 不要.

5. 是……的(shì……de) **: stressing circumstances connected with the action of the main verb.**

When you want to emphasize the place where the action is occurring , the time when an action is occurring, the means of conveyance used, oror the purpose of the action , then place 是 in front of the words you want to stress, and 的 at the end of the sentence or after the main verb.

法杜	是	從甘比亞來	的。	The Gambia is where Fatou is from.
三明治	是	志學做	的。	Zhixue is who made the sandwich.
「年輕」	是	今天教	的。	What was taught today was "young."
這個	是	要送給希京	的。	What is being given to Xijing is this.

● 換你試試看 *It's Your Turn!*
huàn nǐ shìshìkàn

Challenge 1

Please choose the correct pinyin.

1. (　　) 已　　A. yí　　B. yǐ　　C. yì

2. (　　) 覺得　　A. jiào de　　B. juété　　C. jué de

3. (　　) 高興　　A. gāoxìng　　B. gǎoxing　　C. gāoqìng

4. (　　) 可惜　　A. kěxì　　B. kěxǐ　　C. kěxí

5. (　　) 聽說　　A. dīngchuō　　B. tīngshuō　　C. tīngchuō

6. (　　) 不一定　　A. búyīdìng　　B. bùyídìng　　C. bùyīdìng

Challenge 2

I. Pattern drills

A：According to the contents of following pictures, use the pattern
　　"X(的……)比 Y SV" to make a sentence.

花蓮

For example：

花蓮的天氣／台北的天氣　（好）

台北

→花蓮的天氣比台北的天氣好。

- -

a. 日本車／美國車　（貴）

日本車

→

美國車

b.印度菜／中國菜 （好吃）

印度菜

中國菜

→

[菜　cài　food, cuisine]

c.英語系的學生／歷史系的學生　（多）

英語系

→

歷史系

[系　xì department]　[歷史　lìshǐ history]

d.看電影／看漫畫 （有意思）

看電影

→

看漫畫

[電影　diànyǐng movie]　[漫畫　mànhuà caricature, comic]
[有意思　yǒu yìsi　to be interesting]

e.紅色的衣服／黃色的衣服 （好看）

紅色衣服

→

黃色衣服

[衣服　yīfú clothes]　[紅色　hóngsè red]
[黃色　huángsè yellow]

B：Look at the pictures and use the pattern "不比" or "NP1 / VP1 沒有NP2 / VP2那麼+SV" to assemble the words below.

Example :

這個博物館／那個博物館（大）

→這個博物館沒有那個博物館那麼大。

a.哥哥／弟弟（高）

→

b.王先生／王太太（胖）

→

c.日本／台灣（熱）

→

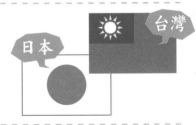

d.我的褲子／你的褲子（長）

→

[褲子 kùzi pants, trousers]

e.雞排／牛排（好吃）

→

[雞排 jīpái chicken steak]　[牛排 niúpái beef steak]

Opposites			
大 小 dà xiǎo big small		輕 重 qīng zhòng light heavy	
胖 瘦 pàng shòu fat thin		快 慢 kuài màn fast slow	
高 矮 gāo ǎi tall short		冷 熱 lěng rè cold hot	
長 短 cháng duǎn long short		多 少 duō shǎo many few	

II. Use the pattern "越來越……" to modify the sentences below.
Example :

我以前不喜歡喝奶茶。我現在喜歡喝奶茶了。
→我越來越喜歡喝奶茶了。

[以前 yǐqián formerly, previously]　[喝 hē to drink]　[奶茶 nǎichá milk tea]

a.哥哥以前不忙。哥哥現在很忙了。

→

b.法杜以前覺得學漢字沒意思。她現在覺得學漢字
　很有意思了。

→

[漢字 hànzì Chinese character]

c.姊姊以前很瘦。她現在很胖了。

→

d.志學以前不認識台灣人。他現在認識很多台灣人了。

→

e.爸爸以前不喜歡去爬山。爸爸現在喜歡去爬山了。

→

Challenge 3

I. Rearrange the following sentences to form a dialogue. Use the numbers 1 through 8 to indicate the correct order.

(　　　) A. 愷俐，早安！

(　　　) A. 愷俐，我的**頭**越來越**痛**了，怎麼辦呢？

(　　　) B. 不客氣。 [頭 tóu head]　[痛 tòng tòng pain; to be painful]

(　　　) A. 但我今天就不能去**上課**了。

(　　　) B. 早啊！　　　　　　　　[上課 shàngkè to take a class]

(　　　) B. 法杜，你應該要去看醫生。

(　　　) B. 別**擔心**，我可以幫你**請假**。 [擔心 dānxīn to worry]

(　　　) A. 真的很謝謝你。　　　[請假 qǐngjià to take a leave]

....

II. Reading comprehension.

Supplementary Vocabulary	
租　zū　to rent	才　cái　only, merely
間　jiān　the measure word for a room	千　qiān　thousand
套房 tàofáng a suite ; a room with a toilet and bath or shower	包括　bāokuò　to include
雅房　yǎfáng　a room to share	費　fèi　expense; charge
家具　jiājù　furniture	水電費　shuǐdiànfèi　expense for utilities
房租　fángzū　rent	網路費　wǎnglùfèi　Internet Fee

志學：我想**租**一**間套房**。
zhìxué　　wǒ xiǎng zū　yìjiān　tàofáng

立山：你現在的房間不好嗎？
lìshān　　nǐ xiànzài de fángjiān bùhǎo ma

志學：那間**雅房**有點小，我 想 找大一點的。
zhìxué　　nàjiān yǎfáng yǒudiǎn xiǎo　wǒ xiǎng zhǎo dà yìdiǎn de

立山：(Points to a picture on a Web page) 這個房間比我的房間還漂亮。
lìshān　　　　　　　　　　　　　　　zhè ge fángjiān bǐ　wǒde fángjiān hái piàoliàng

志學：有沒有**家具**？**房租**貴不貴？
zhìxué　　yǒu méi yǒu jiājù　　fángzū guìbúguì

立山：沒有家具，但是這個房間很便宜，房租才七千元。
lìshān　　méiyǒu jiājù　　dànshì zhège fángjiān hěn piányí　　fángzū cái qīqiānyuán

志學：包括水電費嗎？
zhìxué　　bāokuò shuǐdiànfèi ma

立山：不包括，但是包括網路費了。
lìshān　　bùbāokuò　　dànshì bāokuò wǎnglùfèi le

志學：你可以跟我去看一下嗎？
zhìxué　　nǐ kěyǐ　　gēnwǒ qù kàn yí xià ma

立山：當然可以。
lìshān　　dāngrán kěyǐ

- -

1. (　　) Why does Zhìxué intend to find a new house?
   a. Because his old one is too small.
   b. Because his old one is too expensive.
   c. Because his old one is far from school.

2. (　　) What kind of information does Lìshān provide for Zhìxué?
   a. A house for sale.
   b. A room for rent.
   c. A job opening.

3. (　　) Which is not suitable for Zhìxué's needs?
   a. A room with furniture.
   b. The rent is not expensive.
   c. A room with good ventilation.

4. (　　) How much is the rent per month?
   a. NT$10,000
   b. NT$7,000
   c. NT$5,000

5. (　　) What does Zhìxué imply when he says: "你可以跟我去看一下嗎"?
   a. He thinks that the room can be taken into consideration.
   b. He does not like the room at all.
   c. He thinks that the room is small.

Challenge 4

Find the characters in the green box with the radicals listed in the pink boxes and write them in the green squares below. Each characters should contain the radical to the left of the squares.

部首 Radicals	手 部 shǒu bù		水 部 shuǐ bù		口 部 kǒu bù	人 部 rén bù		火 部 huǒ bù	
意思 Meaning	hand		water		mouth	human		fire	
字形 Forms	扌	手	氵	水	口	亻	人	火	灬
例字 Examples	打	拿	海	漿	吃	你	今	燈	熱

打　河　他　介　拉
喝　水　唱　法　煮
但　災　提　照　叫

人　：　□　　□　　□

手　：　□　　□　　□

水　：　□　　□　　□

火　：　□　　□　　□

口　：　□　　□　　□

聽力練習 *Let's Listen!*
tīnglì   liànxí

Listen to the dialogue and mark correct statements with "T" and incorrect ones with "F".

Supplementary Vocabulary and Phrases
請……吃飯 qǐng…chīfàn to treat somebody to a meal
從今天起 cóng jīntiān qǐ starting today
太……了 tài…le too, very
走吧 zǒuba let's go

(   ) 1. Kǎilì treats Fǎdù to dinner because she wants to welcome Fǎdù.

(   ) 2. Fǎdù is going to be Kǎilì's classmate.

(   ) 3. Fǎdù does not like French food.

(   ) 4. Kǎilì also thinks that the Chinese food is expensive.

(   ) 5. They eventually decide to eat Chinese food.

● 字型練習 *Let's Write!*
zìxíng liànxí

丨 卜 上		

上 上 上
shàng 上 上

丨 厂 厂 厂 厗	馬 馬 馬 馬 馬				

馬 馬 馬
mǎ 馬 馬

′ ′ 彳 彳 彳 彴 彴 彳 彳 從									

從 從 從
cóng 從 從

⺯ ⺯ 幺 幺 糸 糸 紅 經 經 經 經									

經 經 經
jīng 經 經

丨 冂 冂 冋 冋 門 門 門

門 門 門
mén 門 門

丨 冂 冂 冋 冋 門 門 門 門 閂 開 開

開 開 開
kāi 開 開

一 厂 丌 耳 耳 耴 耵 聽 聽 聽 聽 聽

聽 聽 聽
tīng 聽 聽

丶 丨 忄 忙 忙 忙

忙 忙 忙
máng 忙 忙

、	亠	亠	亠	立	产	产	音	音	音	意	意

意　意　意
yì　意　意

丨	冂	冂	曲	田	甲	思	思	思

思　思　思
sī　思　思

﹁	﹁	﹁	臼	臼	臼	與	與	睯	睯	覺

覺　覺　覺
jué　覺　覺

丨	冂	冂	冎	冎	丹	咼	咼	咼	渦	過	過

過　過　過
guò　過　過

Note

第七課 明天是星期幾？
dì qī kè　míngtiān shì xīngqí jǐ

● 對話一 *Dialogue One*
duìhuà　yī

(Lishan has been very busy lately and is feeling overwhelmed. Claire drops by to see if she can offer any help—and she has another mission to complete as well.)

愷俐：立山，你的樣子看起來不太好。怎麼了？
kǎilì　　 lìshān　　　nǐ de yàngzi kàn qǐlái bú tài hǎo　　zěnme le

立山：我最近實在太忙了。因為這幾天要考試，
lìshān　　 wǒ zuìjìn shízài tài máng le　　 yīnwèi zhè jǐ tiān yào kǎoshì

　　　我昨天念了很多書。
　　　 wǒ zuótiān niàn le hěn duō shū

愷俐：辛苦了！
kǎilì　　 xīnkǔ le

立山：而且我從星期一到星期五都要上很多課。
lìshān　　 érqiě wǒ cóng xīngqí yī dào xīngqí wǔ dōu yào shàng hěn duō kè

　　　星期六要語言交換，星期天又要工作。
　　　 xīngqí liù yào yǔyán jiāohuàn　　 xīngqí tiān yòu yào gōngzuò

　　　我好想休息。
　　　 wǒ hǎo xiǎng xiūxí

愷俐：我最近也很忙，只是¹⁸沒有¹⁹你那麼忙。
kǎilì　　wǒ zuìjìn yě hěn máng　zhǐshì méiyǒu nǐ nàme máng

立山：你也要 上很多課嗎？
lìshān　　nǐ yě yào shàng hěn duō kè ma

愷俐：還好²⁰，我只有²¹星期二²²、星期三²³、星期四²⁴的上午²⁵
kǎilì　　hái hǎo　wǒ zhǐyǒu xīngqí èr　xīngqí sān　xīngqí sì de shàngwǔ

　　　有課²⁶，但是²⁷每天下午²⁸都要去補習班²⁹教³⁰英語。
　　　yǒu kè　dànshì měi tiān xiàwǔ dōu yào qù bǔxíbān jiāo yīngyǔ

立山：真好！我從 早上³¹ 到 晚上³² 都要上課呢³³！
lìshān　　zhēnhǎo　wǒ cóng zǎoshàng dào wǎnshàng dōu yào shàngkè ne

愷俐：好辛苦哦！
kǎilì　　hǎo xīnkǔ ó

立山：是啊，而且³⁴作業很多，³⁵真是³⁶受不了。
lìshān　　shì a　érqiě zuòyè hěn duō zhēnshì shòu bù liǎo

●生詞 Vocabulary
shēngcí

1 樣子 appearance
2 起來 by, by way of
3 怎麼了 What happened?; What's up?
4 最近 lately, recently
5 實在 indeed
6 這幾天 these days; in the several days to come
7 考試 exam, test; to take or hold an exam, test, quiz, etc.
8 昨天 yesterday
9 辛苦 to expend considerable effort; toilsome
10 星期一 Monday
11 到 until

12 星期五 Friday
13 星期六 Saturday
14 語言交換 language exchange
15 星期天 Sunday
16 又 again
17 休息 to take a rest
18 只是 however
19 沒有……那麼…… less... than...; not as... as...
20 還好 not really
21 只有 only
22 星期二 Tuesday
23 星期三 Wednesday
24 星期四 Thursday
25 上午 hours before noon;

morning; a.m.
26 課 class, course
27 每天 every day
28 下午 hours after noon; afternoon; p.m.
29 補習班 bushiban, cram school
30 教 to teach
31 早上 morning
32 晚上 evening, night
33 呢 (sentence-final particle used to solicit reactions such as surprise, envy, etc.)
34 作業 homework
35 真是 really
36 受不了 to be intolerable; can't take it

恺俐：真可憐[37]！
kǎilì　zhēn kělián

立山：唉[38]。對了，你找我有事嗎？
lìshān　ai　duì le　nǐ zhǎo wǒ yǒu shì ma

恺俐：啊，差[39]點[40]忘了[41]。下個[42]星期是我的生日[43]，
kǎilì　a　chādiǎn wàng le　xià ge　xīngqí shì wǒ de shēngrì

我想 邀請[44]你來參加[45]我的生日派對[46]！
wǒ xiǎng yāoqǐng nǐ lái cānjiā wǒ de shēngrì pàiduì

立山：是幾月[47]幾號[48]星期幾呢？
lìshān　shì jǐ yuè jǐ hào xīngqí jǐ ne

恺俐：是四月[49]十六號星期一。你有空[50]嗎？
kǎilì　shì sì yuè shíliù hào xīngqí yī　nǐ yǒukòng ma

立山：我看看……那天[51]我 正好[52] 沒事！
lìshān　wǒ kànkàn　nà tiān wǒ zhènghǎo méi shì

恺俐：太好了！那就請你下個星期一 晚上 六點[53]
kǎilì　tài hǎo le　nà jiù qǐng nǐ xià ge xīngqí yī wǎnshàng liù diǎn

來我家哦！
lái wǒ jiā ó

立山：沒問題！
lìshān　méi wèntí

恺俐：那一言為定[54]！
kǎilì　nà yìyán wéidìng

立山：一言為定！
lìshān　yìyán wéidìng

●生詞 *Vocabulary*
shēngcí

37 可憐 to be pitiful
38 唉 (sound of a sigh)
39 差點 nearly, almost
40 忘 to forget
41 下個 next (Sunday, week, month, etc.)
42 星期 week
43 生日 birthday
44 邀請 to invite
45 參加 to take part in, participate
46 派對 party
47 月 month
48 號 date
49 四月 the fourth month, April
50 有空 to have free time, be free, available
51 天 day
52 正好 to happen to
53 點 o'clock
54 一言為定 it's a deal

對話二 *Dialogue Two*
duìhuà èr

(Claire's class decides to visit the Juming Museum during their school vacation. Claire and Joshua have been elected by the class to be in charge of the trip. They are arranging the schedule.)

志學：楊老師 剛剛 說我們幾號去朱銘美術館？
zhìxué　　yáng lǎoshī　gānggāng shuō wǒ men jǐ hào qù zhūmíng měishùguǎn

愷俐：老師說，假期的第二天上午。
kǎilì　　　lǎoshī shuō　jiàqí de dìèr tiān shàngwǔ

志學：我忘了假期是從幾號到幾號。
zhìxué　　wǒ wàng le jiàqí shì cóng jǐ hào dào jǐ hào

愷俐：從三月三十一號到四月五號。
kǎilì　　　cóng sān yuè sānshíyī hào dào sì yuè wǔ hào

　　　所以假期的第二天是四月一號。
　　　suǒyǐ jiàqí de dìèr tiān shì sì yuè yī hào

志學：四月一號不是愚人節嗎？
zhìxué　　sì yuè yī hào bú shì yúrén jié ma

愷俐：是愚人節啊！ (She smiles.)
kǎilì　　　shì yúrén jié a

　　　放心，老師不會騙人的！
　　　fàngxīn　　lǎoshī bú huì piànrén de

生詞 *Vocabulary*
shēngcí

55 剛剛　just now

56 朱銘　Juming (a well-known Taiwanese sculptor)

57 美術館　gallery, fine art museum

58 假期　vacation

59 三月　March

60 三十一　thirty-one

61 愚人節　April Fool's Day

62 放心　to stop worrying

63 騙　to cheat

志學：那就好。我們要幾點集合[64]呢？
zhìxué　　nà jiù hǎo　　wǒ men yào jǐ diǎn jíhé ne

愷俐：我想……我們 早上 八點半[65]，在語言[66]中心[67]
kǎilì　　wǒ xiǎng　　wǒmen zǎoshàng bā diǎn bàn　　zài yǔyán zhōngxīn

門口[68]集合，好不好？
ménkǒu jíhé　　hǎo bù hǎo

志學：好。對了，記得那天 上午 十一點以前要
zhìxué　　hǎo　duì le　　jì de nàtiān shàngwǔ shíyī diǎn yǐqián yào

訂便當。
dìng biàndāng

愷俐：沒問題。參觀[69] 完[70]後[71]，下午五點我們一起
kǎilì　　méi wèntí　　cānguān wán hòu　　xiàwǔ wǔ diǎn wǒ men yìqǐ

回家，OK？
huíjiā

志學：Okay！
zhìxué

愷俐：我有事，先走了。再見！
kǎilì　　wǒ yǒu shì　　xiān zǒu le　　zàijiàn

志學：再見！
zhìxué　　zàijiàn

●生詞 *Vocabulary*
shēngcí

64 集合　to gather

65 半　half; half an hour, thirty minutes

66 語言　language

67 中心　center

68 門口　gate

69 參觀　to pay a visit to

70 完　to finish, be over

71 後　after

數字 *Numbers*
shùzì

零 **0** líng				

一 **1** yī	二 **2** èr	三 **3** sān	四 **4** sì	五 **5** wǔ
六 **6** liù	七 **7** qī	八 **8** bā	九 **9** jiǔ	十 **10** shí
十一 **11** shíyī	十二 **12** shíèr	十三 **13** shísān	十四 **14** shísì	十五 **15** shíwǔ
十六 **16** shíliù	十七 **17** shíqī	十八 **18** shíbā	十九 **19** shíjiǔ	二十 **20** èrshí

二十一 **21** èrshíyī	三十五 **35** sānshíwǔ	七十四 **74** qīshísì	九十六 **96** jiǔshíliù

一百 **100** yì bǎi	一百零八 **108** yì bǎi líng bā
一百五十 **150** yì bǎi wǔshí	兩百 **200** liǎng bǎi
兩百二十二 **222** liǎng bǎi èrshíèr	三百 **300** sān bǎi
五百 **500** wǔ bǎi	九百九十九 **999** jiǔ bǎi jiǔshíjiǔ

日記 Claire White's Diary
rìjì

Dear Diary,

我最近很忙！最近有很多事情：從星期二到星期四都要上課，每天下午還要教英語 and I am also responsible for the trip to 朱銘美術館。朱銘 is a famous Taiwanese sculptor, and I believe that the trip is going to be excellent. But the interesting part is this: The trip will be on 假期的第二天, in other words, 四月一號！在台灣四月一號也是愚人節, the day to fool people around you! That's why 志學 is afraid that 楊老師 is trying to trick him. Ha! 放心，楊老師不會騙人的！

但是 I'm obviously not the busiest one around. 我的鄰居立山比我更忙；我沒有立山那麼忙。他從星期一到星期天、從早上八點到晚上七點都不能休息，真可憐！Since 他有很多課, he has a lot of 作業 to do. But anyway, no matter how busy he is, I still have to 邀請他來參加我的生日派對！我的生日是四月十六號, an Aries. He has promised to come! 立山，放心，if some day 你也邀請我參加你的生日派對，我一定會去的。

白愷俐

尋找部首 *Let's Find Radicals*

xún zhǎo bùshǒu

The form of some radicals can change based on the radical's position in a character. The following table lists seven common radicals that have two forms and shows how they appear in characters.

Radical 部首	人 rén		刀 dāo		心 xīn		手 shǒu		犬 quǎn		玉 yù		肉 ròu	
Meaning 意思	person		knife		heart		hand		dog		jade		meat	
Forms 字形	亻	人	刂	刀	忄	心	扌	手	犭	犬	王	玉	月	肉
Examples 例字	你 他 仇 偶 住	今 企 介 令 傘	利 割 刪 刑 刺	分 切 刃 剪 劈	情 忙 快 怪 怖	愛 忘 想 念 恐	打 找 掉 拉 推	拿 拳 掌 摩 擊	狗 狼 狂 犯 獵	獎 狀 獻 獸 獒	玩 球 現 玫 瑰	璧 瑩 璽	胸 腹 腰 背 臀	腐 臠

● 文字之美 The Beauty of Chinese Characters
wénzì zhī měi

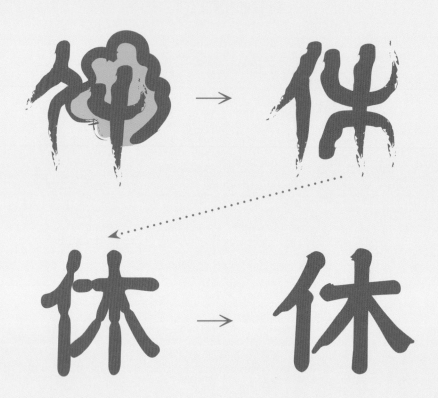

The character "休" (xiū) means to rest or relax. It depicts a person (on the left) leaning against a tree (on the right). Since reclining against a tree can be relaxing, comfortable, and conducive to relieving stress and fatigue, 休 came to mean rest. It is generally combined with 息 (xí) in modern Chinese to form the high-frequency noun/verb compound 休息 (xiūxí).

唐詩之美 *The Beauty of Tang Poetry*
tángshī zhī měi

夜 思 Night Thoughts
yè sī

李 白 Li Bai / Li Bo
lǐ bái

床 前 明 月 光 ， 疑 是 地 上 霜 。
chuáng qián míng yuè guāng　　yí shì dì shàng shuāng

舉 頭 望 明 月 ， 低 頭 思 故 鄉 。
jǔ tóu wàng míng yuè　　dī tóu sī gù xiāng

The moonlight shines before my bed, I thought it was the frost on the floor.

Lifting my head I look at the moon, then I lower my head and think of home.

Li Bai is probably China's best-known poet. He spent most of his life traveling during the Tang Dynasty and many of his poems feature the moon, wine, and Taoist imagery. His ability to effortlessly create beautiful poetry from simple words—unlike his contemporary Du Fu, who strove to use complex language—earned Li Bai the nickname "poetic genius."

In this poem, Li Bai uses ordinary language and imagery to capture a cold, late-night moment. But it is precisely its seemingly unoriginal and random details that allow this poem to resonate so powerfully with readers. In fact, this poem is so widely read that many native Chinese speakers can recite it by the time they are three or four years old.

The poem features the rhyming of 光, 霜, and 鄉. It also contains the contrast of above and below; up and down. On a cold night, unable to sleep, the narrator's gaze and thoughts switch from the moon above to the floor that it illuminates below. Alone in the

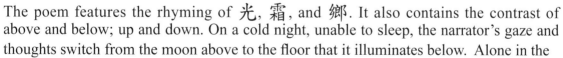

cold, the narrator mistakes brilliant moonlight for frost on the floor. It is noticing this detail that triggers thoughts of home.

No matter where one is or how far that place is from home, the same moonlight shines down on both places. Li Bai captures this notion with simple language and, in so doing, stirs our basic human emotions for home, which lends to the poem's universal appeal.

● 發音 *Pronunciation*
fāyīn

The 一 that changes tones:

ˋ ˇ　　ˊ ˋ　　ˊ ˋ　　ˋ ˊ ˊ ˋ　　ˋ ˇ ˋ ˇ

一起　　一定　　一樣　　一言為定　　下午一點

The 一 that does NOT change tones:

一 ˋ 一 ˋ　　一 ˊ 一　　ˋ 一 一　　ˋ ˇ ˊ 一 ˇ

一月一號　　星期一　　第一天　　上午十一點

1. Most of the ordinal uses of 一, like 第一(first), 一月 (the first month), 一號(the first day) do not have tone change but, 一點 (the first hour) and 一分 (the first minute) are exceptions.

2. When 一 is the unit of a number (like 三十一 thirty-one) other than "one" itself, 一 is always first tone.

e	車	課			
	chē	kè			
e	麼	的	呢	了	個
	me	de	ne	le	ge
e e	怎麼	這麼	這個	哥哥	
	zě me	zhè me	zhè ge	gē ge	
en	陳	分	跟	很	門　人　真
	chén	fēn	gēn	hěn	mén　rén　zhēn
eng	等	更	生	正	烹
	děng	gèng	shēng	zhèng	pēng

這個人很真誠，那個人更真誠。
zhè ge rén hěn zhēnchéng　　nà ge rén gèng zhēnchéng

這個人跟那個人，怎麼都這麼認真！
zhè ge rén gēn nà ge rén　　zě me dōu zhè me rènzhēn

This person is sincere, but that person is more sincere.
Why are both this person and that person so earnest?

● 文法 *Grammar*
wénfǎ

1. 起來 (qǐlái)：

The pattern is used to show the speaker's estimation or assessment of the topic.

Following "起來" is often an adjective or a descriptive, modifying clause. The subject can be omitted.

Topic	*Verb*		*Descriptive Clause*
你的樣子	看	起來	不太好。You don't look too good.
我	想		功課還沒做。 I (just) thought of some homework I haven't done.
她跳舞	跳		好美。She started dancing and it was beautiful.
妹妹的華語	說		像日語。 (My) sister speaks Chinese like she speaks Japanese.

2. 了 (le)

＊In lesson 3, we learned that the particle "了$_1$" can follow a verb or verb phrase and indicates the completion of an action.

＊In this lesson, we see that "了$_2$" always appears at the end of a sentence. It emphatically confirms the completion or realization of some (new) situation.

你吃(飯)了$_1$嗎？Have you eaten? / Have you had something to eat?
我應該會考得很好，因為昨天我念了$_1$很多書。 I should do well on the test because I studied a lot yesterday.
這幾天我們去了$_1$很多地方。I've been to many places in the past few days.
明天要考試，你看書了嗎？Have you studied for the test tomorrow?

是的，我吃了$_2$。Yes. I've eaten. / Yep. I ate.
你志學現在認識很多台灣人了$_2$。Zhixue knows a lot of Taiwanese (people) now.
希京已經很會說華語了$_2$。 Xijing is already quite able to speak Chinese. / Xijing's Chinese is already good.
我到家了$_2$。I'm home.

3. 從……到……(cóng…dào…)

In the construction "從……到……", "從" and "到" can be followed by words indicating either location or time to express distance or duration.

		從……到……		
我		星期一	星期五	都要上很多課。 I have a lot of classes from Monday to Friday.
林**醫生**每天	從	早上	晚上	都在看**病人**。 Dr. Lin sees a lot of patients everyday, from morning to evening.
她晚上		八點	十點	都在**跳舞**。 She was dancing from 8:00 to 10:00 p.m.
		台北	**高雄**	可以坐**高鐵**或飛機。 From Taipei to Kaohsiung you can take high-speed rail or fly.

🍎 [醫生 yīshēng doctor] [病人 bìngrén patient] [跳舞 tiàowǔ to dance]
[高雄 gāoxióng Kaohsiung] [高鐵 gāotiě＝高速鐵路 gāosùtiělù high speed rail]

4. 每……都……(měi……dōu……)

When the pronoun "每" modifies a noun, a measure word should be used before the noun it modifies. For example: 每個朋友. However, before the nouns "天" and "年," a measure word cannot be used, and measure words are optional before "月." For example, we say "每天." "每" is often used in combination with "都."

每……都……
每天下午都要去補習班教英語。 Every afternoon I have to go teach at a bushiban.
我每天都有華語課。 I have Chinese class every day.
我們每(個)月都要去爬山。 I go hiking every month.
台灣每年七月到九月天氣都很熱。 It's hot in Taiwan every year from July to September.

5. 時間表示法(shíjiān biǎoshìfǎ)

In Chinese, if the year, month, and date are given at the same time, this order is followed: **year   month   date   day of the week**

＊Ordinal number + "年"(nián) = year. For example: 2000年 = AD 2008

＊Ordinal number + "月 = month. For example: 五月 = May

＊Ordinal number + "日" or "號" = date. For example, the first day of the month is 一日(號), the second day is 二日(號), and so on. "號" is generally used as the spoken form and "日" is the written form. For example, you would say "四月一號" and write "四月一日" for "April 1."

＊Ordinal number + "星期" The cardinal numbers from one to six follow "星期" to express Monday to Saturday. Generally, the name for Sunday is "星期天" in spoken Chinese and "星期日" in written Chinese.

S	TW (Time-When)	VP	Meaning
金小姐的生日是	一九八五年十二月三十一日。		Ms. Jin's birthday is December 31, 1985.
我	二零零七年七月一日	來台灣。	I came to Taiwan on July 1, 2007.
我們**學校**	九月三日	**開學**。	Our school starts on September 3.
我和愷俐	星期五晚上	**去看電影**。	Claire and I went to see a movie Friday night.

TW (Time-When)	S	VP	Meaning
一九八五年十二月三十一日。	是金小姐	的生日。	December 31, 1985 is Ms. Jin's birthday.
二零零七年七月一日	我	來台灣。	July 1, 2007 is when I came to Taiwan.
九月三日	我們學校	開學。	September 3 is when our school starts.
星期五晚上	我和愷俐	去看電影。	Friday night Claire and I went to see a movie.

[學校 xuéxiào school]   [開學 kāixué school begins / classes start]

[看電影 kàndiànyǐng see a movie / watch a film]

🍎 "星期" means the same as "禮拜" (lǐbài) and "週" (zhōu). Therefore "星期一" is the same as "禮拜一" and "週一", "星期二" is the same as "禮拜二" and "週二", and so on. "星期日（天）" is the same as "禮拜日（天）" and "週日". However, "星期" is used most frequently.

＊Ordinal number + "點" and ordinal number + "分"

When telling someone the time the following rules apply:

9:00	九點	10:05	十點零五分
12:20	十二點二十分	3:30	三點半

年 月 日 星期 點 分 (Year Month Date Week Time)
華語考試時間是七月二十六日上午九點鐘。 The time of the Chinese test is July 26, at 9:00 a.m.
我們星期天十點半去野餐，好嗎？ Let's go on a picnic Sunday (morning) at 10:30, all right?
弟弟：爸媽**什麼時候**到台灣？ Brother: When do mom and dad arrive in Taiwan? 姐姐：他們五月一日上午十點二十分的飛機。 Sister: Their flight arrives May 1 at 10:20 in the morning.
小陳：我們什麼時候去**唱歌**？ Cheny: When are we going singing? 小白：星期五晚上七點。 Whitey: Friday night at 7:00.

🍎 [什麼時候 shéme shíhòu when]　　[唱歌 chànggē to sing]

6. 看看 (kànkàn)

In Chinese, verbs can be repeated. The form for duplicating monosyllabic verbs (V) is "VV" or "V—V." However, the form for repeating disyllabic verbs (AB) is "ABAB," and "一" is never used. For example "看看", "說說", "等一等" and "介紹介紹" are frequently used. Duplicating a verb has the function of implying that an action is of short duration or conveys the idea of giving something a try. In this sense, it is similar to adding "一下" to a verb.

Repeated Verb	Example	Meaning
看→看看	今天你想和我去博物館看看文物展嗎？	Would you like to go with me to the museum today and check out the exhibition?
說→說說	請偉立來跟我們說說如何**學習**華語？	Weili, could you tell us a little about how you learn Chinese?
等→等一等	妳在那裡等一等，我馬上就到。	Wait there for just a minute. I'll be right there.
介紹→介紹介紹	請你介紹介紹你的新室友吧！	How about introducing your new roommate?

[學習 xuéxí to learn]

● 換你試試看 It's Your Turn!
huàn nǐ shìshìkàn

Challenge 1

Please choose the correct pinyin.

1. (　) 剛剛　　A. kāngkāng　B. gānggāng　C. hānghāng

2. (　) 假期　　A. jiāqǐ　　B. jiāqí　　C. jiàqí

3. (　) 星期　　A. xīngqǐ　　B. xīnqí　　C. xīngqí

4. (　) 補習班　A. bǔxíbān　B. pǔxíbān　C. pǔxípān

5. (　) 一言為定　A. yìyán wéidìng　B. yìyán wèidìng　C. yìshuō wéidìng

6. (　) 生日派對　A. shēnrì pàiduì　B. shēngrì pàiduì　C. shēngrì bānduì

Challenge 2

The following is 法杜's weekly schedule.

日期 rìqí / 時間 shíjiān	9月3日 星期一	9月4日 星期二	9月5日 星期三	9月6日 星期四	9月7日 星期五	9月8日 星期六	9月9日 星期日
早上 7:00	起床 qǐchuáng	起床	起床	起床	起床	起床	起床
早上 8:00							
上午10:00	中文課	中文課	中文課	中文課	中文課	花蓮 huālián 旅行 lǚxíng	太魯閣 tàilǔgé
中午12:00							
下午 3:00		書法課	書法課	書法課			
晚上 6:00					我的生日派對	泡溫泉 pào wēnquán	回台北
晚上11:00	睡覺 shuìjiào	睡覺	睡覺	睡覺			

Supplementary Vocabulary and Phrases	
日期　rìqí　date	太魯閣　tàilǔgé　Taroko (a national park in Taiwan)
時間　shíjiān　time	
起床　qǐchuáng　to get up	泡　pào　to soak / to take (a bath)
睡覺　shuìjiào　to go to sleep; to sleep	溫泉　wēnquán　hot spring

I. Use the patterns "從……到……", "每……都……", "S + TW + VP", and "TW + S + VP" to make sentences that answer the questions below. Use the following examples and the schedule above for reference.

法杜的書法課是**從**星期二**到**星期四。
fǎdù　de　shūfǎ　kè shì cóng　xīngqí　èr　dào xīngqí　sì

法杜從星期一到星期五**每**天**都**有中文課。
fǎdù　cóng xīngqí　yī　dào xīngqí　wǔ　měitiān　dōu yǒu　zhōngwénkè

法杜**九月六日**去花蓮。
fǎdù　jiǔ yuè liù　rì　qù huālián

九月六日晚上法杜泡溫泉。
jiǔ yuè liù　rì wǎnshàng fǎdù　pào wēnquán

- -

a. 法杜的中文課是什麼時候？

→

b. 法杜每天都七點起床嗎？

→

c. 法杜的生日是幾月幾日星期幾？

→

d. 法杜幾月幾日星期幾去花蓮旅行？

→

e. 法杜幾月幾日星期幾去太魯閣？

→

II.Please use 早上, 上午, 中午, 下午, 晚上, and 點分, along with 法杜's schedule to make sentences that answer the questions below. Use the following examples as a guide:

法杜星期二**下午三點**有書法課。
　　fǎdù　　xīngqí　èr　xiàwǔ sān diǎn yǒu　shūfǎ　kè

法杜九月十日**晚上六點**回台北。
　　fǎdù　jiǔ yuè　shí　rì wǎnshàng liùdiǎn huí　táiběi

法杜**早上七點**起床。
　　fǎdù　zǎoshàng　qī diǎn qǐchuáng

早上七點，法杜起床。
zǎoshàng qīdiǎn　　　fǎdù　qǐchuáng

----

a.法杜每天的中文課是幾點？
→

b.法杜幾點起床？
→

c.法杜的生日派對是什麼時候？
→

d.法杜什麼時候去泡溫泉？
→

e.法杜從星期一到星期四幾點睡覺？
→

Challenge 3

Sentence building: Add the words in brackets to make a progressively longer sentence.

Example：

我們看電影。
　　 kàn　diànyǐng

🍎 [看電影 kàn diànyǐng see a movie]

（在志學家）→我們在志學家看電影。

（十一點五十分）→十一點五十分我們在志學家看電影。

（晚上）→晚上十一點五十分我們在志學家看電影。

（三十一號）→三十一號晚上十一點五十分我們在志學家看電影。

（十二月）→十二月三十一號晚上十一點五十分我們在志學家看電影。

（二零零八年）→二零零八年十二月三十一號晚上十一點五十分我們在志學家看電影。

---

a.我學中文。

（在台灣）→

（從六月到九月）→

（去年）→

---

b.我會介紹室友給大家。

（新）→

（認識）→

（晚上）→

（明天）→

---

c.他去補習班。

（昨天）→

（下午）→

（三點）→

（半）→

（學西班牙文）→

Challenge 3

d.我要參加派對。

（生日）→

（朋友的）→

（星期五）→

（下個）→

（十二點）→

（中午）→

Challenge 4

Find the characters with these radicals in the two-character compounds below.

部首 Radicals	心 部 xīn bù		女 部 nǚ bù	木 部 mù bù	日 部 rì bù	刀 部 dāo bù	
意思 Meanings	heart		female	wood	sun	knife	
字形 Forms	忄	心	女	木	日	刂	刀
例字 Examples	忙	惠	媽　婆	林　李	明　早	別	分

本之剪楊	來前刀姊	妻機是親	子會她切	意昨最好	思天怕慢	如晚星五	何到期樓

心： □ □ □ □

女： □ □ □ □ □

木： □ □ □ □

日： □ □ □ □

刀： □ □ □ □ □

聽力練習 *Let's Listen!*
tīnglì liànxí

Listen to the dialogue and choose the best answer.

Supplementary Vocabulary and Phrases
後天 hòutiān the day after tomorrow
忙過頭 mángguòtóu over busy; too busy; very busy
香水 xiāngshuǐ perfume
項鍊 xiàngliàn necklace
蛋糕 dàn'gāo cake
逛 guàng to stroll; to ramble; to roam; to browse; sometimes used: 逛(一)逛.
不行 bùxíng to not be allowed; will not do
晚一點 wǎnyìdiǎn a little later
大忙人 dàmángrén busy man; busy woman

1. (   ) Kǎilì's birthday is (a) April 26th. (b) April 16th. (c) April 6th.
(d) April 20th.

2. (   ) Lìshān thinks Kǎilì's birthday (a) is tomorrow. (b) is today.
(c) is the day after tomorrow. (d) was yesterday.

3. (   ) What gift does Fǎdù want to buy for Kǎilì? (a) Perfume. (b) Clothes.
(c) A necklace. (d) A cake.

4. (   ) Where will they buy the presents? (a) At a bakery. (b) At a company.

    (c) At a clothing shop. (d) At a department store.

5. (   ) Who is a busy person? (a) Lìshān. (b) Kǎilì. (c) Fǎdù. (d) Huìměi.

● 字型練習 *Let's Write!*
zìxíng liànxí

一 丁 亓 㠯 写 写 㝵 事

事 事 事
shì 事 事

丨 冂 日 日 旦 旱 旱 旱 旱 最 最
最 最 最
zuì 最 最

一 二 三 手 乇 看 看 看 看
看 看 看
kàn 看 看

一 十 才 木 杧 栏 样 样 楪 様 様
様 様 様
yàng 様 様

| ` | 二 | 言 | 言 | 言 | 訁 | 訊 | 訊 | 訊 | 訊 | 訊 | 說 |

說 shuō 說 說

| 一 | 十 | 卄 | 卅 | 甘 | 其 | 其 | 其 | 期 | 期 | 期 | 期 |

期 qí 期 期

| ` | 丷 | 丷 | 广 | 方 | 方 | 前 | 前 | 前 |

前 qián 前 前

| ` | ` | ` | 爫 | 爫 | 严 | 受 | 受 |

受 shòu 受 受

`	`	氵	氵	汀	沪	沪	派	派			

派	派	派				
	pài	派	派			

丨	冂	冂	冈	冈	冈	岡	岡	剐	剛		

剛	剛	剛				
	gāng	剛	剛			

丨	𠀎	𠀎	馬	馬	馬	馬	馬	馬	馬	騙	騙

騙	騙	騙				
	piàn	騙	騙			

`	冂	冂	日	尸	尸	旦	昪	星			

星	星	星				
	xīng	星	星			

Note

第八課 這本書多少錢？
dì bā kè zhè běn shū duōshǎo qián

對話一 Dialogue One
duìhuà yī

(Higyeong and William are talking about buying presents for Claire's birthday party on April 16.)

希京：偉立，你會去愷俐的生日派對嗎？
xījīng wěilì nǐ huì qù kǎilì de shēngrì pàiduì ma

偉立：我當然會去！你也會去嗎？
wěilì wǒ dāngrán huì qù nǐ yě huì qù ma

希京：會去是會去，可是不知道應該送她什麼禮物。
xījīng huì qù shì huì qù kěshì bù zhīdào yīnggāi sòng tā shé me lǐwù

偉立：女生應該都喜歡花吧？
wěilì nǚshēng yīnggāi dōu xǐhuān huā ba

我打算送她一束玫瑰花，怎麼樣？
wǒ dǎsuàn sòng tā yí shù méiguī huā zěmeyàng

希京：不好，花太貴了，而且你老婆會吃醋。
xījīng bù hǎo huā tài guì le érqiě nǐ lǎopó huì chīcù

偉立：真的嗎？
wěilì zhēn de ma

希京：現在玫瑰花一朵大約四十塊錢。
xījīng xiànzài méiguī huā yì duǒ dàyuē sìshí kuài qián

偉立：**你說得對**，真的很貴。
wěilì　　nǐ shuō de duì　　zhēn de hěn guì

希京：我想**買**一**件好看**的**衣服**給愷俐。
xījīng　　wǒ xiǎng mǎi yí jiàn hǎokàn de　yīfú　gěi　kǎilì

我們女生都很**愛漂亮**，她一定會喜歡！
wǒ men nǚshēng dōu hěn ài piàoliàng　　tā　yídìng huì　xǐhuān

偉立：那我應該送什麼好呢？希京，你有沒有什麼**建議**？
wěilì　　nà　wǒ yīnggāi sòng shé me hǎo ne　xījīng　　nǐ yǒu méiyǒu　shé me jiànyì

希京：嗯……**對**了，聽說愷俐**一直**想要一**本好用**的
xījīng　　ēn　　　dùi le　　tīngshuō kǎilì　yì zhí xiǎngyào yì běn hǎoyòng de

中文**字典**，你可以送一本給她！
zhōngwén zìdiǎn　　nǐ　kěyǐ sòng yì běn gěi tā

偉立：好**主意**！我**決定**了，就送字典給她吧！
wěilì　　hǎo　zhǔyì　　wǒ juédìng le　　jiù sòng zìdiǎn gěi tā ba

希京：那我們一起去買**東西**吧！走吧！
xījīng　　nà　wǒ men　yìqǐ　qù mǎi dōng xī ba　　zǒu ba

偉立：好！
wěilì　　hǎo

●生詞 *Vocabulary*
shēngcí

1 知道 to know	10 朵 (measure word for flowers)	19 愛 to love
2 女生 girl, woman, female	11 大約 about, around	20 建議 advice
3 花 flower	12 四十 forty	21 一直 all the way, all along
4 打算 to plan to	13 塊 dollar (informal)	22 本 (measure word for books)
5 束 bundle, bouquet	14 你說得對 you are right	23 好用 to be easy to use
6 玫瑰花 rose	15 買 to buy	24 字典 dictionary
7 貴 to be expensive	16 件 (measure word for clothing)	25 主意 idea
8 老婆 wife	17 好看 to be good-looking	26 決定 to decide
9 吃醋 to be jealous	18 衣服 clothes	27 東西 thing

對話二 *Dialogue Two*
duìhuà　èr

(William and Higyeong are in a bookstore.)

偉立：希京，你覺得這本字典怎麼樣？
wěilì　　xījīng　　　nǐ　jué de　zhè běn　zìdiǎn　zěn me yàng

希京：我覺得不好，字太小了。
xījīng　　　wǒ jué de　bù hǎo　　zì　tài xiǎo le

偉立：說得也是。那本怎麼樣？字看起來夠大了吧？
wěilì　　shuō de　yěshì　　nà běn zěn me yàng　zì　kàn　qǐlái　gòu dà　le ba

希京：看起來不錯！
xījīng　　　kànqǐlái　　búcuò

偉立：那我就買那本字典好了。
wěilì　　nà　wǒ jiù mǎi　nà běn　zìdiǎn　hǎo le

希京：好啊！不過，多少錢啊？
xījīng　　hǎo　a　　búguò　　duōshǎo qián　a

偉立：我問一下。對不起，請問這本書多少錢？
wěilì　　wǒ wèn　yíxià　　duìbùqǐ　　qǐngwèn zhè běn shū duōshǎo qián

店員：這本六百五十元。
diànyuán　　zhè běn　liù bǎi　wǔshí yuán

偉立：那我要這本。
wěilì　　nà　wǒ yào zhè běn

店員：好的。收您一千元，找您三百五十元。
diànyuán　　hǎo de　　shōu nín　yì qiān yuán　zhǎo nín sān bǎi　wǔshí yuán

　　　　這是您的發票，歡迎再度光臨！
　　　　zhè shì　nín de　fāpiào　　huānyíng　zàidù　guānglín

偉立： ⁵¹接下來，我們要去哪裡呢？
wěilì　　jiēxiàlái　　wǒ men yào qù　nǎlǐ　ne

希京： ⁵²陪我去⁵³挑衣服吧！我知道有一⁵⁴⁵⁵家店，
xījīng　　péi wǒ qù tiāo　yīfú　ba　　wǒ zhīdào yǒu yì jiā diàn

衣服⁵⁶全部都⁵⁷打五折呢！
yīfú　quánbù dōu dǎ wǔ zhé ne

偉立： 真⁵⁸便宜，那我們走吧！
wěilì　zhēn piányí　　nà wǒ men zǒu ba

希京： ⁵⁹出發！
xījīng　　chūfā

●生詞 *Vocabulary*
shēngcí

28 這 this

29 字 Chinese character, word

30 小 to be small, little

31 說得也是 that makes (more) sense

32 那 that

33 夠 enough

34 不錯 to be good

35 好了 it will be better to

36 多少錢 ...how much money?
　　　　...how much does it cost?

37 對不起 excuse me

38 書 book

39 六 six

40 百 hundred

41 五十 fifty

42 元 dollar (formal)

43 好的 OK

44 收 to receive

45 千 thousand

46 找 to give change

47 三 three

48 發票 receipt

49 再度 one more time (literary)

50 光臨 to patronize

51 接下來 next

52 陪 to accompany

53 挑 to pick

54 家 (measure word for stores)

55 店 store, shop

56 全部 all

57 打五折 to give a discount of fifty percent

58 便宜 to be inexpensive, cheap

59 出發 to set off/out

● 數字 *Numbers*
shùzì

一千 **1,000** yì qiān	兩千 **2,000** liǎng qiān	三千 **3,000** sān qiān	五千五百 **5,500** wǔ qiān wǔ bǎi

兩千兩百二十 **2,220** liǎng qiān liǎng bǎi èrshí		七千八百四十 **7,840** qī qiān bā bǎi sìshí

九千九百九十九 **9,999** jiǔ qiān jiǔ bǎi jiǔshíjiǔ

一萬 **10,000** yí wàn	兩萬 **20,000** liǎng wàn	十萬 **100,000** shí wàn	二十萬 **200,000** èrshí wàn

一百萬 **1,000,000** yì bǎi wàn	兩百萬 **2,000,000** liǎng bǎi wàn
兩百二十萬 **2,200,000** liǎng bǎi èrshí wàn	兩百二十二萬 **2,220,000** liǎng bǎi èrshíèr wàn
一千萬 **10,000,000** yì qiān wàn	兩千萬 **20,000,000** liǎng qiān wàn

兩千兩百萬 **22,000,000** liǎng qiān liǎng bǎi wàn
兩千兩百二十萬 **22,200,000** liǎng qiān liǎng bǎi èrshí wàn
兩千兩百二十二萬 **22,220,000** liǎng qiān liǎng bǎi èrshíèr wàn

一億 **100,000,000** yí yì	兩億 **200,000,000** liǎng yì	十億 **1,000,000,000** shí yì

二十億 **2,000,000,000** èrshí yì	一百億 **10,000,000,000** yì bǎi yì
兩百億 **20,000,000,000** liǎng bǎi yì	兩百二十億 **22,000,000,000** liǎng bǎi èrshí yì

兩百二十二億 **22,200,000,000** liǎng bǎi èrshíèr yì

一千億 **100,000,000,000** yì qiān yì	兩千億 **200,000,000,000** liǎng qiān yì

兩千兩百億 **220,000,000,000** liǎng qiān liǎng bǎi yì
兩千兩百二十億 **222,000,000,000** liǎng qiān liǎng bǎi èrshí yì
兩千兩百二十二億 **222,200,000,000** liǎng qiān liǎng bǎi èrshíèr yì

一兆 **1,000,000,000,000** yí zhào	兩兆 **2,000,000,000,000** liǎng zhào

十兆 **10,000,000,000,000** shí zhào

兩百一十三億四千五百六十七萬八千九百零一 **21,345,678,901** liǎng bǎi yīshísān yì sì qiān wǔ bǎi liùshíqī wàn bā qiān jiǔ bǎi líng yī

日記 Claire White's Diary
riji

Dear Diary,

昨天是四月十六號，也是我的 生日！I held a 派對 in the flat where 法杜住 with me. I was so happy that all 我的同學 in 楊老師's class came to bring me such wonderful presents! 希京送了一件很好看的衣服給我 ，我好喜歡喔！希京是女生, so it's no wonder she understands 女生都愛漂亮, and 我很喜歡她的禮物 . The most considerate man, 陳偉立, 送了一本很好用的字典給我. 這本字典看起來很貴, 偉立一定 paid a lot. 法杜送了 a bottle of perfume, 惠美送了 a pair of 漂亮的 earrings, and 立山送了玫瑰花給我. And 志學? He was absurd as usual—he said he wanted to give me a kiss!

楊老師的生日 is coming soon, so I'm thinking about 要送老師什麼禮物. I know 楊老師一定喜歡 cute things, so I may 送老師 a porcelain figurine of a dog I saw in a department store a while ago. The problem is that 一個兩千元…真的太貴了  但是 I think it's worth it!

白愷俐

尋找部首 Let's Find Radicals
xún zhǎo bùshǒu

Some radicals change their form completely when occupying different positions in a character. Other radicals undergo subtle changes in form depending on their position. Among these radicals, the abbreviation of the last stroke (or strokes), for example, changing a long horizontal stroke 一 to a short rising stroke ╱ , or reducing a long falling stroke ╲ to a dot ╲ is what comprises the change in form. The following table presents examples of these radicals.

Radicals 部首	女 nǚ		牛 niú		禾 hé		羊 yáng			豕 shǐ		足 zú		食 shí	
Meanings 意思	female		cattle		crop		goat *			pig		foot		food	
Forms 字形	女	女	牜	牛	禾	禾	𦍌	𦍌	羊	豕	豕	𧾷	足	飠	食
Examples 例字	媽姊姐妹好	妻妾妝妥委	地物牧牲特	牟牢牽犁犀	秋種稻秀租稅	穀穎秀秦	羚羶	美羔善羨義	群	豬	象豪	趾距跑跌踏	蹩	飯餅飲飽餓	養餐饕饗

＊Generally speaking, Chinese speakers usually do not distinguish sheep from goats. Biologically speaking, the word 羊 can refer to many species in the subfamily Caprinae of the family Bovidae.

The five Chinese elements (五行 wǔ xíng) are all radicals. Can you figure out how they change their form?

Radicals 部首	金 jīn		木 mù		水 shuǐ		火 huǒ		土 tǔ	
Meanings 意思	metal		wood		water		fire		earth	
Forms 字形	釒	金	木	木	氵	水	灬	火	圡	土
Examples 例字	釘針鈔鉛銀	鑒鑿	枝杯板材樹	未本末朱李	汗海沒洗澡	永永泉漿	熱烈烹煮焦	灰災炭炸炒	地坡城垃圾	在坐堅基堂

文字之美 *The Beauty of Chinese Characters*
wénzì zhī měi

The character "仙" (xiān) depicts a supernatural being. From the two components of this character, it is clear that 仙 also refers to someone who lives on a mountain. Because mountains are removed from the hustle and bustle of city life, the ancients believed the way to long life was to spend time in the mountains meditating. Over the course of time, those that lived in the mountains—sages and immortals alike—became known as 仙.

諺語的智慧 *The Wisdom of Chinese Proverbs*
yànyǔ de zhìhuì

八 仙 過 海 ， 各 顯 神 通
bā xiān guò hǎi gè xiǎn shén tōng

(Like the) Eight Immortals crossing the sea, each shows his/her divine power.

↓

Everybody using his/her talents to outwit each other to obtain the same objective.

↓

May the best person win.

The Eight Immortals are a group of legendary super-humans in Chinese mythology. Each has a special ability that can be transferred to a tool of power to give life or destroy evil. The Eight Immortals live on a mythical mountain somewhere in the Bohai Sea. They are often depicted together in literature, murals, paintings, sculpture, wood block prints, and even on vases.

呂洞賓 (lǚ dòng bīn) is the leader of the group and often shown wearing scholarly robes and carrying a sword on his back that repels evil sprits. Lü Dongbin is also a poet.

In a Ming Dynasty story entitled The Eight Immortals Cross the Sea (八仙過海 bā xiān guò haǐ), the immortals are on their way to a meeting when they encounter an ocean. Rather than float across on clouds like they usually do, they decide to make things more interesting. Each of them shows off his or her special power to cross the water in a different way. A proverb was born.

In contemporary usage, this proverb is used to describe situations in which several people are after the same objective and use different ways to get it. For example, in an election, you could say, "To get votes, candidate A does X, candidate B does Y, and candidate C does Z. 真是八仙過海 (zhēn shì [really is] bā xiān guò haǐ)."

Other competitive situations that require innovative approaches to succeed, like bidding for a design contract, increasing sales, or pursuing the same handsome boy or pretty girl, could all be summed up by using this proverb. Frequently, the related phrase "大家各憑本事(dàjiā gè píng běn shì)" is used in these situations among the contestants as a bid of good will, and is similar to saying, "You do it that way; I'll do it this way. May the best person win!"

發音 *Pronunciation*
fāyīn

ai	買	塊	愛	百	再	來
	mǎi	kuài	ài	bǎi	zài	lái

ei/ui	對	陪	回	會	美	妹妹
	duì	péi	huí	huì	měi	mèimei

妹 妹 愛 買 菜 。
mèimei ài mǎi cài

(My) younger sister loves to buy food.

妹 妹 帶 了 三 百 塊 。
mèimei dài le sān bǎi kuài

(My) younger sister brought three hundred dollars with her.

妹 妹 來 開 會 。
mèimei lái kāi huì

(My) younger sister is coming to the meeting.

誰 陪 妹 妹 去 派 對 ？
shéi péi mèimei qù pàiduì

Who is going with (my) younger sister to the party?

魏 太 太 帶 妹 妹 回 來 了 。
wèi tàitai dài mèimei huílái le

Mrs. Wei came back with (my) younger sister.

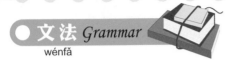

● 文法 *Grammar*
wénfǎ

1. 多少 (duōshǎo)

＊When expressing amounts or quantities in Chinese, one must add a corresponding measure word after the number. For QWs that serve to ask a specific number, the measure word after "多少" can be omitted.

＊"多少" is introduced in this lesson. We saw "幾" in lesson 4 and 7. "多少" and "幾" both enquire about an amount or quantity. The number expressed by "多少" may be large or small; "幾" generally indicates numbers from 1 to 10.

M + 多少 + N ?		
這個漢堡	多少	錢？ How much is this hamburger?
這本書有		頁？ How many pages does this book have?
這間補習班有		學生？ How many students does this bushiban have?
愷俐有		台灣朋友呢？ How many Taiwanese friends does Kaili have?

幾 + (M) + N ?		
你住在	幾	樓？ Which floor do you live on?
你有		位中文老師？ How many Chinese teachers do you have?
你早上有		節課？ How many class periods do you have in the morning?
立山會說		種語言？ How many languages can Lishan speak?

[節 jié period]　　[種 zhǒng kind, type, variety]

2. 吧 (ba)

＊"吧" can be used at end of a statement to indicate that the speaker has an estimate of a situation but is not completely certain about it. There is usually question mark at the end of such a sentence, expressing a mild tone.

＊"吧" can be used at the end of statement to express request, command, consultation, agreement, or suggestion.

女生應該都喜歡花吧？ I think girls should all like flowers. / All girls should like flowers, right?
他今年一月去韓國吧？ I think he's going to Korea in January. / He's going to Korea in January, right?
這本書兩百五十元吧？ I think this book is two hundred fifty dollars. / This book is $350.00, right?
明天要考試吧？ I think there is a test tomorrow. / There is a test tomorrow, right?

我下個月回國吧！ I'll probably go home next month.
好吧！我來幫你吧！ Okay. I'll help you.
我們星期二去看電影吧！ Let's go see a movie on Tuesday.
明天要考試，你還是好好念書吧！ There's a test tomorrow so you'd better study!

3. 給 (gěi)

"給" can be a verb or a preposition. In Chinese, prepositions are generally combined with nouns or pronouns to form prepositional phrases, which appear before verbs as adverbials. The verb "給" can take one or two objects.

S ＋ 給 ＋ O1 ＋ O2 ？
請給我一杯水。　Please give me a glass of water.
我做飯給你吃好嗎？　I'll make something to eat for you, okay?
希京送一件衣服給愷俐。 Xijing gave an article of clothing (as a gift) to Kaili.
請給我看你新室友的照片，好嗎？ Please give me your new roommate's picture to look at, okay?

[杯 bēi cup; a cup of]

4. 量詞 (liángcí)

There are a large number of measure words in Chinese. Everything can be "measured" and that measure is represented by a specific measure word. Here is a list of commonly used measure words with some of the nouns that go together with them.

Measure Words	Matching Nouns
本	書、字典、日記
篇 (piān)	日記
朵	花
束	花
個	人、朋友、家人、學生、國家、字、房間、禮物、工作、蛋糕(dàn'gāo)、包子(bāozi)
名、位	老師、先生、小姐
份 (fèn)	餐、蛋糕、沙拉、三明治、工作
塊 (kuài)	蛋糕、錢
道 (dào)	菜、料理
盤 (pán)	菜、料理、水果、炒麵(chǎomiàn)、炒飯(chǎofàn)、滷味(lǔwèi)
碗 (wǎn)	飯、湯(tāng)
杯 (bēi)	水、奶茶(nǎichá)、咖啡(kāfēi)、可樂(kělè)、酒(jiǔ)
條 (tiáo)	褲子(kùzi)、項鍊(xiàngliàn)
瓶 (píng)	香水(xiāngshuǐ)、可樂(kělè)、酒(jiǔ)
件	衣服
所	學校、醫院
間、家	店、學校、博物館、百貨公司(bǎihuò gōngsī)
部 (bù)	電影
輛 (liàng)	車、公車、高鐵(gāotiě)
架 (jià)	飛機
門	課

種 (zhǒng)	運動、水果、事、東西、人
項 (xiàng)	運動
場 (chǎng)	展覽
首 (shǒu)	歌(gē)
台	電話(diànhuà)
幅 (fú)	畫、國畫(guóhuà)
隻 (zhī)	狗、貓(māo)
枝 (zhī)	筆(bǐ)
雙 (shuāng)	鞋子(xiézi)、筷子(kuàizi)

5. 而且 (érqiě)

This word is used to connect two SVs, verb phrases, prepositional phrases, or short sentences. "而且" indicates additional conditions related to the topic/subject of the sentence. It functions like the optional words "in addition", "moreover", and "also" in the examples below.

	而且	(還／也)	
台灣水果好吃	而且		水又多。Taiwanese fruit is delicious and (in addition) juicy.
這件衣服不好看		還／也	不便宜。This garment is ugly and (moreover) not cheap.
我在台灣旅行		還／也	認識很多台灣人。I travel in Taiwan and I (also) know a lot of Taiwanese.
昨天立山請我吃飯		還／也	送我回家。Yesterday Lishan treated me to a meal and (moreover) took me home.
明天晚上我要上課		還／也	要參加愷俐的生日派對。Tomorrow night I have to go to class and (in addition) attend Kaili's birthday party.

6. 錢的單位 (qián de dānwèi)

The monetary unit in Chinese is "元". The units in other languages/countries include "元", "角"(jiǎo) or "毛"(máo, dime or 1/10 of a yuan) and "分" (fēn, cent or 1/100 of a yuan). In spoken Chinese, yuan can be referred to as "塊". Native speakers often use "塊錢" and frequently omit the last word "錢" in the expression. All the zeroes between two non-zero numerals should be connected by the word "零".

300　元	三百塊（錢）
3,050　元	三千零五十元
30,050　元	三萬零五十元

這枝筆多少錢？ How much is this pen?
這枝筆35元。＝ 這枝筆35塊錢。 This pen is thirty-five dollars.
日本料理三百五十塊錢。 Japanese food is three hundred fifty dollars.
這件衣服三千零五十元。 This article of clothing is three thousand fifty dollars.
這學期學費三萬零五十元。 The tuition this semester is thirty thousand fifty dollars.

[學期 xuéqí a semester; a school term]　　　[學費 xuéfèi school fees; tuition]

換你試試看 *It's Your Turn!*
huàn nǐ　shìshìkàn

Challenge 1

Please choose the correct pinyin.

1. (　　) 多少錢　　A. duōshàoqián　B. duōsháoqián　C. duōshǎoqián

2. (　　) 一朵花　　A. yì duǒ huà　B. yí duǒ huā　C. yì duǒ huā

3. (　　) 一束花　　A. yī shù huà　B. yí shù huā　C. yì shù huā

4. (　　) 全部　　A. juānbù　　B. quánbù　　C. quánbú

5. (　　) 兩百元　A. èr bǎi yuán　B. liǎng bǎi yuán　C. liàng bǎi yán

6. (　　) 歡迎光臨　A. huānyíng guānglín　B. huányíng guānglìng　C. huānyīng guānglín

Challenge 2

$2,000

$1,000

$500

$100

第1課 第2課 第3課 第4課 第5課 第6課 第7課 第8課 第9課 第10課 第11課

 $50   **$10**   **$5**   **$1**

How much money do you see?

a.

→ $ _____

b.

→ $ _____

c.

→ $ _____

d.

→ $ _____

e.

→ $ _____

Challenge 3

Look at the picture and complete the dialogues.

對話一 duìhuà yī (Dialogue One)

$2,500

愷俐：法杜，希京送我一件
kǎilì   fǎdù   xījīng song wǒ yí jiàn

很漂亮的衣服。
hěn piàoliàng de yīfú

可是，我沒有鞋子，
kěshì   wǒ méiyǒu xiézi

好想買一 雙 新鞋子。
hǎo xiǎng mǎi yì shuāng xīn xiézi

法杜：嗯！我也想買新衣服。
fǎdù   ēn   wǒ yě xiǎng mǎi xīn   yīfú

那我們一起去買吧！
nà wǒmen yìqǐ qù mǎi ba

愷俐：小姐，我想買 一 雙 紅色的高跟鞋。
kǎilì   xiǎojiě   wǒ xiǎng mǎi yì shuāng hóngsè de gāogēnxié

店員：高跟鞋在這裡，您 穿 幾號呢？
diànyuán   gāogēnxié zài zhèlǐ   nín chuān jǐ hào ne

愷俐：37號。這 雙 高跟鞋多少錢？
kǎilì sānshíqī hào zhè shuāng gāogēnxié duōshǎo qián

愷俐：小姐，我想買 一 雙 紅色的高跟鞋。
kǎilì   xiǎojiě   wǒ xiǎng mǎi yì shuāng hóngsè de gāogēnxié

店員：這雙＿＿＿＿＿＿＿＿元，我們全部打五折，
diànyuán zhè shuāng   yuán   wǒmen quánbù dǎ wǔ zhé

所以是＿＿＿＿＿＿＿＿元。
suǒyǐ shì   yuán

愷俐：小姐，我可以 試穿 嗎？
kǎilì   xiǎojiě   wǒ kěyǐ shìchuān ma

店員：當然可以，來，這是您的尺寸。
diànyuán   dāngrán kěyǐ lái zhèshì nín de chǐcùn

愷俐：剛好耶！法杜，妳覺得這 雙 鞋怎麼樣？
kǎilì   gānghǎo ye   fǎdù   nǐ jué de zhè shuāng xié zěmeyàng

法杜：很漂亮，看起來還不錯！而且才＿＿＿＿＿＿元。
fǎdù   hěn piàoliàng kàn qǐ lái hái bú cuò érqiě cái   yuán

愷俐：那我就買這 雙 鞋子吧！
kǎilì   nà wǒ jiù mǎi zhè shuāng xiézi ba

對話二 duìhuà èr (Dialogue Two)

$490
$590
$2,000

法杜 fǎdù：愷俐，妳覺得這件上衣和這條裙子怎麼樣？
kǎilì nǐ jué de zhè jiàn shàngyī hàn zhè tiáo qúnzi zěmeyàng

愷俐 kǎilì：很好看。hěn hǎokàn

法杜 fǎdù：這件上衣和這條裙子_____錢？
zhè jiàn shàngyī hàn zhè tiáo qúnzi qián

店員 diànyuán：打折以後，這件上衣_____元，
dǎzhé yǐhòu zhè jiàn shàngyī yuán
這條裙子_____元。
zhè tiáo qúnzi yuán

法杜 fǎdù：嗯！那條褲子呢？
ēn nà tiáo kùzi ne

店員 diànyuán：那條褲子_____元。
nà tiáo kùzi yuán

法杜 fǎdù：嗯！那我買這件白色上衣和這條藍色褲子，一共多少錢？
ēn nà wǒ mǎi zhè jiàn báisè shàngyī hàn zhè tiáo lánsè kùzi yígòng duōshǎo qián

店員 diànyuán：小姐，您的一共_____元。
xiǎojiě nín de yígòng yuán

Supplementary Vocabulary

鞋子	xiézi shoes
雙	shuāng a pair of
紅色	hóngsè red
高跟鞋	gāogēnxié high-heels
穿	chuān to wear
試穿	shìchuān to try on
尺寸	chǐcùn size
剛好	gānghǎo just right
上衣	shàngyī blouse
條	tiáo measure word for skirts
裙子	qúnzi skirt
褲子	kùzi pants
白色	báisè white
藍色	lánsè blue
一共	yígòng total

Challenge 4

Use the table to find the characters with these radicals in the two-character compounds below.

部首 Radicals	犬 部 quǎn bù		肉 部 ròu bù		玉 部 yù bù			金 部 jīn bù		衣 部 yī bù	
意思 Meanings	dog		meat		jade			gold		clothes	
字形 Forms	犭	犬	月	肉	𤣩	王	玉	釒	金	璧	衣
例字 Examples	狗	狀	腿	腐	玫	琴	璧	錢	鑒 鑫	被	裳

珍　珠
褲　裙
鐵　胃
豆　腐

獎　金
珊　瑚
獅　子
狼　狽

監　獄
背　錯
鐘　錶
脫　襪　衫

犬 ： ☐ ☐ ☐ ☐ ☐

肉 ： ☐ ☐ ☐ ☐

玉 ： ☐ ☐ ☐

金 ： ☐ ☐ ☐ ☐ ☐

衣 ： ☐ ☐ ☐ ☐

● 聽力練習 *Let's Listen!*
tīnglì   liànxí

Listen to the dialogue and choose the best answer.

Supplementary Vocabulary and Phrases
為了 wèile in order to, for the purpose of
KTV Karaoke Television
唱歌 chànggē to sing
跳舞 tiàowǔ to dance
棒 bàng to be great, wonderful
歌曲 gēqǔ song, melody
其他 qítā other
訂位 dìngwèi reservation, to make a reservation, reserve a table
請客 qǐngkè to treat

1. (   ) Why does Kǎilì want to treat everybody? (a) She passed the exam. (b) Her mother will be coming. (c) To thank everybody for her birthday party. (d) She got a scholarship.

2. (   ) How does Kǎilì treat everybody? (a) By bringing a cake. (b) By inviting everybody to sing. (c) By cooking a meal. (d) She sings the happy birthday song for everybody.

3. (   ) When will they go to KTV? (a) Monday. (b) Wednesday. (c) Thursday. (d) Friday.

4. (   ) Who can not go to KTV? (a) Xījīng (b) Lìshān (c) Fádù (d) Everybody can go to KTV.

5. (   ) What can they do in the KTV? (a) Sing songs and dance. (b) Read books. (c) Watch a movie. (d) Do some shopping.

● 字型練習 *Let's Write!*
zìxíng liànxí

ㄏ	ㅏ	午	숲	金	釒	釟	錢	錢	錢	錢

錢	錢	錢	
	qián	錢 錢	

ノ	ㄷ	ㅕ	竹	竹	竺	笞	筲	筧	算	算

算	算	算	
	suàn	算 算	

フ	ㄱ	ㅋ	ㄹ	ㅌ	聿	聿	書	書	書	

書	書	書	
	shū	書 書	

ヽ	ㅏ	ㅁ	ㅂ	中	虫	串	眚	眚	青	貴 貴

貴	貴	貴	
	guì	貴 貴	

| ⸜ | ⺊ | ⺊ | 艹 | 苩 | 苗 | 莅 | 萑 | 萑 | 雚 | 歡 | 歡 |

| 歡 | 歡 | 歡 | | | | | | | | | |
| | huān | 歡 | 歡 | | | | | | | | |

| 一 | T | 乛 | 丒 | 严 | 臣 | 臥 | 臤 | 臤 | 臨 | 臨 | 臨 |

| 臨 | 臨 | 臨 | | | | | | | | | |
| | lín | 臨 | 臨 | | | | | | | | |

| 一 | 二 | 干 | 王 | 王 | 玔 | 珇 | 珇 | 珇 | 瑰 | 瑰 | |

| 瑰 | 瑰 | 瑰 | | | | | | | | | |
| | guī | 瑰 | 瑰 | | | | | | | | |

| 一 | 十 | 土 | 圵 | 圵 | 坷 | 珀 | � | 垍 | 塊 | 塊 | |

| 塊 | 塊 | 塊 | | | | | | | | | |
| | kuài | 塊 | 塊 | | | | | | | | |

一 广 斤 丙 而 而

而 而
ér 而 而

丨 冂 冂 月 且

且 且
qiě 且 且

丶 丨 丬 业 业 业 业 业 业 业 对

對 對
duì 對 對

丶 丶 丶 丩 爫 爫 爫 爫 爫 爫 愛 愛

愛 愛
ài 愛 愛

第九課 銀行在哪裡？
dì jiǔ kè　yínháng　zài　nǎlǐ

● 對話一 Dialogue One
duìhuà yī

(Claire wants to wire some money back to Canada, but unfortunately, she can't remember where the bank is.)

愷俐：糟了，銀行怎麼走呢？(William arrives.) 偉立！
kǎilì　zāole　yínháng zěnmezǒu ne　　　　　　　wěilì

你來得正好，你知道銀行在哪裡嗎？
nǐ　láide zhènghǎo　nǐ　zhīdào yínháng zài　nǎlǐ　ma

偉立：不好意思，我不清楚。你可以去問問老師，
wěilì　bùhǎo　yìsi　wǒ bù qīngchǔ　nǐ　kěyǐ　qù wèn wèn lǎoshī

她一定知道。
tā　yídìng　zhīdào

愷俐：可是老師還沒來，你知道老師現在在哪裡嗎？
kǎilì　kěshì lǎoshī háiméi lái　nǐ zhīdào lǎoshī xiànzài zài　nǎlǐ　ma

偉立：老師在辦公室裡。
wěilì　lǎoshī zài bàngōngshì lǐ

愷俐：謝謝你！
kǎilì　xièxie　nǐ

偉立：不客氣！
wěilì　búkèqì

(Claire goes to Ms. Yang's office.)

愷俐：楊老師，不好意思，打擾一下！
kǎilì　　yáng lǎoshī　　bùhǎo　yìsi　　dǎrǎo　yíxià

老師：沒關係，請說！
lǎoshī　　méiguānxi　　qǐng shuō

愷俐：老師知道銀行怎麼走嗎？我想匯錢回加拿大，
kǎilì　　lǎoshī zhīdào yínháng zěmezǒu ma　　wǒ xiǎng huì qián huí jiānádà

但是忘了銀行在哪裡。
dànshì wàngle yínháng zài nǎlǐ

老師：銀行啊？你出大門後，先往左走，過兩個
lǎoshī　　yínháng a　　nǐ chū dàmén hòu　　xiān wǎng zuǒ zǒu　　guò liǎng ge

紅綠燈之後，再右轉，就會看到了。
hónglǜdēng zhīhòu　　zài yòu zhuǎn　　jiù huì kàndào le

愷俐：謝謝老師！您真好，您幫了我大忙呢！
kǎilì　　xièxie lǎoshī　　nín zhēn hǎo　　nín bāng le wǒ dà máng ne

老師：不客氣！
lǎoshī　　búkèqì

● 生詞 *Vocabulary*
shēngcí

1 糟了 oh, no!; oops!
2 銀行 bank
3 怎麼走 how to get to
4 得 manner particle (the part following 得 modifies the action preceding it)
5 清楚 to be clear
6 還沒 not yet
7 辦公室 office
8 打擾 to bother
9 匯 to wire, remit, transfer
10 出 to go out
11 大門 gate
12 往 towards
13 左 left
14 走 to walk
15 過 to pass, go by
16 兩 two (used before measure words)
17 紅綠燈 traffic light
18 之後 after
19 右 right
20 轉 to turn
21 看到 to catch sight of, see

● 對話二 *Dialogue Two*

duìhuà èr

(Although Claire now knows how to get to the bank, she is unable to find her bankbook and seal. She thinks she must have put them somewhere in her flat. She asks her roommate, Fatou, to do her a favor.)

法杜：愷俐，你在做什麼？
fǎdù   kǎilì   nǐ zài zuò shéme

愷俐：我在找我的存摺跟印章，我要匯錢回加拿大。
kǎilì   wǒ zài zhǎo wǒ de cúnzhé gēn yìnzhāng   wǒ yào huì qián huí jiānádà

         你可以幫我找一下嗎？
         nǐ kěyǐ bāng wǒ zhǎo yíxià ma

法杜：好啊。
fǎdù   hǎo a

愷俐：法杜，你幫我看看在不在電視機旁邊的櫃子裡，
kǎilì   fǎdù   nǐ bāng wǒ kàn kàn zài bú zài diànshìjī pángbiān de guìzi lǐ

         我來看一下這邊的抽屜。
         wǒ lái kàn yíxià zhèbiān de chōutì

法杜：沒問題。
fǎdù   méiwèntí

愷俐：糟糕，不在抽屜裡。有可能在飯桌上，我去看看。
kǎilì   zāogāo   bú zài chōutì lǐ   yǒukěnéng zài fànzhuō shàng wǒ qù kàn kàn

法杜：也不在櫃子裡。會不會掉到沙發下面呢？
fǎdù   yě bú zài guìzi lǐ   huì bú huì diào dào shāfā xiàmiàn ne

愷俐：有可能，幫我看看，好不好？
kǎilì   yǒukěnéng   bāng wǒ kàn kàn   hǎo bù hǎo

法杜： 好。 (Searches under the couch.)
fǎdù　　hǎo

這邊該掃了，沙發下有好多垃圾。
zhèbiān gāi sǎo le　　shāfā xià yǒu hǎo duō lèsè

愷俐： 你放心，我今天會掃地。飯桌上也沒有，
kǎilì　　nǐ fàngxīn　wǒ jīntiān huì sǎo dì　　fànzhuō shàng yě méiyǒu

會不會在臥室呢？
huì bú huì zài wòshì ne

法杜： 我們進去找找看。
fǎdù　　wǒmen jìnqù zhǎo zhǎo kàn

愷俐： (Enters the bedroom.) 我找到了，在書桌的抽屜裡。
kǎilì　　wǒ zhǎodào le　　zài shūzhuō de chōutì lǐ

法杜： 恭喜！那快去匯錢吧！地我來掃就好了。
fǎdù　　gōngxǐ　nà kuài qù huì qián ba　　dì wǒ lái sǎo jiù hǎo le

愷俐： 謝謝你！
kǎilì　　xièxie nǐ

●生詞 Vocabulary
shēngcí

22 在 to be (doing something)
23 做 to do
24 找 to look for
25 存摺 bankbook
26 印章 seal
27 好啊 okay
28 電視機 television set
29 旁邊 side; next to
30 櫃子 cabinet, closet
31 這邊 this side, around here
32 抽屜 drawer
33 糟糕 oh no; too bad

34 有可能 maybe
35 飯桌 dining table
36 上 top, on top
37 掉 to fall
38 沙發 sofa, couch
39 下面 the place under something
40 該 should; to need, ought (to do something)
41 掃 to sweep
42 下 under
43 有 there is

44 垃圾 trash, garbage
45 掃地 to clean or sweep the floor
46 臥室 bedroom
47 進去 to go in, enter
48 找到 to find
49 恭喜 congratulations
50 快 to hurry to
51 吧 (sentence-final particle indicating an urging tone)

日記 *Claire White's Diary*
rìjì

Dear Diary,

I received my scholarship a few days ago and 昨天我想匯錢 回加拿大. However, two bad things happened. One is 我忘了 銀行怎麼走, and the other is 我忘了我的存摺跟印章 在哪裡. How could I possibly 匯錢回加拿大 without them?

我問偉立 他知道不知道銀行怎麼走, 他說他不知道, 但是楊老師應該知道. 所以我就去問楊老師, and she told me that 銀行不遠, just simply 出大門後往左走, 過兩個 紅綠燈 之後再右轉, 就會看到了. Were it not for her, I could not have 匯錢回加拿大了.

我在家裡找我的存摺跟印章, and I asked 法杜 to help me. 我們找了櫃子跟抽屜 in the living room, even 沙發下跟 飯桌上, 但是都沒有找到. In the end 我們到臥室裡去找, and 我們找到了, 存摺跟印章在書桌的抽屜裡. How stupid I am! I should have thought to look there first. 謝謝大家,

大家真好, 幫了我一個大忙!

白愷俐

尋找部首 *Let's Find Radicals*
xún zhǎo bùshǒu

Some radicals tend to reside at one single position in a character and seldom move. While studying the following radicals, note that while it is possible for their forms to change, the change is significantly less frequent than that of other radicals.

Radicals 部首	尸 shī	戈 gē	戶 hù	斤 jīn	欠 qiàn	歹 dǎi	皿 mǐn
meanings 意思	lying body	weapon	door plank	ax	yawn	defect	container
Examples 例字	屈居 屋屏 尾屁 屎尿 屍局	戰截 戎戒 我或 成戴 戌戲	扉扇 房扈 扁所	斬斷 斫斯 斯新 斥斧	歌歟 歎歐 欷歔 歡欣 歇欸	死殞 歿殀 殮殯 殘殊 殃殖	盤盒 盆盎 盅盃 盛盈 益盡

Radicals 部首	穴 xuè	竹 zhú	舟 zhōu	走 zǒu	門 mén	雨 yǔ	頁 yè
Meanings 意思	cave	bamboo	boat	moving	portal	rain	head
Examples 例字	窩窪 空窗 穿突 窮究 窄窺	竿筍 筒管 筋節 筆筷 箱笛	船舶 艘航 舵艙 艇艦 般	起趣 超越 趕趁 趟赴 趨	開闢 關閉 闊闖 間閒 閘閣	雪雲 雷電 霜露 霧霞 霉零	頭頂 頰頸 額顏 顧順 領顆

Characters indicated with an "!" are exceptions. Notice the shape and position of a single stroke may vary. For example, the first stroke of 死 is longer than it is when it appears in 殘, and the horizontal stroke in 戈 looks slightly different than it does when appearing in other characters.

文字之美 *The Beauty of Chinese Characters*
wénzì   zhī měi

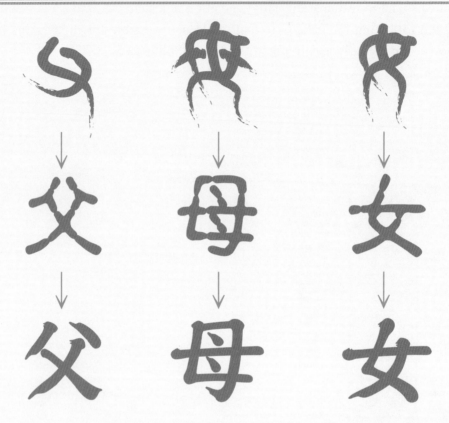

The character "父" (fù) means father. It depicts a hand holding something symbolic of authority. Since fathers have the greatest authority in patrilineal society, "權" (quán) is always in their hands. The character for mother, "母" (mǔ), is formed by adding two dots to the character "女" (nǚ), which means female or woman. The two dots represent the breasts. Because the ancients thought that a mother's distinguishing characteristic is the ability to rear children, they emphasized the breast in creating the character for mother.

LESSON 9

唐詩之美 *The Beauty of Tang Poetry*
tángshī zhī měi

春曉 Spring Morning
chūn xiǎo

孟浩然 Meng Haoran
mèng hàorán

春 眠 不 覺 曉 ， 處 處 聞 啼 鳥 。
chūn mián bù jué xiǎo   chù chù wén tí niǎo

夜 來 風 雨 聲 ， 花 落 知 多 少 。
yè lái fēng yǔ shēng   huā luò zhī duō shǎo

I sleep in late this spring morning; everywhere around me I hear the singing of birds.

I remember the sound of last night's storm; I wonder how many blossoms have fallen.

Although Meng Haoran's poems are overshadowed by those of his contemporary Wang Wei, this particular poem is learned by many native Chinese speakers in elementary school.

In this poem, the narrator wakes to a beautiful spring morning after a good night's sleep—since the weather is cool, the narrator slept well. Looking outside, he or she sees flower petals on the ground from the wind and rain the night before. The narrator likes flowers, and thus thinks it is a shame that they have fallen to the ground. Notice the rhyme of the characters 曉, 鳥, and 少.

This poem can also be read as metaphor for a romantic encounter. The wind and rain of the night before are symbolic of the passion that took place, and the fallen flowers represent the emotion spent. Because of this, the narrator is able to sleep soundly, wakes

up well rested the following morning, and reflects on the events of the previous evening.

No matter the interpretation, parallelism abounds in *Spring Morning*. The first half of the poem has day and the second half night. The second five characters contains the sound of birds, and the third five the sound of wind and rain. And the new life of nature in spring, exemplified by the chirping birds, is accompanied by a loss of life, symbolized by the fallen flowers.

LESSON 9 193

發音 *Pronunciation*
fāyīn

in	銀	印	進	林
	yín	yìn	jìn	lín

ing	清	定	請	零
	qīng	dìng	qǐng	líng

會 議 進 行 著 。
huìyì jìnxíng zhe

The meeting is under way.

英 語 發 音 課 的 講 義 已 經 影 印 好 了 。
yīngyǔ fāyīn kè de jiǎngyì yǐjīng yǐngyìn hǎo le

The photocopies of the handouts for the English pronunciation class are ready.

你 今 天 心 情 好 ， 明 天 心 情 也 一 定 好 。
nǐ jīntiān xīnqíng hǎo míngtiān xīnqíng yě yídìng hǎo

If you are in good mood today, tomorrow you will certainly be in good spirits, too.

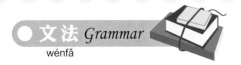

● 文法 *Grammar*
wénfǎ

1. 在 (zài) :

Combined with a noun and a compound locality noun (direction word + suffix), the preposition "在" is used to indicate location. Direction words include: 上, 下, 前, 後, 裡, 外, 左, 右, 旁, 東, 南, 西, 北(běi), 中間(zhōngjiān). Direction words are often used in conjunction with suffixes like 邊, 面, 頭(tóu) to form compound locality nouns. The table below demonstrates how to combine direction words, direction suffixes, and 在 to express the spatial position of objects. Note that "有" can also be used in sentences to express location.

Direction Words	Compound Locality Nouns ~suffix			Examples
	~邊	~面	~頭	
上	上邊	上面	上頭	桌子**上面**有一個花瓶。 There is a vase on the table.
下	下邊	下面	下頭	桌子**下面**有一個垃圾桶。 There is a trash can under the table.
前	前邊	前面	前頭	偉立站在法杜的**前面**。 William is standing in front of Fatou.
後	後邊	後面	後頭	愷俐站在法杜的**後面**。 Claire is standing behind Fatou.
裡	裡邊	裡面	裡頭	一個男人在電梯**裡面**。 A man is inside the elevator.
外	外邊	外面	外頭	電梯**外面**有四個人。 Four people are outside the elevator.
左	左邊	左面		行李在電梯裡面的**左邊**。 The luggage is on the left inside the elevator.
右	右邊	右面		小狗在電梯裡面的**右邊**。 A puppy is on the right inside the elevator.
旁	旁邊			電梯**旁邊**有一張桌子。 There is a table next to the elevator.
中間				法杜站在偉立和愷俐的**中間**。 Fatou is standing between William and Claire.

🍎 [花瓶 huāpíng vase]　[垃圾桶 lèsètǒng trash can; rubbish bin]　[電梯 diàntī elevator; lift]
[行李 xínglǐ baggage; luggage]　[小狗 xiǎogǒu puppy]

前面
qiánmiàn

中間
zhōngjiān

後面
hòumiàn

上面
shàngmiàn

裡面
lǐmiàn

外面
wàimiàn

下面
xiàmiàn

左邊
zuǒbiān

右邊
yòubiān

旁邊
pángbiān

Direction Words	Compound Locality Nouns ~suffix		Examples
	~邊	~面	
東	東邊	東面	花蓮在台灣的**東邊**。 Hualien is in eastern Taiwan.
南	南邊	南面	屏東在台灣的**南邊**。 Pingtung is in southern Taiwan.
西	西邊	西面	台灣的**西面**有台中、彰化。 Taichung and Changhua are in western Taiwan.
北	北邊	北面	台北、基隆、桃園在台灣的**北邊**。 Taipei, Taipei, Keelung, and Taoyuan are in northern Taiwan.

在 ＋ *Place*		
字典	在	櫃子上面。 The dictionary is on the cabinet.
我喜歡坐		教室的前面。 I like to sit in front of the class.
我和希京		花園裡面散步。 Higyeong and I took a walk in the park.
她		外面吃飯。 She is out to eat. / She is outside eating.

🍎 [散步 sànbù to take a walk]

🍎 The combination of a noun with "上"or "裡" often occurs with location words.

For example: 桌子上, 櫃子上, 飯桌上, 抽屜裡, 辦公室裡, 學校裡, 教室裡. The word "裡" cannot be used after proper nouns like the name of a country or a city.

For example: 台灣裡, 美國裡, 台北裡 would be considered strange to native speakers.

🍎 A direction word + 邊、面、頭 combination can follow a noun to indicate locations such as "電視機(的)旁邊", "學校(的)裡面", "教室(的)外面", "加拿大(的)南邊". In these expressions, the particle "的" following the noun is optional.

＊ Combined with a noun, the preposition "在" indicates location. When the phrase is placed before a verb, it indicates the location of the action.

在 ＋ Place ＋ V			
我妹妹	在	台灣	學中文。 My sister is studying Chinese in Taiwan.
媽媽		廚房裡	做飯。 Mom is in the kitchen cooking.
學生們		教室裡	考試。 The students are taking a test in the classroom.
明天我們		哪裡	集合？ Where are we meeting tomorrow?

🍎 [教室 jiàoshì classroom]

＊ 有 and 在 can both be used to indicate the location of something with slightly different effect. 在 is used to show that certain things exist in certain places. 有 is used to show that there is something in a certain place.

For example:

Place ＋ 有 ＋ Indefinite Noun		
我的衣櫃裡	有	很多漂亮的衣服。 My closet contains a lot of pretty clothes.
故宮裡		中國文物。 The National Palace Museum has Chinese artifacts.
中國		萬里長城。 China has the Great Wall.
台北市		101大樓。 Taipei 101 is in Taipei.

Definite Noun ＋ 在 ＋ Place		
很多漂亮的衣服	在	我的衣櫃裡。 There are lots of pretty clothes in my closet.
中國文物		故宮。 There are Chinese artifacts at the National Palace Museum.
萬里長城		中國。 The Great Wall is in China.
101大樓		台北市。 Taipei 101 is in Taipei.

🍎 [萬里長城 wànlǐ chángchéng The Great Wall]　　　[大樓 dàlóu building]

· ·

2. 還 (hái)

In lesson 3, we learned that the particle 還 is an adverb. When placed before a verb, it is used by the speaker to introduce an additional statement to complement the one has just said. This lesson introduces the negative markers "沒(有)" and "不" that are placed after "還" and before the verb to indicate situations that have not yet occurred.

還 ＋ V
昨天我們參觀博物館，還參觀美術館。 Yesterday we visited the museum as well as the art museum.
我剛剛吃了一份(fèn)三明治，還吃了一盤(pán)水果。 I just ate a sandwich and a plate of fruit.
我會騎腳踏車，還會開車。 I can ride a bike as well as drive a car.
希京會說中文，還會說英文。 Higyeong can speak Chinese and English.

🍎 [騎 qí to ride]　　[腳踏車 jiǎotàchē bicycle]

還 ＋ *Negative Marker* ＋ *V*

我還沒(有)複習到第九課。
I still haven't reviewed lesson nine.

我弟弟還沒(有)回台灣。
My brother hasn't yet returned to Taiwan.

我還不認識她，請你介紹一下吧！
I haven't met her yet. Please introduce us!

他還不知道明天要不要考試！
He still doesn't know if we're going to have a test tomorrow or not.

3. 怎麼 (zěnme)

　　"怎麼" is an interrogative adverb. It is often used to ask about the manner, reason, or cause of an action.

怎麼 ＋ *VP (verbal phrase)*		
美術館	怎麼	走？ How do you get to the art museum?
這一句中文		說？ How do you say this Chinese sentence?
他		現在才來？ How can he just be arriving now?
昨天你		沒去參觀故宮呢？ How could you not visit the National Palace Museum yesterday?

🍎 [句 jù sentence]

🍎 "怎麼" and "為什麼" (lesson 5) are both used to ask about the cause of or reason for something. "怎麼" indicates that the speaker is confused or surprised. "為什麼" does not. In addition, "怎麼"can stand alone as a clause.

4. 幫 (bāng)

In the pattern "N1 + 幫 + N2 + V", "幫" expresses that N1 helps N2 to perform an action. N1 may either complete the action together with N2, or perform the task alone.

N1 + 幫 + N2 + V				
請	你	幫	我	送禮物給她。 Help me get her a present.
	媽媽		他	匯錢到台灣好嗎？ Mom, would you help him wire money to Taiwan?
	老師		學生們	複習作業。 The teacher helps the students review the homework.
今天晚上	我		安惠	做飯。 I helped Anhui cook dinner tonight.

5. 先……再…… (xiān…zài…)

The adverbs "先" and "再" are often inserted before verbs to form the construction "先……再……", which emphasizes the order in which the verbs are performed.

先 + V1 + 再 + V2				
我	先	去銀行	再	去學校。 First I went to the bank and then I went to school.
我們		吃飯		討論去哪裡玩！ Let's eat first, then we'll talk about where to go for fun.
愷俐		認識希京		認識法杜。 Claire met Higyeong before before she met Fatou.
老師		複習上一課		上課。 The teacher reviewed the lesson first and then went to class.

6. 中文疑問句的句型 (zhōngwén yíwènjùde jùxíng) : Chinese Question Sentence Pattern

There are five types of questions in Chinese: (1) Particle Questions, (2) Interrogative Pronoun, (3) Tag Question, (4) V Negative V or A Negative A, and (5) Alternative Questions.

(1)**"嗎"和"呢"的疑問句** : **Particle Questions with "嗎" and "呢"**

Questions with "嗎" and "呢" are a simple and commonly used type of question. The person who asks this kind of question has some idea concerning the answer.

你知道法杜住在哪裡**嗎**？	Do you know where Fatou lives?
你昨天怎麼沒來上課**呢**？	How come you didn't come to class yesterday?
他喜歡爬山**嗎**？	Do you like to go hiking?
你生日是幾月幾日**呢**？	When is your birthday?

(2)**疑問代詞疑問句** : **Interrogative Pronoun**

These are questions with "哪裡", "什麼", "誰", "哪", "怎麼", "多少" and "幾". This is how to specifically ask where, what, who, which, how, how much, and how many.

這本書**多少**錢？	How much is this book?
你住在**幾**樓？	Which floor do you live on?
這件衣服**怎麼**樣？	How about this item of clothing?
你今天晚上想吃**什麼**？	What would you like to eat tonight?

(3)**附加疑問句** : **Tag Question**

These are questions ending with "好嗎", "好不好", "是嗎", "是不是", "對嗎", "對不對", "可以嗎". They are short statements that function to ask for confirmation or a suggestion, and are added to affirmative statements.

你喜歡運動，**對不對**？	You like to exercise, right?
我們一起回家，**可以嗎**？	Let's go back together, okay?
她在台灣學習中文，**是不是**？	Isn't she in Taiwan studying Chinese?
我們在語言中心門口集合，**好不好**？	How about we meet in front of the language center?

(4) 正反疑問句：V Negative V or A Negative A

This type of question is also often used. This is a type of question that requires a "yes" or "no" answer.

你女朋友**會不會**做飯？	Can your girlfriend cook? / Does your girlfriend know how to cook?
她**有沒有**兄弟姊妹？	Does she have any siblings?
你**認識不認識**楊老師？	Do you know Yang Laoshi?
你**有沒有**什麼建議？	Do you have any suggestions?

🍎 [兄弟姊妹 xiōngdì jiěmèi brothers and sisters; siblings]

(5) 選擇疑問句：Alternative Questions

This type of question contains two or more choices. The person replying, therefore, needs to choose one of the options in his or her response.

你們的中文課是上午還是下午？	Is your Chinese class in the morning or in the afternoon?
志學去爬山還是去買衣服？	Did Joshua go hiking or go clothes shopping?
希京是日本人、中國人還是韓國人？	Is Higyeong Japanese, Chinese, or Korean?
我們去吃中國菜還是法國菜？	Are we going to eat Chinese food or French food?

● 換你試試看 *It's Your Turn!*
huàn nǐ   shìshìkàn

Challenge 1

Please choose the correct pinyin.

1. (　　) 銀行　　　A. yínháng　　B. yíngxíng　　C. yínxíng

2. (　　) 匯錢　　　A. huìqián　　B. fíqián　　C. huìjián

3. (　　) 紅綠燈　A. hónglǜdēng　B. hónglùdēng　C. hónglǜděng

4. (　　) 右轉　　　A. yóuzhuàn　　B. zuǒzhuǎn　　C. yòuzhuǎn

5. (　　) 旁邊　　　A. pāngbiān　　B. pángbiān　　C. pǎngbiàn

6. (　　) 不好意思　A. búhǎo yìsi　B. bùhǎo yìsi　C. búhào yìsi

Challenge 2

Describe the map below by completing the sentences.

A. 台灣在哪裡？

中國在台灣的_____邊。

菲律賓在台灣的_____邊。　　🍎 [菲律賓 fēilǜbīn
The Philippines]

台灣在中國的_____邊。

日本和_____都在台灣的北邊。

台灣在韓國和菲律賓的_____。

B. 愷俐的家在哪裡？
　　　　jiā zài nǎ lǐ

Ex：愷俐的家在 公車 站和郵局的對面。
　　　　zài gōngchē zhàn hàn yóujú de duìmiàn

北

百貨公司 bǎihuògōngsī	電影院 diànyǐngyuàn	書店 shūdiàn
		商店 shāngdiàn
銀行	餐廳 cāntīng	郵局 yóujú	公車站
博物館	補習班	★愷俐的家

學校

Supplementary Vocabulary	
對面 duìmiàn in front of ; across from	餐廳 cāntīng restaurant
百貨公司 bǎihuògōngsī department store	商店 shāngdiàn store
電影院 diànyǐngyuàn cinema; theater	郵局 yóujú post office
書店 shūdiàn book store	

1. 銀行在哪裡？銀行在餐廳的＿＿＿＿＿，百貨公司
　 yínháng zài nǎ lǐ　yínháng zài cāntīng　　　　　　bǎihuògōngsī
　 的＿＿＿＿＿。
　　 de

2. 百貨公司在哪裡？ 百貨公司在＿＿＿＿＿＿。
　 bǎihuògōngsī zài nǎ lǐ　bǎihuògōngsī

3. 學校在哪裡？ 學校在＿＿＿＿＿＿＿＿。
　 xuéxiào zài nǎ lǐ　xuéxiào zài

4. 郵局在哪裡？ 郵局在＿＿＿＿＿＿＿＿。
　 yóujú zài nǎ lǐ　yóujú zài

5. 餐廳在哪裡？ 餐廳在＿＿＿＿＿＿＿＿。
　 cāntīng zài nǎ lǐ　cāntīng zài

Challenge 3

Complete the sentences according to what you see in the pictures.

A. 語言中心怎麼走？
　　yǔyán zhōngxīn zěnme zǒu

Ex1：從學校大門直走，過了操場後，就會看到展覽館。
　　　cóng xuéxiào dàmén zhí zǒu　　guò le cāochǎng hòu　　jiù huì kàn dào zhǎnlǎn guǎn

　　　語言中心就在 展覽館 的 樓上。
　　　yǔyán zhōngxīn jiù zài　zhǎnlǎn guǎn　de　lóushàng

Ex2：從學校大門往北走，先過了操場後，就可以看到
　　　cóng xuéxiào dàmén wǎng běi zǒu　xiān guò le cāochǎng hòu　jiù kě　yǐ kàn dào

　　　書店和展覽館。語言中心在書店和展覽館的樓上。
　　　shūdiàn hàn zhǎnlǎn guǎn　　yǔyán zhōngxīn zài shūdiàn hàn zhǎnlǎn guǎn de lóushàng

1. 語言中心教室
2. 書店
3. 展覽館
4. 圖書館 túshūguǎn
5. 研究室 yánjiùshì
6. 老師辦公室
7. 醫學系教室
8. 警衛 jǐngwèi
9. 體育館 tǐyùguǎn
10. 英文系教室
11. 中文系教室
12. 商店
13. 銀行
14. 餐廳
15. 操場 cāocháng

學校大門口

Supplementary Vocabulary	
體育館　tǐyùguǎn　gym	研究室　yánjiùshì　study room
操場　cāochǎng　field; grassy area	圖書館　túshūguǎn　library
警衛　jǐngwèi　guard booth; security office	

1.書店怎麼走？
　shūdiàn zěnme zǒu
從學校大門直走，＿＿＿＿＿＿＿＿＿＿＿＿。
cóng xuéxiào dàmén zhí zǒu
書店就在＿＿＿＿＿旁邊。
shūdiàn jiù zài　　　　　pángbiān

2.從　中文　系教室到圖書館怎麼走？
　cóng zhōngwén xì jiàoshì dào túshūguǎn zěnme zǒu
先往＿＿＿＿＿＿＿，再＿＿＿＿＿＿＿，
xiānwǎng　　　　　　　　zài
就會看到了。圖書館就在研究室的＿＿＿＿＿。
jiù huì kàn dào le　túshūguǎn jiù zài yánjiùshì de

3.從老師辦公室到銀行怎麼走？
　cóng lǎoshī bàngōngshì dào yínháng zěnme zǒu
從老師辦公室到銀行先＿＿＿＿＿＿＿，
cóng lǎoshī bàngōngshì dào yínháng xiān
再＿＿＿＿＿＿，就會看到了。銀行就在商店
zài　　　　　　　　jiù huì kàn dào le　yínháng jiù zài shāngdiàn
和餐廳的＿＿＿＿＿＿。
hàn cāntīng de

4.從醫學系教室到體育館怎麼去？
　cóng yīxué xì jiàoshì dào tǐyùguǎn zěnme qù
先＿＿＿＿＿＿＿，再＿＿＿＿＿＿＿。
xiān　　　　　　　　zài
體育館就在＿＿＿＿＿旁邊。
tǐyùguǎn jiù zài　　　　　pángbiān

5.從語言中心到老師辦公室再到餐廳怎麼走？
　cóng yǔyán zhōngxīn dào lǎoshī bàngōngshì zài dào cāntīng zěnme zǒu
從語言中心到老師辦公室＿＿＿＿＿＿＿。
cóng yǔyán zhōngxīn dào lǎoshī bàngōngshì
再從老師辦公室到餐廳＿＿＿＿＿＿＿。
zài cóng lǎoshī bàngōngshì dào cāntīng

B. 愷俐要怎麼到每一個地方？
　　kǎilì　yào　zěnme　dào　měiyíge　dìfāng

Ex：從愷俐的家怎麼到百貨公司呢？
　　cóng　kǎilì　de　jiā　zěn me　dào　bǎihuògōngsī　ne

從愷俐的家往西走，過兩個紅綠燈右轉後，再過
cóng　kǎilì　de　jiā wǎng xī　zǒu　　guò liǎng ge hónglǜdēng　yòu zhuǎn hòu　zài guò

一個紅綠燈，你就會看到百貨公司。百貨公司在
yí　ge hónglǜdēng　　nǐ　jiù　huì　kàn dào　bǎihuògōngsī　　bǎihuògōngsī　zài

銀行的對面。
yínháng　de duìmiàn

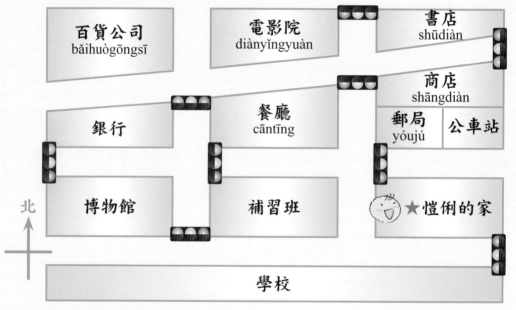

1.從愷俐的家怎麼到銀行？
　cóng　kǎilì　de　jiā zěn me　dào yínháng

2.從博物館怎麼到公車站？
　cóng bówùguǎn zěn me dào gōngchēzhàn

3.從學校怎麼到書店？
　cóng xuéxiào zěn me dào shūdiàn

Challenge 4

Find the characters with these radicals in the two-character compounds below.

部首 Radicals	牛 部 niú bù		豕 部 shǐ bù		禾 部 hé bù		足 部 zú bù		食 部 shí bù	
意思 Meanings	cattle		pig		crop		foot		food	
字形 Forms	牛	牛	豕		禾		𧾷	足	飠	食
例字 Examples	物	牢	豬	豪	私	禿	趴	蹩	飯	餐

豬　肉　　豪　飲　　種　稻　　走　路
牛　餅　　物　象　　跑　跳　　餐　館
特　長　　清　秀　　吃　飽　　跟　蹤
牢　手　　租　稅

牛 ： ☐ ☐ ☐ ☐

豕 ： ☐ ☐ ☐

禾 ： ☐ ☐ ☐ ☐

足 ： ☐ ☐ ☐ ☐

食 ： ☐ ☐ ☐ ☐

聽力練習 *Let's Listen!*
tīnglì liànxí

Listen to the dialogue and choose the best answer.

Supplementary Vocabulary			
皮皮	pípí Pipi (a Chinese pet name)	重要	zhòngyào to be important
關門	guānmén to close a door	跑	pǎo to run
回來	huílái to come back	出去	chūqù to go out; get out
不見	bújiàn to be gone	床	chuáng bed

1. (　　) What are they looking for? (a) The mother. (b) The husband. (c) The dog. (d) The wife.

2. (　　) Where did the husband say it might be? (a) In the garden. (b) Under the bed. (c) In the room. (d) He didn't say.

3. (　　) Who goes outside to look for it? (a) Both the husband and the wife. (b) Only the husband. (c) Only the wife. (d) None of the above.

4. (　　) Why is the husband tired? (a) Because he is looking for something. (b) Because he is cooking. (c) Because he just came home from work. (d) None of the above.

5. (　　) In the end, where is the thing they are looking for? (a) On the bed. (b) Under the bed. (c) In the garden. (d) At the store.

● 字型練習 Let's Write!
zìxíng liànxí

| ` | `` | `` | ㅛ | 米 | 米 | 粘 | 粘 | 粘 | 糟 | 糟 |

糟 糟 糟
zāo
糟 糟

| 一 | 十 | 才 | 木 | 木 | 村 | 材 | 林 | 埜 | 埜 | 楚 | 楚 |

楚 楚 楚
chǔ
楚 楚

| 一 | 立 | 立 | 立 | 辛 | 刻 | 勃 | 勃 | 勃 | 勃 | 辦 | 辦 |

辦 辦 辦
bàn
辦 辦

| 一 | 一 | 戶 | 币 | 币 | 乕 | 雨 | 雨 | 雷 | 雪 | 電 |

電 電 電
diàn
電 電

一 十 扌 扩 扩 扩 护 挀 摳 撄 撄 擾

擾 擾 擾
rǎo
擾 擾

一 一 冫 氵 氵 汀 汀 汇 汇 淮 匯

匯 匯 匯
huì
匯 匯

厂 百 亘 車 車 軒 軒 軒 輔 輔 轉 轉

轉 轉 轉
zhuǎn
轉 轉

十 圭 圭 封 封 封 封 幫 幫 幫 幫

幫 幫 幫
bāng
幫 幫

一 十 扌 扌 扐 找 找

找 找 找
zhǎo
找 找

、 亠 六 立 立 产 产 音 音 音 章

章 章 章
zhāng
章 章

丿 𠂉 𠂊 𠂊 𠂇 𠂉 𠂊 𠂋 𠂌 飯 飯

飯 飯 飯
fàn
飯 飯

′ 𠂇 宀 自 自 𠂤 鱼 鼻 鼻 㫃 邊 邊

邊 邊 邊
biān
邊 邊

第十課 我可不可以試試看？
dì shí kè wǒ kě bù kěyǐ shìshì kàn

對話一 *Dialogue One*
duìhuà yī

(Interested in Chinese culture, Joshua has decided to learn calligraphy. He is practicing calligraphy in the language center when when Claire comes in.)

愷俐：嗨[1]，志學！你在做什麼？
kǎilì　　hāi　　zhìxué　　nǐ zài zuò shéme

志學：喔，嚇[2]我一跳。我在練習寫[3]書法[4]。
zhìxué　　o　　xià wǒ yí tiào　　wǒ zài liànxí xiě shūfǎ

愷俐：哇，你的字好漂亮！你學了多久[5]了？
kǎilì　　wā　　nǐ de zì hǎo piàoliàng　　nǐ xué le duójiǔ le

志學：快[6]一年[7]了。
zhìxué　　kuài yì nián le

愷俐：好厲害哦！我可不可以試試[8]看[9]？
kǎilì　　hǎo lìhài o　　wǒ kě bù kěyǐ shìshì kàn

志學：可以啊。
zhìxué　　kěyǐ a

愷俐：那你可不可以教我？
kǎilì　　nà nǐ kě bù kěyǐ jiāo wǒ

志學：好是好，不過我還沒教¹⁰¹¹過人。
zhìxué　　hǎo shì hǎo　　búguò wǒ hái méi jiāo guò rén

愷俐：你這麼¹²聰明，一定沒問題的。
kǎilì　　nǐ zhè me cōngmíng　yídìng méi wèntí de

志學：好¹³吧！¹⁴一開始，要先把毛筆洗¹⁸一洗。
zhìxué　　hǎo ba　　yì kāishǐ　　yào xiān bǎ máobǐ xǐ yì xǐ

(Claire cleans the brush.) 愷俐：¹⁹好了。²⁰然後呢？
　　　　　　　　　　　　kǎilì　　hǎo le　　ránhòu ne

志學：然後把²¹紙²²放好。(Claire puts the paper down.)
zhìxué　　ránhòu bǎ zhǐ fàng hǎo

志學：²³接著，這樣²⁴握²⁵筆，你看。
zhìxué　　jiē zhe　　zhèyàng wò bǐ　　nǐ kàn

(Joshua demonstrates writing a character. Then Claire writes a character.)

愷俐：是不是這樣？
kǎilì　　shì bú shì zhèyàng

志學：沒錯！你學得很快呢！
zhìxué　　méi cuò　　nǐ xué de hěn kuài ne

●生詞 *Vocabulary*
shēngcí

1 嗨 hi
2 嚇……一跳 to surprise
3 寫 to write
4 書法 calligraphy
5 多久 how long
6 快 almost
7 年 year
8 試 to try
9 看 to try (something)
10 過 to have (done something); to have the experience (of doing something)
11 人 other people
12 聰明 to be smart, bright, clever
13 吧 (sentence-final particle expressing the acceptance of a conclusion)
14 一開始 in the beginning
15 要 do (as in "Do be careful!")
16 把 (disposal marker—used before object and followed by verb)
17 毛筆 brush pen
18 洗 to wash
19 好了 done
20 然後 (and) then
21 紙 paper
22 放 to put
23 接著 next
24 握 to hold
25 筆 pen

對話二 *Dialogue Two*
duìhuà　èr

(Claire goes to a department store to buy some new clothes.)

26 **專櫃小姐**：Hello. May I help you?
zhuānguì xiǎojiě

愷俐：你好，我會說中文。
kǎilì　　nǐhǎo　　wǒ huì shuō zhōngwén

專櫃小姐：那太好了。請問需要什麼嗎？
zhuānguì xiǎojiě　　nà tài hǎo le　　qǐngwèn xūyào shé me ma

愷俐：我想買 27**上衣**跟 28**牛仔褲**。可以 29**麻煩**你 30**幫**我把
kǎilì　　wǒ xiǎng mǎi shàngyī gēn　niúzǎikù　　kěyǐ　máfán　nǐ bāng wǒ bǎ

31 32 33**那條淺藍色**的牛仔褲 34**拿**給我看嗎？
nà tiáo qiǎnlánsè　de　niúzǎikù　ná gěi wǒ kàn ma

專櫃小姐：沒問題。(She hands Claire the jeans.)
zhuānguì xiǎojiě　méiwèntí

愷俐：謝謝。小姐，請問我可不可以試試看？
kǎilì　xièxie　xiǎojiě　qǐngwèn wǒ kě bù kěyǐ shìshì kàn

專櫃小姐：35**試穿**當然可以！來，我 36**帶**你去 37**試衣間**。
zhuānguì xiǎojiě　shìchuān dāngrán kěyǐ　lái　wǒ dài nǐ qù shìyījiān

愷俐：謝謝你！(Claire tries on the jeans.)
kǎilì　xièxie nǐ

專櫃小姐：小姐，這條牛仔褲好 38**適合**你哦！
zhuānguì xiǎojiě　xiǎojiě　zhè tiáo niúzǎikù hǎo shìhé nǐ o

愷俐：真的嗎？我也覺得，看起來 39**好像變得**更年輕了 40
kǎilì　zhēn de ma　wǒ yě jué de　kàn qǐlái hǎoxiàng biànde gèng niánqīng le

專櫃小姐：我們有一⁴¹款上衣，跟這條牛仔褲很
zhuānguì xiǎojiě　　wǒmen yǒu yì kuǎn shàngyī　gēn zhè tiáo niúzǎikù hěn

搭⁴²配，你要不要看一看？
dāpèi　　nǐ yào bú yào kàn yí kàn

愷俐：太好了！麻煩你囉⁴³！
kǎilì　tài hǎo le　máfán nǐ luo

●生詞 Vocabulary
shēngcí

26 專櫃小姐 counter sales woman
27 上衣 top, blouse
28 牛仔褲 jeans
29 麻煩 to trouble (someone)
30 幫 to help
31 條 (measure word for trousers, pants, jeans, etc.)
32 淺 light (color)
33 藍色 blue
34 拿 to take, to hold in the hand
35 試穿 to try on
36 帶 to lead
37 試衣間 fitting room
38 適合 to fit; be suitable
39 好像 seems, seems like
40 變得 to become
41 款 type, style
42 搭配 to go well
43 囉 (combination of le 了 and o 喔)

日記 Claire White's Diary
riji

Dear Diary,

今天我看到志學 在練習書法. 他寫得真好！

我問他他學了多久了, 他說他學了快一年了. *Seeing* 志學

do it, 我也想試試看, 所以 *I borrowed a* 毛筆 *from him,*

寫了一個字看看. 我寫了「白」字, 也就是我的姓. 他說

我學得很快, 也寫得很好！ 我想我也是 *a genius!*

下課之後, 我到 *a department store* 去買新上衣 跟

牛仔褲. 專櫃小姐很親切, *I asked her to hand me* 一條淺藍色

的牛仔褲, 她說我可以試穿, *and showed me the way to the* 試

衣間. *I found* 那條牛仔褲很適合我, 我看起來好像變得

更年輕了！ *Finally* 我買了牛仔褲跟一件上衣.

真好！我愛 ♥ *shopping!*

白愷俐

● 尋找部首 *Let's Find Radicals*
xún zhǎo bùshǒu

Some radicals, although very common, do not make words in modern SMC by themselves. That is, the radical itself does not really have a meaning, but it still provides a concept to all the characters that take it as radical; as a result, it is still very useful to be familiar with them. Take a look at the following radicals and the characters in which they appear.

Radicals 部首	冫 bīng	勹 bāo	宀 mián	广 yǎn	彳 chì	攴 pū	疒 chuáng
Meanings 意思	ice	encompass	house	shelter	left step	hit	disease
Examples 例字	冬冰 冷冶 凋凍 凜冽 凝	包匈 勺勾 勻勿 匆甸 匍匐	宇宅 家室 宮容 安定 守宿	店庫 府庭 廊廁 廚廟 廣廠	從往 後得 循復 徒徑 很德	收攻 改放 政故 敗敢 救教	病症 疼痛 疾疫 疤痘 痙癒

Radicals 部首	糸 mì	艸 cǎo	虫 huǐ	辵 chuò	隹 zhuī	髟 biāo
Meanings 意思	thread	grass	small animal	motion	short-tailed bird	hair
Examples 例字	絲線 紗綢 縫紉 紡織 紅綠	草葉 花莖 蔬菜 茶菇 落苦	蟲蛇 蚊蠅 蝴蝶 虹蛋 蛙蝕	進退 過迎 迷送 遠近 迅速	雞雀 隻雙 雌雄 雜集 雛難	髮鬃 鬍鬚 髯髭 鬢髻 鬆

Study how each radical changes its form in different characters.

文字之美 *The Beauty of Chinese Characters*
wénzì　zhī　měi

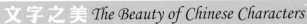

"子" (zǐ) means infant. The character depicts the two arms of a baby sticking out from its swaddling clothes. Because the baby's body and legs are wrapped up and cannot be seen, his or her head looks especially large. It is for this reason that the top part of 子 is exaggerated in size.

● 諺語的智慧 *The Wisdom of Chinese Proverbs*
yànyǔ de zhìhuì

不入虎穴，焉得虎子
bú rù hǔ xuè　yān dé hǔ zǐ

(If you) don't enter the tiger's den, how (can you) get the tiger cub?

↓

You need to take risks to get what you want.

↓

Nothing ventured, nothing gained.

This is a very fundamental proverb that nearly every Chinese native speaker will use from time to time. It is generally used to encourage someone to do something potentially risky or scary when that person is not yet sure about doing it or is just worried about it.

For example, your friend might be nervous about an upcoming performance and tell you that he or she might make a mistake, and might even be thinking about not going through with it. To encourage your friend, you can use this proverb.

This proverb can stand on its own. You need not worry about adding anything before or after it. You can just stay it to show your support and your understanding of the situation.

The character "焉" in this proverb comes from classical Chinese and has a range of meanings including "how", "why", "when", "here", "there", and "so that." It is most commonly used in written Chinese today, but does show up from time to time in spoken Chinese in the form of proverbs and set phrases. Another common and useful one is "心不在焉 (xīn bú zài yān)". The literal translation "mind not here" conveys the meaning of being "preoccupied" or "distracted", as in "I'm a little preoccupied". If you are having trouble concentrating on something, you can say, "我心不在焉".

● 發音 *Pronunciation*
fāyīn

b	把	筆	幫	變
	bǎ	bǐ	bāng	biàn

p	漂	配	陪	爬
	piào	pèi	péi	pá

m	沒	明	毛	麻
	méi	míng	máo	má

f	放	煩	飛	分
	fàng	fán	fēi	fēn

我 怕 表 妹 也 沒 別 的 辦 法 了 。
wǒ pà biǎomèi yě méi bié de bànfǎ le

I am afraid that my cousin does not have another idea, either.

婆 婆 賣 的 薄 棉 被 ， 又 白 又 便 宜 。
pópo mài de bó miánbèi yòu bái yòu piányí

The thin quilt that the old woman sells is white and inexpensive.

伯 伯 想 麻 煩 爸 爸 剝 葡 萄 皮 。 比 較 方 便 嘛 ！
bóbo xiǎng máfán bàba bō pútáo pí bǐjiào fāngbiàn ma

Uncle would like to trouble Dad to peel grapes for him. That's more convenient, isn't it?

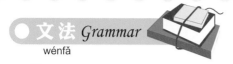

● 文法 *Grammar*
wénfǎ

1. 把 (bǎ)

"把" is common in Chinese. In the "把-construction", the noun following "把" is both the object of "把" and the object of the verb. Most sentences utilizing the 把-construction denote the subject's disposal or impact upon the object, with the result of the disposal or impact indicated with the complement following the verb.

Following the verb there is always a complement or other descriptive elements.

S + 把 + Object + V				
楊老師	把	書	放在桌子上。	Ms. Yang put the book on the table.
愷俐		三明治	吃完了。	Claire took the sandwich and ate it. / Claire ate the sandwich.
我		房間	掃乾淨了。	I swept the room clean.
法杜		電視機	打開了。	Fatou turned on the TV.

🍎 [乾淨 gānjing to be clean, neat]

＊This type of "把" sentence commonly indicates giving a certain object to a certain person.

S + 把 + Object (something) + V + Object (somebody)				
希京	把	禮物	送給	愷俐了。 Higyeong took the gift and gave it to Claire.
店員		錢	找給	志學了。 The clerk got Joshua his change.
我		存摺	拿給	媽媽了。 I gave the passbook to mom.
學生		作業	交給	老師。 The student turned in the homework to the teacher.

🍎 [交 jiāo to give]

＊When "請" is used with "把", the subject is often omitted. For example:

(S) + 請 + 把 + Object + V			
請	把	書	翻到第八頁。 Please open (the book) to page eight.
		門	打開。 Please open the door.
		飯	吃完。 Please finish the food.
		這些水果	洗一洗。 Please wash this fruit.

2. 多 (duō/duó)

"多" has two tones. The first tone is used in general sentences, such as "很多" (hěnduō) and "差不多" (chābùduō). The second tone is used with question sentences, such as "多久" (duójiǔ) and "多大" (duódà). In Chinese, the interrogative adverb "多" can be placed before a SV, to inquire about the exact level or degree of a particular state. The form is "多 + SV".

多 + SV	
多久	A: 從我家到學校很遠。 It's far from my house to school. B: 坐公車要多久？ How long do you have to ride the bus? A: 大約五十分鐘。 About fifty minutes.
多便宜	A: 這本字典很便宜。 This dictionary is quite inexpensive. B: 有多便宜？ How inexpensive is it? A: 才九十九元。 It's only ninety-nine dollars.
多好吃	A: 我媽媽做的菜很好吃！ The food my mom makes is really tasty! B: 有多好吃？ How tasty is it? A: 我已經吃三碗飯了。 I've already eaten three bowls.
多大	A: 故宮博物院很大。 The National Palace Museum is really big. B: 有多大？ How big (is it)? A: 參觀一天都不夠。 Visiting for one day isn't enough (to see everything).

🍎 [分鐘 fēnzhōng a minute]   [碗 wǎn a bowl]

3. 得 (de) and 的 (de)

The structural particles "得" and "的" indicate what precedes it is subordinated to another structure.

＊ "得" is placed between a verb and a regulative or directional complement to indicate whether a certain result will be realized or not.

V/A		+ 得	
他	走	得	很遠。He walks/walked really far.
妹妹的書法	寫		很好。Sister writes calligraphy really well.
我女朋友唱歌	唱		很好聽。 My girlfriend sings beautifully.
你	說		太快，我聽不懂。 You speak too quickly; I don't understand.

＊The structural particle "的" only occurs after an attributive modifier. For example:

Noun as attributive	法杜**的**衣服很漂亮。 Fatou's clothes are really pretty.
Adjective as attributive	新**的**衣服在房子裡。 The new clothes are in the room.
Possessive as attributive	我們**的**學校在台北。 Our school is in Taipei.
Relative pronoun as attributive	你昨天買**的**那件牛仔褲。 That pair of jeans you bought yesterday.

4. 試試看 (shìshì kàn)

In lesson 7, we learned the particle "看看". The form for reduplicating monosyllabic verbs is "VV" or "V一V", for example "想想" or "想一想" and "等等" or "等一等". In this lesson, the pattern is "VV看." For example, "試試看". Reduplication of a verb has the function of implying a short duration for that action or expressing the idea of giving something a try.

In comparing "VV" and "VV看". "VV" emphasizes action that is more relaxed, free, and perhaps without purpose. "VV看" emphasizes action that has a definite purpose.

VV 看	
寫寫看	我來**寫寫看**這個中文字。I'll try to write this character.
唱唱看	你來**唱唱看**中文歌，好嗎？ Try singing this Chinese song, okay?
說說看	請她**說說看**台灣旅行的經驗。 Please ask her to talk a little bit about her Taiwan travel experiences.
問問看	你可以**問問看**志學，這句西班牙文怎麼說。 You can ask Joshua how to say this sentence in Spanish.

[唱 chàng to sing] [歌 gē song] [旅行 lǚxíng travel] [經驗 jīngyàn experience(s)]

● 換你試試看 *It's Your Turn!*
huàn nǐ shìshìkàn

Challenge 1

Please choose the correct pinyin.

1. (　　) 練習　　A. liànxí　　B. lièxí　　C. liànxì

2. (　　) 寫書法　　A. xué shūfǎ　　B. xiě shúfá　　C. xiě shūfǎ

3. (　　) 聰明　　A. cóngmíng　　B. cōngmíng　　C. sōngmǐng

4. (　　) 牛仔褲　　A. liúzikù　　B. niúrénkù　　C. niúzǎikù

5. (　　) 適合　　A. shìhé　　B. sīhé　　C. sīhè

6. (　　) 麻煩　　A. máfán　　B. māfān　　C. màfàn

Challenge 2

Pattern drills with 把-construction, directional complements, and VV看.

I. 把　Example：存摺／找到　→　我把存摺找到了。

1. 晚飯／做好

→

2. 作業／寫完

→

3. 課文／念了一次

→

4. 咖啡／喝完 [咖啡 kāfēi coffee] [喝 hē to drink]

→

5. 衣服／洗好

→

II. 把　Example：**專櫃小姐／牛仔褲／我**
　　　　　→ 專櫃小姐把牛仔褲拿給我。

1. 老師／生詞／我們
→

2. 我／錢／店員
→

3. 店員／便當／我
→

4. 男朋友／花／女朋友
→

5. 哥哥／車／弟弟
→

III. 把　Example：**書本／放／桌上** → 請把書本放在桌上。

1. 車／停／家門口
→

2. 錢／存／銀行裡
→

3. 衣服／放／櫃子裡
→

4. 今天教的生詞／寫／紙上
→

5. 書／放／抽屜裡
→

IV. VV看 Example：來／這個／想想看／我／問題
→ 我來想想看這個問題。

1.我的／你來／中文／寫寫看／名字

→

2.吃吃看／我做的／大家／日本料理

→

3.這杯／很好喝的／你／喝喝看／咖啡

→

4.單字的／試試看／這個／造句／志學

→

5.我來／學學看／中文歌／怎麼／唱

[歌 gē song, melody] [唱 chàng to sing]

→

Challenge 3

Combine the words to form sentences.
Example： 穿穿看／很漂亮／你／這一件／衣服
→ 這一件衣服很漂亮，你穿穿看。

1.存摺／我／放在／了／把／抽屜裡

→

2.請／幫／我／找找看／我的／印章

→

3.媽媽／做／很好吃／得／的／中國菜

→

4.請／書／拿／把／給／我

→

5.中文課／楊老師／教／得／很好／的

→

Challenge 4

Find the characters with these radicals in the two-character compounds below.

部首 Radicals	宀 部 mián bù	糸 部 mì bù		艸 部 cǎo bù	广 部 yǎn bù	辵 部 chuò bù
意思 Meanings	house	thread		grass	shelter	motion
字形 Forms	宀	糸	糸	艹	广	辶
例字 Examples	室 寶	素	紙	英 草	床 庫	這 逛

| 紐約 | 客廳 | 起床 | 花蓮 | 邊線 | 舊家 | 結婚 |
| 安康 | 廁所 | 草莓 | 連續 | 廠商 | 教室 | 進度 |

宀 : ☐ ☐ ☐ ☐

糸 : ☐ ☐ ☐ ☐ ☐

艸 : ☐ ☐ ☐ ☐

广 : ☐ ☐ ☐ ☐ ☐

辵 : ☐ ☐

● 聽力練習 *Let's Listen!*
tīnglì   liànxí

Listen to the dialogue and choose the best answers.

Supplementary Vocabulary
改變 gǎibiàn to change
小桌子 xiǎozhuōzi small table
位子 wèizi place, seat
搬 bān to move
移 yí to move
動手 dòngshǒu to start doing sth.; get to work
電話 diànhuà telephone
桌巾 zhuōjīn tablecloth

1. (   ) What are they moving? (a) A television set and small table. (b) A small table and sofa. (c) Only a small table. (d) Only a sofa.

2. (   ) What is next to the sofa? (a) A television set. (b) A small table. (c) A telephone. (d) A tablecloth.

3. (   ) What direction did they move the television set? (a) To the left. (b) To the right. (c) They didn't move it. (d) They moved it forward.

4. (   ) What do they put on the small table? (a) A book. (b) A cloth. (c) A television set. (d) A telephone.

5. (   ) What does Fǎdù provide? (a) A book. (b) A tablecloth. (c) A television set. (d) A telephone.

● 字型練習 *Let's Write!*
zìxíng liànxí

丶 亠 亖 言 言 言 言 訂 訂 訂 訊 試

試 試 試
shì 試 試

ㄥ ㄥ ㄠ ㄠ ㄠ 糸 紅 紅 紅 絅 絅 紳 練

練 練 練
liàn 練 練

丨 丬 口 口 吐 吐 吓 吓 咔 咔 嚇 嚇

嚇 嚇 嚇
xià 嚇 嚇

丨 冂 口 口 무 무 무 趴 趴 趴 跳 跳 跳

跳 跳 跳
tiào 跳 跳

一 丁 扌 扩 护 护 护 捤 捤 捤 握

握 握 握
wò
握 握

丿 ク 夕 夕 夘 外 然 然 然 然 然

然 然 然
rán
然 然

乚 幺 幺 幺 幺 幺 紅 紅 紙 紙

紙 紙 紙
zhǐ
紙 紙

一 丆 丌 耵 耳 耳 耴 聊 聊 聊 聦 聰

聰 聰 聰
cōng
聰 聰

一 丁 扌 扌 扣 扣 把

把 把 把
bǎ   把 把

丨 冂 日 旦 早 是 是 是 是 題 題 題

題 題 題
tí   題 題

丿 ⺀ ⺊ ⺮ ⺮ ⺮ 竻 竺 笁 筀 筆

筆 筆 筆
bǐ   筆 筆

丶 亠 亖 言 言 信 絬 結 結 綪 綪 變

變 變 變
biàn   變 變

第十一課 我的頭好痛
dì shíyī kè wǒ de tóu hǎo tòng

● 對話一 *Dialogue One*
duìhuà yī

(Claire and Fatou are watching television in the living room of their flat. Suddenly, Fatou doesn't feel well.)

法杜 ： 噢¹！ (Holds head.)
fǎdù   òu

愷俐 ： 法杜，怎麼了？
kǎilì   fǎdù zěnme le

法杜 ： 我覺得很不舒服²。我的頭³好痛⁴！
fǎdù   wǒ jué de hěn bù shūfú   wǒ de tóu hǎo tòng

愷俐 ： 你去看過醫生⁵了嗎？
kǎilì   nǐ qù kàn guò yīshēng le ma

法杜 ： 還沒。
fǎdù   háiméi

愷俐 ： 那我們現在就去看醫生吧！
kǎilì   nà wǒmen xiànzài jiù qù kàn yīshēng ba

●生詞 *Vocabulary*
shēngcí

1 噢 ouch
2 舒服 to be comfortable
3 頭 head
4 痛 to ache, hurt
5 醫生 doctor, physician

(In a clinic near their flat.)

醫生：你好，請問你哪裡不舒服？
yīshēng　nǐhǎo　qǐngwèn nǐ nǎlǐ bù shūfú

法杜：我的頭好痛。
fǎdù　　wǒ de tóu hǎo tòng

醫生：來，我看看……。
yīshēng　lái　wǒ kànkàn

(Several seconds pass.)

愷俐：是不是感冒[6]了？
kǎilì　shì bú shì gǎnmào le

醫生：不是，她沒發燒[7]、也沒咳嗽[8]，應該不是感冒。
yīshēng　bú shì　tā méi fāshāo　yě méi késòu　yīnggāi bú shì gǎnmào

法杜：我有頭痛[9]的毛病[10]，在甘比亞的時候[11]就 常常[12]
fǎdù　　wǒ yǒu tóutòng de máobìng　zài gānbǐyà de shíhòu jiù chángcháng

頭痛了。
tóutòng le

醫生：放心，問題[13]不大，我一定會把你治好[14]。
yīshēng　fàngxīn　wèntí bú dà　wǒ yídìng huì bǎ nǐ zhì hǎo

(After being diagnosed, Claire and Fatou wait for the prescription to be filled.)

愷俐：幸好[15]，醫生說你的頭痛
kǎilì　xìnghǎo　yīshēng shuō nǐ de tóutòng

不嚴重[16]，吃幾天的藥[17]就
bù yánzhòng　chī jǐ tiān de yào jiù

會好[18]了。
huì hǎo le

● 生詞 shēngcí *Vocabulary*

6 感冒　flu, to catch a cold
7 發燒　to have high temperature
8 咳嗽　to cough, cough
9 頭痛　headache
10 毛病　ailment
11 時候　moment, period of time
12 常常　often
13 問題　problem, issue
14 治好　to cure

● 生詞 shēngcí *Vocabulary*

15 幸好　fortunately
16 嚴重　to be serious, grave
17 藥　medication
18 好　to recover

法杜：我覺得當 醫生 **能救人**，真好。
fǎdù　　wǒ jué de dāng yīshēng néng jiù rén　zhēn hǎo

我以後一定要 **成為** 一位好醫生。
wǒ yǐhòu yídìng yào chéngwéi yí wèi hǎo yīshēng

愷俐：**加油**！
kǎilì　jiāyóu

(A nurse in the pharmacy calls Fatou to come pick up the medication.)

護士：賈法杜小姐！
hùshì　jiǎ fǎdù xiǎojiě

法杜：(Goes to the window-counter.) 是！
fǎdù　　　　　　　　　　　　　shì

護士：這 **種** 藥三餐飯後吃，另一 種 藥**睡前**吃。
hùshì　zhè zhǒng yào sāncān fànhòu chī lìng yì zhǒng yào shuìqián chī

記得這幾天不要**喝冰水**！
jìdé zhè jǐ tiān bú yào hē bīng shuǐ

法杜：好，謝謝你！
fǎdù　hǎo　xièxie nǐ

對話二 *Dialogue Two*
duìhuà èr

(Ready for class, Ms. Yang walks into the classroom where she finds Claire sitting alone.)

老師：愷俐，早安！
lǎoshī　kǎilì　zǎoān

愷俐：楊老師，早安！
kǎilì　yáng lǎoshī zǎoān

老師：**奇怪**了，**怎麼**只有你一個人？**其他**同學呢？
lǎoshī qíguài le zěnme zhǐyǒu nǐ yí ge rén qítā tóngxué ne

愷俐：法杜 **生病**(36) 了，她頭痛不舒服，所以沒來。
kǎilì　　　fǎdù　shēngbìng　le　　tā tóutòng bù shūfú　　suǒyǐ méi lái

老師：那偉立呢？他不是**一向**(37)都很**健康**(38)嗎？
lǎoshī　　nà wěilì ne　　tā bú shì yíxiàng dōu hěn jiànkāng ma

愷俐：聽說他也 生病 了。好像是**胃痛**(39)吧！
kǎilì　　tīngshuō tā yě shēngbìng le　　hǎoxiàng shì wèitòng ba

他一直**拉肚子**(40)。
tā　yìzhí　lā　dùzi

老師：不會吧！那希京呢？
lǎoshī　bú huì ba　　nà xījīng ne

愷俐：希京上**樓梯**(41)的時候**不小心**(42)**跌倒**(43)，**扭到腳**(44)了。
kǎilì　xījīng shàng lóutī de shíhòu bù xiǎoxīn diédǎo　niǔ dào jiǎo le

● **生詞** *Vocabulary*
shēngcí

19 能　can; to be able to, have the ability to; be allowed to

20 救　to save

21 成為　to become

22 加油　keep up the good work; I (or we) support you (lit. add oil/fuel)

23 護士　nurse

24 種　sort, type, kind

25 餐　meal

26 飯　meal, rice

27 另　other, another

28 睡　sleep

29 前　before

30 喝　to drink

31 冰　ice; cold

32 水　water

33 奇怪　to be strange, weird

34 怎麼　how come

35 其他　other

36 生病　to get sick

37 一向　as always

38 健康　to be healthy

39 胃痛　stomachache

40 拉肚子　to have diarrhea (lit. to pull belly)

41 樓梯　stairs, flight of stairs

42 不小心　carelessly, by mistake

43 跌倒　to be tripped up, fall down

44 扭到腳　to sprain one's ankle

老師：真**慘**，那志學呢？志學不會也**出事**了吧！
lǎoshī zhēn cǎn nà zhìxué ne zhìxué bú huì yě chūshì le ba

愷俐：志學**最**可憐，他**出車禍 受傷** 了。
kǎilì zhìxué zuì kělián tā chū chēhuò shòushāng le

他們現在都在**醫院**裡。
tāmen xiànzài dōu zài yīyuàn lǐ

老師：**天啊**？**怎麼會**這樣？希望他們都**早日康復**！
lǎoshī tiān a zěnme huì zhèyàng xīwàng tāmen dōu zǎorì kāngfù

愷俐：老師也要 **保重 身體** 喔！
kǎilì lǎoshī yě yào bǎozhòng shēntǐ o

● **生詞** *Vocabulary*
　shēngcí

45 慘　to be miserable

46 出事　to get into trouble

47 最　the most

48 出車禍　to be involved in a car accident

49 受傷　to be injured

50 醫院　hospital

51 天啊　oh my goodness

52 怎麼會　how could that happen

53 早日康復　to recover very soon
　　　　　(formal, idiomatic)

54 保重　to take good care of

55 身體　body

日記 *Claire White's Diary*
riji

Dear Diary,

昨天法杜頭痛，我和她一起去看醫生。醫生看過之後，說法杜沒感冒，頭痛也不嚴重，真是太好了！之後，我跟法杜去拿藥。護士說，法杜每天三餐飯後都要吃藥，睡前還要吃另一種藥，而且不可以喝冰水。

第二天，我上中文課的時候，同學都沒來。我知道法杜生病了，可是其他人呢？噢，*originally* 一向都很健康的偉立胃痛；希京不小心扭傷了腳；志學最慘了，他出了車禍。希望大家都早日康復。好想大家喔！

白愷俐

● 尋找部首 *Let's Find Radicals*
xún zhǎo bùshǒu

Since some radicals look very similar to other radicals, it is important to know how to distinguish them. Take a close look at the following radicals and try to tell the differences between them. Notice also how each radical can change form in different characters.

Radicals 部首	日 rì	曰 yuē	月 yuè	肉 ròu	犬 quǎn	豕 shǐ
Meanings 意思	sun	speech	moon	meat; flesh	dog; canine	pig
Examples 例字	旦 早 晒 旺 旭 旬	書 曹 替 曾 會 曲	朋 服 朦 朧 朗 期	肌 肚 肝 肥 背 胃	犯 狂 狗 狐 獒 獎	豬 豚 豪 豢

Radicals 部首	豸 zhì	夊 yǐn	衣 yī	示 shì	邑 yì	阜 fù
Meanings 意思	reptile	shuffle	clothing	sign	state	mound
Examples 例字	豺 豹 貂 貍 貓 貌	廷 延 建	衫 袖 被 初 袋 裏	社 祖 祝 神 禁 祭	邦 郊 郡 郎 那 邪	防 阻 限 降 院 阿

LESSON **11**

● 文字之美 *The Beauty of Chinese Characters*
wénzì zhī měi

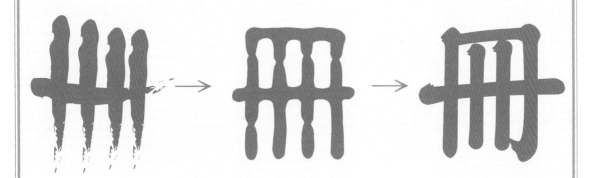

The character "冊" (cè) depicts bamboo strips woven together to form a book. The vertical strokes represent the bamboo strips, and the horizontal stroke shows the string that holds the strips together. In the past, characters could be written on the bamboo strips, and then the book would be rolled up for easy storage.

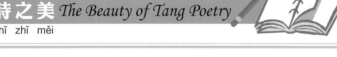

唐詩之美 The Beauty of Tang Poetry
tángshī zhī měi

遊子吟 Chant for a Traveling Son　　　孟郊 Meng Jiao
yóu zǐ yín　　　　　　　　　　　　　mèng jiāo

慈母手中線，遊子身上衣。
cí mǔ shǒu zhōng xiàn　yóu zǐ shēn shàng yī

臨行密密縫，意恐遲遲歸。
lín xíng mì mì féng　yì kǒng chí chí guī

誰言寸草心，報得三春暉。
shéi yán cùn cǎo xīn　bào dé sān chūn huī

Thread in my mother's hand, clothes on her traveling son.

Just before sewing the meticulous stitches, she fears it will be long before I return.

Who says that an inch of grass can repay three springs of sunshine?

Meng Jiao (751–814) lived a life of poverty. Unable to pass the Tang civil service exams and gain a government post, he traveled throughout Hubei, Hunan, and Guangxi and wrote over five hundred poems. Friendship and family relations are important themes in some of his poetry.

This poem features two basic images: thread and clothes. In older times, mothers often made clothing for their children. In lines one and two of this poem, Meng describes the narrator's mother making clothes for her son. They both know he is going to live away from home, and probably for a long time, so the mother puts a lot of effort into her work to make sure the clothes are well-made. They are going to last. This way, no matter where the son travels, he will have the clothes and be reminded of his mother's love.

Of course the mother wishes her son would stay nearer to home, but she can accept her son's travels—her love is what has allowed him to grow and leave the house with confidence. Line three is a metaphor that expresses this concept, and by saying it, the narrator admits that a mother's love cannot be repaid. In fact, the idiom "寸草春暉" comes from this line in the poem, and can be used as a reminder, for example on Mother's Day, of the importance of motherly love.

發音 *Pronunciation*
fāyīn

Compare the following sounds:

	unaspirated affricate (affricate with slight puff of air)	aspirated affricate (affricate with strong puff of air)	fricative
alveolo-palatal (followed by i and ü)	**j** 救 加 健 接 jiù jiā jiàn jiē	**q** 前 奇 其 淺 qián qí qí qiǎn	**x** 幸 向 小 洗 xìng xiàng xiǎo xǐ
alveolar (followed by i, u, o, a, and e)	**z** 早 在 糟 左 zǎo zài zāo zuǒ	**c** 餐 慘 聰 存 cān cǎn cōng cún	**s** 嗽 掃 四 三 sòu sǎo sì sān

姊 姊 算 錢 算 了 三 十 七 次 。
jiě jie suàn qián suàn le sānshíqī cì

Sister has counted the money thirty-seven times.

謝 小 強 在 學 怎 麼 自 己 洗 澡 。
xiè xiǎoqiáng zài xué zěme zìjǐ xǐzǎo

Xie Xiaoqiang is learning how to take a bath on his own.

孫 小 姐 最 近 在 想 ， 早 餐 要 怎 麼 做 才 好 。
sūn xiǎojiě zuìjìn zài xiǎng zǎocān yào zěme zuò cái hǎo

Recently, Miss Sun has been thinking about a good way to make breakfast.

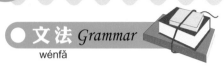

● 文法 *Grammar*
wénfǎ

1. 過 (guò) : to compare; compared to; than

＊In Chinese, "過" is often used to express the experience of having done something.

"過" must be placed immediately after a verb. The basic pattern is:

S + V + 過			
我的哥哥	住	過	台灣。 My older brother has lived in Taiwan.
偉立	學		中文。 Weili has studied Chinese.
我	吃		感冒藥了。 I've taken (the) cold medicine.
我的爸爸和媽媽	參觀		故宮博物院。 My parents have visited the National Palace Museum.

＊The negative form is "沒(有)……過". The negative pattern is:

S + 沒(有) + V + 過				
弟弟	沒(有)	住	過	台灣。 (My) younger brother hasn't lived in Taiwan.
法杜		吃		滷味。 Fatou hasn't eaten lǔwèi.
姊姊		去		歐洲。 (My) older sister hasn't been to Europe.
我		聽		她要參加我的生日派對。 I haven't heard whether she's going to attend my birthday party.

🍎 [弟弟 dìdi younger brother]   [滷味 lǔwèi soy marinated food]

＊There are two question sentences that use "過". One is "有沒有 + V + 過", and the other is "……過……沒 (有)". They are frequently two ways of asking the same thing, but the second pattern can also express a slightly different meaning, depending on context. For example:

S + 有沒有 + V + 過				
陳老師	有沒有	去	過	甘比亞？ Has Ms. Chen (ever) gone/been to The Gambia?
你的妹妹		來		台灣？ Has your younger sister (ever) come/been to Taiwan?
你		寫		書法？ Have you (ever) written Chinese calligraphy?
你		看		電影？ Have you (ever) seen/watched a movie?

S + V + 過 + 沒有				
陳老師	去	過	甘比亞	沒(有)?	Has Ms. Chen (ever) gone/been to The Gambia? Did Ms. Chen go to The Gambia?
你的妹妹	來		台灣		Has your younger sister (ever) come/been to Taiwan? Did your younger sister come to Taiwan?
你	寫		書法		Have you (ever) written Chinese calligraphy? Did you write the Chinese calligraphy?
你	看		電影		Have you (ever) seen/watched a movie? Did you watch a movie?

🍎 [電影 diànyǐng movie]

2. 的時候 (de shíhòu) 、 **現在** (xiànzài) 、 **以後** (yǐhòu) 、 **以前** (yǐqián)
Words expressing time, such as "⋯⋯的時候", "現在", "以後" and "以前" can function as adverbials to indicate the time that an action or state occurs. It can describe things that occur in the past, the future, as well as ones that happen consistently.

* 的時候 (de shíhòu) is similar in meaning to "when", "while", and "during" in English—the period of time when an action or event takes place. For example:

⋯⋯的時候		
在美國	的時候	我每個月都去爬山。 While I was in the U.S., I went hiking every month.
考試		老師常常走來走去。 During the test, the teacher kept walking around the room.
天氣熱		我喜歡喝冰水。 When it's hot / During hot weather, I like drinking ice water.
生病		要記得多多休息。 When (you're) sick, remember to get more rest.

🍎 [天氣 tiānqì weather]   [熱 rè to be hot]

* 現在 (xiànzài) is similar to the English time expressions "(right) now", "at the present time", and "currently", although "now" in English is often unstated and implied by context.

		現在	
我們	現在	就去吃飯。We're going to go eat now.	
志學		很忙。Zhixue is busy right now.	
		法杜華語說得很好。Fatou speaks Chinese really well now.	
		我頭好痛。My head hurts. / I have a headache.	

* 以前(yǐqián) and 以後(yǐhòu) mean "before" and "after" in English. A specific moment or action modifier may be inserted directly before "以後" or "以前" to make a sentence expressing "before/after something happen(s/ed), …". For example:

		以前
來台灣	以前	我不會說華語。 Before I came to Taiwan, I couldn't speak Chinese.
回國		我要會說華語。 Before I return to my country, I need to be able to speak Chinese.
三個月		我的妹妹在俄羅斯念書。 Three months ago, my younger sister studied in Russia.
回家		我和愷俐要一起去買東西。 Before we go home, Claire and I need to go shopping.

		以後
來台灣	以後	他開始學習華語。 After he came to Taiwan, he started studying Chinese.
認識你		我華語說得更好了。 After I met you, my Chinese got better.
吃飯		再吃藥。 Take the medicine after eating.
下課		我們一起去唱歌。 After class, we can go singing.

[學習 xuéxí to learn]　[唱歌 chànggē to sing]

3. 就 (jiù)

In lesson 5, we learned that "就" has two meanings. 就1 means "just" or "right". 就 2 is a relational adverb. In this lesson, we review those two usages and learn two more.

* 就1: Functions like "just" and "right" in English. Also similar to "indeed". Used for emphasis, it can either confirm a fact, or stress that something stated is exactly what it is.

她**就**是我們的老師。	She (indeed) is our teacher.
生病**就**要看醫生。	When (you're) sick, just see a doctor.
這裡**就**是我的家。	This is my house, right here.
今天**就**是中秋節。	Today is (indeed) Mid-Autumn Festival.

🍎 [中秋節 zhōngqiūjié Mid-Autumn Festival; The Moon Festival]

* 就2: Often used to suggest that an action occurs quickly or early. It is also used to indicate that one action or event takes place immediately after a previous one.

我們現在**就**去醫院。	Let's get to the hospital.
你剛來怎麼**就**要走。	You just got here; how can you be leaving already?
我早上六點**就**起床。	I got up at six this morning.
妳喜歡這一件衣服**就**買吧！	You like that garment, so just buy it!

🍎 [起床 qǐchuáng to get up]

* 就3: Functions as an adverb that links a previous statement with its conclusion.

立山下課以後，**就**去工作。　　After Lishan got out of class, he went to work.
既然大家都認識，我**就**不介紹了。 Since everyone knows each other, I won't make introductions.
你覺得身體不舒服，**就**在家裡休息。 If you don't feel well, just rest at home.
你不會的問題，**就**問老師。 Just ask the teacher about the stuff you don't understand.

* 就4: As an adverb, "就4" often connects two verbs or verbal phrases and expresses that the second takes place as soon as the first is completed.

我回家**就**寫作業。	As soon as I got home I did my homework.
我叫張志學，叫我志學**就**好。	
My name's Zhāng Zhìxué, but you can (just) call me Zhìxué.	
他們到了醫院**就**打電話給楊老師。	
As soon as they got to the hospital they called Ms. Yang.	
爸爸一到台灣**就**去參觀故宮。	
(My) dad visited the National Palace Museum as soon as he got to Taiwan.	

🍎 [打電話 dǎ diànhuà to make a phone call]

4. 身體 (shēntǐ) **Parts of the Body**

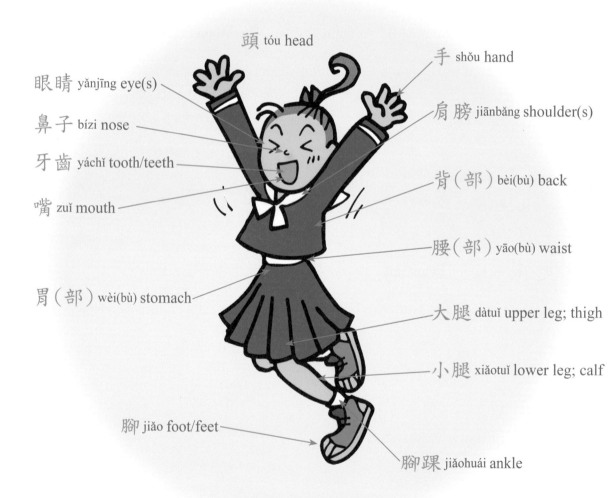

頭 tóu head
手 shǒu hand
眼睛 yǎnjīng eye(s)
肩膀 jiānbǎng shoulder(s)
鼻子 bízi nose
牙齒 yáchǐ tooth/teeth
背（部） bèi(bù) back
嘴 zuǐ mouth
腰（部） yāo(bù) waist
胃（部） wèi(bù) stomach
大腿 dàtuǐ upper leg; thigh
小腿 xiǎotuǐ lower leg; calf
腳 jiǎo foot/feet
腳踝 jiǎohuái ankle

5. 身體的病痛 (shēntǐ de bìngtòng) **Bodily Pains**

In Chinese, we often use "痛" (tòng) and "痠" (suān) to describe where we have aches, pain, soreness, or where something hurts.

頭痛 tóutòng headache

流鼻涕 liúbítì runny nose

打噴涕 dǎpēntì to sneeze

眼睛痛 yǎnjīngtòng my eye(s) hurt(s)

肩膀痛 jiānbǎngtòng shoulder pain; my shoulder hurts

牙痛 yátòng toothache

嘴破 zuǐpò cold/canker sore

胃痛 wèitòng stomachache

肚子痛 dùzitòng stomachache

腰痠 yāosuān lower back pain; my lower back is sore

腳痛 jiǎotòng foot pain; my foot hurts

腿痛 tuǐtòng leg pain; my leg hurts

腿痠 tuǐsuān my leg is sore

LESSON 11

換你試試看 It's Your Turn!
huàn nǐ shìshìkàn

Challenge 1

Choose the correct pinyin.

1. ( ) 不舒服　A. bùshūfú　B. búshūfú　C. bǔshūfú
2. ( ) 感冒　A. gǎnmào　B. gānmào　C. gànmào
3. ( ) 頭痛　A. tòutóng　B. dóudòng　C. tóutòng
4. ( ) 健康　A. jiànkān　B. jiǎnkàng　C. jiànkāng
5. ( ) 咳嗽　A. késhù　B. gèsòu　C. késòu
6. ( ) 嚴重　A. yánzōng　B. yánzǒng　C. yánzhòng
7. ( ) 加油　A. jiāyóu　B. qiāyóu　C. xiāyóu
8. ( ) 其他　A. jītà　B. qítā　C. xǐtǎ
9. ( ) 跌倒　A. diédào　B. tiándào　C. diédǎo
10. ( ) 早日康復　A. cǎorì gāngfù　B. zǎorì gāngfù　C. zǎorì kāngfù

Challenge 2

Pattern drills.

I.　上過　有沒有　找過　參觀過　吃過　看過

Example: 你 ＿＿上過＿＿ 書法課沒有？

1. 你 ＿＿＿＿＿＿ 醫生了嗎？
2. 同學們 ＿＿＿＿＿ 去歐洲旅行過？
3. 你 ＿＿＿＿＿＿ 晚飯沒有？
4. 你在找存摺嗎？你 ＿＿＿＿＿ 抽屜沒有？
5. 昨天你的爸爸媽媽有沒有＿＿＿＿＿ 故宮？

II.

晚上六點的時候	以後	現在	以前
吃飯的時候		放假的時候	

Example: ___晚上六點的時候___ ，媽媽在廚房裡做飯。

1. _____ 這本字典打六折。

2. 下課 _____ 我們一起去醫院看志學。

3. _____ ，你會做什麼？

4. 睡覺 _____ 記得要吃藥。

5. _____ ，我喜歡看電視。

III.

就帶	就上課	就是	就睡覺
就去	就學		

Example: 我們 ___就帶___ 水果去看志學。

1. 偉立 _____ 我的鄰居。

2. 愷俐下課以後 _____ 補習班教英文。

3. 早上八點我 _____ 。

4. 我一到台灣 _____ 中文。

5. 我昨天晚上九點 _____ 。

Challenge 3

Reading comprehension drill. Try to guess the meaning from contextcontext and the picture to answer the questions.

醫生：林小姐，你哪裡不舒服呢？
yīshēng lín xiǎojiě nǐ nǎlǐ bùshūfú ne

安惠：醫生，我一直流鼻水和咳嗽，全身都不舒服。
ānhuì yīshēng wǒ yìzhí liúbíshuǐ hàn késòu quánshēn dōu bùshūfú

醫生：從什麼時候開始呢？
yīshēng cóng shéme shíhòu kāishǐ ne

安惠：今天早上。
ānhuì jīntiān zǎoshàng

醫生：有沒有發燒、頭痛呢？
yīshēng yǒu méiyǒu fāshāo tóutòng ne

安惠：沒有。
ānhuì méiyǒu

醫生：還有沒有哪裡不舒服？
yīshēng hái yǒu méiyǒu nǎlǐ bù shūfú

安惠：我想沒有吧！
ānhuì wǒ xiǎng méiyǒu ba

醫生：那妳只是小感冒。這 種 藥妳帶回去吃，
yīshēng nà nǐ zhǐ shì xiǎo gǎnmào zhè zhǒng yào nǐ dài huí qù chī

一天四次，三餐飯後和睡前。
yì tiān sì cì sān cān fàn hòu hàn shuì qián

我給妳三天份的藥。記得要多休息喔！
wǒ gěi nǐ sān tiān fèn de yào jì de yào duō xiūxí o

安惠：謝謝你，醫生！
ānhuì xièxiè nǐ yīshēng

感冒藥

林 安 惠 先生
小姐

用法：
每日 4 次 3 日份　　　C.C
每飯後及睡前服用　　1 包
　　　　　　　　　　　粒

每　　　小時服用　　C.C.
　　　　　　　　　　包
　　　　　　　　　　粒

陳醫生診所
台北市忠孝東路三段888號
電話：02-2456-7890
中華民國 98 年 9 月 15 日

Question drill.

1. ( ) Who doesn't feel well? A. Chen Weili. B. Dr. Chen. C. Lin Anhui.
2. ( ) When did Anhui start having a runny nose and cough? A. Yesterday morning. B. The day before yesterday. C. This morning.
3. ( ) What kind of medicine does the doctor give Anhui? A. Antacid B. Cold medicine. C. He doesn't give her any medicine.

4. (　　) How many times a day should Anhui take the medicine? A. Four times.
B. Three times.　　C. Once

5. (　　) How many days should Anhui take the medicine?　　A. Four days.
B. Three days.　　C. One day.

6. (　　) When should Anhui take the medicine?　A. Before each meal and at bedtime.　B. After meals and before bedtime.　C. While eating.

Challenge 4

Find the characters with these radicals in the in the two-syllable words below.

部首 Radicals	疒 部 chuáng bù	曰 部 yuē bù	月 部 yuè bù	虫 部 huǐ bù	隹 部 zhuī bù
意思 Meanings	disease	speech	moon	small animal	short-tailed bird
字形 Forms	疒	曰	月	虫	隹
例字 Examples	痛 病	會 曲	有 朋	蟲 蛋	雞 隻

書畫　集合　雞蛋　病蟲　朦朧　最近　更會　高雄
蜜蜂　雖然　痠痛　蝴蝶　期望　朋友　歌曲　癌症

疒：□□□□□

曰：□□□□

月：□□□□

虫：□□□□□□

隹：□□□

● 聽力練習 *Let's Listen!*
tīnglì   liànxí

Listen to the dialogue and choose the best answers.

Supplementary Vocabulary		
台大醫院	táidà yīyuàn	National Taiwan University Hospital
病房	bìngfáng	sickroom

1. (   ) Where is Zhìxué staying? (a) At home. (b) National Taiwan University Hospital. (c) National Taipei University Hospital. (d) None of the above.

2. (   ) When will Zhìxué's friends visit him? (a) This morning. (b) Tomorrow morning. (c) Before class. (d) After class.

3. (   ) Which sickroom is Zhìxué staying in? (a) 1288. (b) 12. (c) 1280. (d) 128.

4. (   ) What will Zhìxué's friends bring? (a) Flowers. (b) Money. (c) Fruit. (d) Nothing.

5. (   ) How much money does Ms. Yáng give to Kǎilì? (a) One hundred dollars. (b) One thousand dollars. (c) Five hundred dollars. (d) Ten thousand dollars.

字型練習 Let's Write!
zìxíng liànxí

丶 丶丶 氵 汀 汸 泸 浐 流 流

流 流 流
liú
流 流

′ ′′ 冂 白 自 自 鼻 鼻 畠 鼻 鼻

鼻 鼻 鼻
bí
鼻 鼻

一 厂 厂 厂 戸 戸 豆 豆 豆 豇 頭 頭

頭 頭 頭
tóu
頭 頭

丶 丨 冂 日 田 田 円 胃 胃 胃

胃 胃 胃
wèi
胃 胃

`丶 ﹀ ㄔ ㄔ ネ 衤 衤 衤 衤 祸 祸 禍`

禍 禍 禍
huò   禍 禍

`丨 口 口 呂 呂 呂 足 足 跃 跃 跌 跌`

跌 跌 跌
dié   跌 跌

`丶 十 艹 艹 苩 芮 莤 萮 蒅 蕠 藥 藥`

藥 藥 藥
yào   藥 藥

`丨 口 口 口' 吖 吐 咳 咳 咳`

咳 咳 咳
ké   咳 咳

丶 口 口 吖 吓 吒 呏 咏 味 味 嗽 嗽

嗽 嗽 嗽
sòu
嗽 嗽

一 丆 互 至 医 医 殹 殹 殹 殹 醫

醫 醫 醫
yī
醫 醫

丨 刀 月 月 目 盯 盯 盱 盰 肺 脏 睡

睡 睡 睡
shuì
睡 睡

丶 忄 忄 忄 忄 忰 忰 㥄 憐 憐 憐

憐 憐 憐
lián
憐 憐

第十二課 我希望明年能去日本留學
dì　shíèr　kè　　wǒ　xīwàng　míngnián néng qù　　rìběn　　liúxué

● **對話一** *Dialogue One*
　　duìhuà　yī

(Several days before New Year's Eve, Ms. Yang's class is enjoying coffee in a café near the language center. They are talking about the future.)

老師：時間過得真快，一年又過了！
lǎoshī　　shíjiān　guò de zhēn kuài　　yì nián yòu guò　le

　　　　我先祝福大家，新年快樂！
　　　　wǒ xiān　zhùfú　dàjiā　　xīnnián　kuàilè

全班：老師，新年快樂！
quánbān　　lǎoshī　　xīnnián　kuàilè

老師：那我們今天就來談談新年的新希望。
lǎoshī　　nà　wǒmen　jīntiān　jiù　lái　tántán　xīnnián　de　xīn　xīwàng

　　　　愷俐，你先來。
　　　　kǎilì　　　nǐ xiān lái

愷俐：我希望明年能去日本留學。
kǎilì　　wǒ xīwàng míngnián néng qù　rìběn　liúxué

　　　　聽說日本很漂亮！
　　　　tīngshuō　rìběn　hěn piàoliàng

● **生詞** *Vocabulary*
　shēngcí

1 時間　time
2 祝福　to wish, bless
3 快樂　to be happy
4 全　whole
5 班　class
6 談　to talk about
7 希望　wish, hope

法杜： **換**我了！我希望以後可以當一位好醫生。
fǎdù huàn wǒ le wǒ xīwàng yǐhòu kěyǐ dāng yí wèi hǎo yīshēng

老師：很好！偉立，你呢？
lǎoshī hěn hǎo wěilì nǐ ne

偉立：我希望我可以跟我老婆一起**搬**到**鄉**下去住。
wěilì wǒ xīwàng wǒ kěyǐ gēn wǒ lǎopó yìqǐ bān dào xiāngxià qù zhù

老師：鄉下**空氣**好，人又親切，我也喜歡鄉下。
lǎoshī xiāngxià kōngqì hǎo rén yòu qīnqiè wǒ yě xǐhuān xiāngxià

希京，你呢？
xījīng nǐ ne

希京：**如果**可以的話，我想**留**在台灣念**研究所**。
xījīng rúguǒ kěyǐ dehuà wǒ xiǎng liú zài táiwān niàn yánjiùsuǒ

老師：我記得你說過想 念 **政治**，對吧？
lǎoshī wǒ jìde nǐ shuō guò xiǎng niàn zhèngzhì duì ba

希京：沒錯！
xījīng méicuò

愷俐：老師，她騙你的！她 **真正** 的願望是——
kǎilì lǎoshī tā piàn nǐ de tā zhēnzhèng de yuànwàng shì

交到一個男朋友，然後**趕快**結婚！
jiāo dào yí ge nánpéngyǒu ránhòu gǎnkuài jiéhūn

● **生詞** *Vocabulary*
shēngcí

8 換 to take turn; it's one's turn to	14 研究所 graduate institute/ school/program	18 交 to make friends with, befriend
9 搬 to move		
10 鄉下 countryside	15 政治 politics	19 到 (success marker; it shows that the preceding verb is successfully accomplished)
11 空氣 air	16 真正 to be real, actual, authentic, genuine, honest	
12 如果 if		20 趕快 right away
13 留 to stay	17 願望 wish	21 結婚 to get married

希京： 你 ²² 少 ²³ 胡說！ (She blushes; everyone laughs.)
xījīng　　　nǐ shǎo húshuō

志學： (Raises his hand.) 我也要說我的願望！
zhìxué　　　　　　　　　wǒ yě yào shuō wǒ de yuànwàng

老師： 來，請說！
lǎoshī　　lái　qǐng shuō

志學： 我要跟 ²⁴ 愷俐在一起！
zhìxué　　wǒ yào gēn　kǎilì　zàiyìqǐ

同學： 哇！ (Everyone starts to whistle and cheer.)
tóngxué　　wā

愷俐： (Blushes.) 我……我什麼都不知道啦！
kǎilì　　　　　　wǒ　　wǒ shéme dōu bù zhīdào　la

● 對話二 Dialogue Two
duìhuà èr

(After class, Claire dines with Higyeong. Higyeong asks Claire about her New Year's resolution.)

希京： 愷俐，你想去日本留學呀？
xījīng　　kǎilì　　nǐ xiǎng qù　rìběn　liúxué　ya

愷俐： 是啊！
kǎilì　　shì　a

希京： 真可惜，為什麼你不 ²⁵ 考慮來韓國呢？
xījīng　　zhēn kěxí　　wèishéme　nǐ bù　kǎolǜ lái hánguó ne

韓國也很漂亮啊。如果你來的話，
hánguó yě hěn piàoliàng a　　rúguǒ　nǐ lái dehuà

還可以住我家哦！
hái　kěyǐ zhù wǒ jiā　ó

恺俐：謝謝你，可是我對日本有一份特別的感情。
kǎilì　　xièxie nǐ　　kěshì wǒ duì rìběn yǒu yí fèn tèbié de gǎnqíng

希京：怎麼說？
xījīng　　zěmeshuō

恺俐：這是祕密，你別跟別人說哦。其實，我的
kǎilì　　zhè shì mìmì　　nǐ bié gēn biérén shuō ó　　qíshí　　wǒ de

初戀情人是日本人。所以我對日本情有獨鍾。
chūliàn qíngrén shì　rìběn rén　　suǒyǐ wǒ duì　rìběn qíngyǒu dúzhōng

希京：原來如此。那志學怎麼辦？
xījīng　　yuánlái rúcǐ　　nà zhìxué zěmebàn

恺俐：看他的表現囉！
kǎilì　　kàn tā de biǎoxiàn luo

希京：好吧！新年快到了，我用成語祝福你吧！
xījīng　　hǎo ba　　xīnnián kuài dào le　　wǒ yòng chéngyǔ zhùfú nǐ ba

我祝你──早生貴子！
wǒ zhù nǐ　　zǎoshēng guìzǐ

●生詞 Vocabulary
shēngcí

22 少 don't (do something)!
23 胡說 to babble, talk nonsense
24 跟……在一起 to be dating someone
25 考慮 to consider
26 對 toward
27 份 (measure word for a feeling or a serving of food)
28 特別 to be special
29 感情 feeling
30 怎麼說 Why is that?
31 祕密 secret
32 別 please don't (do something)
33 別人 other people
34 其實 in fact; actually

35 初戀 first love
36 情人 lover
37 情有獨鍾 to have a particularly good feeling (idiomatic)
38 原來如此 Oh, I see.
39 看 to depend
40 表現 expression, behavior, performance
41 用 to use
42 成語 Chinese idiomatic expression
43 祝 to wish
44 早生貴子 May you soon have a noble child! (idiomatic)

愷俐：早生貴子？你說⁴⁵錯了啦！我還沒結婚呢。
kǎilì　zǎoshēng guìzǐ　nǐ shuō cuò le　la　wǒ hái méi jiéhūn ne

希京：⁴⁶唉呀，我要說的是「早日康復」啦！
xījīng　āiya　wǒ yào shuō de shì　zǎorì kāngfù　la

愷俐：我又沒生病！我想，
kǎilì　wǒ yòu méi shēngbìng　wǒ xiǎng

你要說的是「⁴⁷早日學成」吧！(They laugh.)
nǐ yào shuō de shì　zǎorì xuéchéng　ba

● 生詞 *Vocabulary*
shēngcí

⁴⁵ 錯　to be wrong　　　　　　　　　　⁴⁶ 唉呀　Oops!

⁴⁷ 早日學成　Hope you complete your studies soon. / Here's to learning it quickly. (idiomatic)

日記 *Claire White's Diary*
riji

Dear Diary,

　　新年快到了。今天上課的時候，老師要大家說說新年的新希望。我說我希望明年能去  日本留學。法杜希望以後可以當一個好醫生。偉立很喜歡鄉下，他希望明年能搬到鄉下去住。希京希望明年能在台灣念政治研究所。其實，除了讀書之外，她真正的願望是交個台灣的男朋友，然後趕快結婚　　　　！志學的願望……算了，我不想說！

　　希京問我為什麼不去韓國留學。我誠實地跟她說了心中的秘密，希望她別告訴志學才好。

白愷俐

● 成語 *Chinese Idiomatic Expressions*
chéngyǔ

一 心 一 意
yìxīn　　yíyì

"一心一意" is used to describe someone who is concentrating on something and not distracted. It can be used as an adverb followed by the particle "地".

他 一 心 一 意 地 做 完 工 作。
tā　yìxīn　　yíyì　　de zuò wán gōngzuò

Single-mindedly, he finished the job.

一 石 二 鳥
yìshí　　èrniǎo

If a plan is "一石二鳥", it can achieve two separate goals with a single effort. This idiom can be used as an adjective with the particle "的".

這 真 是 個 一 石 二 鳥 的 好 計 畫。
zhè zhēn shì ge　yìshí　　èrniǎo　de hǎo　jìhuà

This is really a good plan; we can kill two birds with one stone.

三 生 有 幸
sānshēng　yǒuxìng

If you feel honored when meeting someone important, you can say that you are "三生有幸". Notice that it can be used after the verb, "是".

能 認 識 你, 我 真 是 三 生 有 幸。
néng rènshì　nǐ　　wǒ zhēn shì sānshēng yǒuxìng

It is my utmost pleasure to meet you.

四季如春
sìjì　rúchūn

"四季如春" means that a place, in terms of climate, is very pleasant; the four seasons are all like spring. This idiom can be used as an adjective with the particle "的".

普羅旺斯是個**四季如春**的地方。
pǔluówàngsī　shì　ge　sìjì　rúchūn　de　dìfāng

The climate in Provence is like spring year-round.

五體投地
wǔtǐ　tóudì

"五體投地" means to put (oneself) in a humble and submissive posture or position. It can be used as an adverb after the particle "得".

我真是佩服你佩服得**五體投地**呀！
wǒ zhēn shì　pèifú　nǐ　pèifú　de　wǔtǐ　tóudì　ya

I admire you so much that I throw myself on the ground before you!

六神無主
liùshén　wúzhǔ

If someone is overwhelmed by worry or fear and does not know what to do, we can say that he or she is "六神無主". It functions as an adverb with the particle "得".

這場意外把小陳嚇得**六神無主**，好可憐！
zhè chǎng yìwài　bǎ xiǎochén xià de　liùshén　wúzhǔ　hǎo　kělián

This accident scared Cheny out of his wits—poor child!

七上八下
qīshàng bāxià

If you are agitated, perturbed, or in an unsettled state of mind, then you are feeling "七上八下". It can modify words that are related to feeling, such as "心情".

最近發生很多事，我的心情也跟著七上八下。
zuìjìn fāshēng hěn duō shì wǒ de xīnqíng yě gēn zhe qīshàng bāxià

There has been so much going on lately that I'm at sixes and sevens.

亂七八糟
luànqī bāzāo

If something is a mess, you can say it is "亂七八糟". It can also be used as an adverb with the particle "得".

你怎麼把房間弄得亂七八糟的？
nǐ zěme bǎ fángjiān nòng de luànqī bāzāo de

How come you messed up your room like this?

九牛一毛
jiǔniú yìmáo

You can describe something as "九牛一毛" if it is an insignificant part of an enormous whole. Notice that it can be used after the verb, "是".

他很有錢，這些錢對他來說不過是九牛一毛。
tā hěn yǒuqián zhè xiē qián duì tā láishuō búguò shì jiǔniú yìmáo

He is so rich that, for him, this amount of money does not matter at all.

十全十美
shíquán shíměi

You can call something "十全十美" if it goes perfectly for you.

This idiom can be used after the verb, "是".

十全十美的一天！

今天真是十全十美的一天！
jīntiān zhēn shì shíquán shíměi de yì tiān

Today has been a perfect, perfect day!

● 文法 *Grammar*
wénfǎ

1. ⋯⋯的話 (…dehuà)；如果⋯⋯ (rúguǒ…)；
   如果⋯⋯的話 (rúguǒ…dehuà)

* "⋯⋯的話" expresses the conditional mood. The condition is placed before "的話". This structure is frequently used with "如果⋯⋯", and becomes "如果⋯⋯的話"

⋯⋯的話		
有機會	的話，	我想去歐洲。 If there is the opportunity, I'd like to go to Europe.
大家都可以		我們就去吃日本料理。 If it's alright with everyone, let's go eat Japanese food.
你會做菜		法杜就會喜歡你。 If you can cook, Fatou will like you.
書法要寫得好		就要每天練習。 To be good at calligraphy, it takes daily practice.

如果……

如果	你不知道，可以問老師。
	If you don't know, you can ask the teacher.
	明天你要來，請打電話給我。
	If you want to come tomorrow, please give me a call.
	我是你，就不會這樣做。
	If I were you, I wouldn't do it this way.
	休息可以馬上好，我就不要吃藥了。
	If all I need is rest, then I won't take medicine.

如果……的話

如果	你會說中文	的話，	我們就可以多多認識。
			If you can speak Chinese, then we can get to know each other better.
	你喜歡		我就買這一件衣服給你。
			If you like it [an article of clothing], I'll buy it for you.
	你到家		請打電話給我。
			If you get home, please give me a call.
	你有空		可以教我英文嗎？
			If you have time, could you teach me English?

2. 去 (qù) 、 來 (lái) 、 到 (dào)

The verbs " 去, 來, 到 " can function alone or combine with other verbs to serve as directional complements.

＊去 (qù) : When the action proceeds away from the speaker, " 去 " is the correct complement to use.

去		
明年偉立想搬	去	鄉下住。
		Next year, William wants to move to the countryside.
我們要幾點		愷俐家參加生日派對呢？
		What time do we have to go to Claire's birthday party?

	去	參觀美食展覽。 Yesterday I went to a food exhibition.
昨天我		
上個月我哥哥		中國玩。 Last month my (older) brother went to China (for pleasure).

* 來 (lái) : This is the appropriate complement to use when the action proceeds towards the speaker. For example:

來		
你	來	台灣的話，可以打電話給我。 If you come to Taiwan, you can give me a call.
你幾點		我家呢？ What time will you come to my house?
法杜		台灣已經六個月了。 Fatou has been in Taiwan six months already.
大家拿出課本		。 Take out your textbooks, everyone.

* 到 (dào) : This complement is suitable to express the arrival to any place from anywhere.

到		
我剛	到	家。 I just got home.
早上八點他就		學校了。 He got to school at 8:00 this morning.
他想搬		鄉下。 He wants to move to the countryside.
我姊姊星期日		台灣。 My (older) sister arrived in Taiwan on Sunday.

3. 跟 (gēn)

In lesson 3, we learned "和" (hàn/hé). This is a common conjunction used for nouns and pronouns. "和" and "跟" correspond to the English words "and" and "with", depending on context. When the prepositional phrase "跟 + NP" is placed before a verb as an adverbial modifier, it is generally used with the adverb "一起"; together they form the phase "跟 + NP + 一起".

跟 + NP		
我	跟	楊老師學習中文。 I study Chinese with Ms. Yang.
偉立		安惠結婚三年了。 William and Anhui have been married three years.
我爸爸		媽媽都在美國工作。 My mom and dad both work in the United States.
老師		大家介紹台灣很多漂亮的地方。 The teacher introduced lots of pretty places in Taiwan to everyone.

跟 + NP + 一起			
惠美	跟	我	一起 |去看展覽。 Huimei and I went to the exhibition together.
志學		愷俐		練習書法。 Joshua and Claire practice calligraphy together.
老師		我們		去醫院看志學。 The teacher went with us to see Joshua in the hospital.
我		法杜		住在台北市。 Fatou and I live together in Taipei.

4. 對 (duì)

The prepositional phrase "對" introduces the person or thing that is the object of a particular subject. For example:

	對 + NP	
希京	對	台灣男孩情有獨鐘。 Higyeong has a thing for Taiwanese men.
老師		我們很好。 (Our) teacher is so nice to us.
醫生		我說，生病要多喝水、多休息。 The doctor told me to drink a lot of water and get plenty of rest when you're sick.
我		中國文物很有興趣。 I'm really interested in Chinese antiques.

🍎 [興趣 xìngqù interest]

5. 別 (bié)

In Chinese, "別" means "don't", as in "do not do sth." It can be used to admonish someone to refrain from doing something.

別	
別	擔心我，我會好好地在家裡休息。 Don't worry about me—I'll just rest at home.
	跟別人說我的秘密。 Don't tell anyone my secret.
	客氣，就當自己的家。 Don't be polite; make yourself at home.
	生氣了！ Don't be angry!

🍎 [擔心 dānxīn to worry] [生氣 shēngqì to be angry]

6. 祝福語 (zhùfúyǔ) Expressions of wishes and blessings

All of these idiomatic expressions are suitable to say or write in each situation.

General Purpose	
萬事如意 wànshì rúyì	I hope everything goes smoothly. / Good luck.
心想事成 xīnxiǎng shìchéng	May all your wishes come true.

New Year's

| 新年快樂 xīnnián kuàilè | Happy New Year. |
| 恭喜發財 gōngxǐ fācái | Wishing you wealth and prosperity. |

For Travel

旅途愉快 lǚtú yúkuài	Have a nice trip.
一帆風順 yìfán fēngshùn	Have a smooth trip.
一路順風 yílù shùnfēng	Bon voyage.
珍重再見 zhēnzhòng zàijiàn	Take care and see you when you get back.

For Learning and Study

| 學業進步 xuéyè jìnbù | Keep up the good work. / May you continue to progress. |
| 早日學成 zǎorì xuéchéng | Hope you complete your studies soon. / Here's to learning it quickly. |

For Birthday

| 生日快樂 shēngrì kuàilè | Happy birthday. |
| 長命百歲 chángmìng bǎisuì | Here's to a long life. / And many more. |

For Wedding

天作之合 tiānzuò zhīhé	You're a match made in heaven.
幸福美滿 xìngfú měimǎn	Wishing you happiness and all the best.
百年好合 bǎinián hǎohé	Here's to many good years to come.
早生貴子 zǎoshēng guìzǐ	May you soon have a noble child.

Health-related

| 早日康復 zǎorì kāngfù | Get well soon. |
| 身體健康 shēntǐ jiànkāng | Here's to good health. |

● 換你試試看 *It's Your Turn!*
huàn nǐ shìshìkàn

Challenge 1

Choose the correct pinyin for each item.

1. ( ) 希望　　A. xīwàng　　B. xìwàng　　C. xīwāng

2. ( ) 留學　　A. ròuxué　　B. liúxué　　C. liúxiě

3. ( ) 祝福　　A. zhùfú　　B. zhùfù　　C. zúfú

4. ( ) 研究所　A. yèjiùshuō　B. yánjiùshuō　C. yánjiùsuǒ

5. ( ) 願望　　A. yuánwàng　B. yuànwàn　　C. yuànwàng

6. ( ) 早日學成　A. zǎorì xuéchéng　B. zǎorì xiéchéng　C. zhǎorì xuéchéng

7. ( ) 初戀　　A. chūliàn　　B. cūliàn　　C. chùdiàn

8. ( ) 一份　　A. yīfèn　　B. yífèn　　C. yìfèn

9. ( ) 原來如此　A. yuánlái rúcǐ　B. yuánlài rúcì　C. yuánlái rúzǐ

10. ( ) 成語　　A. chéngyǔ　　B. chènyǔ　　C. chéngyú

Challenge 2

Sentence Completion

Complete the sentences below with the appropriate idioms from the box.

一石二鳥	身體健康	新年快樂	旅途愉快	十全十美
五體投地	早日學成	幸福美滿	情有獨鍾	早日康復

1. 愷俐要去日本留學了，我們祝福她＿＿＿＿＿＿＿。

2. 我妹妹又漂亮又聰明，真是一個＿＿＿＿＿＿的女生。

3.新的一年來了，我祝福大家 ＿＿＿＿＿＿＿＿＿＿＿。

4.在台灣，可以學中文也可以吃美食，

真是 ＿＿＿＿＿＿＿＿＿＿。

5.我姐姐要結婚了，祝福他們 ＿＿＿＿＿＿＿＿＿＿＿。

6.偉立感冒生病、希京不小心跌倒、志學車禍

受傷，我希望他們可以 ＿＿＿＿＿＿＿＿＿。

7.下個月楊老師要去中國玩，先祝福楊老師

＿＿＿＿＿＿＿＿＿。

8.最近我女朋友常常生病，真希望她 ＿＿＿＿＿＿＿。

9.志學對愷俐 ＿＿＿＿＿＿＿＿＿。

10.他來台灣五個月，中文就說得那麼好，我真是佩

服得 ＿＿＿＿＿＿＿＿＿ 呀！

Challenge 3

I. Pattern drills with ……的話；如果……；如果……的話
Example： **你去美國 ／ 可以住我家 （如果……）**
　　　→ 如果你去美國，可以住我家。

1.你找到存摺 ／ 請打電話給我。（如果……的話）
→

2.你不舒服 ／ 記得要去看醫生。(……的話)

→

3.我是你 ／ 我就會每天送她回家。(如果……)

→

4.你喜歡台灣 ／ 就留下來住。(……的話)

→

5.明天你想去美術館 ／ 我們一起去好嗎？
(如果……的話)

→

- -

II. Pattern drills with ……去；來；到。
Example：志學邀愷俐一起／故宮參觀 (去)
　　　 → 志學邀愷俐一起去故宮參觀。

1.他是什麼時候 ／ 台灣的？(來)

→

2.我 ／ 日本看好朋友 (去)

→

3.你幾點 ／ 學校呢 (到)

→

4.請幫我把東西 ／ 拿上 ／ 好嗎 (來)

→

5.你 ／ 美國 ／ 記得打電話給媽媽（到）

→

III. Pattern drills with 跟 + NP + 一起；跟 + NP。
Example： **我找不到我的存摺 ／ 印章 （跟）**
   → 我找不到我的存摺跟印章。

1.我 ／ 我女朋友 ／ 常常 ／ 去爬山
（跟……一起）

→

2.你 ／ 星期六 ／ 星期日 ／ 都有空嗎（跟）

→

3.上次假期 ／ 愷俐 ／ 志學 ／ 去看展覽
（跟……一起）

→

4.我 ／ 哥哥 ／ 要／ 去日本留學（跟……一起）

→

5.我會說／中文／日文／英文（跟）

→

Challenge 4

Find the characters with these radicals in the two-character compounds below.

部首 Radicals	冫 部 bīng bù	示 部 shì bù		彳 部 chì bù	邑 部 yì bù	阜 部 fù bù
意思 Meanings	ice	sign		left step	state	mound
字形 Forms	冫	示	礻	彳	阝	阝
例字 Examples	冬 凍	祭	社	得 很	那 都	院 阿

基隆 神祕 很忙 祝福 車票 往復 冷清 往後
冰凍 陳郎 陸上 部隊 祭祖 陰陽 鄭部 待價

冫 : ☐ ☐ ☐

示 : ☐ ☐ ☐ ☐ ☐ ☐ ☐

彳 : ☐ ☐ ☐ ☐ ☐

邑 : ☐ ☐ ☐

阜 : ☐ ☐ ☐ ☐ ☐ ☐

聽力練習 Let's Listen!

tīnglì liànxí

Listen to the dialogue and choose the best answer for each question.

Supplementary Vocabulary
101大樓　yīlíngyī dàlóu　The Taipei 101 building
淡水　dànshuǐ　Danshui (located in northern Taiwan)
九份　jiǔfèn　Jiufen (located in northern Taiwan)
花蓮　huālián　Hualien City and County (located on the east coast of Taiwan)
高雄　gāoxióng　Kaohsiung City and County (located in southern Taiwan)
小吃　xiǎochī　snack(s); appetizer(s); side-dish(es)
小籠包　xiǎolóngbāo　steamed dumpling(s); small steamed bun(s)
珍珠奶茶　zhēnzhū nǎichá　bubble tea; pearl milk tea
滷味　lǔwèi　soy marinated food
雞排　jīpái　fried chicken chop
遊學　yóuxué　travel study

1. (　　) How long has Kǎilì been in Taiwan? (a) Almost one year. (b) Over one year. (c) Almost two years. (d) One and half years.

2. (　　) What is the reason for Kǎilì to come to Taiwan? (a) Taiwan is a friendly country. (b) To learn Chinese. (c) There are many good places in Taiwan. (d) All of the above.

3. (　　) Where has Kǎilì traveled in Taiwan? (a) Taipei 101. (b) Everywhere from west to east. (c) Everywhere from north to south. (d) All of the above.

4. (　　) What kind of snacks does Fǎdù like to eat? (a) Fried chicken. (b) Pearl milk tea. (c) Steamed dumplings. (d) All of the above.

5. (　　) What is Kǎilì's impression of Taiwan? (a) It's a very busy place. (b) It's very crowded. (c) It's a good place for overseas study. (d) It's very boring.

● 字型練習 *Let's Write!*
zìxíng liànxí

| ` | ㄴ | ㄷ | 血 | 幼 | 㘎 | 留 | 留 | 留 | | |

留 留 留
liú 留留

| ` | ㇇ | ㇕ | 礻 | 衤 | 礻 | 礻 | 礻 | 祸 | 福 | 福 |

福 福 福
fú 福福

| 一 | 丁 | 扌 | 扩 | 扩 | 扨 | 捗 | 捗 | 搬 | 搬 | 搬 |

搬 搬 搬
bān 搬搬

| 一 | 厂 | 厂 | 斥 | 盾 | 盾 | 盾 | 咸 | 感 | 感 | 感 |

感 感 感
gǎn 感感

LESSON 12 279

| ✓ | ⼃ | ⼫ | 白 | 伯 | 纟 | 纟白 | 纟白 | 纟樂 | 纟樂 | 樂 | 樂 |

樂 樂 樂
lè 樂 樂

| ⼂ | ⼂ | ⼂ | ⼂ | 氵 | 沪 | 波 | 波 | 波 | 婆 | 婆 |

婆 婆 婆
pó 婆 婆

| 一 | 十 | 土 | 耂 | 老 | 考 |

考 考 考
kǎo 考 考

| ⼂ | ⼂ | 占 | 广 | 庐 | 庐 | 虍 | 虍 | 虍 | 虍 | 慮 | 慮 |

慮 慮 慮
lù 慮 慮

| ` | ' | ' | 宀 | 宀 | 宀 | 宀 | 宷 | 宲 | 宲 | 實 | 實 |

實　實　實
shí
實　實

| ' | = | 言 | 信 | 结 | 结 | 结 | 絲 | 絲 | 戀 | 戀 | 戀 |

戀　戀　戀
liàn
戀　戀

| 一 | 厂 | 万 | 成 | 成 | 成 |

成　成　成
chéng
成　成

| l | 刀 | 月 | 日 | 旫 | 旫 | 旫 | � | 時 | 時 |

時　時　時
shí
時　時

生詞總表
Vocabulary

A

a 啊 ah 3
āgēntíng 阿根廷 Argentine 5
ǎi 矮 short 6
ai 唉 (sound of a sigh) 7
ài 愛 to love 8
āiya 唉呀 oops 12
ānhuì 安惠 Anhui (name of the wife of Chen Weili) 2

B

bā 八 eight 4
bǎ 把 (disposal marker) 10
ba 吧1 (guess marker, "S吧？" shows that the speaker is suspecting S to be true) 4
ba 吧2 (sentence-final particle of an urging tone) 9
ba 吧3 (sentence-final particle with a tone accepting a conclusion) 10
bàba 爸爸 dad, father 5
bái 白 Bai (Chinese surname) 2
bǎi 百 hundred 8
bǎihuògōngsī 百貨公司 department store 6
báisè 白色 white 8
bàn 半 half; half an hour, thirty minutes 7
bān 搬 to move 10
bān 班 class 12
bān 搬 to move 12
bāng 幫1 to help 4
bāng 幫2 for, to help 10
bàng 棒 great, wonderful 8
bāngmáng 幫忙 to help with something 6
bàngōngshì 辦公室 office 9
bāokuò 包括 to include 6
bǎozhòng 保重 to take good care of 11
bāozi 包子 steamed stuffed buns 8
bēi 杯 cup; a cup of 8
běi 北 North 9
běibiān 北邊 the side of North 9
bèi(bù) 背(部) back 10
bèitòng 背痛 backache 10
běn 本 (measure for book) 8
bǐ 比 than 6
bǐ 筆 pen 8, 10
biànde 變得 to become 10
biǎoxiàn 表現 performance 12
bié 別 please don't (do something) 12
biérén 別人 other people 12
bié zhème shuō 別這麼說 never mind, there's

no need to apologize 6
bǐjiào 比較 (contrastive) more 6
bīng 冰 ice 11
bìngfáng 病房 sickroom 11
bìxū 必須 must 5
bízi 鼻子 nose 10
bówùguǎn 博物館 museum 4
bù 不 not 1
bù 部 8
búcuò 不錯 good 8
búguò 不過 but 6
bùhǎo yìsi 不好意思 excuse me 6
bú huì ba 不會吧 oh no; how could it be possible? 4
bújiàn 不見 disappear; vanish 9
bú kèqì 不客氣 you're welcome 1
bùrán 不然 if not so, otherwise 4
bǔxí bān 補習班 bushiban, cram school 7
bù xiǎoxīn 不小心 carelessly 11
bùxíng 不行 to not allowed; will not do 7
búyòng 不用 not to have to 4
(tā) búzài (她)不在 (she) is not in 4

C

cāi 猜 to guess, suppose 5
cái 才1 (main clause marker, it indicates that the proposition in the subordinate clause is a must in order to verify the proposition in the main clause) 5
cái 才2 only, merely 6
cài 菜 food, cuisine 6
cān 餐 meal 11
cǎn 慘 to be miserable 11
cānguān 參觀 to pay a visit to 7
cānjiā 參加 to take part in, participate 7
cāochǎng 餐廳 restaurant 9
cāocháng 操場 playground, playing-field 9
cóng 從 from 6
cóng jīntiān qǐ 從今天起 (starting) from today 6
cōngmíng 聰明 to be smart, bright, clever 10
cuìyùbáicài 翠玉白菜 Jadeite Cabbage with Insects 4
cúnzhé 存摺 bankbook 9
cuò 錯 to be wrong 12

Ch

chābùduō 差不多 not much difference 6
chādiǎn 差點 nearly, almost 7
chàng 唱 to sing 10
chángcháng 常常 often 11
chànggē 唱歌 sing 4
chángmìng bǎisuì 長命百歲 Wishing you a long life 12
chǎofàn 炒飯 fried rice 8
chǎomiàn 炒麵 fried noodles 8

chē　車　car　4
chén　陳　Chen (Chinese surname)　2
chéngshì　城市　city　6
chéngwéi　成為　to become　11
chéngyǔ　成語　Chinese idiomatic expression　12
chī　吃　to eat　3
chīcù　吃醋　to be jealous　8
chǐcùn　尺寸　size　8
(wǒ) chídào le　(我)遲到了(I) am late　2
chōutì　抽屜　drawer　9
chū　出　to go out　9
chū chēhuò　出車禍　to be involved in a car accident　11
chuān　穿　to wear　8
chuáng　床　a bed　9
chūfā　出發　to set off　8
chúfáng　廚房　kitchen　3
chúle...zhīwài　除了……之外　eside, other than　3
chūliàn　初戀　first love　12
chūnjuǎn　春捲　spring rolls　3
chūqù　出去　to go out; to get out　9
chūshì　出事　to get into trouble　11

D
dà　大　to be big　4
dǎ diànhuà　打電話　make a phone call　4
dǎ pēntì　打噴嚏　to sneeze　10
dǎ wǔ zhé　打五折　to give a discount of fifty percent　8
dài　帶　take somebody　3
dài　帶　to lead　10
dàjiā　大家　everyone; everybody　2
dàlóu　大樓　building　9
dàmángrén　大忙人　a busy man; a busy woman　7
dàmén　大門　gate　9
dàn　但　but　5
dàn'gāo　蛋糕　cake　7
dāng　當　to be, take the role as　3
dāngrán　當然　of course, surely　6
dāngzhēn　當真　to take seriously　4
dànshì　但是　but　5
dànshuǐ　淡水　Danshui County is in the North of Taiwan　12
dānxīn　擔心　to worry　6
dānzì　單字　vocabulary　5
dào　道　(measure word for dishes)　8
dào　到1　to arrive at　4
dào　到2　until　7
dào　到3　(success marker; it shows that the verb before it is successfully accomplished)　12
dàodì　道地　to be authentic　5
dāpèi　搭配　to go well　10
dǎrǎo　打擾　to bother　9

dǎsuàn　打算　to plan to　8
dàtuǐ　大腿　thigh　10
dàyuē　大約　about, around　8
de　的1　of, 's　2
de　的2　(affirmation marker, "S的！" shows that the speaker is sure that S will be true)　4
de　的3　(adjectival marker)　5
de　得　manner particle (the part following 得 is modifying the action preceding it)　9
dehuà　的話　if　5
děng　等　to wait, await　6
dì　第　(ordinal prefix), -th　5
dìdi　弟弟　young brother　10
diǎn　點　o'clock　7
diàn　店　store　3
diàn　店　store, shop　8
diànhuà　電話　telephone; phone number　4
diànshìjī　電視機　television set　9
diàntī　電梯　elevator; lift　9
diànwán yóuxì　電玩遊戲　videogame　5
diànyǐng　電影　a movie　10
diànyǐngyuàn　電影院　cinema; theater　9
diào　掉　to fall　9
diédǎo　跌倒　to be tripped up, fall down　11
dìfāng　地方　place　5
dìngwèi　訂位　reservation, make a reservation, reserve a table　8
dōngbiān　東邊　East side　9
dòngshǒu　動手　to start doing sth.; to get to work　10
dōngxi　東西　something　3
dōngxī　東西　thing　8
dōu　都　both, all　3
duì　對1　yes; you're right　4
duì　對2　toward　12
duìbùqǐ　對不起1　I'm sorry!　2
duìbùqǐ　對不起2　excuse me　8
duìle　對了　by the way; ah yes　3, 4
duìmiàn　對面　opposites somewhere　9
duō　多　many; much　4
duǒ　朵　(measure for flower)　8
duōduō zhǐjiào　多多指教　nice to meet you; let's get along; (lit.) give me much advice　5
duójiǔ　多久　how long　10
duōshǎo qián　多少錢　how much money　8

E
èluósī　俄羅斯　Russia　5
en　嗯　um　5
èr　二　two　2
érqiě　而且　moreover　4
èrshí　二十　twenty　6

F
fǎdù　法杜　Fatou (name of a Gambian girl)　5
fàn　范　Fan (a Chinese surname)　6

283

fàn　飯　meal　11
fān dào　翻到　to turn to (page...)　5
fàng　放　to put　10
fāngbiàn　方便　to be convenient　6
fàngjià　放假　to take a day off　4
fángjiān　房間　room　6
fàngxīn　放心　to stop worrying　7
fángzū　房租　rent (for a room, a flat)　6
fànzhuō　飯桌　dining table　9
fāpiào　發票　receipt　8
fāshāo　發燒　to have high temperature　11
fāshēng　發生　to happen, occur　6
fèi　費　expense; charge　6
fēijī　飛機　airplane　4
fēil bīn　菲律賓　9
fēizhōu　非洲　Africa　5
fèn　份　portion (measure for feeling or a serving of food)　8, 12
fēngyè　楓葉　maple leaves　4
fēnsàn　分散　to disperse　5
fēnzhōng　分鐘　a minute　10
fú　幅　(measure word for pictures, paintings, prints, etc.)　8
fùqīn(fù)　父親(父)　father　2
fùxí　複習　to review　5

 G

gāi　該　should; to need, owe (doing something)　9
gǎibiàn　改變　to change　10
gānbǐyà　甘比亞　The Gambia　5
gāng　剛　just　3
gānggāng　剛剛　just now　7
gānghǎo　剛好　just right　8
gānjìng　乾淨　clean, neat　10
gǎnkuài　趕快　in a hurry; to hurry　3
gǎnkuài　趕快　hurriedly　12
gǎnmào　感冒　flu, to catch a cold　11
gǎnqíng　感情　feeling　12
gāo　高　tall　1
gāo　高　high　3
gāogēnxié　高跟鞋　high-heels　8
gāotiě　高鐵　= gāosùtiělù　高速鐵路　high speed rail　7
gāoxìng　高興　to be happy　6
gāoxióng　高雄　Kaohsiung City or County (in the south of Taiwan)　12
gè　各　each, every　5
ge　個　(measure word for countable things)　6
gē　歌　a song　8
gěi　給　(dative marker)　3
gēn　跟　with　4
gēn ... zài yìqǐ　跟……在一起　to be dating someone　12
gèng　更　even more　5

gēqǔ　歌曲　a song, a melody　8
gèwèi　各位　Everybody!; Ladies and Gentlemen!　2
gōngchē　公車　bus　4
gōngxǐ　恭喜　congratulations　9
gōngxǐ fācái　恭喜發財　12
gōngzuò　工作　to work　5
gòu　夠　enough　8
guāi　乖　well-behaved　2
guàng　逛　to stroll; to ramble; to roam　7
guānglín　光臨　to patronize　8
guānmén　關門　to close a door　9
gùgōng　故宮　National Palace Museum　4
guì　貴　expensive　2
guì　貴1　your (polite)　2
guì　貴2　to be expensive　8
guìzi　櫃子　cabinet, closet　9
guó　國　country, nation, state　5
guò　過1　to pass, go by　9
guò　過2　to have (done something); to have the experience (of doing something)　10
guóhuà　國畫　Chinese painting　4

 H

hāi　嗨　Hi!　10
hái　還　still; even; further　3
hái hǎo　還好　not really　7
háiméi　還沒　not yet　9
hàipà　害怕　be afraid of　5
hàn/hé　和　and　3
hànbǎo　漢堡　hamburger　5
hánguó　韓國　Korea　3, 5
hánguó rén　韓國人　Korean　3
hànzì　漢字　Chinese character　6
hǎo　好1　to be fine, good　1
hǎo　好2　so　3
hǎo　好3　to recover　11
hào　號　date　7
hǎoa　好啊　OK　9
hǎochī　好吃　delicious　3
hǎode　好的　OK　8
hǎokàn　好看　to be good-looking　8
hǎole　好了1　to be all right　3
hǎole　好了2　it will be better to　8
hǎole　好了3　done　10
hǎoxiàng　好像　seemingly　10
hǎoyòng　好用　to be easy to use　8
hē　喝　drink　6
hē　喝　to drink　11
hěn　很　quite　1
(wǒ)hěn gāoxìng rènshì nǐ/nín　(我)很高興認識你/您　Nice to meet you　2
hóngl dēng　紅綠燈　traffic light　9
hóngsè　紅色　red　8
hòu　後　after　7
hòumiàn　後面　at the back; behind　9

hòutiān 後天 the day after tomorrow 7

huā 花 flower 8

huālián 花蓮 refers to Huālián Xiàn 花蓮縣, County of Hualien (on the east coast of Taiwan) 4

huàn 換 to take turn; it's one's turn to 12

huānyíng 歡迎 welcome 4

huāpíng 花瓶 vase 9

huásuàn 划算 affordable; profitable 6

huáyǔ 華語 Chinese (the language) 2

huāyuán 花園 garden 6

huí 回 to go/come back to 4

huílái 回來 come back 9

huíjiā zuòyè 回家作業 homework 5

huì 會1 to be going to; will 3

huì 會2 to be able 4

huì 匯 to remit 9

huìměi 惠美 Huimei (name of a girl) 4

hùshì 護士 nurse 11

húshuō 胡說 to babble, talk nonsense 12

J

jǐ 幾 which (number) 4

jià 架 (measure word for machines) 8

jiā 家1 home 4

jiā 家2 (measure for store) 8

jiǎ 賈 Jia (a Chinese surname) 6

jiājù 家具 furniture 6

jiàn 見 to meet 5

jiān 間 the measure word for a room 6

jiàn 件 (measure for clothing) 8

jiānádà 加拿大 Canada 5

jiānbǎng 肩膀 shoulders 10

jiānbǎngtòng 肩膀痛 shoulders hurt 10

jiànkāng 健康 to be healthy 11

jiànyì 建議 advice 8

jiǎo 腳 foot/fee 10

jiāo 交 to give 10

(nǐ) jiào ... jiùhǎole (你)叫……就好了 Just call ... 2

jiǎohuái 腳踝 ankle 10

jiǎotàchē 腳踏車 bicycle 9

jiǎotòng 腳痛 leg hurt 10

jiārén 家人 families 4

jiāyóu 加油 keep up the good work; I (or we) support you (lit. add oil, or add fuel) 11

jiào 叫 to be called as 2

jiāo 教 to teach 7

jiāo 交 to make friends with, befriend 12

jiàozuò 叫做 to be called as 6

jiàqí 假期 vacation 7

jiārén 家人 family members 5

jìdé 記得 to remember 5

jié 節 period 8

jiéhūn 結婚 to get married 12

jiějie 姊姊 elder sister 2, 5

jièshào 介紹 to introduce 5

jiēxiàlái 接下來 next 8

jiēzhe 接著 next 10

jíhé 集合 to gather 7

jīhuì 機會 chance, opportunity 5

jīlóng 基隆 9

jìn 進 to enter 3

jǐngwèi 警衛 a guard 9

jīngyàn 經驗 experience(s) 10

jìnqù 進去 to go in, enter 3, 9

jīn 金 Jin (Korean surname) 5

jīnnián 今年 this year 6

jīntiān 今天 today 4

jīpái 雞排 chicken cutlet 6

jìrán 既然 since, now that 5

jiù 就1 right 3

jiù 就2 (main clause marker, indicating that the condition in the subordinate clause suffices to verify the proposition shown in the main clause) 3

jiù 救 to save 11

jiǔ 酒 bear 8

jiǔfèn 九份 Jiufen County is in the North of Taiwan 12

jù 句 a sentence 9

juéde 覺得 to feel, think, consider that 5, 6

juédìng 決定 to decide 8

K

kāfēi 咖啡 8

kāi 開1 to drive 4

kāi 開2 to open 6

kǎilì 愷俐 Kaili (Chinese name of Claire White, a Canadian girl) 1

kāishǐ 開始 to start, begin 5

kāixué 開學 the school begin 7

kàn 看1 to see 4

kàn 看2 to try to 10

kàn 看3 to depend 12

kàn diànyǐng 看電影 see a movie 3

kàn shū 看書 reading 4

kàndào 看到 to catch sight of 9

kǎo 考 to test in 5

kǎol 考慮 to consider 12

kǎoshì 考試 exam, test; to take or hold an exam, test, quiz, etc. 7

kè 課 class, course 7

kělè 可樂 8

kělián 可憐 to be poor, pitiable 7

kèqì 客氣 polite; modest 5

késòu 咳嗽 to cough, cough 11

kěshì 可是 but 3

kěxí 可惜 a pity 6

kěyǐ 可以 can 4

kòng 空 leisure; free time 4

kōngqì 空氣 air 12

KTV Karaoke Television 8

kuài 快1 to be fast, quick 5

kuài　快2　to hurry to　9
kuài　快3　almost　10
kuài　塊　chunk　8
kuài　塊　dollar (informal)　8
kuàilè　快樂　to be happy　12
kuàizi　筷子　chopsticks　8
kuǎn　款　type, style　10
kùzi　褲子　pants　6

la　啦　(cause marker, "S啦！" shows that the speaker needs the addressee to carry out S)　4
lā dùzi　拉肚子　to have diarrhea (lit. to pull belly)　11
lái　來1　to be about to; to let oneself　2
lái　來2　to come　5
(wǒ)láizì ...　(我)來自……　(I) come from ....　2
láizì　來自　to come from　5
làn　爛　to be poor　4
lánsè　藍色　blue color　8, 10
lǎopó　老婆　wife　8
lǎoshī　老師　teacher　1
le　了　(perfective aspect marker)　3
lèi　累　tired　1
lèsè　垃圾　trash, garbage　9
lèsètǒng　垃圾桶　ash can　9
lǐ　裡　inside　4
lí　離　distant from　4
liàng　輛(measure word for cars)　8
liǎng　兩　two (used before measure words)　9
liǎnhóng　臉紅　to blush　3
liànxí　練習　to practice　4
liàolǐ　料理　cuisine (especially Japanese, Korean or Chinese)　5
lǐbài　禮拜　week　7
lìhài　厲害　to be awesome　4
lǐmiàn　裡面　inside　4, 9
lín　林　Lin (Chinese surname)　2
lìng　另　other, another　11
língqián　零錢　change　5
línjū　鄰居　neighbor　1
lìshān　立山　Lishan (name of a boy)　4
歷史　history　5
liù　六　six　8
liú　留　to stay　12
liúbítì　流鼻涕　running nose　10
liúxué　留學　to study abroad　5
lǐwù　禮物　gift, present　6
lóu　樓　floor, story　4
lóutī　樓梯　stairs, flight of stairs　11
luo　囉　(combination of le 了 and o喔)　10
lǚtú yúkuài　旅途愉快　Have a nice trip.　12
lǔwèi　滷味　soy marinated food　8
lǚxíng　旅行　travel　4

M

ma　嗎　(interrogative marker)　6
máfán　麻煩　to trouble　10
māma　媽媽　mom, mother　3, 5
mǎi　買　to buy　8
mànyìdiǎn　慢一點　slowly　4
máng　忙　to be busy　1, 6
mángguòtóu　忙過頭　over busy; very busy　7
māo　貓　cat　8
máobǐ　毛筆　brush pen　10
máobìng　毛病　ailment　11
mǎshàng　馬上　right away, at once　6
měi　美　to be beautiful　3
méi cuò　沒錯　that's right　5
méiguānxi　沒關係　never mind　2
méiguī huā　玫瑰花　rose　8
měiguó　美國　the United States　5
mèimei　妹妹　younger sister　5
měishí　美食　delicacies　3
měishùguǎn　美術館　gallery, fine art museum　7
měitiān　每天　everyday　4
měi tiān　每天　every day　7
méi wèntí　沒問題　no problem　3
méi xiǎngdào　沒想到　to one's surprise　3
méi yìsi　沒意思　to be boring　4
méi yǒu　沒有　no; not to have　5
méiyǒu nàme　沒有……那麼……　less... than...; not as... as...　7
měishù　美術　art　5
men　們　(plural marker, denoting a group of people)　5
mén　門　door　6
ménkǒu　門口　gate　7
mìmì　祕密　secret　12
míngfēn　明芬　Mingfen (name of a girl)　4
míngnián　明年　next year　5
míngtiān　明天　tomorrow　3, 5
míngzi　名字　name (full name or given name)　2
mǔqīn(mǔ)　母親(母)　mother　2

N

ná　拿　to take, hold in hand　10
nǎ　哪2　which　5
nà　那1　then (concluder)　3
nà　那2　that　8
na　哪1　ah (following finals which end with "n" sound)　4
nǎichá　奶茶　milk tea　6
nǎlǐ　哪裡　where　5
nán　難　difficult　5
nán měizhōu　南美洲　South America　5
nánbiān　南邊　9
nánpéngyǒu　男朋友　boyfriend　4
ne　呢1　(interrogative marker)　1

ne 呢2 (sentence-final particle used to solicit reactions such as surprise, envy, etc.) 7
néng 能 can; to be able to, have the ability to; be allowed to 11
nǐ 你 you 1
nǐ shuōde duì 你說得對 you are right 8
nián 年 year 7, 10
niàn 念 to study 5
niàn yánjiùsuǒ 念研究所 attend at a graduate school 3
niánqīng 年輕 young 6
niànshū 念書 to read books; to study 5
nǐhǎo ma 你好嗎？ How are you? 1
nín 您 you (honorific) 5
nínhǎo 您好 Hello! (polite) 1
niǔ dào jiǎo 扭到腳 to sprain one's own ankle accidentally 11
niúpái 牛排 beef steak 6
niúzǎi kù 牛仔褲 jeans 10
nuówēi 挪威 Norway 5
nǚér 女兒 daughter 2
nǚshēng 女生 girl, woman 8

ó 哦 oh 3
o 喔 oh 3
òu 噢 ouch 11
ōuzhōu 歐洲 Europe 5

pá shān 爬山 to go hiking in the mountain; to go mountain climbing 3
pàiduì 派對 party 7
pán 盤 plate 8
pàng 胖 fat 6
pángbiān 旁邊 side 9
pǎo 跑 to run 9
pào 泡 to dunk 7
péi 陪 to accompany 8
pèiǒu 配偶 spouse 2
pēngrèn 烹飪 cooking (literary/formal) 3
piān 篇 piece of writing 8
piàn 騙 to cheat 7
piányí 便宜 to be inexpensive, cheap 2, 8
piàoliàng 漂亮 to be pretty 2, 5
pípí 皮皮 PiPi is Chinese name of a pet 9
píng 瓶 bottle 8
píngcháng 平常 usually 3
píngdōng 屏東 Pingtung County (in southern Taiwan) 9

Q
qí 騎 to ride 9
qī 七 seven 4
qiān 千 thousand 6

qiān 千 thousand 8
qián 錢 money 4
qiǎn 淺 light (color) 10
qián 前 before 11
qiánmiàn 前面 front 9
qǐchuáng 起床 awake up 7
qíguài 奇怪 to be strange 11
qǐlái 起來 by, by way of 7
qǐng 請1 to invite 2
qǐng 請2 please 5
qǐng...chīfàn 請……吃飯 to treat somebody to a meal 6
qīngchǔ 清楚 to be clear 9
qǐngjià 請假 to take a leave 6
qǐngkè 請客 to treat 8
qīngmíngshànghétú 清明上河圖 Along the River During the Ching-Ming Festival 4
qíngrén 情人 lover 12
qǐngwèn 請問 may I ask...? 2
qǐngwèn nǐ yǒu shéme shì ma 請問你有什麼事嗎？ Would you like to leave a message? 4
qǐngwèn nín zhǎo nǎ wèi 請問您找哪位？ Who would you like to speak with? 4
qíngyǒu dúzhōng 情有獨鍾 to have particularly good feeling (idiomatic) 12
qīnqiè 親切 to be kind; to be agreeable 5
qíshí 其實 in fact 12
qítā 其他 other 8, 11
qù 去 to go 3
quán 全 whole 12
quánbù 全部 all 8
qúnzi 裙子 skirt 8

ránhòu 然後 then 10
rè 熱 to be hot 6
rén 人1 person, people 5
rén 人2 other people 10
rènshì 認識 to know 2
rènzhēn 認真 to be earnest 2
rìběn 日本 Japan 5
rìqí 日期 date 7
rúguǒ 如果 if 12
rúhé 如何 how 3

S
sān 三 three 8
sànbù 散步 to take a walk 9
sangmén 嗓門 sound of human voices 2
sānmíngzhì 三明治 sandwich 3
sānshíyī 三十一 thirty one 7
sān yuè 三月 March 7
sǎo 掃 to sweep 9
sǎo dì 掃地 to clean the floor, sweep the floor 9
sì 四 four 4

sìshí 四十 forty 8
sì yuè 四月 the fourth month, April 7
sòng 送 to give as a present 6
suān 痠 10
suànle 算了 forget it 3
suì 歲 years 6
suǒyǐ 所以 so 3, 4

 Sh

shāfā 沙發 sofa, couch 9
shālā 沙拉 salad 3
shàng 上1 to go up to 4
shàng 上2 top, on top 9
shāngdiàn 商店 store 9
shàngkè 上課 to go to school 4
shàngkè 上課 to take a class 6
shàngmiàn 上面 above; over; on top of; on the surface of 9
shàngwǔ 上午 hours before noon; morning, forenoon; a.m. 7
shàngyī 上衣 top, blouse 8, 10
shǎo 少 don't (do something)! 12
shéi 誰 who? 2
shéme 什麼1 what? 2
shéme 什麼2 anything 3, 6
shéme 什麼時候 shíhòu when 7
shēngbìng 生病 to get sick 11
shēngqì 生氣 angry 12
shēngrì 生日 birthday 7
shēngwù 生物 biology 5
shēntǐ 身體 body 11
shēntǐ jiànkāng 身體健康 good health 12
shì 是 to be 1
shì 事 event, incident, thing 6
shì 試 to try 10
shìchuān 試穿 to try on 8
shìchuān 試穿 to try on 10
shìhé 適合 to fit 10
shíhòu 時候 moment, period of time 11
shíjiān 時間 time 7, 12
shíjiǔ 十九 nineteen 6
shíliù 十六 sixteen 5
shìyījiān 試衣間 fitting room 10
shìyǒu 室友 roommate 6
shízài 實在 indeed 7
shīzhàng 師丈 the husband of someone's teacher 2
shòu bù liǎo 受不了 to be intolerable 7
shōu 收 to receive 8
shǒu 首 first 8
shǒu 手 hand 10
shòu 瘦 thin 6
shōufèi 收費 fee (literary/formal) 3
shòushāng 受傷 to be injured 11
shū 書 book 8
shù 束 bundle, bouquet 8

shuài 帥 handsome 5
shuāng 雙 a pair of 8
shūdiàn 書店 boos store 9
shūfǎ 書法 calligraphy 10
shūfú 舒服 to be comfortable 11
shuì 睡 sleep 11
shuǐ 水 water 11
shuǐdiànfèi 水電費 utility 6
shuǐguǒ 水果 fruit 3
shuǐjiǎo 水餃 dumplings 3
shuìjiào 睡覺 to sleep 7
shǔjià 暑假 summer vacation 4
shùnbiàn 順便 conveniently 5
shuō 說 to speak 4
shuō de duì 說得對 That's right! 3
shuōbúdìng 說不定 chances are; maybe 6
shuōde yěshì 說得也是 that makes (more) sense 8
shuōhuà 說話 saying, talking, or speaking 5

T

tā 他 he 1
tā 她 she 2
tài... le 太……了 too, very 6
tài 太 too; really 3
táiběi 台北 Taipei 3
táidà yīyuàn 台大醫院 National Taiwan University Hospital 11
tàilǔgé 太魯閣 Taroko. Taroko National Park 7
tàitai 太太 wife; Mrs. 2
táiwān 台灣 Taiwan 3, 5
táizhōng 台中 9
tán 談 to talk about 6, 12
tāng 湯 8
táocí 陶瓷 china 4
tàofáng 套房 a suite; a room with a toilet (a studio) 6
tǎolùn 討論 to discuss, talk about 5
táoyuán 桃園 9
tèbié 特別 to be special 12
tècháng 特長 ability 4
tiān 天 day 7
tiān a 天啊 oh my goodness 11
tiānqì 天氣 weather 6
tiānzuò zhīhé 天作之合 12
tiāo 挑 to pick 8
tiáo 條 (measure for trousers, pants, jeans, etc.) 8, 10
tiàowǔ 跳舞 dance 4
tǐyùguǎn 體育館 a gymnasium; a gym 9
tīngshuō 聽說 I heard that; somebody told me that 6
tòng 痛 to ache, hurt 6, 11
tóngxué 同學 classmate, student 2
tóu 頭1 side (suffix indicating directions) 9

tóu　頭2　head　6, 11
tóutòng　頭痛　headache　10, 11
tuǐsuān　腿痠　10
tuǐtòng　腿痛　10
túshūguǎn　圖書館　library　9

W

wā　哇　wow!　3
wàiguó rén　外國人　foreigner　4
wàimiàn　外面　outside　9
wán　玩　to play, enjoy oneself　5
wán　完　to finish, be over　7
wǎn　碗　a bowl　8
wàng　忘　to forget　7
wǎng　往　towards　9
wǎnglùfèi　網路費　Internet fee　6
wànlǐchángchéng　萬里長城　Great Wall　9
wǎnshàng　晚上　evening, night　7
wànshì rúyì　萬事如意　Everything is lovely and satisfactorily all the luck.　12
wǎnyìdiǎn　晚一點　a few time later　7
wèi　位　a measure word for respected person (or showing a polite way)　3
wèi　位　measure for person (polite)　5
wèi(bù)　胃(部)　stomach　10
wèizi　位子　place, seat　10
wèilái　未來　future　4
wěilì　偉立　Weili (name of one of Claire's classmates)　2
wèishéme　為什麼　why　5
wèitòng　胃痛　stomachache　10, 11
wèn　問　to ask　6
wèn wèntí　問問題　to ask questions　2
wēnquán　溫泉　hot spring　7
wèntí　問題　problem　11
wénwù　文物　cultural relic　4
wénxué　文學　literature　5
wǒ　我　I, me　5
wò　握　to hold　10
wǒmen　我們　we　2
wòshì　臥室　bedroom　9
wǔ　五　five　4
wùjià　物價　price of commodities　6
wǔshí　五十　fifty　8

X

xì　系　faculty; department　5
xǐ　洗　to wash　10
xià　下　under　9
xià...yí tiào　嚇……一跳　to surprise　10
xià yí wèi　下一位　the next one　2
xiàcì　下次　next time　3
xiàge　下個　next (Sunday, week, month, etc.)　7
xiàkè　下課　to finish class; to dismiss the class　5
xiàmiàn　下面　place under　9

xiān　先　first　5
xiǎng　想　want; would like to　3
xiǎng　想1　to want to　4
xiǎng　想2　to think　4
xiǎng　響　to ring　5
xiàng　項　item　8
xiàngliàn　項鍊　necklace　7
xiāngshuǐ　香水　perfume　7
xiāngxià　鄉下　countryside　12
xiānshēng　先生　sir　1
xiànzài　現在　now　2
xiǎo　小　to be small, little　8
xiǎochī　小吃　local snack　12
xiǎogǒu　小狗　puppy　9
xiǎohái　小孩　children　3
xiǎojiě　小姐　lady　1
xiǎolóngbāo　小籠包　Steamed dumpling; small steamed bun　12
xiǎotuǐ　小腿　shank　10
xiǎozhuōzi　小桌子　small table　10
xiàwǔ　下午　afternoon; p.m.　7
xiàyǔ　下雨　rain　4
xībiān　西邊　9
xiě　寫　to write　10
xièxie　謝謝　thank you　1
xiézi　鞋子　shoes　8
xǐhuān　喜歡　to like　3
xījīng　希京　Xijing (name of a Korean girl)　5
xīn　心　heart　4
xīn　新　to be new　5
xíng　行　to be fine　4
xìng　姓1　surname, family name　2
xìng　姓2　to have the surname of　2
xìnghǎo　幸好　fortunately　11
xìngfú měimǎn　幸福美滿　12
xínglǐ　行李　baggage; luggage　9
xīngqí　星期　week　7
xīngqí èr　星期二　Tuesday　7
xīngqí liù　星期六　Saturday　7
xīngqí sān　星期三　Wednesday　7
xīngqí sì　星期四　Thursday　7
xīngqí tiān　星期天　Sunday　7
xīngqí wǔ　星期五　Friday　7
xīngqí yī　星期一　Monday　7
xìngqù　興趣　Interests　4
xīnkǔ　辛苦　to pay a lot of effort　7
xīnshuǐ　薪水　wages; salary　6
xīnxiǎng shìchéng　心想事成　12
xiōngdì jiěmèi　兄弟姊妹　sibling　5
xiūxí　休息　to take a rest　7
xīwàng　希望1　to hope　3
xīwàng　希望2　wish, hope　12
xué　學　to learn　3, 5
xuéfèi　學費　school fees; tuition　8
xuéhuì　學會　to acquire the skill of　4
xuéqí　學期　a semester; a school term　8
xuéshēng　學生　student　1

xuéxí 學習 to learn 7
xuéxiào 學校 school 2
xuéyè jìnbù 學業進步 Studies progresses 12
xūyào 需要 to need 6

Y

ya 呀 ah (following monophthongal finals or finals which end with "i" sound) 4
yáchǐ 牙齒 tooth 10
yǎfáng 雅房 a room to share 6
yǎnjīng 眼睛 eyes 10
yǎnjīngtòng 眼睛痛 10
yánjiùshì 研究室 research room 9
yáng 楊 Yang (Chinese surname) 2
yàngzi 樣子 appearance, mien 7
yánjiùsuǒ 研究所 graduate institute 3, 12
yánzhòng 嚴重 to be serious, grave 11
yāo 邀 to invite 4
yāo(bù) 腰(部) waist 10
yào 要1 will; to want to 4
yào 要2 do (as in "Do be careful!") 10
yào 藥 medication 11
yāoqǐng 邀請 to invite 7
yāosuān 腰痠 backache 10
yátòng 牙痛 toothache 10
yàzhōu 亞洲 Asia 5
yèshì 夜市 nightmarket 3
yě 也 also 1
ye 耶 yeah! 3
yè 頁 page 5
yěcān 野餐 to go on a picnic 3
yī (yí; yì) 一 one 4
yí 咦 (exclamation uttered when surprised) 6
yí 移 to move 10
yì kāishǐ 一開始 in the beginning 10
yìdiǎn 一點 a little bit 5
yídìng 一定 must 4
yìfán fēngshùn 一帆風順 Have a nice trip. 12
yīfú 衣服 clothes 6
yīfú 衣服 clothes 8
yí ge rén 一個人 alone 5
yígòng 一共 total 8
yǐhòu 以後 later on 5
yǐjīng 已經 already 6
yìndù 印度 India 5
yīnggāi 應該 should, to be supposed to 5
yīngwén 英文 English 4
yīngyǔ 英語 English, the English language 5
yínháng 銀行 bank 9
yīnwèi 因為 because 5
yīnyuè 音樂 music 5
yìnzhāng 印章 seal 9
yìqǐ 一起 together 3
yīshēng 醫生 doctor, physician 11
yíxià 一下 in a short while 5
yíxiàng 一向 as always 11

yīxué 醫學 medical science 5
yīxué 醫學 medical science, medicine 5
yìyán wéidìng 一言為定 that's a deal 7
yíyàng 一樣 the same as 5
yīyuàn 醫院 hospital 11
yìzhí 一直 all the way, all along 8
yòng 用 to use 12
yǒu 有1 to have 4
yǒu 有2 there be 3, 9
(qǐngwèn nǐ) yǒu shé me shì ma (請問你) 有什麼事嗎？ Would you like to leave a message? 4
yòu 又 again 7
yòu 右 right 9
yòubiān 右邊 the right, right side 9
yóujú 郵局 post office 9
yǒukěnéng 有可能 maybe 9
yǒukòng 有空 to have free time, be free, available 3, 7
yǒuqù 有趣 to be interesting 5
yóuxué 遊學 travel study 12
yǒuyìdiǎn 有一點 a little bit 4
yú 於 at, in, on (literary) 5
yuǎn 遠 to be far 4
yuán 元 dollar (formal) 8
yuánlái 原來 originally, actually 3
yuánlái rúcǐ 原來如此 oh, I see. 12
yuànwàng 願望 Wishes 4
yuànwàng 願望 wish 12
yuè 月 month 7
yuè...yuè... 越……越…… the more..., the more... 6
yùndòng 運動 to do exercise 3
yùqì 玉器 jade 4
yúrén jié 愚人節 April Fool's Day 7
yùxí 預習 preview 3
yǔyán 語言 language 7
yǔyán jiāohuàn 語言交換 language exchange; language exchange partner 5, 7

Z

zài 在 to be (somewhere) 3
zài 在 to be (doing something) 9
zài 載 to give (somebody) a ride or a drive 4
zài 再 one more time 5
zài shēnbiān 在身邊 to be around 5
zàidù 再度 one more time (literary) 8
zàijiàn 再見 goodbye 1
zàishuōyícì 再說一次 say again 4
zǎo 早 ＝早安 2
zǎoān 早安 good morning 1
zāogāo 糟糕 oh no; too bad 9
zàojù 造句 making sentences 5
zāole 糟了 oh, no!; oops! 9
zǎoshàng 早上 morning 7
zǎoshēng guìzǐ 早生貴子 May your have a noble baby soon! (idiomatic) 12

聽力練習
Let's Listen!

第一課　早安，您好！

II.Choose the best description for each dialogue.

1.

鄰居：小姐，早安！
　　　xiǎojiě　zǎoān

愷俐：先生，早安！你好嗎？
　　　xiānshēng zǎoān　nǐ hǎo ma

鄰居：我很好，你呢？
　　　wǒ hěn hǎo　nǐ ne

愷俐：我也很好，謝謝！
　　　wǒ yě hěn hǎo　xièxie

2.

老師：老師好！
　　　lǎoshī hǎo

愷俐：你好，你是學生嗎？
　　　nǐhǎo　nǐ shì xuéshēng ma

老師：我是學生。他也是學生嗎？
　　　wǒshì xuéshēng　tā yě shì xuéshēng ma

愷俐：他不是學生，他也是老師。
　　　tā bú shì xuéshēng　tā yě shì lǎoshī

3.

愷俐：先生，早安！您好嗎？
　　　xiānshēng zǎoān　nín hǎo ma

鄰居：不好，我很忙。
　　　bù hǎo　wǒ hěn máng

愷俐：你很累嗎？
　　　nǐ hěn lèi ma

鄰居：我很累。
　　　wǒ hěn lèi

第二課　您貴姓？

II.Listen to the dialogue and answer the questions. (True/ False)

愷俐：老師好。對不起，我遲到了！
　　　kǎilì　lǎoshī hǎo　duì bù qǐ　wǒ chí dào le

老師：愷俐啊，沒關係。請坐請坐。
　　　lǎoshī　kǎilì a　méi guānxī　qǐng zuò qǐng zuò

師丈：妳好，妳好。
　　　shīzhàng nǐ hǎo　nǐ hǎo

老師：愷俐，這是我先生，他叫林俊傑。
　　　lǎoshī　kǎilì　zhèshìwǒxiānshēng tā jiào línjùnjié

　　　妳叫師丈就好了。
　　　nǐ jiào shīzhàng jiù hǎole

愷俐：您好，我叫白愷俐。我來自加拿大，
　　　kǎilì　nín hǎo　wǒ jiào bái kǎilì wǒ lái zì jiānádà

很高興認識您。
hěn gāoxing rènshì nín

師丈：我也很高興認識妳。
　　　lǎoshī　wǒyě hěn gāoxing rènshì nǐ

愷俐：這漂亮的女生是誰呢？
　　　kǎilì　zhè piàoliàng de nǚshēng shì shuí ne

老師：這是我的女兒。她叫婷婷。
　　　lǎoshī　zhè shì wǒ de nǚér　tā jiàotíngtíng

老師：婷婷……要叫姐姐喔！
　　　lǎoshī　tíngtíng … yàojiào jiějie　o

婷婷：姐姐好。
　　　tíngtíng　jiějie hǎo

愷俐：嗯！很乖，很乖。
　　　kǎilì　en　hěnguāi　hěnguāi

老師，師丈：哈！哈！哈！
　　　lǎoshī shīzhàng　hā　hā　hā

愷俐：哇！老師，您的家很大，很漂亮呢！
　　　kǎilì　wa　lǎoshī　nín de jiā hěndà　hěnpiàoliàngne!

　　　這房子很貴嗎？
　　　zhè fángzi hěn guì ma

師丈：不貴、不貴。這房子很便宜。
　　　shīzhàng búguì　búguì　zhè fángzi hěn piányí

第三課　我喜歡爬山

II. Listen to the dialogue and mark the correct statements with "T" and the incorrect ones with "F".

希京：請問你是立山嗎？
　　　xījīng　qǐngwèn nǐ shì lìshān ma

立山：是的，我就是。妳是金希京小姐，
　　　lìshān　shi de　wǒ jiù shì　nǐ shì jīn xījīng xiǎojiě

　　　對不對？
　　　duì bú duì

希京：對啊！你好，我來自韓國。
　　　xījīng　duì a　nǐ hǎo　wǒ lái zì hánguó

立山：原來你是韓國人喔！妳好，我姓高
　　　lìshān　yuánlái nǐ shì hánguórén ō　nǐ hǎo　wǒxìnggāo

　　　名立山。
　　　mínglìshān

　　　叫我立山就好了。
　　　jiào wǒ lìshān jiù hǎo le

　　　對了，我帶妳去吃小吃，如何？
　　　duì le　wǒ dài nǐ qù chī xiǎochī　rúhé

希京：小吃是什麼？小小的飯嗎？
　　　xījīng　xiǎochī shì shí me　xiǎoxiǎo de fàn ma

立山：哈哈不是喔！那裡就有小吃，走吧！
　　　lìshān　hā hā búshì ō　nà lǐ jiù yǒu xiǎochī zǒu ba

希京：喔，我認識它們—包子、炒麵、
　　　xījīng　ò　wǒ rènshì tāmen　bāozi chǎomiàn

　　　炒飯，炒飯真的好好吃！
　　　chǎofàn　chǎofàn zhēn de hǎo hǎo chī

立山：我平常都來這裡吃東西，
　　　lìshān　wǒ píngcháng dōu lái zhè lǐ chī dōngxī

　　　炒飯也是我最喜歡的小吃了。
　　　chǎofàn yě shì wǒ zuì xǐhuān de xiǎochī le

　　　除了炒飯之外，
　　　chú le chǎofàn zhī wài

這裡的 水 餃 也 很 好 吃 喔！
zhè lǐ de shuǐjiǎoyě hěn hǎo chī ō

希京：太好了，我們 趕 快 進 去 吃吧！
xījīng　tài hǎo le　wǒmen gǎnkuài jìn qù chī ba

立山：志學 說 得 對，妳 真 的 很 愛 吃 美 食。
lìshān　zhìxuéshuōde duì　nǐzhēndehěn ài chīměishí

　　　 等 等 我 啊！
　　　 děngděng wǒ a

第四課　我會說華語

II.Listen to the dialogue and choose the best answer.

惠美的姊姊：喂，請 問 您 找 哪位？
huìměi de jiějie　wèi　qǐngwènnín zhǎo nǎ wèi

愷俐：您 好，我 想 找 惠美。
kǎilì　nín hǎo　wǒ xiǎng zhǎo huìměi

惠美的姊姊：對不起，她不在。請 問 你 有
huìměi de jiějie　duì bù qǐ　tā bú zài　qǐngwèn nǐ yǒu

　　　　　 什麼 事 嗎？
　　　　　 shéme shì ma

愷俐：您好，我是愷俐，妳們 的 新 鄰居。
kǎilì　nínhǎo　wǒ shì kǎilì　nǐmen de xīn línjū

惠美的姊姊：喔，你 就 是 住 在 四樓 的
huìměi de jiějie　ō　nǐ jiù shì zhù zài sì lóu de

　　　　　 外國人，對不對？
　　　　　 wàiguórén　duì bú duì

　　　　　 您好，我是 惠美 的 姊姊。
　　　　　 nín hǎo　wǒ shì huìměi de jiějie

愷俐：我 想 邀 請 惠美 跟 我 一起 去 看
kǎilì　wǒ xiǎng yāoqǐng huìměi gēn wǒ yì qǐ qù kàn

　　　 展 覽。可以 請 她 打 電話給 我 嗎？
　　　 zhǎnlǎn　kěyǐ qǐng tā dǎ diànhuàgěi wǒ ma

惠美的姊姊：好。她有妳的 電話 嗎？
huìměi de jiějie　hǎo　tā yǒu nǐ de diànhuà ma

愷俐：有，謝謝 您。
kǎilì　yǒu　xièxie nín

惠美的姊姊：愷俐，沒 想 到 你 的 中 文
huìměi de jiějie　kǎilì　méi xiǎng dào nǐ de zhōngwén

　　　　　 這 麼 厲害！
　　　　　 zhè me lìhài

　　　　　 歡 迎 你 有 空 來 坐坐！
　　　　　 huānyíng nǐ yǒu kōnglái zuòzuò

愷俐：謝謝，再見。
kǎilì　xièxie　zàijiàn

惠美的姊姊：不客氣，再見。
huìměi de jiějie　bú kèqì　zàijiàn

第五課　你是哪一國人？

Listen to the dialogue and mark correct statements with "T" and incorrect ones with "F".

法杜：我 覺得 今天 的 考試 有 一 點 難，
fǎdù　wǒ jué de jīntiān de kǎoshì yǒu yì diǎn nán

　　　 你 呢？
　　　 nǐ ne

志學：我 覺得 不 難！因為 我 的 語言 交 換
zhìxué　wǒ jué de bù nán! yīnwèiwǒde yǔyán jiāohuàn

昨天 幫 我 練習了 造句，
zuótiān bāng wǒ liànxí le zàojù

所以 考試 的 時候，就 不 害怕 了。
suǒyǐ kǎoshì de shíhòu　jiù bú hài pà le

法杜：你的語言 交換？
fǎdù　nǐ de yǔyán jiāohuàn

志學：語言 交換 就是 language exchange
zhìxué　yǔyán jiāohuàn jiùshì

partner。

法杜：他 是 哪 一國 人？
fǎdù　tā shì nǎ yìguó rén

志學：我的語言 交換是台灣人,念資訊科
zhìxué　wǒ de yǔyán jiāohuànshì táiwānrén niàn zīxùn kē

　　　 學的，我們 除了 練習 中 文之外，
　　　 xué de　wǒmen chú le liànxí zhōngwénzhīwài

　　　 還常常 討論 電玩 遊戲 呢！
　　　 hái chángcháng tǎolùn diànwán yóuxì ne

法杜：哇！真 有趣。
fǎdù　wā　zhēn yǒuqù

志學：那 你 想 不 想 要 語言 交 換
zhìxué　nà nǐ xiǎngbùxiǎng yào yǔyán jiāohuàn

法杜：想 啊，但是 我 要 交 換 什麼
fǎdù　xiǎng a　dànshì wǒ yào jiāohuàn shéme

　　　 語言 呢？
　　　 yǔyán ne

志學：中 英 交換，怎麼 樣？
zhìxué　zhōngyīng jiāohuàn　zěmeyang

法杜：我 會 說 英文，但是 不 會 教 英 文
fǎdù　wǒ huì shuō yīngwén　dànshì bú huì jiāo yīngwén

　　　 耶！
　　　 ye

志學：妳 真 客氣，妳 的 英 文 一定 沒 問題。
zhìxué　nǐ zhēn kèqì　nǐ de yīngwényídìngméiwèntí

　　　 既然 你 有 興趣，我 明 天 就 幫 你
　　　 jì rán nǐ yǒu xìngqù　wǒ míngtiān jiù bāng nǐ

　　　 找 一位 很 帥 的 語言 交換。
　　　 zhǎoyí wèi hěn shuài de yǔyán jiāohuàn

法杜：志學，等一下！我的語言 交換 必須
fǎdù　zhìxué　děng yí xià　wǒ de yǔyán jiāohuànbì xū

　　　 是 女 生 啦！
　　　 shì nǚ shēngla

第六課　她是我的室友

Listen to the dialogue and choose the best statements.

愷俐：法杜，妳今天晚上 想 吃什麼？
kǎilì　fǎdù　nǐ jīntiān wǎnshàngxiǎng chī shéme

　　　 我 請 妳 吃飯。
　　　 wǒ qǐng nǐ chīfàn

法杜：啊？為什麼妳要 請我吃飯？
fǎdù　a　wèishéme nǐ yào qǐng wǒ chīfàn

愷俐：因為 從 今天起，你 就是 我的室友
kǎilì　yīnwèi cóng jīntiān qǐ　nǐ jiù shì wǒdeshìyǒu

　　　 了。
　　　 le

法杜：呵呵，好哇！那我們 要 吃什麼？
fǎdù　hēhē　hǎo wā　nà wǒmen yào chīshéme

293

愷俐：妳想 吃 中國 菜還是法國 菜？
kǎilì　nǐ xiǎng chī zhōngguó cài hái shì fǎ guó cài

法杜：我都喜歡耶，不知道哪一個比較好。
fǎdù　wǒdōuxǐhuānyé　bùzhīdào nǎ yí ge bǐ jiǎohǎo
　　　但我覺得 中國 菜比法國 菜便宜
　　　dàn wǒ jué de zhōngguócài bǐ fǎguó cài piányí

愷俐：哇！妳人真好，我也覺得法國 菜太
kǎilì　wā　nǐ rénzhēnhǎo　wǒyě juéde fǎguó cài tài
　　　貴了，那我們 就 吃 中國 菜好了。
　　　guì le　nà wǒmen jiù chī zhōngguócài hǎole

法杜：謝謝你 請 我 吃飯。
fǎdù　xièxie nǐ qǐng wǒ chīfàn

愷俐：不客氣，那我們 走吧！
kǎilì　bú kèqì　nà wǒmen zǒu ba

第七課　明天是星期幾？

Listen to the dialogue and choose the best answer

法杜：立山，愷俐的 生日你要送 什麼呢？
fǎdù　lìshān　kǎilì de shēngrì nǐ yàosongshéme ne

立山：愷俐的 生日不是後天嗎？
lìshān　kǎilì de shēngrì bú shì hòutiān ma
　　　我 明天再買禮物。
　　　wǒ míngtiān zài mǎi lǐwù

法杜：不是後天，是 明天。
fǎdù　bú shì hòutiān　shì míngtiān

立山：我記得她的 生日是四月十六日，不
lìshān　wǒ jì de tā de shēngrì shì sì yuè shí liù rì　bú
　　　是嗎？
　　　shì ma

法杜：是的，明天就是四月十六日星期
fǎdù　shìde　míngtiān jiùshì sì yuèshíliù rì xīngqí
　　　一。
　　　yī

立山：真的嗎！我 忙 過頭了。怎麼辦？
lìshān　zhēndema　wǒ mángguò tóu le　zěmebàn
　　　我還沒買，要送 什麼呢？
　　　wǒ hái méi mǎi　yào song shéme ne

法杜：我 想 要送 香 水給她，你呢？
fǎdù　wǒ xiǎng yào song xiāngshuǐ gěi tā　nǐ ne
　　　衣服、項鍊 或 蛋糕都可以呀！
　　　yīfú　xiàngliàn huò dàngāo dōu kěyǐ ya

立山：嗯……
lìshān　en…

法杜：我 等一下要去百貨公司 逛 逛，
fǎdù　wǒ děng yí xià yào qù bǎihuògōngsī guàngguàng
　　　你要不要跟我一起去看看呢？
　　　nǐ yàobúyào gēn wǒ yì qǐ qù kànkàn ne

立山：好吧！可是我 晚一點還要去工
lìshān　hǎoba　kěshì wǒ wǎn yì diǎn hái yào qù gōng
　　　作。
　　　zuò

法杜：好的好的，大忙 人！
fǎdù　hǎodehǎode　dà máng rén

第八課　這本書多少錢？

Listen to the dialogue and choose the best answer.

愷俐：謝謝你們大家上星期一來參加我的
kǎilì　xièxie nǐmen dàjiā shàngxīngqíyī lái cānjiā wǒde
　　　生日派對！
　　　shēngrì pàiduì

立山：不客氣！大家都是 同學嘛！
lìshān　bú kè qì　dàjiā dōu shì tongxué ma

法杜：是啊！而且妳人又很好。
fǎdù　shì a　érqiě nǐ rén yòu hěnhǎo

愷俐：為了謝謝大家，我們 這星期五去
kǎilì　wèi le xièxiè dàjiā　wǒmen zhè xīngqíwǔ qù
　　　KTV唱歌 好不好？
　　　chànggē hǎobùhǎo

法杜：好啊！聽說 台灣 的KTV很不錯，
fǎdù　hǎo a　tīngshuō táiwān de　hěnbúcuò
　　　我們可以在裡面 唱歌、跳舞 和
　　　wǒmen kěyǐ zài lǐ miàn chànggē　tiàowǔ hàn
　　　吃東西。
　　　chī dōngxī

希京：嗯！台灣的KTV比 韓國 還棒，
xījīng　en　táiwān de　bǐ hánguó hái bàng
　　　各國的歌曲都 有。
　　　gè guóde gēqǔ dōu yǒu

立山：我也想 去，可是這 星期五我有
lìshān　wǒ yě xiǎngqù　kěshì zhè xīngqí wǔ wǒ yǒu
　　　事，真可惜！
　　　shì　zhēn kěxí

希京：沒 關係！下次你再和我們一起去
xījīng　méi guān xi　xià cì nǐ zài hànwǒmen yì qǐ qù
　　　唱歌。
　　　chànggē

愷俐：好吧！其他人都可以的話，我就去
kǎilì　hǎo ba　qí tā rén dōu kě yǐ de huà　wǒ jiù qù
　　　訂位了。
　　　dingwèi le

法杜：愷俐，一個人大約多少 錢？
fǎdù　kǎilì　yí ge rén dàiyuē duōshǎoqián

愷俐：不用 錢，我請客！
kǎilì　bú yòng qián　wǒ qǐng kè

希京、法杜：哇！謝謝愷俐！
xījīng　fǎdù　wā　xièxiè kǎilì

第九課　銀行在哪裡？

Listen to the dialogue and choose the best answer.

安惠：皮皮來吃飯！……皮皮，皮皮！咦！
ānhuì　pípí lái chīfàn　pípí　pípí　yí
　　　皮皮呢？
　　　pípí ne

偉立：我不知道，我 剛 回家。
wěilì　wǒ bù zhī dào　wǒ gāng huíjiā

安惠：皮皮吃飯囉！……快來吃飯！
ānhuì　pípí chīfàn luō　kuài lái chīfàn
　　　咦！老公，你剛 回來沒關門嗎？
　　　yí　lǎogōng nǐ gāng huí lái méiguānménma

偉立：啊！我 忘 了！今天 工作 好 累…
wěilì　　a　　wǒwàng le　jīntiān gōngzuò hǎo lèi…

安惠：那皮皮 會不會 不見了？
ānhuì　nà pípí huì bú huì bú jiàn le

偉立：我 不 知道
wěilì　wǒ bù zhīdào

安惠：好吧！現在 找 皮皮比較 重要…
ānhuì　hǎoba　xiànzài zhǎo pípí bǐ jiào zhòngyào

　　　皮皮！皮皮！
　　　pípí　　pípí

偉立：皮皮 會不會 跑 出去 外 面 了？
wěilì　pípí　huìbúhuì　pǎo chūqù wàimiàn le

安惠：是嗎？那偉立，你 快 出去 找找 看。
ānhuì　shì ma　nà wěilì　nǐ kuàichūqùzhǎozhǎokàn

偉立：我 去 花 園 找 找，
wěilì　wǒ qù huāyuán zhǎozhǎo

　　　它最喜歡 去 那裡 了。
　　　tā zuì xǐhuān qù nà lǐ le

安惠：那我 去 房 間 裡找 找。
ānhuì　nà wǒ qù fángjiān lǐ zhǎozhǎo

偉立：皮皮！皮皮回家啦！
wěilì　pípí　　pípí huíjiā lā

安惠：偉立，皮皮在這裡。皮皮在 床
ānhuì　wěilì　pípí zài zhèlǐ　pípí zài chuáng

　　　底下啦！皮皮，出來 吃飯。
　　　dǐ xià lā　pípí　chūlái chīfàn

第十課　我可不可以試試看

Listen to the dialogue and choose the best answers.

愷俐：法杜，我 想 改變一下 客廳裡
kǎilì　fǎdù　wǒ xiǎng gǎibiàn yí xià kètīng lǐ

　　　小 桌子的 位子，好不好？
　　　xiǎozhuōzi de wèizi　hǎobùhǎo

法杜：好啊！那 電視 呢？
fǎdù　hǎo a　nà diànshì ne

愷俐：也一起 改變 吧！
kǎilì　yě yìqǐ gǎibiàn ba

法杜：愷俐，妳 想 怎麼 改變 呢？
fǎdù　kǎilì　nǐ xiǎng zě me gǎibiàn ne

愷俐：我 想 把 小桌子 搬到 沙發 旁 邊。
kǎilì　wǒ xiǎng bǎ xiǎozhuōzi bāndào shāfā pángbiān

法杜：把 電視 往 左 邊移一點 好 嗎？
fǎdù　bǎ diànshì wǎng zuǒbiān yí yì diǎn hǎo ma

愷俐：好啊！現在 我們 就 動手 吧！
kǎilì　hǎo a　xiànzài wǒmen jiù dòngshǒu ba

法杜：沒 問題！
fǎdù　méi wèntí

愷俐：現在 客廳 看起來好 大喔！
kǎilì　xiànzài kètīng kànqǐ lái hǎo dà　o

法杜：是啊！
fǎdù　shì a

愷俐：還可以把 電話 放 在 小 桌子上。
kǎilì　hái kěyǐ bǎ diànhuà fang zài xiǎozhuōzi shàng.

法杜：對了，我把上次買 的 桌巾拿出來。
fǎdù　duì le　wǒ bǎshàngcì mǎi dezhuōjīnná chūlái

愷俐：這樣 我們 的 客廳 看 起 來就 更
kǎilì　zhèyàngwǒmen de kètīng kàn qǐ lái jiù gèng

漂 亮 了。
piào liàng le

第十一課　我的頭好痛

Listen to the dialogue and choose the best answers.

楊老師：愷俐，你 知道 志學 是 在 哪一所
yang lǎoshī kǎilì　nǐ zhīdào zhìxué shì zài nǎ yì suǒ

　　　　醫院 嗎？
　　　　yīyuàn ma

愷俐：知道，在 台大醫院。
kǎilì　zhīdào　zài táidà yīyuàn

楊老師：哪一間 病 房 呢？
yang lǎoshī nǎ yì jiān bingfáng ne

愷俐：1288 病 房，在 12 樓。
kǎilì　yīèrbābā bìngfáng　zài shíèr lóu

楊老師：你們 都 去 看 過 他 了 嗎？
yang lǎoshī nimen dōu qù kàn guò tā le ma

希京：還 沒有！下課 以後，我們 要一起 去
xījīng　hái méiyǒu　xià kè yǐhòu　wǒmenyàoyì qǐ qù

楊老師：那我 和 你們 一 起 去看 他
yanglǎoshī nà wǒ hàn nǐmen yì qǐ qùkàn tā

愷俐：老師，我們 要帶什麼 去比較 好呢？
kǎilì　lǎoshī　wǒmenyàodàishéme qù bǐ jiǎohǎone

楊老師：嗯！我 看 就帶 水果 去吧！
yang lǎoshī en　wǒ kàn jiù dài shuǐguǒ qù ba

希京：水果 好吃 又 健康。
xījīng　shuǐguǒ hǎochī yòu jiànkāng

愷俐：那等 一下 中 午 休息我就 去 買 水
kǎilì　nà děng yí xià zhōngwǔ xiūxí wǒ jiù qù mǎi shuǐ

　　　果。
　　　guǒ

楊老師：愷俐，這 一千元 給妳去 買 水果
yang lǎoshī kǎilì　zhè yìqiānyuán gěi nǐ qù mǎishuǐguǒ

愷俐：謝謝 老師
kǎilì　xièxie lǎoshī

第十二課　我希望明年能去日本留學

Listen to the dialogue and choose the best answer for
each question.

法杜：愷俐，你来台灣 多久 呢？
fǎdù　kǎilì　nǐ lái táiwān duójiǔ ne

愷俐：快 一年 了。
kǎilì　kuài yì nián le

法杜：哇！快 一年了。你 為什麼 想 来
fǎdù　wā　kuài yì nián le　nǐ wèishéme xiǎng lái

　　　台灣 念 書呢？
　　　táiwān niàn shū ne

愷俐：因為聽 說 台灣 人 很 親切，
kǎilì　yīnwèi tīng shuō táiwān rén hěn qīnqiè

　　　而且我也 希望 可以 把 中 文 學 好
　　　érqiě wǒ yě xīwàng kěyǐ bǎ zhōngwén xué hǎo

法杜：我也 是。
fǎdù　wǒ yě shì

愷俐：其實，在 這一年裡，我 還去了 很多
kǎilì　qíshí　zài zhè yì niánlǐ　wǒ hái qù le hěn duō

好 玩 的地方。
hǎo wán de dìfāng

法杜：那你去哪裡玩 了？
fǎdù　　nà nǐ qù nǎlǐ wán le

愷俐：我去了101 大樓、淡水、九份、
kǎilì　　wǒ qù le yīlíngyī dàlóu　dànshuǐ　jiǔfèn

　　　花蓮 和 高 雄，從 南到北，
　　　huālián hàn gāoxióng cóng nándàoběi

　　　從 西到 東，我 都 去過 了。
　　　cóng xī dào dōng　wǒ dōu qù guò le.

法杜：那你喜歡 台 灣 的 小 吃嗎？
fǎdù　　nànǐ　xǐhuān táiwān de xiǎochī ma

愷俐：當然 喜歡！台 灣的 小 吃 好 好吃
kǎilì　　dāngrán xǐhuān　táiwān de xiǎochī hǎo hǎo chī

　　　哦！
　　　ó

法杜：是啊！小 籠 包、珍珠 奶茶、滷味、
fǎdù　　shì a　　xiǎolóngbāo zhēnzhū nǎichá　lǔwèi

　　　雞排，我 都 喜歡 吃。
　　　jīpái　　wǒ dōu xǐhuān chī

愷俐：對啊！台 灣 真 是一個 遊學的 好地
kǎilì　　duì a　　táiwān zhēn shì　yí ge yóuxué de hǎo dì

　　　方。
　　　fāng

聽力練習解答

Answer for the Listening

第一課　早安！您好！

I. Listen and circle the right tones.
1. jiě
2. yé
3. dà
4. shēng
5. mǒ
6. kē

II. Choose the best descryiption for each dialogue.
1. C
2. A
3. B

第二課　您貴姓？

I. Listen and circle the right tones.
A. xí
B. zhāi
C. miào
D. qǐng
E. yī

II. Listen to the dialogue and mark the correct statements with "T" and the incorrect ones with "F".
1. T
2. F
3. F
4. T
5. F

第三課　我喜歡爬山

I. Listen and circle the right tones.
A. yè
B. cán
C. chū
D. hǒng
E. fáng

II. Listen to the dialogue and mark the correct statements with "T" and the incorrect ones with "F".
1. T
2. F
3. T
4. F
5. F

第四課　我會說華語

I. Listen and circle the right tones.
A. yǎo
B. huǐ
C. yuán
D. yīng
E. kè

II. Listen to the dialogue and choose the best answer.
1. B
2. B
3. A
4. A
5. A

第五課　你是哪一國人？

Listen to the dialogue and mark correct statements with "T" and incorrect ones with "F".
1. T
2. F
3. T
4. F
5. F

第六課　她是我的室友

Listen to the dialogue and mark correct statements with "T" and incorrect ones with "F".
1. T
2. T
3. F
4. F
5. T

第七課　明天是星期幾？

Listen to the dialogue and choose the best answer.
1. b
2. c
3. a
4. d
5. c

第八課　這本書多少錢？

Listen to the dialogue and choose the best answer.

1. c
2. b
3. d
4. b
5. a

第九課　銀行在哪裡？

Listen to the dialogue and choose the best answer.

1. c
2. a
3. b
4. c
5. b

第十課　我可不可以試試看？

Listen to the dialogue and choose the best answer.

1. a
2. b
3. a
4. d
5. b

第十一課　我的頭好痛

Listen to the dialogue and choose the best answer.

1. b
2. d
3. a
4. c
5. b

第十二課　我希望明年能去日本留學

Listen to the dialogue and choose the best answer for each question.

1. a
2. d
3. d
4. d
5. c

Note

國家圖書館出版品預行編目資料

實用生活華語不打烊. 初級篇／楊琇惠著.
 －－二版.－－臺北市：五南圖書出版股份
有限公司, 2023.08
 面；　公分
 ISBN 978-626-366-333-6（平裝）

1.漢語　2.讀本

802.86　　　　　　　　　　112011409

1XZS　華語系列

實用生活華語不打烊（初級篇）

編 著 者 ― 楊琇惠(317.4)

文字編輯 ― 鄒蕙安、Brian Greene（葛偉立）、郭馨維

美術設計 ― 黃甄嫻

發 行 人 ― 楊榮川

總 經 理 ― 楊士清

總 編 輯 ― 楊秀麗

副總編輯 ― 黃惠娟

責任編輯 ― 魯曉玟

插　　畫 ― 鄭雯允

錄音人員 ― 林姮伶、范雅婷、盧俊良

封面設計 ― 黃聖文、姚孝慈

出 版 者 ― 五南圖書出版股份有限公司

地　　址：106台北市大安區和平東路二段339號4樓

電　　話：(02)2705-5066　　傳　真：(02)2706-6100

網　　址：https://www.wunan.com.tw

電子郵件：wunan@wunan.com.tw

劃撥帳號：01068953

戶　　名：五南圖書出版股份有限公司

法律顧問　林勝安律師

出版日期　2010年 2 月初版一刷（共四刷）
　　　　　2023年 8 月二版一刷
　　　　　2024年 5 月二版二刷

定　　價　新臺幣430元

經典永恆・名著常在

五十週年的獻禮──經典名著文庫

五南，五十年了，半個世紀，人生旅程的一大半，走過來了。

思索著，邁向百年的未來歷程，能為知識界、文化學術界作些什麼？

在速食文化的生態下，有什麼值得讓人雋永品味的？

歷代經典・當今名著，經過時間的洗禮，千錘百鍊，流傳至今，光芒耀人；

不僅使我們能領悟前人的智慧，同時也增深加廣我們思考的深度與視野。

我們決心投入巨資，有計畫的系統梳選，成立「經典名著文庫」，

希望收入古今中外思想性的、充滿睿智與獨見的經典、名著。

這是一項理想性的、永續性的巨大出版工程。

不在意讀者的眾寡，只考慮它的學術價值，力求完整展現先哲思想的軌跡；

為知識界開啟一片智慧之窗，營造一座百花綻放的世界文明公園，

任君邀遊、取菁吸蜜、嘉惠學子！